FIRST
TEMPTATION

OTHER BOOKS BY LEAF GRAHAM

Garden of Evil (*Unhallowed* book 2)

FIRST TEMPTATION

UNHALLOWED BOOK I

LEAF GRAHAM

OVERVIEW  PUBLISHING

Cover art: Leaf Graham

Published by Overview Publishing.

Graham, Leaf
 First Tempation: Unhallowed Book 1 / Leaf Graham.
— First Edition
    p. cm.

ISBN: 979-8-9916221-3-4 (hc)
ISBN: 979-8-9870778-5-6 (pbk)
ISBN: 979-8-9870778-6-3 (ebook)

Printed in the United States of America.

10 9 8 7 6 5 4 3 2 1
First Edition

Dedicated to my followers

at Fanfiction.net and Archive of Our Own.

Find more *Unhallowed* fun at
https://www.patreon.com/UnhallowedGarden.

There is an old illusion.

It is called good and evil.

– *Friedrich Nietzsche*

Content Advisory

This book and the *Unhallowed* series are works of speculative fiction that cross the boundaries between erotic horror, dark urban fantasy, and apocalyptic storytelling. Themes and subjects explored, such as fallen angels and witchcraft, may be triggering or offensive to some readers.

Unhallowed contains explicit sex and violence, and refers to rituals, religious beliefs, and magic that do not represent ideas of the real world.

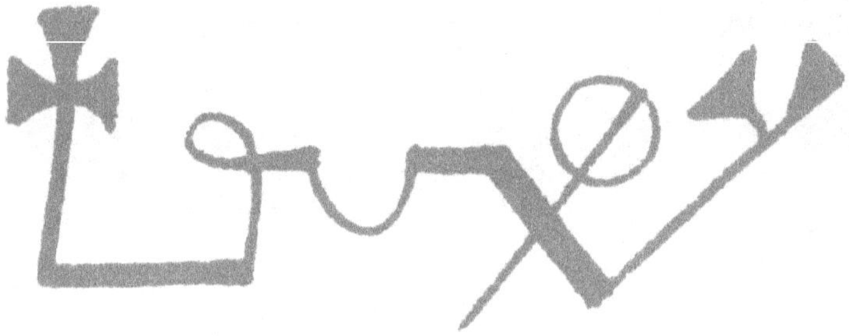

CHAPTER 1

The neighbor's dog was out of his yard again. Despite the hazards of life in a decaying neighborhood outside the Walls, the promise of adventure outweighed the danger. His owner tried to dog-proof the yard, yet he always found a way to slip out. Especially on nice autumn days like today, when the cool breeze carried scents too enticing for a bored Corgi to ignore.

Raina saw the little brown-and-white dog as she pulled her rickety wooden cart up the cracked sidewalk. The stubby-legged pooch sat outside the weathered gate of a splintery fence that framed an equally splintered house.

"You know you're not supposed to be out here," Raina said, bringing her cart to a stop. She put her hands on her hips to try and look stern. "It's not safe."

The dog gave her a hopeful wag of his curled tail. His tongue lolled in a goofy grin. Her stern act wasn't fooling him. When she approached him, he got to his feet. Did a silly, stamping dance outside the gate.

"Impatient rogue, aren't you? You really shouldn't sneak out if you can't get back in."

Smiling at the dog's antics, she reached over the fence and lifted the latch. The gate swung inward, its rusty hinges whining from the effort of opening. The pup trotted into the yard with a satisfied air of entitlement.

"All right, Brom." She latched the gate behind him. "No more escape artistry. Charlie should be home soon."

She was talking to Corgi butt. Brom was already prancing up to the front porch.

Charlotte—Charlie to her friends—was one of Raina's regular laundry clients. Out of necessity the old lady still worked as a picker in the fields. She didn't have time or energy to work and keep up with her wash. Raina always cut her a discount. It wasn't the best financial decision, but the money Charlie saved went to feeding Brom.

Taking up the handles of her wagon, Raina got it moving again. Several bags of dirty clothes from her neighbors weighed the cart down. A week's worth of work. Before her mother died, they could wash the same amount in half the time.

"Hey, Raina," a man's voice greeted.

Inwardly, she sighed. Outwardly, she put on a polite smile for the man who hurried across the street to catch up with her.

"Hi, Maurice."

A solitary evening at home was nothing to look forward to, but she would rather be alone than have his company. It wasn't that she disliked him. As an acquaintance, he was fine. But beneath his friendly exterior lurked an insecure, self-centered man blind to his own egotistical ways.

Worse, he didn't bathe often, and he didn't brush his teeth—at all. A flurry of white flakes from his unwashed scalp crusted his shoulders. Granted, there were worse crimes than bad hygiene. But standing downwind of him on a hot day was enough to make a person gag.

What he lacked in physical appeal was not made up for in personality. His constant need for approval was tedious, as were his clumsy attempts to court her. Their conversations always went the same way. He would greet her. They would make small talk. He would try again to ask her out. She would find another way to politely decline.

"How've you been?" He fell into step with her.

"I've been busy." She walked quicker.

Fallen leaves crunched under the pitted wheels of her cart as it rumbled along.

"Say, I was wondering if you might want to grab a bite to eat tonight." Maurice raised his voice so she could hear him over the noise of the wagon. It was impossible to sound casual while talking so loudly.

She glanced at him, her smile unwavering. "I've got an awful lot of laundry I need to do. But thanks. I appreciate the offer."

He glanced back and took stock of the full cart. It was a potential opportunity for him. "You want me to carry some of that for you?"

"No, thanks. I've got it."

She turned up the walkway to her front porch. He tagged along behind her, shadowing her as he did so often. His dogged loyalty was admirable if unwanted.

"You sure?" he tried again. "Maybe I could help you wash—"

"Oh, no." She hauled the cart up onto the porch. "Thanks, but I don't need any help. I'm kind of set in my way of doing things. You know? Another person would only slow me down."

She'd made the mistake of letting him assist her once when she needed to rehang some curtains. While he was quick to offer help he wouldn't follow instructions. Wanting to do things his way, he pulled the rod bracket clean out of the wall. What should have taken a few minutes took four hours. It also left the curtains at an unattractive slant.

Despite refusing his offer, when she paused outside her door and saw his hopeful look, she wavered.

"Maybe we could get some lunch this weekend..."

Maurice brightened. "Oh, that'd be great, Raina. Just let me know when and I'll clear my schedule."

He was trying to impress her with how accommodating he could be, but the desperation made her weary. She wished it didn't bother her. He wasn't a bad guy. Just... too needy.

Raina didn't need anyone. She was through with relationships. Her last one had been a toxic mess. Her boyfriend counted on the fact that she needed him. Preyed on her fear of being alone after her mother died. The months before she finally broke it off were a nightmare. Strings of dark days she spent furious or heartbroken from the moment she woke until she slept again.

It took two years to restore herself after leaving him. Two years to remember what happiness was. The last thing she wanted now was a man who needed constant validation and someone to tell him when to wash.

She went to let herself into her house and stopped short. There was a note tacked to the center of the door. She tugged it free.

Maurice was ever at the ready. "That's from the landlord."

One guy owned the whole block. He was a hefty older man who only came around if someone needed maintenance done or if they missed a rent payment.

Raina scanned the short letter and bristled in outrage. "He's sold the neighborhood?"

"He wants us all out in two weeks," confirmed Maurice. "Can you believe it? Talk about a jerk move."

"He can't do that!" Raina objected. "I have a lease agreement till the end of the year!"

"I don't think he cares. He had some ritzy-lookin' dude here with him earlier checking the place out. I think it's a done deal."

"Well, they'll have to kick me out," said Raina. "Because I'm not leaving until my lease is up. I mean, two weeks? That's ridiculous! That's not enough time to find a new place to live!"

Maurice looked skeptical. "You should probably start searching. I have my eye on someplace near the old amusement park. That old hotel they converted...um. The ghost apartment building. You know the one? Where all the celebrities died back in the day? Maybe you could—"

"I've got to get to work," she said. "I'll see you tomorrow."

She unlocked the door and started tossing bags of laundry into the front hall. Maurice lingered on the sidewalk a bit longer then drifted away.

—

Over the next two weeks, Raina saw the landlord on three occasions. Each time he tried to convince her to leave. Each time she countered him with the contract he'd signed. The first two meetings were cordial. The third time he came to her house he insisted she needed to be out in two days. It was strange but he seemed more concerned than belligerent. Almost... afraid.

"I'm sorry," he said for the umpteenth time. He mopped sweat from his greasy bald head with an old handkerchief. "The lease is void. You're going to have to leave by Saturday."

"You can't kick me out, Eli," she insisted. "I'll go to the magistrate if you try. Now get out."

She held the door open for him. He shot her a last forlorn look then left.

His expression haunted her when she was no longer in the heat of the moment. It was so out of place given the situation. She chalked it up to financial difficulties or some other pressure in his private life. Whatever it was, it was no concern of hers.

—

That evening she prepped a bath to soak her weary body. Like most of her neighbors, she heated her water over a firepit in the back yard. It wasn't a lifestyle choice: The local government rationed electricity in and around New Salem.

Within the protective Walls that surrounded the settlement, power was easier to access and budgeted more generously. Outside the triple barricade things were tight. Energy was strictly rationed, with rolling blackouts during peak hours. Most of the houses in the area didn't even have a water heater hooked up. Hers didn't.

It took several trips back and forth from the firepit to fill the tub to a decent level. It was the same process for the laundry. Just a different thing to wash. When the water was deep enough, she shed her clothes and eased herself into the tub.

She just got comfortable when the bathroom light went out. Plunged into darkness, she sat there for a few moments in dead silence. She had no pets and New Salem had little weather in late fall apart from the sudden drop in temperature. The house was as still as a tomb.

As seconds stretched without the light coming back on, she grumbled a curse and climbed out of the tub. Of all the times for there to be a blackout. She had emergency candles stashed all over the house. She could take a couple from the bedroom and bathe by candlelight. Pretend she was at a spa. Turn a negative to a positive. She wasn't about to waste the hot water.

She fumbled for the towel rack and, finding the towel, she wrapped it around herself. It was threadbare from age and did little to keep the cold off her wet skin. Shivering, she tugged open the door.

Bright blue-white LED light blinded her.

"There she is." A man's voice muffled and gruff. "Get her!"

Hands grabbed her. Rough, hostile hands. One pressed a foul-smelling cloth over her nose and mouth, smothering her in chemical odor. She struggled to free herself. The hands gripped tight. Raina held her breath against the terrible smell. Something solid struck her middle. The air left her in a rush.

She couldn't hold breath she didn't have. The need to breathe overcame her. She gasped, sucking in more of the chemical smell. The world swam and she slipped into darkness.

—

Raina woke shivering, forced to consciousness by a jolt that went straight through to her bones. She tried to move and found she was bound hand and foot. Naked and gagged, she was trapped inside a crate designed to hold a large dog or small livestock. The sensation of the box hitting the ground was what woke her.

The side opened. Cold air rushed in.

Two hooded people grabbed her and pulled her out. Holding her between them by her arms they dragged her over the rough pavement. Bound as she was, she couldn't walk. Cold and battered, Raina looked around frantically, fear growing like a sick and thorny flower in the pit of her stomach. The ball gag prevented her screaming for help.

They were in New Salem's grungy town square. Her captors hauled her to where three blood-stained altars stood before an imposing chapel. The First Church. Home to the largest religious order in town, one that called itself the Post-Angelicans.

The old church was of Gothic design. To either side of its recessed doors long red banners hung, trimmed in white and emblazoned with black dragons. The symbol of the Lord Prince of New Salem. It was him the Church was devoted to.

A small crowd gathered around. Some wore the robes of Church acolytes, bald individuals in hooded gray robes. Others were random drunks from nearby bars. Ugly, cruel faces surrounded her, jeering and hooting. Some called for her blood. None knew her.

Three standing torches lit the area, one behind each altar. The hooded people brought Raina to the central altar—the largest and most gore-stained of the three. They lifted and tossed her onto the cold stone where they tied her arms and legs to thick iron rings set into the surface. Crunching her eyes shut, she willed herself to wake up. This had to be a nightmare. The coppery scent of blood and the icy, hard press of the altar against her bare skin couldn't be real.

"*Domine!*" a woman's voice called out somewhere behind her head. The Prophet of New Salem, leader of the First Church. The power in her exclamation quieted the onlookers. "*Exaudi orationem nostrum!*"

Raina opened her eyes to a starry sky above. The gory altar beneath her was freezing, but it was fear that made her tremble.

Arms came into view above her, robed in dark red velvet. Slender hands clutched a long, curved knife. The sharp tip was pointed straight at Raina's abdomen. Terror seized her and she struggled against her bonds, yanking with all her might. The ropes bit into her wrists and ankles, refusing to loosen.

The ceremonial weapon came down. With a sudden flash of motion and a clang of metal on metal, the knife disappeared, dashed away by a bigger blade. A man with a dark brown ponytail wielded the machete.

"Your Lord will take his sacrifice alive today." His words were confident, almost jovial. Yet despite his casual tone, he meant what he said.

The gathered crowd buzzed with surprised whispers.

"But sir—" the Prophet said, both subservient and peeved.

"No buts," the man dismissed. "Untie her and bring her to me." He fished in his pocket and tossed a handful of coins onto the altar. "That should recoup your loss."

The hooded people untied her from the altar and pulled her up. They kept her hands bound but freed her ankles so she could walk. Seizing her arms, they yanked her away from the altar. She stumbled and the rough pavement raked her bare feet. Her captors didn't care. They took her to the man who had interrupted her execution.

Despite the fact the Prophet had called him "sir" he wore common clothing. Faded jeans and an untucked ivory shirt hugged his muscular frame. His black leather jacket was well-worn and covered in scuff marks. Only his motorcycle boots looked new.

The hooded men shoved her at him. She looked up expecting to see cruelty. Instead, she saw warmth in his brown eyes.

"Let's go," he said to her. Then he bent and scooped her up over his brawny shoulder.

In a testament to his strength, he carried her out of the town square that way. Not a dignified way to leave, but it was a short trip. He took her out the southern gateway and over to a dust-coated black motorcycle that was parked on the sidewalk. Setting her down on the seat, he stooped to make eye contact with her.

"I'm going to take off your gag now," he said. "Please don't make me regret it."

He removed the ball gag. She took a deep breath. Swallowed. The gag had prevented that as well as speech.

"What's your name?" he asked.

"R-Raina," she stammered, teeth chattering from the cold.

He shrugged off his jacket. "Raina, I'm Troy and this might be your luckiest day... or your worst ever. I guess it depends on how you look at it."

He draped the coat over her shoulders. It was large on her and smelled like him, though not in an unpleasant way. He untied her hands. As soon as the bonds were of,f she shoved her arms into the satin-lined sleeves. They still carried the heat from his body.

He mounted the motorcycle behind her, straddling it expertly. His arms fenced her in as he reached for the handlebars.

"Sit tight," he said. The motorcycle roared to life. "It's going to be a chilly ride."

CHAPTER 2

The ride was more than chilly. Where the jacket didn't cover Raina's skin, the wind attacked. In a matter of minutes, she went from cold to numb, to burning. In a way, it was a blessing. The discomfort stopped her dwelling on the fact that she was sitting on the motorcycle with nothing between her and the seat.

Hunkered down against the icy air, she was half frozen by the time they reached their destination, a blocky three-story hotel. Built in the mid-1800s, the building's age showed in its design and its cracked and crumbling exterior.

A multitude of dark, arched windows gazed solemnly out at the street, taking in their arrival as it had witnessed so many visitors before them. A handful of dusty windows were lit, obscured by overgrown trees in need of trimming. A curved sign above the entrance proclaimed the place the Bradford Hotel.

Troy shut off the motorcycle, bringing sudden stillness to the cobblestone plaza. Scores of blackbirds flocked in the open space. They perched in the autumnal trees and lined the rooftop of the hotel. Alert, the birds watched the pair in eerie silence.

"Here," he said.

He lifted Raina off the bike. Carried her over to the wide sidewalk in front of the double doors where he set her on her feet. The icy concrete underfoot only increased her shivering. He held one of the doors open and ushered her inside.

"Where do you live?" he asked as the door swung shut on a pivot arm behind them.

An unintentionally loaded question.

"N-near the graveyard." She pulled the jacket tight. Though the temperature was nicer inside than out, without his body heat to help keep her warm, her shaking was uncontrollable. "J-just outside the Walls. But... I don't know if it's m-my home anymore."

He led the way across a small, antiquated foyer that smelled every bit as old as it looked. To the right was the hotel lobby, a broad room lit by a central fire pit. The fire was surrounded by cream-colored wingback chairs and loveseats. There were a few people in the room, some near the fire and some seated at the bar on the far side of the lobby.

Raina eyed the fire, envious, and adjusted her death grip on the leather jacket. She was painfully aware of her nudity beneath it. Though the firepit beckoned, she didn't want to get close to the people clustered around it. The coat was just long enough to hide her so long as she didn't bend over or make any sudden moves. There was a real risk of flashing someone.

"Why not?" prompted Troy when she didn't continue.

Brought back to the conversation, she looked at him. "Oh. The landlord s-sold the place. He was t-trying to evict me when those g-goons you rescued me from kidnapped me. At least, I think they're the same ones..."

"Well, I paid for you," he said brightly. They reached a wide flight of carpeted stairs, split in the center, which led to the floor above. "So, any claim they had on your debts is gone."

Raina wasn't sure how to take that. "I wasn't in debt," she corrected. Then: "Are you saying you own me n-now?"

"Own?" Troy blinked, surprised. "No. I meant nobody does. But if you have no home and nowhere to go, I'm sure the prince won't have a problem with you staying here. If you want to."

The twin sets of carpeted stairs curved above a pair of windowed doors to the courtyard. Globe lanterns on the walls shed amber light on blue-gray carpet flattened by years of use. Although it was rough and thin, the aged wool was better to walk on than the frigid marble tile in the foyer.

"The prince?"

"Prince Michael, our Lord of the Unified Settlements," said Troy with a grandiose flair.

Raina detected an irreverent sense of amusement in his words. It was the same way he spoke to the Prophet in the town square. Like it was all one big joke to him. As in the square, she didn't get the impression it was directed at her, though. Weird.

"You're not—You're not the Prince?" she stammered. "I thought—"

Troy laughed and started up the stairs. "Hell no. I wouldn't want the job, either. Too much work."

Raina flushed, embarrassed. Everything had happened so fast she hadn't processed his earlier introduction. It was all a terrifying blur. At least he didn't seem offended by the mistake. She found herself liking him, beyond appreciating his help.

"Sorry. I thought because those people let you take me..." She fluttered a hand to wave away the awkwardness. "Thank you, by the way. For saving me."

"Don't mention it," he dismissed. "I'm Troy. One of Michael's inner circle. The Prophet doesn't like me, but she wouldn't risk her position arguing over a token sacrifice. No offense."

"None taken." There was no prestige in being a sacrifice, token or otherwise.

Halfway up the stairs, a shared landing brought the twin flights of steps together to form a single unit. Troy and Raina continued up and had almost reached the top when another man came into view above them.

Tall and poised, he wore a tailored black outfit that blended elements of suit and toga. His wavy blond hair was longer than Troy's, falling to mid-back and restrained in a similar low ponytail. He was handsome, but there was something more there. A presence that commanded attention. He looked down at the pair on the stairs, scrutinizing Raina in particular. His intense, penetrating gaze captivated her. Meeting his dark eyes sent a jolt through her on par with the way the crate struck the ground earlier.

"Who is this?" he asked. His mellow tone belied the intensity of his gaze.

"Her name's Raina." Troy touched her elbow to signal she should come up the last steps with him. "Raina, this is Prince Michael."

The prince put her in mind of the Renaissance paintings in her mother's collection of art books—especially those eyes and lips. He was compelling yet intimidating, mysterious. Being near him was like peering into the depths of an unexplored mineshaft from the very edge.

"Hello." Self-conscious, she immediately second-guessed her greeting. She'd never met someone of such prestige before.

Doing so while mostly nude threw off her social instincts. "Uh, Sir. Highness."

Troy coughed to cover an inappropriate laugh. The prince ignored the reaction.

"Michael is fine," he said. He turned his attention to Troy. "Your thoughts?"

The dark-haired man shrugged and leaned against the banister. "Those yokels at the Church were going to sacrifice her. I thought you might want her alive."

Michael assessed the newcomer, not at all shy about his study. "One of the better decisions you've made lately."

"She was kicked out of her house. I figured she could stay here for a bit while she sorts things out. Maybe work in the kitchen or something?"

"What sort of experience do you have?" the prince asked her.

Raina fidgeted. She again wished she were wearing something more than the borrowed coat. Of all the socially painful and awkward encounters she'd had in life, this ranked number one by far. No contest.

Hopefully, he wouldn't notice she had nothing else on.

"I, um, do laundry," she said. "I run a business washing clothes for folks in my neighborhood. It doesn't pay much, but it keeps me fed and all." She couldn't bring herself to say "housed".

"Michael wears a lot of expensive sh–stuff," said Troy, correcting his natural tendency toward the crude for the sake of first impressions. "Think you can handle silk without destroying it?"

"Velvet and leather," added Michael.

"I know all about materials and their care." If there was one thing Raina understood, it was clothing. "I can also mend and make clothes, with or without a pattern."

The prince nodded thoughtfully. Then he turned to Troy again. "See that she's cleaned and dressed. Just... don't let Pietre know about her yet."

Dressed? Cleaned? Raina wasn't an object to be cleaned. "I can dress myself."

Michael's eyes traveled down her form and back up. He didn't need to say anything. His poignant look said it all.

He'd noticed.

Raina hugged the jacket tighter. A hot blush warmed her face and ears, stinging her skin as it burned off the chill from outside. She was no longer as cold, but she was far more uncomfortable. Of the two, she preferred to freeze.

"You can assume laundry duties starting tomorrow," he said. "Troy will introduce you to Beth. She runs the laundromat downstairs. She can show you the ropes."

"Thank you."

Raina silently cursed herself for being so overwhelmed by the situation and Michael's presence. She must look like such a rube. One that couldn't even clothe herself. She wanted to come across as clever or witty. She was neither of those things now. Worst introduction ever.

"After you get her situated," Michael said to Troy. "Come find me. There are things we need to discuss."

He took a last keen look at Raina and then proceeded down the stairs. She couldn't help staring at him as he passed.

Troy put a gentle hand on her shoulder.

"Let's get you to a room."

———

The hallway at the top of the stairs branched out to the left and right, pale beige corridors lit by electric amber sconces. Troy led Raina to the left. They passed several brown wooden doors before stopping at one. The door was unlocked. It swung open with a groan of antique hinges when he turned the old-fashioned knob.

The air within the room was stale. Thick with age and disuse. Troy hit a switch and a standing lamp in the corner came on to shed light over a cozy L-shaped room. A door to the left opened to a small bathroom and a closet was on the right. Beyond the short entryway, the room widened into a tidy sleeping area with a double-sized bed.

Other typical hotel furnishings fleshed out the room. The dresser and mirrored sideboard looked original to the hotel. There was also a table with two chairs older than Raina. Heavy curtains of a retro-mod design blanketed the lone window near the bed. A fat lamp took up the bedside table.

A gray layer of dust coated everything.

"This was Desiree's room," Troy said, putting his hands on his hips as he looked around. "She's... not with us anymore. You can use whatever's in here. I don't know if her clothes will fit you, but I figure something might. Anything's better than nothing. Yeah?"

"I couldn't agree more," Raina said, sincere.

At the moment she would agree to just about anything if it meant getting something more to wear than a borrowed jacket. The cold was catching up with her again, making her joints stiff and her fingers numb.

"Dinner's usually around seven," he went on. "About a half hour from now, give or take. Breakfast is six to eight in the morning. You're on your own for lunch, but you can help yourself to what's in the kitchen. There's a bell that sounds the hour so you should be able to keep the time."

Satisfied he'd laid the ground rules, he started toward the door. "See you at dinner?"

"Wait," Raina said. She wanted to get dressed, but there was so much she didn't understand. "I, uh, have some questions..."

"Can it keep till later? I've got to go to talk to Michael."

Most of what she wanted to know could wait. But. "Just one thing. Is there a key? For the room?"

Even though he knew the answer, he patted his pockets anyway. "Nah. That's gone. No clue where it is. We can change the knob if you want, but nobody steals anything around here."

She nodded slowly, absorbing that tidbit. "All right. Thanks. See you at dinner, then."

He gave her a winning smile then let himself out. Left alone, she looked around the quiet room. A sense of sorrow haunted the place. Neglect and... something else. Regret? Loneliness?

To shake the vibe that permeated the living space, she tried to wrap her mind around everything that had happened to her. She wanted to give her situation the attention it was due. Everything had happened so fast she felt a bit like a rock tumbling down a steep incline. If she wanted to direct that fall, she needed to know where she was and where she was going. And that started with getting cleaned up and dressed.

CHAPTER 3

The bar on the ground floor of the Bradford Hotel was a historic picture of the past. The black cherry wood was authentic, polished to a deep shine. Elegant pediments and intricate inlays gave it Victorian grace. It had seen great times and terrible tragedies and propped up many drunks and call girls over the years.

Michael sat on one of the leather and brass stools, looking through a sheaf of papers in a recycled folder. A glass of bourbon stood at the ready near his elbow. Half of it was already in his stomach.

As Lord Prince of New Salem and regent of the new world, he was always busy. There was always something that needed his attention. There was no such thing as a day off.

The folder of papers he held contained the business he needed to oversee the next day. Each day he received a new folder full of new problems and choices. Each week the folder grew thicker. Most of it was bureaucratic: Municipal requests and assessments, reports, important news from other settlements. Sometimes there were legal issues the judge Michael appointed couldn't resolve.

With the number of difficult cases on the rise, he considered appointing a council of magistrates instead of just one. He didn't have time to sort out complicated custody issues and murder trials. As much as he would like to do everything and be everywhere at once, that sort of omnipresence was beyond him.

For now.

"Hey," Troy greeted as he slid up onto the bar stool next to him.

Grateful for the interruption, Michael closed the folder and dropped it on the bar. He reached for his glass. "Did you get the girl settled in?"

"Pretty much." Troy signaled to the bartender and motioned to Michael's bourbon. "Cute, isn't she?"

The prince sipped his drink. The bartender placed an identical glass of brown liquor in front of Troy, who raised it in silent thanks, then took a thirsty gulp from it.

"You didn't bring her here because of her looks."

"No." Troy grinned. "But it doesn't hurt that she's hot. Am I right?"

"You sound like a teenager," scoffed Michael. "I'm more interested in her potential."

"She's got a good spark. I can't believe the Church was just going to off her." Troy had another swig from his glass. "You thinking about training her?"

Michael ran a thumb over the rim of his tumbler. "Possibly. I don't know. I need to find out what, if anything, she can do. Or if it's raw potential. Either way, she'll be an asset..." He trailed off. A thin line appeared between his brows.

"To help you get your powers back?"

Michael's mood darkened. He leveled a black look at his companion. "I haven't lost everything." Disgruntled, he looked back down at his glass. Swirled the liquor to watch it spin. "The Coven has helped me relearn some of what I lost. It's just not... fast enough."

He belted down most of his drink. Setting the tumbler aside, he reached for a thin silver case on the bar. Pulled a black cigarette from it and lit it. The clove-laced tobacco was hard to come by for anyone outside his court. He should indulge the vice less, but he took comfort from the familiar act of smoking.

Troy looked at him with muted sympathy. "It'll come. Even if it doesn't, you have more than enough influence to keep people in line."

Michael wasn't reassured, nor did he want to be. "I don't care about influence. I want to be able to move and see like I used to. I'm practically blind and lame like this. I'm sick of being so curtailed!"

He was also aware he was no match for a serious threat if one arose. He'd been lucky so far, but his luck was bound to run out eventually. He bit back a swell of irritation and puffed on his cigarette. Brooding.

"Well. Hopefully, Raina can help that," Troy said.

He lifted his glass in a toast and held it there. Looked at the prince expectantly.

Finally, Michael lifted his glass. He sighed. "Here's to hoping." He tossed back the last swallow of bourbon and set his glass down again. Waved off a refill the bartender tried to give him.

"Sometimes I envy you and Pietre," Michael said then. He tapped his cigarette in the well-used ashtray on the bar.

Troy set his empty glass down. When the bartender tipped the bottle of bourbon toward his glass, he accepted with a smile.

"Pietre I get, I guess," he said. "But... me?"

An ironic smile tickled the corners of Michael's mouth. "Both of you. I run things, yet you have all the freedom."

"Heavy is the head that wears the crown," quoted Troy. He swiveled on his bar stool, rotating so he could see the prince without having to turn his head. "I think you're overestimating how much freedom either of us has, though."

"I thought it would get easier," Michael continued, not acknowledging the other man's opinion. "After we locked up the nephal and got things settled, I thought things would just... go back to what they used to be. Or something like it. But there's no going back, is there? Life moves persistently forward. Before long, no one will even remember what it used to be like."

"There's always books..."

Michael made a face. He had no faith in society's literacy. "How many people are reading these days? Or writing? I'm pretty sure the major publishers went down when Radio City became a permanent marsh."

Troy tipped his head, conceding the point. Then he got thoughtful, stroking the five o'clock shadow on his chin. "Maybe you should start your own publishing house. Recruit writers from the remnants of society. You could call it the Post-Apocalyptic Press. PAP."

"Just what I need: More work."

Despite his dour tone, Michael's smile broke free. The notion and suggested name were ridiculous enough to crack his mood. His friend had a knack for knowing what to say at times like this.

"Start a tabloid," Troy went on, warming to his joke. "You could call it the PAP Smear."

Michael snorted. "I think there's enough garbage in the world already." He lifted his glass and caught the bartender's eye. "Give me another."

—

An old but beautiful clawfoot bathtub was the focal point of Raina's bathroom. A green and white striped curtain sheathed it, hung on a curved brass rod that was mounted to the ceiling. The tub supplied hot running water—a rarity for someone used to boiling water to wash in. Even if she weren't cold and dirty from her encounter with the altar, she'd want to try it out.

A soak would be lovely, but with dinnertime so close, a quick shower would do to get the grime off and warm her bones. She could soak later, before bed. It would give her time to process things better before she tried to sleep.

She stuck a hand under the water to test it was hot, then she stepped in. Pulled the shower curtain tight to the wall on both sides to keep the steamy heat in. She positioned herself under the shower head and sighed. The heat felt glorious. She shut her eyes and tilted her head back to let the water spill over her.

The hot spray was delightful at first but as her mind wandered, thoughts of the men who broke into her house began to creep in. Her eyes flew open. Paranoid, she yanked the striped curtain back with a rattle of metal rings.

The door to the bathroom was still shut. She was still alone.

Relieved, she tugged the curtain closed again before too much water hit the floor. She was reassured but the magic of the shower was dispelled. She hoped that it wouldn't become a recurring issue. Then she tried to put such thoughts from her mind. It was time to get clean.

She reached for the soap. It was dry and cracked from lack of use, though a few scrubs with a wet washcloth revived it. The bubbly suds had a sweet herbal musk. She gave herself a thorough rub-down and rinse, then tried some of the shampoo. It was in better condition than the soap and made the thickest lather she'd put in her hair.

Slowly, she started to relax.

Once she was clean, she turned off the water and stepped out onto the cold tile. Probably should have thrown a towel down. There were plenty on the shelf. At home, she rationed her towel use, reusing the same threadbare bath towel several times before taking another to save herself more washing. One towel lived on the floor as a stand-in rug.

She wrapped herself up in one of the thick, thirsty bath towels from the shelf. It smelled of too much time in a linen closet but was remarkably soft. Nicer than the ones back home, for sure. She decided it was just as well she hadn't put one on the floor. They were too nice to walk on.

Hoping to find some absorbent powder or antiperspirant, Raina peeked in the bathroom cabinets. There were several bottles of assorted sizes beneath the sink. Lotions and facial cleansers, dusting powders, and a wooden box of scented oils in small vials.

It was difficult to tell how old the items were, but the ones she tested smelled fine. And she tried several. Unused to such luxury, she wanted to smell and sample everything.

At first, she felt wrong for helping herself to someone else's stuff, but Troy had said she could use whatever she wanted. The owner was gone. It would be a shame to let it all go to waste.

She rubbed on a creamy pumpkin body lotion which left her skin soft and perfumed. She sniffed the back of her hand several times, enjoying the scent as she checked out the other products. It was a guilty source of pleasure going through all the luxurious items. Despite knowing she could use them it felt like a naughty secret. Like she was low-key stealing.

Though the lotion she had on was lovely, she couldn't resist trying on one of the oils. There were so many lovely scents to choose from. She daubed a few drops of jasmine at the base of her throat where the collarbone dipped. A few more drops went on her wrists. She'd never been so pampered. It was like a beautiful dream.

When she was done playing with the goops and liquids, she stepped out of the bathroom and into the unfamiliar room again. The cold was already starting to seep in again. She needed something to wear. Again, she felt like an intruder when she opened the closet and dresser. It was just strange to pick through someone else's things. But going naked was not an option. She'd already had more than enough of that.

There wasn't a lot of color variety in Desiree's wardrobe. She had worn a lot of black. Raina found a few colorful items, though, much of it what her mother had called jewel tones. She pulled a few of them out to piece together an outfit.

Garments with the most color won: A red and purple circle skirt with black fringe, a blue long-sleeved top, and some warm fuzzy purple socks. Desiree's shoes didn't fit her, and she couldn't bring herself to wear another woman's undergarments. Going without panties was unpleasant, but not as much as borrowing a pair.

She looked at herself in the full-length wall mirror that was near the door. Though her outfit lacked style or cohesion, the clothes were close enough to her size for comfort. She told herself the mismatched pieces leant her a boho fortune-teller vibe. It worked if she didn't think about her missing underwear.

A distant bell clanged seven. An uncharacteristic stab of stage fright jolted her.

"There's nothing to be nervous about," she told herself. "It's just dinner."

Her reflection didn't believe the false confidence. Her hands trembled and her heart was pounding.

Why was she so nervous? It wasn't the lack of underwear. Not really. It was like performance anxiety, only she wasn't performing. There was nothing to memorize and no one would be judging her. Or would they?

It was more than her wardrobe that was preying on her. It was fear of the unknown jangling her nerves. She had no idea what to expect at the meal. Her aversion to new experiences surfaced in that fear of the unknown.

She hated doing things for the first time, even fun things. First times were always rough, not knowing the rules or expectations. How would she pay for food? Would it go on some tab? Who would she sit with? Or would she be alone, a stranger in a strange crowd..? She wished she'd had a chance to ask Troy. But he had said he would see her at dinner. She could ask him when she found him. If she could find him.

Why couldn't life bypass firsts? If she could skip straight past beginner to novice, things would be much more enjoyable.

She took a last look at her reflection. Eyed her mismatched outfit again and decided to commit to it. If she changed now, she would get caught in a loop of self-doubt and never get out of the room.

No one would know she wasn't wearing panties.

She took a deep breath and stepped into the hallway. Pausing at the top of the stairway, she caught the sound of activity from the first floor. Distant voices and the clatter of furniture and dishware. Steeling herself, she headed down the stairs and into uncharted territory.

CHAPTER 4

The hotel lobby was deserted. Down the hall to Raina's right the dining area bustled with life, giving off tantalizing scents that wafted into the foyer. Raina's stomach growled as her appetite kicked in. Following her nose, the lovely smells brought her to a large room with a long buffet set up near the arched entrance. At a glance, the spread was decadent.

There were several round tables in the room, most of them occupied. Troy and Michael sat at one close to the back, near an unmarked door. Two other people were at the table with them: A man with gray-streaked brown hair and a mature platinum-blonde woman whose outfit and posture spoke of wealth. Both wore black. Many people in the room did. Fancy and funerary.

Catching sight of Raina, Michael lifted a hand, gesturing for her to come over. The silent invitation came as a surprise and a relief. No need to sit alone.She crossed the room to his table, feeling eyes on her from all directions. Her mind raced for something clever to say to the prince and his group. When in her element she could be quite a conversationalist, engaging and even funny. Under pressure, she drew a blank. She'd never been able to pull off charming on demand.

As she approached the table, she donned a confident smile to hide her nerves. The older man to Michael's right returned it with a gentle one of his own. The blonde woman eyed her, openly critical, and lit a long black cigarette.

"Good evening, Raina." Michael gestured to the two open chairs at the table. "Please join us."

She took the chair nearest Troy. It was either that or sit next to the woman.

"Thank you," said Raina. Polite, but not clever. Where was her wit when she needed it?

"I see you found something to wear," Troy observed.

She plucked at the skirt, self-conscious. "I did. Not exactly my usual style, but my things are back at the house. I hope they are, anyway. Oh! I left your jacket upstairs. I'll give it back to you after dinner."

"Sure. Whenever." He wasn't fussed about it.

"Troy said something about you losing your home," Michael said after a sip of red wine.

Word traveled fast.

"I was renting a place outside the Walls," Raina said. "I had a few more months left on the agreement, but for some reason the owner wanted me out this weekend. Then this afternoon, some guys broke in and grabbed me. Next thing I know, I'm on the sacrificial altar downtown." She paused to shoot Troy a grateful look. "Thankfully, Troy stepped in."

The older man at the table looked concerned. The blonde woman's dark eyes flashed heatedly—her only outward reaction. Troy smiled.

"Credit to Love's Pub," he said. "If it weren't for their two-for-one Happy Hour, I wouldn't have even been there."

"All things for a reason," said Michael. He had another sip from his glass.

Something occurred to Raina. "I need to go back and get my stuff before the landlord sells it or throws it away. I don't have much, but I want my mother's necklace. And a few other things..."

Her lack of underwear sprang to mind again.

"You're planning to go back there alone?" asked the older man, his concern growing.

"Yes. I need my stuff. Everything I own is there."

"Going by yourself doesn't sound wise," he said. "After what happened. You have no idea what—or who—might be there."

"She doesn't have to go alone," Troy pointed out.

"Father Jeremiah, always looking out for the welfare of others," said Michael. He rubbed his chin, thoughtful. "I've been meaning to take a tour of the outskirts. Things have changed while I was away."

"We could do a lap around the city," suggested Troy. "Pick up her stuff while we're out."

"Mm," said Michael noncommittally. "Let's get some food. I'm ravenous. We can discuss the matter more after we've eaten."

"I'm just having wine." The blonde woman exhaled clove-spiced cigarette smoke.

"Already full up on butterflies and June bugs, Ligeia?" Michael teased.

Raina found it an odd thing to say, but Ligeia simply huffed a short laugh laced with smoke.

"I don't like the food here," she said.

Michael rose from his chair. Troy and Jeremiah followed suit, so Raina got up and went with them over to the lavish buffet. A small table at one end held clean dinner plates and flatware rolled up in gray napkins waited in a large basket. So formal. Raina was well out of her league.

She was going to watch what the others did and take her cues from them, but Father Jeremiah motioned her ahead. Michael and Troy grabbed plates and napkin rolls, so she did too.

Exploring the buffet table was a lot like looking through the bathroom cabinets. Large platters displayed all manner of foodstuffs: Thin slices of cheese and meat, fresh fruit, an assortment of breads and flavored butters. Further down the table, silver lids covered unmarked chafing dishes. Beneath the lids were a variety of items, from roast chicken to chunks of raw red meat soaked in blood. There were vegetable dishes and something that resembled chopped-up omelet. There was also a Dutch oven with a ladle held in place by a flat lid. No one in Raina's group touched it.

After she loaded her plate with things she could identify, she peeked into the Dutch oven. She used the ladle to stir the contents. Some sort of soup? Something surfaced in the brown broth: Fleshy gray eyeballs. Recoiling in disgust, she slapped the lid down again.

"Not my favorite either," Father Jeremiah commented behind her.

She gave him a wan smile. "Yeah. I think I'll, uh. Pass on the soup."

The four of them returned to the table. Ligeia finished her cigarette while they were gone. A fresh glass of red wine sat before her on the table. Another glass of it had appeared at Raina's seat in her absence. She tried wine once at a wedding and wasn't fond of it—or any alcohol. But she wasn't going to be choosy when her hosts were so generous.

Despite what Ligeia said, the food was quite good. Better than Raina's normal fare. She avoided the wine as long as she could, but eventually, the need to wet her throat overcame her aversion. The wine was also better than what she had in the past, though still not something she would choose for herself.

"Are you going to come when we tour the outskirts?" Michael asked Jeremiah as they ate.

The prince only had the raw, blood-soaked meat chunks on his plate. He skewered the cubes with his fork and devoured them at a rapid pace. Raina tried not to stare, but the wolfish display was hard to ignore.

"I wasn't planning to," said Jeremiah. "Unless you want me to. How long do you expect it to take?"

"Is time an issue?"

Jeremiah's expression soured. "I'm not comfortable leaving the twins for long. They've... been a handful and Lenore isn't... Well, you know how she gets."

Michael's expression darkened. "Yes. I do." He paused. "I don't expect to be gone longer than a few hours." He looked over at Raina. "How much do you need to move from your house?"

Raina swallowed the bite of bread she was working on and took a quick sip of wine to clear her mouth. "Oh. Um. Well. I don't know. I haven't found a new place to live yet."

"You could live here," Troy offered. Then he looked at Michael. "Right?"

Michael tipped his head in an abbreviated nod. It didn't seem to matter to him one way or the other.

"Oh, I wouldn't want to impose," Raina said, flustered by the charitable offer. It was one thing to stay a day or two, but to live there? It hardly seemed possible.

"It wouldn't be an imposition," said Michael. "Though we don't have room for large furniture."

The wine was strong. Only a few sips in she found it difficult to think clearly. Was there anything sizable in her house she couldn't bear to part with? The furniture belonged to her mother — cheap second-hand and third-hand pieces. The couch and kitchen table were well worn and stained, the rugs the same. The bookshelf was on the verge of collapse. It would likely fall apart if moved.

"We should bring Lou and Bud along," Troy mused. "It'd make packing and porting quicker."

Michael finished his meal and pushed the red-smeared plate away. "Agreed. We'll start with the move, then tour the outskirts and head back. If we go after breakfast, we'll be back before evening."

"I'll let Lenore know," said Jeremiah. He drank the last of his wine.

"Are you coming too, Auntie?" Michael asked.

The blonde woman lit a cigarette even though others were still eating. "You're doing this tomorrow?"

"Yes."

Ligeia tipped her head back and exhaled a plume of smoke upward. "Pass. I have things to do."

"What about the laundry?" Raina said.

The others looked at her curiously.

"What about it?" Troy said, not following.

Raina smiled, giddy from the wine. "I was going to meet Beth. About doing laundry."

"That can wait. You can start after we return," Michael decided. He polished off his drink then and pushed his chair out, readying to leave the table. "We'll head out after breakfast."

Although he'd eaten quickly, Raina had expected he would spend more time lingering at the table. She wasn't sure why his leaving disappointed her, but it did.

"Have a good night," she said. Again, her words were inadequate.

He flashed her a quick smile. "And you."

Their eyes met and Raina felt an inexplicable little thrill. She blamed the wine.

Jeremiah also got up, though he hadn't finished his food. The two men left together. Troy stretched and looked across the room at the buffet. His plate was empty. Only a few lonely crumbs remained.

"I think I'm going to hit the dessert table," he said, rising from his seat. "You ladies want me to grab you anything while I'm up?"

Ligeia wrinkled her nose delicately. "I've already made my feelings about the food known."

Unfazed, Troy looked at Raina. She shook her head.

"No, thank you. I haven't finished what I have and I'm almost full."

"All right," he said. "But the devil's food cake is delish."

"I'm fine," Raina asserted with a smile.

Troy sauntered away to survey the desserts. Raina watched him go then turned her attention back to her plate. The food was so rich. There was no way she could finish it. She nibbled and poked at the piles, determined to make them smaller before she gave up.

"So," Ligeia said. "What's your situation? I don't see a ring."

Raina wore no rings or bracelets. They got in the way when she was washing clothes. "Oh. No. I'm not married. Or engaged. Or anything, really. It's just me."

"You live alone?"

"Mm-hm. It was my mother and me, but she... uh. She died. Five years ago, now."

Raina forced down another bite of ambrosia salad and had to throw in the towel. Defeated by indulgence, she set her fork aside. Stuffed.

"And this is the first time you've had problems?" Ligeia said with a touch of incredulity.

"My neighbors are decent folk. I can't say the same about my landlord, but the neighborhood itself has been mostly safe. Up until now."

The older woman made a soft, scoffing sound. "The world is a hungry beast. It's only a matter of time before it devours those who can't protect themselves."

Was that an insult? Raina wasn't sure. "I'm not going to hook up with someone just to feel safe," she said.

"There's nothing wrong with having a roommate," the older woman pointed out. "Better than that, though? Learn how to defend yourself."

"Are you talking about martial arts?" asked Raina. "Or keeping a weapon? I have—"

"I'm talking about personal power. Give me your hand."

Raina's hand obediently presented itself as though pulled on a string. Surprised by the involuntary action, she tried to retreat but Ligeia grabbed her wrist. She pressed Raina's fingers away from the palm and scrutinized it.

"Here." Ligeia lightly drew her index finger over the lines she saw. "Fate. Head. Heart."

As her fingertip moved across Raina's skin, the lines she touched glowed red. The faint light was warm, not at all uncomfortable. When Ligeia finished tracing the lines on her palm, the light connected to form a star.

"Oh, wow," Raina breathed, amazed.

"Fortune's Star. It signals you have strong potential in you. You just need to learn how to use it. It's better than any man-made weapon."

She let go of Raina's wrist. The glowing star faded.

"How did you do that?" Raina said.

Ligeia snorted a derisive laugh. "That parlor trick? Child's play. I can teach you far more important things. Things that will keep you alive."

Troy returned with two plates of treats, one in each hand. Both were full nearly to spilling. As he passed her, Raina found herself at eye level with his hips. His blue jeans were well worn. The faded denim conformed to the shape of his crotch. Suddenly aware of where she was looking, she put her attention back onto her plate. Pushed it away. Even looking at food made her feel fuller. Troy settled into his chair beside her. Rearranged a few things on his plate so he could see them better and decide the order he would eat them.

"Is there a dessert you didn't get?" Ligeia criticized.

Troy grinned at her. "When they put out so many tempting sweets, I just can't say no to any of them. Don't worry. I'll give them a good home."

He dug into a piece of pie topped with a pile of whipped cream.

"It disgusts me you can eat like that without gaining a pound," the woman grumped. She put her cigarette out in the crystal ashtray that sat next to her wine glass.

Troy had a bite of another dessert and made an intense "Mmmmm" sound. "Raina, you have to try this. You ever had a brookie?"

She looked at the thing he was holding. The bar of cake was brown on top and tan on the bottom.

"What is it?"

"Brownie and cookie together." He broke off a section and offered it to her.

She hesitated. His avid desire to share was difficult to resist. She took the chunk. It crumbled a little between her fingers. She shoved it in her mouth to keep it off her lap. It was decadently sweet.

"Isn't it the best thing you've had in your mouth?" prompted Troy.

Ligeia snickered. Troy shot her a look that tried to be disapproving even as he fought a sly smile.

Raina swallowed. "It's super sweet."

"Want some more?" he asked, ready to break off another piece.

"Oh, no," she said. "I'm full. Beyond full. But thank you. I think I'm going to head up to my room and get some rest. It's been... quite a day."

Disappointment showed on his face. Instantly she regretted her choice. Though tipsy, she wasn't so tired that she couldn't spend more time with him. But she didn't want to look indecisive, so she stuck with the plan and got to her feet. She could spend more time with him tomorrow when they went to get her stuff.

"Rest well," he said and continued to eat.

"It was nice to have dinner with you, Troy," she said. "It was nice to meet you, Ligeia."

The woman slid her a placid sidelong look. "A pleasure, dear. Sleep well."

CHAPTER 5

The floor was tricky for Raina to navigate thanks to the wine. It took concentration to make it to the hall without tripping or bumping into anything. Which was silly because she hadn't had much of it. While she wasn't a habitual drinker, she had alcohol before and never gotten a buzz on so quickly.

In the dining room, the wine had made her giddy. Now that she was up and moving, everything wanted to spin and shift. Though the lack of coordination amused her and was good reason to head to bed, she regretted calling it a night so early. She couldn't shake the notion she was missing an opportunity. What that might be was beyond her ability to imagine now.

When she got to the stairs, she paused to steady herself. Looked up at winding trek that loomed before her. The stairs seemed to have grown. They appeared steeper. Longer. A mountain of steps that led into the great beyond. Taking a secure hold on the handrail, she started up.

It was an adventure in slow motion. Every third step or so, one of her feet went astray. Fortunately, the banister was stable and a tight grip on it kept her from falling. Her awkwardness made her laugh. It was a good thing she only had half a glass of wine.

"Are you all right?"

An unfamiliar voice with a thick Austro-Bavarian accent drew her attention upward. She saw a middle-aged man coming down the stairs toward her. He had golden hair cut blunt at his shoulders. He wore a black poet's shirt and black pants. His feet were bare. The lack of footwear was an odd choice compared to his nice clothes.

"Oh, I'm fine," she assured him. "Just having a bit of... gravity."

He smiled. "I see. Do you need assistance? I wouldn't want you to fall."

She fluttered a hand, nearly knocking herself over with the motion. "Oh, no. I'm fine. Just fine. It's fine."

To prove it she started to climb again, gripping her friend the banister. Whoever made handrails was a saint. This one was particularly nice, sturdy pine wood smooth from years of use. It fit well in her hands.

"All the same, I believe I'll accompany you." The man joined her, setting his pace to hers.

"That's sweet of you. I'm Raina, by the way. You have no shoes."

"Raina." He rolled her name over his tongue, savoring it. "Lovely. My name is Pietre. I prefer not to wear shoes."

"Nice to meet you, Pietre," she said. She was about to say more about his missing footwear when something dawned on her. She paused to squint at him. "Pietre?"

He stopped when she stopped. "Yes."

"Ohh," Raina said, her eyes widening. Michael told Troy not to tell Pietre about her. Or something to that effect. "Michael mentioned you."

Amused by her reaction, his smile took on a devilish cast. "Did he now? And what did he say?"

Probably not a good idea to tell him. Michael might not like it if she blabbed. "Not much." It was true: The prince hadn't said anything about Pietre, really. "He was talking to Troy."

She resumed her upward trek. Pietre went with her, watching her hawk-like.

"You're a guest of Michael's then?" he asked.

"I am. More or less. Maybe Troy's guest? I'm not sure."

Distracted, she tripped on the second to last step. The railing stopped her fall. Pietre placed a hand on her back to help steady her. He did nothing inappropriate yet there was something unwholesome about his touch. Made her feel weird.

"Careful," he cautioned. "It's a long fall from here."

"I'm good."

Getting her balance, Raina pushed on and made it to the second-floor landing stumble-free. She was acutely aware of how his hand continued to linger on the small of her back.

"I'm fine, really," she said, moving away from the hand. "I'm just.... going to my room. Over there."

She made a loose wave in the direction of her room then headed down the hall, fighting more gravity as she went. Though the floor tried its best to make her fall she got to her door without losing her balance.

"Good night, Raina." He didn't raise his voice, yet she heard him as clearly as if he were standing right behind her.

She glanced back. He was still by the stairs. She gave him a little smile and a wave which he returned. Then she slipped into her room. It wasn't until she shut the door that she realized he now knew which one was hers. Suffering a bout of paranoia, she locked the door and put the security bolt in place.

A wave of exhaustion swept over her as she moved away from the entry. Alone and tipsy, the entire day caught up with her all at once. She staggered to the bed and sank down on the edge of the mattress. Soon she was on her back watching the ceiling spin.

She wanted to plan for the next day. At the very least, she should change into clothes better suited for bed. She did neither. Lying down was too wonderful.

The room swayed gently, lulling her. Rocked her into a heavy, dreamless sleep.

...

Gray light sifted through the space between the thick retro-print curtains. Raina didn't recognize the room when she first opened her eyes. The morning bell sounded seven o'clock and everything from the previous day came rushing back to her. Most of it, anyway. Things got hazy around midway through dinner.

She did remember the plan to go back to her house after breakfast, though. That was enough to spur her to action. She rolled out of bed and hurried through morning clean-up.

There was toothpaste and a toothbrush in the bathroom. She was okay with using the toothpaste, but she used her finger as a stand-in for a toothbrush. On par with borrowing underwear, the idea of using someone else's brush made her stomach turn. She could do a better job once she had her own again.

As she rummaged through the closet, a wave of melancholy rolled over her, accompanied by a faint headache. The headache she blamed on the wine. The mood was all her. She hated giving up on her home. She didn't have a choice but walking away felt like defeat. She was giving up on what was rightfully hers. Though the house was run down, it was where her mother had spent her final years.

Going from the downtrodden rental to the posh Bradford Hotel was both amazing and a culture shock. The amenities were luxurious. The people were admittedly peculiar but welcoming for the most part. It all felt like a bizarre dream. Like someone else's life. It was also scary to dwell too long on the idea that she was effectively homeless and depending on strangers to get by. Powerful strangers.

Politics were foreign to her. How the ruling class lived was beyond her modest upbringing. Their world was far removed from the one she came from. She knew a few key roles and that those who filled them had strange abilities, and that was about it.

Raina did see how they handled the Great Flood. When the ocean was rising, New Salem's government issued an order for everyone to make camp in the new town square near the First Church. The order applied to everyone inside the Walls and those outside as well. She and her mother had joined the camp, taking only what they could carry. Less than three hours after the evacuation order, violent weather brought a massive mega-tsunami to New Salem.

Devastating tidal waves crashed into the city, the biggest of which was reckoned to be over 1,800 feet high. Michael shielded the camp so that the epic wall of water passed harmlessly over and around them. Downtown was spared while the rest of Los Angeles was submerged for days. A modern-day Passover.

Raina would never forget what it was like, surrounded by the stormy ocean on all sides. Watching cars, trees, and even buildings swirl by while those beneath the dome remained safe and dry. The destruction was astounding, as was the knowledge that one person was responsible for diverting the water. Michael kept them all safe, and his council made sure everyone stayed fed and calm in the days that followed.

It never occurred to Raina that she might one day meet the ruling class face to face. Yet in a single evening, she had met and dined with the highest tier in New Salem—and the nation. They had even invited her to live with them. Her! Some nobody from beyond the Walls.

She was living in paradise with the elite...but for how long?

Troy made it sound as though she could stay indefinitely. At least until she got a new place. Which wouldn't happen until she had money. What little she had saved was at her old house, and it wasn't enough to afford a new home. Not even an apartment. It was part of why she'd resisted moving. She could barely afford the rent on the old place.

She got dressed, again selecting the most colorful items she could find. Then she ran her hands through her long curly hair. It was too tangled to finger-comb. She needed a hairbrush. She would be sure to grab hers along with everything else important that was back at the house.

Melancholy reared up again, chased by a futile desire for normalcy. She didn't want to be uprooted. She didn't want to leave behind the things she and her mother had shared. She was afraid of this new path. It led into the vast unknown. A blank slate she didn't know what to write on. She also faced tough decisions about what to keep from the house. The same decisions she'd avoided when she chose to fight eviction. She wasn't ready to let go, yet she had no choice. Staying there simply wasn't an option. It was time to move on to whatever this weird life held next for her.

Irritated with her own self-pity, she dabbed her moist eyes with the hem of her borrowed shirt. Tried to put thoughts of loss and upheaval from her mind. Moping wouldn't help. And her situation could certainly be worse.

She dug around in the sideboard for a comb or brush. Something to tame her bed-tousled hair. She found a hair pick and another item: A pretty little book. The cover was light brown leather with an ornate foreign design burnt into it. Swirls and jagged angles made up the border. Stars and crosses featured in the central design. Tied at the side, the well-worn book looked vaguely religious.

Curiosity overcame the blues. She untied the book and opened it. Flipped through a few pages and discovered it was a sketchbook. The thick, handmade pages bore illustrations of plants and animals, abandoned buildings, and lots of people. The artist was quite talented. Most of the images were very realistic. Toward the back, she found several drawings of Michael rendered in many ways. Here, he lounged in a chair in a fine suit. On another page was he bent over a desk or table, writing studiously. Another showed him sleeping on his stomach, his bare torso tangled in blankets that barely covered him.

Raina smiled. The book was none of her business, but the sketches were compelling. Hooked, she turned the page. The next picture brought a different vibe. The lines were bolder, heavier. It was a depiction of a nude man on a cross in front of the Church downtown. His head was down. He looked dead.

The next sketch was half-finished. It focused on two cages, the nearest of which held a man in ragged clothing. He glared hatefully out from behind the bars at the viewer. At Raina. The person in the other cage had their back to the artist. Their features and gender were obscured.

Raina shut the sketchbook and shoved it back into the drawer it came from. The disturbing drawings could be fiction. Yet other sketches depicted things that were real, such as the exterior of the Bradford Hotel. There was a distinct possibility those last pictures were real, too. Likely, even. The negative vibe she got from them sure was.

She saw no name in the book. It likely belonged to the former occupant of the room. Desiree. Troy said the woman was no longer with them. What did he mean? Who was the man on the cross? And the people in the cage? Why were they locked up? Why had the artist drawn them? A multitude of questions surrounding the drawings tumbled together in her mind. She gave the drawer a last uneasy glance and then left the room.

CHAPTER 6

The morning meal was as odd as dinner the night before. Metal trays held piles of standard breakfast foods such as eggs and ham, set alongside covered dish filled with raw meat. There was another crock of something Raina chose to avoid, not wishing to have a repeat "soup" incident so early. She went with a safer bet: Pancakes smothered in chocolate and caramel, and crispy thick-cut bacon on the side.

She sat at Michael's table again with the same group of people from the previous night. As she ate, the sketchbook preyed on her thoughts. Now and then she stole a glance at Michael. He was the last subject the artist sketched before the pictures turned grim. Did he know anything about the caged people?

The third time she looked his way he caught her. She quickly looked away, embarrassed. Tried to focus on her food even though she was pretty sure he was still looking at her. She risked a quick peek to check. Sure enough, their eyes met. She suffered another rush of self-consciousness and that same little flutter of excitement she got last night when he was getting ready to leave.

She gave him a smile in an attempt to normalize the situation. He smiled back then returned to the raw meat on his plate. She looked away again, resolving to keep her eyes anywhere but on him. Being conscious of what she was looking at, however, made it more difficult to look around casually.

To occupy herself, she analyzed what the other people at the table wore. Troy and Jeremiah had on similar clothes as yesterday. Jeremiah wore a simple black button-down shirt, pants, and loafers. Troy was in a faded black t-shirt with the words "I Don't Know How but They Found Me" emblazoned on it in pink, old blue jeans, and his motorcycle boots.

Ligeia and Michael were the only ones who'd noticeably altered their outfit choices. Ligeia wore a black strapless dress and blazer, black silk stockings, and pointy Mary Jane heels that accented her long legs. Michael had on a black watered silk shirt and a loose black coat. A blood-red ascot added a splash of color. His pants were snug-fitting black velvet that conformed nicely to his shape... and Raina realized she was staring at him again.

She looked back at her plate but not before he noticed.

—

When breakfast was over it was time to head out. The group that was going on the excursion to Raina's house included herself, Michael, Troy, Jeremiah, and two additional men, Bud and Lou. Lou was tall, Bud was shorter. Both were equally burly, and neither was inclined to smile.

They left the hotel in three vehicles. The workmen took a small box truck, Troy rode his motorcycle. Michael drove a sleek, fancy car he said was a converted Bugatti Chiron.

Raina didn't know much about cars. She hadn't seen many up close and had ridden in even fewer. Her lack of knowledge didn't prevent her appreciating the Bugatti, though. Low to the ground and shiny black with red detailing, its tapered design put her in mind of a snake or a dragon. Even though she was clueless about cars, she could tell it was a superior machine.

She expected Jeremiah to ride with Michael, but the prince insisted she go with him to tell him where to go. The vehicle had no rear seats, so Jeremiah rode in the box truck with Bud and Lou. It was either that or double up with Troy on the motorcycle.

"My house is south of Calvary Cemetery," Raina told Michael as they took off down the long, straight stretch of weathered freeway and sped toward what used to be East Los Angeles. "The one with the high brick wall."

"I know the one," he said. "Last time I saw it, weeds were growing on the sides of the walls."

"It's gotten worse. Whole honeysuckle bushes are growing there now. Looks pretty when they bloom, but they're tearing the bricks apart. I don't expect they walls will last much longer."

Michael pressed the gas pedal down. The throttle opened wide, and the vehicle revved up. They shot down the cracked pavement at an exhilarating speed. The engine was surprisingly quiet, the ride luxuriously smooth. The world flew by outside.

"I've never gone this fast," Raina said. It was both exciting and scary to see the scenery blur.

Michael glanced over at her and smiled. "We could go faster," he said. "But we don't want to leave our friends too far behind."

She looked in the side mirror. The truck was out of sight. Troy's motorcycle was a spot on the horizon. She turned to look at Michael once more. Studied his profile. Her mother's art books sprang to mind again. Lyra had loved all kinds of art, particularly Renaissance sculpture and paintings—a trait she passed on to her daughter.

"You're not what I expected," she admitted on impulse.

He threw her a quick look, one eyebrow arching. "Really. And what did you expect?"

She plucked at her borrowed skirt self-consciously. Which was silly. She didn't typically care about what anyone thought of her. She shouldn't make an exception for him because he was handsome or politically important. And yet she did care. She found herself wanting him to like her, which was even more ridiculous. There was no room in her life for silly crushes.

"I don't know," she said. "I guess I expected someone... older, I suppose. More reserved. Or... I don't know."

In truth, she hadn't heard much about the Lord Prince. She knew he was the leader of the nation. He was powerful. Unreachable. Some said he killed people or had them killed. The altar in the town square seemed to support those dark rumors.

"The people in the square," she ventured. "Troy... he stopped them killing me. They said—the Prophet. She said I was a sacrifice for—for you."

Michael eased off the gas pedal. The world outside the windows slowed.

"The fanatics at the Church came up with that ritualistic nonsense," he said, his humor evaporating. "It has nothing to do with me or my wishes."

She knew she should be careful what she said, but after what happened she was puzzled and wanted answers. There was too much she didn't understand.

"Why do you let them do it?"

A furrow appeared between his brows. His eyes remained steadfastly locked on the road ahead. "It keeps them busy and out of my hair."

"It doesn't bother you that they're hurting others?"

"I don't have time to worry about such things. I have bigger issues to deal with."

"What issues?" She wondered if those issues had anything to do with people in cages.

"Keeping this city functioning, for one." The car sped up again. "Trade doesn't flow on its own. Laws don't enforce themselves. Diplomacy doesn't happen without someone playing diplomat."

"Can't you delegate some of that to other people?"

"I do," he said. "But those people need managing. When it comes to a choice between meeting with delegates about our food supplies or meeting with the Prophet about her rituals, food takes precedence."

Raina had a feeling there was more he wasn't saying, but her questions obviously bothered him. They were close to their destination, so she decided to drop it. For now.

They rode in silence until they reached the first Wall, which cut across the freeway. It separated New Salem from the rest of the world. Constructed from debris of ruined buildings and rusty metal shipping containers, the interior Wall was wide enough for a person to walk along the top. It towered thick and tall, casting long shadows over the buildings nearby.

It was the most formidable of three barricades the city had erected over the years. A unit of guardsmen had to lift a heavy door for them to drive through it. Michael stopped at the guard station to tell them there were two more vehicles in the convoy. Then they were through.

The next two Walls were smaller than the interior one. The middle one was more of a fence than a wall. The gate there was easier to lift and manned by only two people. The outer Wall was even less impressive, made of piled junk strung together with barbed wire. The wheeled chain-link gate was unguarded and left open most of the time.

The freeway beyond the Walls was sun-bleached white. Cracked and littered with dirt, leaves, and fallen branches, it was completely desolate. Uncanny because of its empty size.

"At the third exit ahead," Raina said. "Turn left."

Michael eased up on the gas once more, preparing for the turn. Troy's motorcycle came tearing down the road behind them. He slowed as he got closer to the car so he wouldn't overshoot them. She looked out the window at him. He wore a leather jacket, though not the one he'd loaned her when they met. It was still in her room. He lifted one hand in a salute. She waved back.

"Thank you," she said as she looked over at Michael again. "For everything. I really appreciate your time and help."

He flicked a look at her and the crease between his brows eased. "I'm a believer in 'all things for a reason'. You're here with me for a purpose."

"How do you mean?"

He slowed further as the blanched offramp narrowed into a street. Old graffiti brought color to the fence along the south side. Years of exposure to the elements had faded the spray paint to chalky pastel. They passed an old mattress dumped on the sidewalk. A pack of scrawny dogs sniffed around it. One lifted its leg to mark the mattress as the car passed.

"We can discuss it later," he said. "Where is your house?"

She gazed at him quizzically, but he was firm in his resolve to keep the topic a mystery. She looked out the windshield. Got her bearings.

"Two streets down and to the right," she said. "It's the third house on the north side of the road."

———

If the area had seen better days, it was a long time ago. A sense of long-term neglect infested the neighborhood, predating the end of the old world. Where there was paint on the water-damaged houses, it was peeling badly. A few had caved in on themselves, with huge holes in the roofs and gaping windowpanes that held no trace of glass. Scraggly weeds choked patchy yards. Generations of poverty and years of neglect gave the area its character.

They pulled up alongside a crumbling curb nearly destroyed by previous earthquakes. Michael put the car into park and looked out at the dilapidated old house. Its roof was intact, but the porch was sagging noticeably. A few large black birds flapped in and settled on the badly weathered rooftop.

"No offense," Michael said, eyeing the place critically. "But I don't think you're losing much here."

Raina wasn't offended. The state of the place was beyond her control. "It's what Mom and I could swing."

"Was she kidnapped too?"

"Oh. No. She died a while back. A few months after the Great Flood. I've been living on my own for about five years now."

She didn't feel the need to mention her ex-boyfriend. He didn't deserve it.

"I see," said Michael. He didn't give her sympathy or seem to think any was needed. Instead, he looked at the house again. "Let's go on up. Troy will lead the others here. He's already doubled back."

Most people offered condolences when they learned about her mother's death or asked how she died. While it was a relief to avoid another round of social awkwardness it struck Raina as peculiar that it didn't seem to matter to him.

She pushed open the car door and slid out of her seat into the warm sunshine. A pleasant breeze rustled the branches of trees. The coastal weather was insolently unaware of her situation.

Michael got out as she came around to the sidewalk on his side. He led the way up the concrete path that divided the front yard into two poorly tended dirt patches. Raina caught herself watching the confident way he strode up the walk. She needed to stop looking at him so much. He was going to get the wrong idea.

More black birds flew up to join their brethren atop the house. Were they ravens or crows? She could never remember which was which.

Stepping up onto the porch, they found the front door bolted with a thick padlock fixed through a new latch. Raina grabbed the lock and tugged. It didn't budge.

"Not yours?" Michael said.

She shook her head. "No." She gave the lock a sour glare. "We can try the back door..."

"Mm," Michael said. "My guess is it's locked too."

Before she could offer another suggestion, he put out a hand and made a twisting motion in the air. The lock shuddered and the U-shaped clasp snapped apart. The lock dropped to the porch with a sharp clatter.

Raina looked from the lock to Michael in surprise. She knew he had strange powers but seeing him use them right in front of her was quite an experience.

"Can we just... do that?"

Michael flashed her a charming smile. "We just did." He waved an arm and the door swung open on its own. "After you."

"Thanks," she said, dazzled by the display.

She stepped inside and immediately stopped. The bookshelf in the entry hall was ravaged, its contents thrown on the floor.

"What the..?" she said.

Michael came in behind her and, seeing the mess, brushed ahead of her. He passed close enough for her to catch a whiff of his scent: Fine cologne and the spicy clove cigarettes his aunt smoked, along with a masculine undertone that was all him.

"Anybody here?" he called.

The house was dead silent.

Raina followed him into the living room. It, too, had been ransacked. Couch cushions tossed about. Broken dishes littered the floor Even the pictures were ripped from the walls.

"I've only been gone one night," protested Raina, victimized all over again.

"It doesn't take long to loot a place," Michael said. "You should gather what you came for."

She nodded and headed toward her bedroom, dreading what she would find.

CHAPTER 7

Raina's bedroom was a wreck. Everything she owned was on the floor. Clothes were strewn everywhere. Her bed was torn up, the mattress gutted and flipped up against the wall. Every dresser drawer was pulled out and emptied. A tornado would do less damage.

Numb, she bent to gather a few of her wrinkled garments. "Bastards."

Troy's motorcycle roared up out front and shut off.

"They sure did work this place over," observed Michael.

He helped her pick up her clothes, draping them over his arm. When he found a pair of blue panties in the clutter he paused.

"I don't have anything worth stealing," she objected. The initial shock was fading to anger. "Did they have to throw everything on the floor?"

Noticing what he held she snatched the underwear from him, flushing hotly. She stuffed the underpants into the wad of clothes she held. "You can just put stuff, um, on the bed. Bedframe."

She happened to glance into the bathroom and her heart sank. Abandoning her armload of clothing on the box spring, she hurried over. The small room was destroyed. Linens, toiletries, everything was in a heap on the floor. Anxiety growing, she dug around.

"They took all my jewelry," she said. "Most of it's just— it's not important really. But my mother's necklace..! They took my mother's necklace!"

She kept pawing through the scattered stuff just in case, growing more frantic as she did.

"What does it look like?" Michael asked from the doorway.

"It's a, um. It's a steel chain." She gestured at her chest to imply the length. "It has a pendant with a glass front that shows her picture. A memory locket thing. It has tiny letters in it: M-O-M. They have little crystals on them. But they're not real. Just... just cheap glass things. But there's a small lock of her hair in it. A memory mento."

"Memento mori," he corrected gently.

"It's all I have left of her!"

Michael looked around at the mess. "They probably took whatever they thought they could sell."

She finished tearing through the counter drawer and slammed it in frustration. "Who would buy a picture of someone else's mother?"

"You might be surprised." he nudged the junk on the floor with the toe of his boot. "Perhaps it will turn up."

Raina sagged to sit down on the toilet, close to tears. She needed a moment to collect herself. Outside, the truck rolled up. Its rumbling engine vibrated the windows before it shut off.

"I'll deal with this after I pick up my clothes," she decided, her tone flat. She looked up at him. "Do you know where someone might sell stolen jewelry?"

"No. But I might be able to find someone who does."

She latched onto the idea to keep herself from sinking into angry despair. She had to keep going. There would be time later to process everything.

"You guys in here?" Troy called from the front of the house.

"Back here," Michael said.

He didn't raise his voice, but Troy seemed to hear him anyway as he soon arrived at the bedroom doorway. Raina recalled meeting Pietre on the stairs the night before. He'd used that same voice trick on her.

"What happened?" Troy marveled.

"Thieves. Vandals," Michael said. "Could be the people who took Raina. They put a padlock on the front door." He looked at her. "Your landlord. Would he do something like this?"

She shook her head slowly. "I don't think so? He's old. In bad shape. Not the type, I don't think." She sighed and her shoulders drooped. "But then I also didn't think he was the type to kick out his contracted tenants either."

"Do you know how to reach him?"

"I know where he lives."

"Thinking about paying him a visit?" asked Troy. He sounded as though he liked the idea.

"I think it might be in order." Michael retreated from the bathroom. He surveyed the bedroom again. "He may know who broke in. Have Bud and Lou bring in a couple of boxes. I'm going to check out the rest of the house with Father Jeremiah."

———

It took a couple of hours but eventually Raina packed everything that was worth saving. Her necklace and anything remotely valuable in the house was gone. Whoever stole her things also took several knives, all her matches, and raided the pantry for nonperishables.

She took a few moments to change. Once she was in her own clothes she felt better despite the state of her house. Even though she'd packed several boxes, stuff still covered the floor. Ironic how much she owned that wasn't worth salvaging. Perhaps she should have let go of a few things sooner.

Lou and Bud loaded Raina's boxes into the truck. Michael and Jeremiah joined her and Troy in the living room.

"We should take the boxes back to the hotel. The truck will slow us down." Michael turned his attention to Raina, who was taking a last wistful look around. "Do you want to go with them? Or with us?"

The question pulled Raina out of her glum slump. "To talk to my ex-landlord?"

Michael nodded. "The longer we wait, the more time there is for your necklace to disappear for good."

"What about your tour of the outskirts?"

He shrugged. "It will keep." He looked at Jeremiah. "Do you want to pair up with Troy?"

Jeremiah winced. "Not particularly. No reflection on your driving, Troy. I just can't stand the bugs in my face."

"They're not so bad today." Troy grinned and made a picking motion at his teeth.

"Even still..." Jeremiah looked at Michael. "Unless you need me, I'd rather head home. Or I could go back with the guys and take my car to meet you."

Michael considered and shrugged again. "I don't expect we'll need you for this. I'll send word if we do."

"Sounds good," Jeremiah said. "I'll head back to the mansion."

———

The ride to the landlord's house was a quick one. He didn't live far from Raina's neighborhood and Michael drove fast. Unburdened by the truck, Troy kept pace with the car on his motorcycle. They weren't racing precisely, but there was some friendly jockeying taking place.

"Is he your brother?" she asked. They didn't look like brothers, but one never knew.

She kept a hand on the door to steady herself as they whipped around a corner. She kept her attention on him. Looking out the window made her nervous at this high speed.

"Troy?" Michael said. "No. I don't have any siblings."

"I'm an only child, too," said Raina. "Runs in my family."

"I wish I could say the same," Michael smirked. "My family is glutted with sibling rivalry. Lots of twins, too."

"Twins? How fun."

Michael snorted a laugh. "Double the displeasure."

Outside, Troy pulled ahead. Michael took manual control of the gears and shifted up. The engine thrummed as he nosed ahead of the motorcycle.

"Really?" Raina said. "That's too bad. I always heard having a twin was fun. Secret languages and all."

"Have you known any twins?"

She thought about it. "Once, when I was little."

"How'd they get along?"

"Well, now that you mention it... They got in a fight over who was better friends with me."

One corner of Michael's mouth turned up in a wry smile. "Sounds about right."

"Up on the left," Raina said, spying the house. It was coming up fast. "The beige and blue one."

Michael slowed the car. With a smooth motion, he pulled the car up to the low sidewalk and killed the engine. Troy parked behind him.

"What's the guy's name?" Michael asked.

"Eli. Eli Conroy."

"Let me do the talking," he said.

Their eyes met and again she got that silly little thrill. She clamped down on it. She had no business finding him attractive just because he was helping her. She wasn't interested in complicating her situation with thoughts of relationships, and he was far above her station.

He got out of the car and shut the door. Raina slid out on her side and waited on the sidewalk for the men to join her. Though they were close to her in age, they were not her peers. They had more responsibilities, power, and connections than she could imagine. They were leaders. She couldn't even keep a roof over her head.

They followed a path made of paving stones up to the front door, Michael in the lead. A small flock of blackbirds flew ahead of them to perch in a dead tree and along the eaves of the roof. Troy scoped out the neglected yard as their group stepped under the canopy that shaded the porch. Michael rapped on the door. At the second strike of his knuckles, it creaked inward.

There was a pregnant pause. Troy and Michael shared a look, then the prince glanced back at Raina. She was as surprised as they were.

Cautious now, Troy pushed the door all the way open. Three flies buzzed out of the house. With them came a foul scent of something rotten. Like spoiled meat.

"Oh, ugh!" Raina exclaimed when the rancid odor reached her.

"Not good," said Troy. He knew that scent.

Michael frowned. He was no stranger to the smell either. "Be ready," he murmured to Troy. Then he entered the house.

Troy followed, flexing his fingers like he was going to grab something. Raina took up the rear, hugging herself. The foul stench of decay grew stronger as they moved down the entry hall toward the living room. Though sickeningly putrid, it didn't prepare them for the sight they found.

A body hung over the hearth, hands nailed to the mantle, throat cut from ear to ear. Coals from a recent fire still glowed in the fireplace. The corpse was stripped naked. Left shut up in the warm house, it rotted quickly. Raina gasped. The horrible funk in the air made her instantly regret it. She looked away from the gruesome spectacle.

"Your landlord?" Michael asked.

Raina forced herself to look at the dead man's ashen face and winced. She averted her eyes again. "Yeah. That's him. Oh, God. It's so awful."

The smell was so strong she could taste it. She lifted the collar of her blouse and pressed it over her nose and mouth.

"So much for asking him anything," remarked Troy. He waved a hand before him but that did nothing to abate the smell.

"Did the Church do this?" Raina said, backing toward the open door and the fresh air filtering in through it.

Michael was the only one immune to the rot. He stared at the dead man thoughtfully. "No. They're not opposed to crucifixion, but this isn't their work. Someone else did this."

"Should I burn the body?" asked Troy.

After consideration, Michael said: "No. We need other eyes on this if we're to learn who did it. Gather the others. Have them meet us at the mansion. If someone is crucifying people in my city, I want to know who. And why."

———

They shut the door behind them as they left. Michael took a plastic bag from his coat pocket and took a piece of charcoal out of it. He drew a sigil in the center of the door and muttered some arcane words Raina didn't understand.

"What's he doing?" she asked Troy.

"Putting up a ward. Keeps people out."

Michael finished what he was doing and put the charcoal back in the bag. He dropped it into his pocket. "If anyone messes with the house, it'll give them a shock they won't forget."

They went back to their vehicles. Troy took off in the direction they had come. Michael steered his car the opposite way. He still drove fast, but not at the breakneck speed he'd reached on the way there.

Raina hoped the disgusting smell would leave her, but it persisted. It was cloying. Fatty and noxious, it lingered in her throat and nose and clung to her skin.

"How did you do that thing with the door?" she asked.

"What, the ward?"

"Yes."

"It's a trick Pietre taught me," Michael dismissed.

"Do you have a trick to get rid of this stink?" She waved a hand over herself in a futile attempt to dust it off.

Michael chuckled. "Not a fan of the smell of death?"

"Absolutely not." Raina scrunched her nose. "It's disgusting. I can't believe it doesn't bother you."

"I've smelled it too many times, I suppose. I'm used to it."

He reached over her. Popped open the glove box and pulled out a small, unmarked glass bottle. He placed it in her hand, his fingers brushing hers. It was a whisper of a touch, but in that instant, she noticed how warm his skin was. A riot of intimate notions sprang up unbidden. Thoughts of touching him again, kissing, caressing...

"I could never get used to that disgusting smell," she said to distract herself from the impure ideas.

The bottle had a spray pump. She spritzed a squirt on the front of her blouse and sniffed. It was the cologne Michael was wearing.

"You might be surprised at what a body can accustom itself to," he said. Then: "Would you like to learn how to do it?"

"Get used to the smell of death? No, thanks."

"No," he smiled. "The ward. I could teach you."

"You could?" Raina perked up. "I mean... do you think I can learn?"

"I believe so. You have the potential, I can tell. Troy sensed it too. It's why he rescued you."

That was sobering. She gave herself another spritz of cologne and put the bottle back in the glove box. "Oh. I guess I thought he saved me out of some sort of... I don't know."

"Troy's no hero." Michael's tone was casual. "Though he does have a soft spot for damsels in distress. In your case, he knew you could be useful."

Useful. The description didn't sit well with Raina. "Well. Either way, I'm glad he stopped those people."

"Why does that bother you?" Michael asked, picking up on her discomfort. "Being useful is something many people aren't."

"I don't know." On the spot, she laced her fingers in her lap to stop herself fidgeting. "It just sounds so... cold."

"Cold, hm?" he reflected. "I see."

She expected him to say something else. He didn't. He just turned on the car stereo. The vintage sound of Creedence Clearwater Revival's "Run Through the Jungle" crackled through the speakers thanks to New Salem's only local radio station.

CHAPTER 8

The sleek black car coasted up to a venerable building that sprawled across a plot of land big enough for two houses. Three stories, the Remington mansion towered over the single-level homes around it. Its size and ornate Victorian design dominated the neighborhood.

Late morning sun washed out the red brick exterior. Several blackbirds took perch around the estate as Michael and Raina got out of the Bugatti. Rows of stained-glass windows were dark eyes in the brick exterior. Raina got the distinct impression the house was watching her.

Michael paused on the leaf-strewn sidewalk and looked up. Many of the birds settled in the gnarled limbs of a large tree in front of the house. The autumn breeze stirred faint, tinkling notes from a rusty windchime that dangled from a crooked branch. A lone raven took wing to circle above them. After two passes, it gave a sharp caw and flew off.

Michael watched it, then shifted his attention to Raina.

He smiled. "Welcome to my home."

———

The massive front door swung open silently at Michael's approach without the need for him to raise a hand. Though he'd performed a similar trick at her house, the move reinforced the mysteriousness of the old place.

He let Raina into a foyer with intricate wood paneling and dark brown floorboards. Sunlight filtered through stained glass windows beside the door, dappling the walls blue and green. A short hall extended from the foyer to a boxy flight of stairs that led up to the floors above. A wooden newel post stood at the bottom of the steps, its top darkened from years of people touching it. To the right and left, wide arched doorways opened into a dining room and a sitting room, both done in dark tones.

A musky scent of age permeated the house and there was a palpable energy that hung in the air. A heavy sense of history. Old buildings often held an interesting vibe Raina noticed. A couple of locations made her dizzy with their latent energy.

This place had a strong presence though she would be hard-pressed to describe it if asked. It was as though the house itself had a personality. A sentience. And it was aware of her. It had an ambience of mystery to it that intrigued and intimidated Raina. Much like Michael himself.

He led her to the sitting room where Jeremiah sat on a long dark green couch. Two little boys played on the Persian rug between him, and a coffee table made of brass-framed glass.

The boys were twins, about five years of age, with fair hair that curled softly around their cherubic faces. They wore button-down shirts and shorts, light green and white. Nice clothing, but still in the realm of play clothes. They were tracing the pattern of the rug with toy cars. Both boys looked up when Raina and Michael came into the room.

"Daddy!" one chirped, dropping his car.

He started to get to his feet, but his brother grabbed his shirt and pulled him back down. The two glowered at each other for a moment then the boy who'd done the pulling looked up at Michael.

"Hello," he said politely.

Michael looked down at the twins. "Hello. Have you been good for Father Jeremiah and Mother Lenore?"

The boys hesitated a beat, then said in unison: "Yes."

Michael looked to Jeremiah for confirmation. The man tipped his head, his lips thinning to a repressed line.

"For the most part," he agreed.

Raina looked from the twins to Michael. He was full of surprises. "They're your children?"

He looked at her and bobbed his head in a single nod. "Gabriel, Zachariel," he said, motioning to each in turn. "This is Raina. She's... a friend."

Surely he called her a friend because it was the easiest way to explain her presence to them. But Raina appreciated the designation anyway.

"Hello," the boy identified as Zachariel said to her the same way he had to Michael.

Gabriel eyed her suspiciously then picked his car up again. He busied himself playing with it. Raina could relate. She never liked meeting her mother's friends when she was a child.

"You're married?" she asked Michael.

He fiddled with one of his rings, a gold band set with a small purple stone that he wore on his left pinkie finger. "No. Their mother passed away the day they were born. We were never married."

It was obvious the subject was an awkward one for him, though he didn't seem sad. Neither did the twins, who had tuned out the conversation and were playing again.

"I'm sorry for your loss," Raina said automatically. Then: "Wow. You're a father."

Michael pursed his lips. "They are my sons. Jeremiah and Lenore, my grandmother, mind them for me. I'm a busy man."

"Boys," Jeremiah said. "Why don't you go to the kitchen and see if Cailleach has a snack for you? The grownups need to have a chat."

Though he worded it like an invitation, there was only one correct response. The kids, uninterested in adult conversation, gathered up their toys and trotted out. Raina watched them go.

"How old were you when you had them?" she asked when they were out of the room. She immediately wished she hadn't. It was an awfully personal question.

Michael hesitated, then said: "Twenty. They... weren't planned."

Reina realized his earlier remark about troublesome twins had a much deeper meaning.

"They're cute," she said. "They look a lot like you."

He smiled and she cringed inside at her choice of wording. She hadn't meant to imply anything about him. To avoid more awkwardness, she found herself a seat near the tiled fireplace. Resolved to think about what she was going to say before saying it.

The front door opened with a burst of sunlight and thumped shut. Troy came to the sitting room where he lingered in the doorway. Ligeia swept in past him, dressed to kill as always. Another woman followed her in. She was skinny and looked to be about Ligeia's age. Her black hair was cut in a blunt bob with bangs that skimmed her peaked brows. Heavy black eyeliner framed her eyes. She wore a form-fitting black knit dress and a black leather cincher belt that narrowed her waist waspishly. Her tapered stiletto heels were vicious.

"Raina," Michael said. "This is Trixie. She's a liaison between the larger factions in New Salem. My voice to the masses."

"Hi," Raina said, lifting her hand in a slight wave.

Trixie looked her over. Smiled. "Hello." Then, to Michael: "Troy said you might be training her?"

"We'll see," Michael replied noncommittally.

Pietre came into the room dressed much as he had been when Raina met him before, right down to his bare feet. Three individuals were with him, their relation obvious. The triplets were close to her age and had a haunted worldliness to their hollow eyes. Milk-white skin and hair the color of old straw. The two women wore loose ivory peasant dresses. Their brother wore a muslin poet's shirt and loose trousers, also ivory.

"Raina, this is Pietre," said Michael. "He and Ligeia are the High Priest and High Priestess of New Salem's Coven."

Though she had met Pietre before, Raina didn't mention it. Her memory of the encounter was hazy. A formal introduction freed her from the secret of the meeting. She could dismiss it and start fresh. She gave him a quick smile. He smiled back. There was nothing quick about it.

"Pietre, Raina is my guest." Michael went on. "With him are his apprentices Tisi—" The triplet woman in braids bobbed her head. "Alec—" The man lifted a hand. "—and Meg."

Meg stared at Raina, unblinking. The look wasn't hostile. It was like she was looking right through Raina. Eventually, she blinked and looked over at Michael.

"We have a mystery to investigate," Michael told the group. "Troy and Raina went with me to her landlord's house this morning to ask him about things taken from her home. Someone else got to him before us. They had quite a time with the fellow."

"How do you mean?" Pietre prompted, instantly engaged. Enthusiastic, even.

"They crucified him on his fireplace," Troy supplied.

Michael made a face. He'd wanted to do the big reveal in his own style. "It was a mess."

"And a strong statement," put in Jeremiah, frowning deeply. The subject troubled him.

"I'm sorry I missed that," said Pietre, sounding truly disappointed. "Is he still there?"

Michael nodded. He started to pace before the fireplace, his hands clasped behind his back. "We didn't touch anything. I warded up the place so no one else can get in. You're welcome to check it out yourself. I was hoping you would."

"Delightful!" Pietre said.

Ligeia rolled her eyes in disgust and lit a cigarette.

The triplets listened to the conversation but didn't share Pietre's reaction. They weren't reacting to what was being said at all. Both the warlock's behavior and that of the triplets struck Raina as odd. They were a strange collective indeed.

"Find out what you can," Michael said. "The more information, the better."

"Ahh," said Pietre. "A hunt I can appreciate. The children and I haven't been on one in too long."

"I'll leave it to you then," said the prince. "Find out if there's any kind of a signature or claim. I want to know who did it and why."

"Of course."

"I need to get with you about another matter later." Michael maintained his slow pace before the hearth. "But first, I want this mystery put to rest."

He shifted his attention to Trixie. "Visit the Church. Find out what they know. Someone delivered Raina to the Prophet. I want to know who they are and if they're the ones who took her from her home." Then, to Ligeia: "Would you check with the Coven?"

"I can," agreed Ligeia, exhaling smoke. "But I can assure you we had nothing to do with it."

"I believe you," agreed Michael. "But someone might have heard something."

She nodded.

He looked at Jeremiah next. "I need you to talk to the Order. I don't expect they're involved either, but it's a stone to turn."

Father Jeremiah's expression flickered. "I don't think the Order had anything to do with it either. But I suppose now is a good time to tell you Jacob's been..." He trailed off, uncomfortable.

Michael peered at him. "Has your grandson been acting out?"

Raina looked at Jeremiah in surprise. He didn't look old enough to be a grandfather. He must have gotten an early start too, a pattern she was beginning to recognize within the group. Watching them work together was fascinating. Discovering their nuances equally so. If she'd known, she would have paid more attention to politics.

"Not exactly," said Jeremiah, oblivious to her scrutiny. "It's that... well. He and several other children have been hanging around the abandoned theater in old downtown. He said they're 'learning things'."

"Hm. Find out what they're up to," Michael decided. "And ask Jacob if they've heard anything about the dead landlord while you're at it."

Jeremiah bowed his head in a nod. "And the Society?"

Michael helped himself to a black cigarette from the silver case that sat on the end table between him and Ligeia. "I thought I would pay them a visit." He lit the cigarette and exhaled clove-scented smoke. He looked at Raina. "Want to come?

"The Society?" Raina asked.

"The best of the worst."

The description was hardly enticing. "I should probably go back to the hotel and deal with my stuff."

"We moved everything to your room," Jeremiah supplied helpfully. "Nothing is unpacked but it should all be there for you to sort through."

She smiled at him, appreciating the courtesy. "Thank you. That's very kind of you."

She didn't need the help, but having it made the whole ordeal more bearable. And easier. No need to worry about how she was going to get all those boxes upstairs.

"All right, then," Michael said. "Troy, would you take Raina back to the hotel?"

"Sure," he agreed. "You want me to ask around downtown while I'm at it? Someone at Love's Pub might have heard something..."

Michael was unimpressed. "Just don't get drunk. I might need you later today."

"I'll stick to mead," Troy promised. He looked at Raina. "You want to hit the pub on the way to the hotel?"

She didn't. After the wine last night, she had even less interest in alcohol than before. But his expression was so hopeful she found it difficult to say no. Why was she such a sucker for that look? Especially from men. It was a flaw she should work on.

"I don't mind," she said.

"Great! Let's go."

CHAPTER 9

The trip to Love's Pub on Troy's motorcycle was nicer than the first time Raina rode with him. He loaned her his jacket again, but it was for safety rather than necessity as the temperature was fair by day. She intended to return this jacket as soon as they got back to the hotel. The other one was still in her room. She didn't want to start a collection.

She sat behind Troy this time, her arms around his waist. Since the ride wasn't chilly when she was fully clothed, she could take in the way the machine moved beneath her. It was fun. Her whole body shifted with the curves in the road, making her more a part of the experience. In town he drove slower than Michael tended to. Speed wasn't necessary; they were only minutes away from the town square.

Even at a relaxed pace, though, her long hair whipped about, lashing her cheeks and neck. She wished she had a ponytail holder to tame it. She found if she ducked behind his shoulders the wind didn't pull at her hair as much. It meant having to put her cheek against his back. Hopefully, he didn't mind.

The motorcycle stopped in front of a squat warehouse that had been converted to a public bar. A variety of colorful handmade signs layered the front of Love's Pub. Drink specials and food ads covered the multipaned windows. There were also joke signs such as "Soup of the Day: Tequila" and "Rum before noon makes you a pirate, not a drunk". The front door was propped open for easy access.

"Want some lunch while we're here?" Troy asked as he led the way. "They've got great fried fish."

Stepping inside, Raina had to pause to let her eyes adjust to the dimness. The smell of fried food was strong. It was a busy place. Almost every table was taken.

"Sit yourself wherever," a man behind the bar called to them over voices and the clatter of dishes.

"There's a spot," Raina said, pointing to a small, lopsided table in the back.

They headed that way. The chairs were mismatched. The tabletop was a chunk of concrete with a resin coating. Sitting down, she ran her fingers over the surface. The slab had numbers stamped on it, filled with resin. Like the mansion they'd left, the concrete had an aura of history to it.

"I wonder where this is from," she mused.

Troy looked at the table, not sure what fascinated her. "Looks like a piece of the sidewalk."

"It looks old."

Troy grabbed a paper menu from a clamp near the wall where the salt and pepper shaker lived.

"Oh, hey. They've got Reubens now," he said. He slid the paper over to her. "Have what you want. I'll catch the tab."

"Thanks," she said. "That reminds me... Do I need to pay for the food I've been eating at the hotel? Or will it come out of my pay for laundry when I start?"

He blinked at her wide-eyed, then grinned. "You don't need to worry about that. We work on a... trade system. Service for goods. You do what you're supposed to, you get room and board. You want money? You have to do more."

"What sort of 'more'?" she asked, trying not to sound suspicious. Trading services for goods she understood. Equal exchange was easy. Money in return for undefined "more" did not make sense.

"Well, take me for instance. I do what Michael needs me to do, and he provides me with the things I need and want. Food, gas, drinks. But if, say, somebody in town wants me to find someone for them? They pay me. Somebody wants me to take a message to Michael? They pay."

"So... Within the, uh, the group, you're... what's it called?"

"Socialists?" Troy shrugged. "I suppose. I try to avoid putting titles on things. Too messy. If you want something, just ask me. I'll make sure you get it. If it's unreasonable or something I can't get, I'll tell you."

The bartender came over and slapped some napkins down on the table. Gave them each a smile that deepened the wrinkles around his eyes.

"What can I getcha?" he asked.

"Pulled pork sandwich with fries," Troy said. "And your biggest mug of Buck's Orange."

The beer was a local favorite, named after the founder of the First Church who passed away some years back.

Raina glanced at the menu. "Um. The fried fish," she decided since Troy recommended it.

"And to drink?" the bartender prompted.

"Oh. Just water, please. And could you tell me... what's this from?" She patted the table.

The bartender eyed it. It was obvious he didn't get many people asking about his furniture. "The table? It's a bit of the old railroad platform. Got tore up when the flood hit. We found it in the loading area, so we brought it back here. My buddy turned it into a table. He's pretty handy with resin casting."

"It looks old."

"Yeah. I think the concrete was laid back in the 1930's. Over a hunnert years old now." He gave them both a nod. "Be back soon with your orders."

Once he left, Troy looked at her, impressed. "You called it."

She smiled and studied the imprint in the concrete. "Old things and me get along. Sometimes I feel like I was born at the wrong time."

"No time is the right time," he said philosophically. "Every age has its problems."

"I suppose you're right about that," she had to admit.

"Besides. If you were born in 1930, we never would have met."

She gave a little laugh. "True."

There was a lull where she took in the interior of the pub. The walls were as cluttered inside as out. Lots of old photos and fishing equipment. A mixed bag of patrons chatting happily. All the tables looked different.

"How did you meet Michael?" she said as the silence stretched.

Troy shifted in his chair. "Long story. But you could say I was... destined to be here. Working with him."

"Cryptic," she said. "All things for a reason, huh? So, you believe in destiny?"

"I believe in what I've experienced. Which is... a lot. I've seen some crazy shit."

She leaned forward, intrigued. "Like what?"

A waitress brought their drinks around. When she left, Troy said: "Ghosts. Monsters. Demons. Powers you wouldn't believe unless you saw it. Shit that makes the Disasters seem like playtime."

"I was fifteen when the Disasters started," said Raina. "Mother wouldn't let me go outside for months."

"Smart." Troy had a deep pull from his beer stein.

"Yeah, but I got so tired of being shut up all the time. I thought she was afraid of the fog. The shamblers and crawlers didn't scare me. They were gross, but they didn't do much. You know? So, one night I sneaked out."

"Seriously?" Troy boggled. "During the Disasters?"

She sipped her water and nodded. Setting the glass down, she curled her fingers around it. Distantly noticed the cloudiness of the liquid as she thought back to that trying time. The time when the whole world changed.

"I thought she was just being protective," she said. "I didn't know how bad it had gotten."

"What happened?"

She made a face. "I found out."

Then she related to him the experience she'd had that unsettling night.

***

11 years ago

The foggy night streets were empty. Stillness cloaked the sleeping neighborhood, giving the impression nothing existed beyond the fog. It was creepy, but it was only weather. Nothing to be afraid of. Though it was past midnight Raina, 15 years old at the time, wanted soda from the convenience store.

She cut through the trailer park behind her house, ducking between the silent mobile homes. It was strange to see the neighborhood so void of life. Flat darkness smothered everything, and the area was dead silent. And yet there was a creeping sense of something alert to her passing. It was as though the fog itself was stalking her.

No one followed her yet she suffered the urge to hurry. To make herself invisible. She slipped through a low wire fence and out of the trailer park.

An open dirt lot lay between her and the road. Though the street had light fixtures, none were working. The only source of light came from the shop on the corner. The hazy fog choked it to a faint spot. She hurried that way.

As the sidewalk came into view she caught movement out of the corner of her eye. A silhouette coming through the fog toward her. Her first guess was a large man on a wobbly bicycle. As the shape got closer, she realized there was no bicycle.

The thing emerged from the fog. It was massive, standing over six feet tall. It had the appearance of three people chopped up and fused together. Extra limbs stuck out at unnatural angles. Its misshapen mouth gaped and dripped viscous black fluid between irregular teeth.

It staggered toward her, making a hideous, tortured sound no human could utter.

***

"Holy shit," Troy breathed, his eyes widening.

"I thought it was a sick joke. You know?" said Raina. "Somebody in a costume. Then I got a whiff of it. It was... stomach-turning. I ran the whole way back home expecting it to jump on me at any second. I didn't look back. Nothing that would slow me down, you know? It smelled just like my landlord's house did. Might be why I freaked out when we found him."

"You were fine," he assured her. "It was awful. A lot of folks I know would have completely lost their shit seeing that."

He reached over and took her free hand. Squeezed it. Though his grip was gentle, the contact jolted her with a strong current of electricity. It wasn't painful but it was a surprise. She startled. He let go.

"Sorry," he said.

"No. It's okay," she said apologetically. "I guess I'm just not used to people touching me."

Even as she said that she knew it wasn't true. His touch had carried energy that transferred to her when they connected. It was electric but not static—more like a vibration than a zap.

"I'm kind of a touchy-feely person," admitted Troy. "I grew up in an orphanage. Religious place. Not a lot of meaningful physical contact. Nothing good, anyway."

"I would've thought a religious orphanage would be big on hugs and things."

"Not these people."

Their food arrived, effectively pausing their conversation. They ate in silence for a few minutes before Raina's curiosity got the better of her.

"Who was Desiree?" she asked. When Troy looked at her funny, she clarified: "I mean. To your group? I guess I'm sort of wondering what happened to her."

He smudged his messy fingers on his napkin. "She was a member of the Coven. Had a... falling out with Pietre and Ligeia."

"So, she left?"

He thought about how to answer. His hesitation only fed her curiosity.

"You could say that," he said at last. He took a big bite out of his sandwich.

The vague answer was unsatisfying. "Are they both in charge? What sort of falling out did they have with her? Did they do something to her? Why did Michael tell you not to let Pietre know about me when you first brought me to the hotel?"

Holding up a hand to stave off her barrage of questions, he chewed and swallowed the lump of food.

"Whoa," he said with a crooked grin. He had a dollop of barbecue sauce at the corner of his mouth. "Let's see. Um. Ligeia is the High Priestess. Pietre's a warlock and technically outranks her as High Priest, but she's the shot-caller of the group. Witches are matriarchal."

Raina stared at the spot of red sauce on his face as she ate, wanting him to wipe it away. He didn't notice it.

"The Coven's been around for a long time. Came here from Louisiana or Florida. Someplace east. Desiree came with them. She released some prisoners Pietre and Ligeia had. I don't really know what happened with all that. You'd have to ask them."

"Do they have anything to do with the Society?" she asked between nibbles of her fish plank.

He shook his head and reached for his mug. He drank down a swig. The sauce stayed put. "Nah. The Society's... they're a bunch of people who were super-wealthy before everything went to shit coupled with another group who made it big afterward. Hedonists. They're a pretentious crowd, but they throw great parties."

Raina couldn't stand it any longer. "You've got something on you," she said, touching the left corner of her mouth.

He blinked and touched the left side of his mouth.

"Other side."

Troy swiped a finger over the right side.

She laughed. "You missed it."

He tried again, this time with three fingers.

"You're still missing."

He put his tongue out and tried to lick the offending smear but didn't reach it. Watching him try was pretty funny, though.

"Here," she said. She grabbed her napkin. "Let me."

She rose with the intent to smudge the spot off, putting her free hand down to lean toward him. The concrete slab of a table shifted under the added weight and gravity took over. Before she knew what was happening, it tipped. His plate and hers slid toward her.

Troy grabbed the table and stopped it from falling over, but it was too late for the food. The plates and drinks rocketed off the tabletop and dumped their contents down her front. The dishes clattered on the floor.

For a moment, the whole pub looked at her and Troy. He stared at her in shock. She dripped.

"You okay?" His care was genuine, but he was already starting to grin.

She looked down at herself and the mess on the floor. "Yeah. I need a few napkins."

"Yeah," he said. The grin escaped. "You got some on you."

The waitress bustled over with a couple of wet rags. Raina helped her pick up the dishes while Troy mopped the tabletop.

"Sorry. I'm so sorry for this," Raina said, her face burning.

"It's all right," the waitress said. She handed the other rag to Raina. "That's for you. I'll bring more for the floor."

She hurried off. Raina swabbed her front but there was no help for the barbecue sauce. It had already set in. Even a good wash probably wouldn't remove it. The stain would be with her forever. Troy wiped off her chair with a rag and patted it dry with a paper napkin.

"I guess it's true what they say," he said. "No good deed goes unpunished."

She tried one more time to sop up the red sauce on her skirt then gave up. "Lunch is on me." The best way to get past making a fool of herself was with humor.

He laughed. "And here I was going to treat you."

The waitress came back with more rags. The bartender followed her with a fresh tray of food and drinks he set down on the table.

"No additional charge," he said.

"Oh, you didn't have to do that," Raina demurred, touched by his generosity.

"Quite all right," the bartender smiled. "Gotta treat our regulars right." That last he aimed at Troy.

Once the waitress got the floor mopped up she left them to their meal. Damp and smelling of beer and sauce, Raina could feel the mess starting to congeal. She wasn't going to let it put her off her food, though. She dug in. The fish was piping hot and crisp.

"I guess it's a good thing we were going to the hotel after this."

"All things for a reason," Troy said and bit into his fresh sandwich. It left a smudge of sauce on his cheek.

CHAPTER 10

When they got back to the hotel Troy offered to help her sort her stuff, but she declined. She wasn't sure how she would handle sifting through the remnants of her life. Crying in front of others was one of her least favorite things to do. She hated showing that kind of weakness to anyone.

She let herself into her room and found the boxes stacked neatly near the sideboard. She stared at them. A ripple of vertigo made her head swim. Unpacking was a daunting challenge. Doing it meant she accepted her home was gone. Taken. Her attempts to become self-sufficient and independent had failed. Her life as she knew it truly was over. And she had no idea what the road ahead would bring.

Overwhelmed, she ducked into the bathroom and stripped down. Getting the food off her would improve her immediate situation and give her time to think.

As Michael had pointed out, the house itself wasn't a huge loss. It was her lack of control over the situation that mattered. The future was a yawning chasm of uncertainty before her. What would she do? Where would she go? What was her endgame?

"At least I have some direction this time," she muttered to herself as she gathered her soiled clothes. When her mother died, she had been completely lost for the first couple of weeks.

As she rinsed her shirt in the tub, she decided she needed to get her proverbial land legs under her. Stabilize. Right now, there was no "normal". She had to find a new baseline before she could take productive steps toward a new future.

She rinsed her skirt next. The clothes needed proper washing, but she'd likely do that herself when she started working in the laundry room. So, it made sense to pre-clean them as best she could. Doing laundry for the hotel would pay for her room and board. And she had the help of the prince to discover what happened to her mother's necklace. After she had closure on that matter, she could concentrate on putting her life back together.

After hanging her wet clothes up on the shower curtain rod, she threw on a robe from Desiree's closet. Then she tackled the boxes, looking for clothes to put on first.

The first box was the worst of the lot. Unpacking it painfully cemented her new reality. After she got dressed, she started the task of truly unpacking. She had to blink through a few emotional tears, but she didn't stop. If she did, starting again would be even harder. Moving things to dresser drawers and cabinets was therapeutic. Eventually she found a rhythm to help her flow through the task.

By the third box, she was no longer struggling with the upheaval. Acceptance came inch by inch. As she relaxed into the satisfaction of organization, her mind wandered to other things. Namely, Michael and Troy.

They were the most interesting people she'd met in a long time. Close to her age yet unlike anyone she grew up around or the people from her neighborhood. Both men were confident and secure in who they were. But there the similarities ended.

Michael was proper, well-dressed, and proud. The epitome of a modern prince. He smelled and looked good. Still, it bothered her that she wanted him to notice her. There was no good reason to want that and yet she did. She had stuffed the urge down as far as she could, but she couldn't deny it.

Then there was Troy. Dusky where Michael was fair. Roguishly relaxed and a bit vulgar. He was easy to talk to. She noticed at lunch that he stopped censoring himself. Comfortable enough to be himself and not care about cursing in front of her.

Though she preferred not to use crass language herself, casual swearing didn't bother her. She heard worse from her mother's boyfriends—and from her mother too. Lyra's swearing had amused her. Fond of alliteration, her curses were devilishly creative. A summer favorite was "hotter than the hinges of Hades." And, in winter: "It's colder than a witch's tit in a brass bra."

Another box was empty. She flattened it down and cracked into the next one. The first thing she pulled from it was her mother's old black lace shawl. Raina ran her fingers over the delicate design. She had worn it and her mother's necklace to Lyra's funeral.

Her heart constricted as she thought of the missing necklace again. She draped the shawl over a coat hanger. Straightened it out so it wouldn't slip right off again.

"It's just a necklace," she told herself in vain. The words were hollow.

Her mom wouldn't want her so hung up on a piece of jewelry. Memory lived in the heart, she would say. Still, the loss hurt. The lock of her mother's hair it carried was the only thing left of Lyra in the world.

Raina hung the shawl in the closet to protect it. Then she carried another armload of wrinkled clothing over to the bed to fold. She tried not to think about her mother, but when she pushed the sadness back, Michael crowded in again.

It was pointless to dwell on him so much. She was sure he wasn't thinking about her. A man of his standing had many people demanding his time and consideration. Raina was a drop in the ocean of his existence. She certainly wasn't the only woman fascinated with him. Desiree's sketchbook said he lived in her thoughts, too.

Raina glanced over at the sideboard where the sketchbook was hidden. Was the image of Michael asleep drawn from life or imagination? Was he wearing anything under those sheets?

Annoyed with herself, she forced her attention back to the clothes she was folding. Once she finished, she put the stack into a dresser drawer. The boxes held only what she would need. She left behind several things she never used. Some of it she had forgotten she had. Her drawers were much tidier than they had been in years because of the forced downsizing.

Opening the next box exposed the art books she'd salvaged. She arranged them on the sideboard. As she did, she told herself she wasn't going to fall into silly infatuation simply because she'd met some interesting guys. That's all it was: They were interesting. Strictly platonic acquaintances. She was a nobody in their elite circle. Potentially "useful" but unimportant.

After she got the books arranged to her liking, she flattened the empty box and started on the next one. She found the snow globe her mother bought her when they went to the Queen Mary in Long Beach years ago. The "haunted" ship was fun, though the only things haunting it were the drunk crew and visitors desperately seeking to be scared.

Raina smiled and gave the globe a shake. Artificial snow whirled around the miniature boat within. Then something skittered over her hand: A hairy brown spider. Startled, she dropped the souvenir and vigorously shook her hand. The action flung the spider somewhere. She didn't know where. It also broke her grip on the snow globe. It fell and shattered on the floor. Water and fake snowflakes spread over the old floorboards.

"Crap," she muttered.

Another memory lost and a new mess to clean. Worse, there was a creepy spider on the loose in her room. She grabbed a towel from the bathroom and dropped it over the puddle. She sopped it up and recoiled when a sting of pain lanced her right hand. Examining the injury, she found a bit of glass lodged there.

"Nice going, Raina," she chided herself.

She carefully plucked the shard out and went to find a bandage. It was definitely not her day.

...

"Hi," Raina greeted from the doorway of the laundry room. "Excuse me. Are you Beth?"

After she finished cleaning up the broken snow globe, she finished unpacking. Afterward she went to find Troy to introduce her to the laundry lady but, failing that, she found her own way to the basement laundry room. She brought her lunch-stained clothes and the soggy towel with her.

The brightly lit room had a bank of large washing machines and a row of dryers. A table near the door served as a folding table. Several clothing racks and a wide ironing board stood at the ready.

The woman she addressed was stout, shorter than her, thin-haired, and dour of face. Sensibly dressed for her work. She gave Raina a bland once-over.

"Yeah. Laundry chute's for drops. It gets done in the order it comes in unless you're Michael's family."

"I don't, er. I'm not here to get my stuff washed." She fidgeted with the wad of dirty clothes. "I just brought this with me because I, uh, had an accident earlier. With lunch." The woman stared at her. Raina felt her ears heating up. "Michael sent me to help you. To work. I've had lots of experience doing laundry."

Beth looked skeptical. "Fine." She made it sound like she was doing Raina a favor. "It's pretty simple: You grab the laundry from the drop. Sort it into the triple bin. Whites and lights. Reds. Darks. Handwash goes on the counter. Know how to use industrial machines?"

Raina looked at the machines in question. "I've never used one," she admitted. "But they look easy enough."

"I'll walk you through the first load. Drop your stuff in the right basket then grab the load of darks and we'll get started."

—

Working with Beth was strictly business. She didn't smile or joke or chat. She was brusque and unfriendly, though good at what she did. She took Saturdays off. Raina agreed to pick up the slack that day. They would both work Monday to Friday, with Raina coming in before and after lunch in four-hour shifts.

Though Raina adapted, her performance was far from flawless. At home, she did laundry by hand. Learning to run the machines was a curve. Beth showed her how to fill the soap dispenser and set the dial.

Raina paid attention, yet when it came time for her to do a load on her own, the machine wouldn't start. She fiddled with it, hoping it would miraculously get over whatever problem it was having. She finally had to ask for help. When Beth came over, she jammed her fists against her wide hips.

"Did you follow all the steps?" Her tone said the answer was an obvious "no".

It would have been nice if she just told Raina what was wrong so they could get on with things. "I thought I did." She studied the machine again. It looked the same as it did the last five times that she looked at it.

"You missed one."

Raina stared harder at the machine as she recounted in her head everything she was supposed to do. She still came up blank. She checked her frustration. "I figured I probably did," she said, putting on a smile. "But I can't think of what."

Beth eyed her, perhaps thinking of torturing Raina longer. Then she relented and reached over to flip a trigger on the side of the large door.

"You didn't lock it down."

Ugh. Of all the simple, stupid mistakes to make. "Oops."

"If you don't lock it and it runs," Beth went on as though she were speaking to a child. "The door pops open. Water gets all over. Got to lock it down before it'll run."

"Right. Can't believe I forgot that."

Beth didn't say anything. She went back to her work. Raina turned back to her machine. This time when she punched the start button, the engine revved up. Soon water was sloshing in the washer.

———

At the five o'clock bell, they shut down the laundry room. Although Raina's legs were tired and her back was stiff, it was comforting to have a routine again. She trudged upstairs, thinking of her old clients who were now without laundry service. Likely those who refused to leave were also forcibly evicted. Or worse.

She hadn't seen anyone else prepped for sacrifice. Nor did she see anyone in the neighborhood when she went there with Troy and Michael. Not even Maurice. Hopefully, everyone made it out okay.

When she got to her room, she let herself in and kicked off her shoes. Then she started a hot bath. Her aching back and legs would thank her for a soak. She found a bottle of bubble bath under the sink and poured a couple of capfuls under the faucet, then a third cap as an afterthought. Soon she was sliding under a heavenly blanket of bubbles.

She hoped the bath would relax her, but she had to keep her injured hand out of the water. Though small, the wound didn't need bubble bath to irritate it. The bloody stone altar crept in on her peace too. Every time she closed her eyes for long, there it was. She didn't understand why Michael allowed such a thing if he didn't approve of it.

There was a knock at the door in the main room. She didn't react at first, debating whether to get out of the tub or pretend she didn't hear it.

Another knock.

With a soft groan of protest, she hauled herself out of the tub. Wrapped herself up in a fluffy white towel. Bubbles slid down her legs onto the floor as she left the bathroom.

Looking through the peephole she saw Michael. She wasn't in a state to receive company, but she didn't want to keep him waiting longer, so she opened the door. She tried to keep her wet body behind it, one hand clutching the towel.

"Hi," she said with a crooked smile. "You, uh, caught me in the bath."

A flicker of interest passed over his features. "I found out something about your missing necklace. But it can wait until dinner."

Her necklace! "No, it's all right." She opened the door all the way. "Please come in." Then, remembering her state of undress: "I'll just throw something on."

At the sudden exposure, Michael's eyes wandered down her towel-wrapped body. "If you prefer."

Catching the look, she ducked back into the bathroom.

"I'll be right out," she said, shutting the door.

She looked down at herself. Her long hair was wet from shoulders to waist. The towel she gripped around her middle was askew. She was a mess. Between this and her jacketed arrival, any hope she had of making a decent impression was shot.

Toweling off, she threw on the clothes she'd set aside for after bathing. A long-sleeved ivory top with bell-shaped cuffs and a pair of once-red flare pants faded with age. She pinned her damp locks back with a hair clip. Brushing would take too long. She was still a mess, but a more presentable mess.

When she came out of the bathroom, she found Michael sitting at the table next to the bed, looking through a pocket-sized notebook. He put it away when he saw her.

"You didn't have to rush."

She waved a hand. "I didn't want to keep you waiting."

"If that's the case, you didn't have to get dressed."

She came over and sat down on the bed across from him, catching a glimmer of mischief in his dark eyes.

"We've already had one conversation with me underdressed," she said. "I don't want to set a precedent."

"I wouldn't mind." His smile only enhanced the mischief.

She was being baited. Was he trying to embarrass her? Flirt? Both? "I think once is my limit."

"A shame."

"You said you heard something about my necklace?" Changing the subject meant not having to figure how to respond to that.

"I did. I spoke with Holly Walker, the Society's most social butterfly. She believes she can help. There's a big get-together coming up. She would like to meet you there."

Raina cocked her head. "A party? Where and when?"

He shifted and relaxed back in the chair. "This weekend at the old Beverly Hills Hotel. Starts at nine bells."

The idea of going to a Society party alone was scary. "Do you think they'd mind if I went with someone?"

He shrugged. "I doubt it, as long as your guest fits the theme. Who were you thinking of inviting?"

That stumped her. Who, indeed? "I... hadn't. I just got as far as 'not alone'." She smiled sheepishly.

Michael rubbed his chin, the light dusting five o'clock shadow skritching under his fingertips. "I could take you if you like."

She blinked several times, stunned. The prince was offering to take her to the ball. She suffered a childish surge of joy and promptly clamped down on it. "That... that would probably make things easier. If you don't mind, that is."

He smiled. No mischief now. The expression softened his chiseled features. "I wouldn't offer if I did."

"What should I wear?" Most of her clothes were casual and Desiree's wardrobe was tasteful but not classy. "I've never been to a fancy party before. I don't even own a nice dress."

"Ligeia says every woman should own a little black dress," the prince advised. "But I'm sure there's a theme. The Society adores them. I'll find out what it is. We can get you something to wear tomorrow."

"Oh. Okay. Sounds good," she said, trying to be casual. Inside, she was riding a wave of nervous excitement. "Oh. I met Beth today. We figured out a schedule. I'm done by five if that works."

She had no money. If she were to buy something, she would need his help, further indebting her. Though Troy said it wasn't an issue for her to get what she needed she hated taking advantage. At least Michael knew she was earning her stay.

"That's fine," he said. "The shop I'm thinking of keeps late hours." He got to his feet. "I'll let you get back to your bath."

She nodded and got up too. She walked him to the door. "Thanks. For the, uh. The help. I know I keep saying that..."

She didn't like being in a position to rely on another person, but she wasn't going to be an ingrate about it.

"You're welcome. See you in a bit."

She closed the door behind him and leaned against it. Her emotions were in a twist. On the one hand, she didn't want to keep depending on Michael to get things done. On the other, he was going to take her to a Society party!

She wandered back to the bathroom and stripped down, lost in her reeling thoughts. It wasn't until she was neck-deep in the tub again that she noticed the water had cooled.

CHAPTER 11

"The triplets were sixteen the first time they did the ritual with me," Pietre said. "They slept for eighteen hours or so afterward, but apart from that, they were fine."

The warlock shared a table with Michael, Troy, and Trixie at their usual spot in the dining room. The others had their food already. Michael was waiting for Raina. To tide him over, he had a glass of bourbon for an appetizer.

"They had training," he pointed out.

Pietre cut into his rare steak. Hot blood trickled in a red rivulet over the white plate. "Only a month. They were no worse for wear compared to when you performed the ritual with them later. You were rougher on them than I was, and they survived." He popped the morsel into his mouth.

Michael remembered that night well. While the triplets were battered and unconscious afterward, time healed all wounds. It hadn't bothered him then. Why did it bother him now? Raina was in good health. Her circumstances proved she was resilient. Yet he was hesitant.

"There are three of them," he said. "There's only one of her. She should have more than the basics down before we go and drain her. You know the risks."

Pietre shrugged. "It's your choice. But the sooner you conduct the ritual the sooner you will regain your strength. You're taking her to the Society gala, yes?"

"The masquerade?" Troy perked up.

"Mm. Yes," said Michael. He sipped his bourbon and sucked his teeth to savor the spicy burn.

"Perhaps after that, we should get started," Pietre suggested. "Ligeia said she would help."

"Are you going?" Trixie asked Troy.

He glanced at the black-haired woman then returned to his meal. "Possibly. Why?"

She pushed her food around but didn't eat. She was busy side-eyeing Troy. "I've never been to one of Holly's masquerades. Would you dance with me if I go?"

Troy grinned. "I didn't know you liked to dance."

"Every now and then." Trixie favored him with a fetching smile. Trying to close the deal.

"Do we know what the theme is?" Troy asked Michael around a mouthful of potatoes.

"Not yet. I'll find out from Holly tomorrow. I'll be taking Raina to find something to wear."

"I could do that," Trixie volunteered. "Save you some time. Besides, it's tradition that girls shop together for these things."

While Michael fancied the idea of watching Raina try on outfits for him, he had work to do first if he wanted to steal time to go to the party. Practicality won.

"All right," he said. "Take her to Eclipsed Chamber. Put it on the account."

———

The next day Michael held court at the First Church. He had several people in his employ who were devoted to keeping the municipal wheels of New Salem turning. But some things, out of necessity, required his attention. As such he held court every week, sometimes twice a week if needed.

On any given court day Michael met with officials and emissaries in the chapel. Oversaw legal proceedings. Passed judgment and made decisions. Not the most glamorous side of life as Lord Prince, but vital. If he could pass the duties on to someone else, he would. As of yet he'd found no one he trusted enough. Even those closest to him had defects that made them less than ideal to trust with so much. They simply wouldn't do things the way he would.

Five chairs occupied the dais at the front of the chapel. The central and biggest was his. The chairs to either side were for his inner circle. That day, his aunt Ligeia was the only one joining him. Spectators and civilians sat in the first three rows, waiting for their turn to go before the Lord Prince with their legal issues.

The first order of business was always a meeting with the Chancellor, a short man with thinning hair and handmade spectacles. Michael's Private Secretary, a gray-robed acolyte of the Church, handed folders to the official while the prince summarized the contents for him. The man was capable of reading them, but a summary cleared any immediate questions about Michael's decisions without their having to meet again.

"Yes to the request from Santo Feo for the pigs," Michael said. "But we can only provide seventy-five, not one hundred. Yes to the water tax increase. Doctor Hugo needs to hire more help.

His chief maintenance worker fell into the retaining tank last week. The Leviathan ate him. He needs replacing. Not to mention the whole facility needs repairs. Make sure Hugo knows he can hire out now."

Michael paused to reflect. He was missing something. He did a quick mental checklist and found it.

"Also: No to mandatory schooling for children. If parents wish to educate their offspring themselves, it's their right. We'll make an exception for children such as Jacob after the Conservatory is formed."

The Chancellor jotted down a few notes, nodded, and left. It was the Magistrate's turn next.

"What have you got for me, Justice?" Michael said. "Not much, I hope."

The Magistrate was a tall, older man dressed in formal judicial robes. His long face was deeply etched with the lines of experience. "Just one matter, my Lord. A civil issue I thought you should arbitrate. It could set precedence."

He handed Michael a docket that held the facts of the case. Any civil case that had a potential death penalty went through the prince. Less than that was up to the Magistrate's best judgment. Michael reviewed the docket. The case, an avoidable tragedy, involved a child-sitter and the death of a toddler.

An irresponsible teen mother was in the habit of leaving her child in the care of a nanny for weeks at a time while she spent her time with friends. Unemployed, the young woman lived with her parents. They were both factory workers who didn't want to waste their off hours raising their grandchild.

Though the toddler's family hadn't done their part in protecting the child, Michael ruled in their favor. The child died on the nanny's watch and because of her actions. He gave the defendant until nightfall to leave town. Then the death warrant went into effect. The law said only the wronged family could kill the defendant, so it would be on them to enforce the ruling.

It was a tough system, but it kept order in New Salem.

"I'm surprised you sided with them," Ligeia said once they were gone. "If the child had been home with the family—"

"He would have been just as neglected," Michael finished for her. "Justice was served when he was taken from them. They won't go after the nanny. The mother's parents are too old and lazy to hunt her, and the mother is too young and naive. The nanny will have to forge a new life somewhere else. All are punished."

Ligeia made a soft noise in the back of her throat. "I would have put them all to death. New Salem doesn't need their kind. Any of them."

He reached over and touched her hand, his expression sincere. "Auntie, you know I would never stand between you and your passions. If they happen to turn up dead, I'll see it as divine providence."

His words sparked a small, grudging smile. "I won't go against your ruling. But I do appreciate your generosity, my dear."

———

That afternoon the Society sent word: The theme of the party was ancient gods and goddesses. Far from a typical toga party, attendees needed to dress to impress. The Society had exacting standards, and they expected the prince's entourage to go further beyond.

Raina finished her work and joined Trixie for a trip to the shop Michael recommended. The storefront was up in the Hills, so they took a pedicab: A bicycle strapped to a two-wheeled carriage. The driver was strong. His tree trunk calves, and massive thighs had seen many miles with riders in tow. The ride was smooth and swift. Fun, too. The autumn wind played through Raina's hair as the city whisked by. It made the silence between her and the other woman pleasant rather than awkward.

When they arrived at the Eclipsed Chamber, Trixie paid the driver a few coins of the local currency—silver tokens stamped with the seal of the dragon. She promised him more of the same if he waited for them. Then they went inside.

The interior of the boutique was overwhelming. It had one section devoted to leather items mostly in red and black. Beside it was a section where bright colors and feathers reigned supreme. Corsetry made up another department. Throughout the shop glass cases housed chains and products that made Raina stare. She couldn't even guess the purpose of some of the items. Everywhere she turned were ball gags, handcuffs, and spiked metal.

"This way," Trixie said, heading toward the back. Away from the glass cases.

Raina hugged herself and followed, taking it all in with large eyes. Sex permeated every inch of the shop. It showed on mannequins equipped with strap-ons and in the artwork squeezed in between products. The back wall held a jaw-dropping variety of paddles, quirts, and crops.

"I'm glad I came here with you instead of Michael," she said.

Trixie glanced back. "Oh?"

"There are a lot of, um. Adult things here."

The other woman laughed at her prudishness. "Nothing will jump out and bite you. Relax."

She led Raina to a corner that hosted a variety of costume items. She pawed through bodysuits and leotards, rejecting several.

"Let's find you something first," she said. "I'm thinking... Egyptian goddess. Sound good?"

Raina made herself stop staring at the wooden torsos in bondage gear displayed along the top of the back wall. "Um. Sure. Yeah. I'm good with whatever so long as it fits the theme."

"Easy enough."

Trixie grabbed a few things and held them up for Raina's inspection. "Isis?" She flapped a golden leotard with a feathery cape. "Bastet?" She held up a black leather half-mask with gold detailing. She offered a dark blue catsuit next, one with a sprinkling of silvery stars. "Or Nut?"

Raina looked at them. "What can we get to go with the Bastet mask?"

Trixie put the gold leotard and blue catsuit back and looked around. "Up to you," she said. "Toga? Unitard? Bikini? You could go in chains and nothing else if you want."

"Only chains?" Raina blinked rapidly. "I couldn't do that."

Trixie giggled. "At the Society's parties, you could show up naked covered in gold paint. You just have to make it look expensive."

Raina cast about, hoping for inspiration. She saw a display of oversized dildos that made her regret it. The apocalypse did a number on major appliances and pencil supplies, but there was no shortage of phalluses it seemed.

"Ah. I think I want some kind of shoulder thing. And maybe a dress?"

"You're no fun," Trixie accused. "I think I saw something over in lingerie that might work."

—

Raina picked a white diaphanous open-sided slip dress to wear under a strapless black leather corset. Her accessories were a gilded neck-and-shoulder collar and gold armbands. A pair of gold platform sandals completed the outfit.

For herself, Trixie assembled an Aphrodite costume. It included a form-hugging silk wrap that showed more than it covered and a pair of gold sandals like Raina's. At the front counter, she picked up a long blonde wig made of human hair.

"We have a wrist cape that'd go better with your outfit than the armbands," the clerk said to Raina during check out.

Raina fingered the gold arm bands. A wrist cape might be fun. "Could I see it?"

He smiled and ducked out from behind the counter. He was gone only a minute or so then came back with a wad of white cloth and four short black leather cuffs. "Try these," he said.

He helped Raina into the accessory, snapping the cuffs on her upper arms and wrists. Then he pointed her toward a full-length mirror.

"Oh, wow!" she exclaimed. "It's so pretty."

Each side had a narrow length of white gauze looped through brass O-rings. The fabric connected the upper bands to the wrist cuffs. She turned this way and that, flapping her arms to watch the draped fabric flow. The gauzy cloth fluttered nicely, and it matched the dress she chose.

"Do you want them?" the clerk asked.

Raina didn't have to think about it. "Definitely."

The clerk helped her pop them back off and bundled them up. Carried them over to the pile of merchandise where Trixie was waiting impatiently.

"Do you want the gold armbands for your outfit?" the clerk asked Trixie.

"No," she said with disdain. She didn't want Raina's cast-offs. "I have something at home I'm going to use. Just ring the rest up so we can get going. Put it on the account."

———

That night, it was Michael, Troy, and Raina at the table for dinner. The buffet was another unusual assortment of delicious offerings mingled with things that didn't even qualify as food, such as a chafer dish filled with sauteed snails. It didn't matter that they were in garlic wine butter. Snails were for birds. The dessert table made up for the oddities with some seasonal pies, including pumpkin.

"Were you and Trixie able to get down to the shop?" Michael asked once they got their meals to the table.

He was having his typical plate of raw, blood-soaked meat. Raina had yet to see him have anything else other than alcohol.

"Yes," she said. "That was... quite a store."

Troy smirked. "Never been to the Eclipsed Chamber before?"

She shook her head. "I didn't even know it existed."

Michael's left brow twitched, and he hid a smile behind the act of shoving another bite of meat into his mouth. It was a sly look. He seemed to be having fun at her expense.

She eyed him. "You did that on purpose, didn't you?"

Troy snorted a laugh. Michael let his smile loose.

"I thought you might find it... fun." He said it with so much false innocence, she knew he'd deliberately set her up.

"Bondage gear and giant penises," she said dryly, prompting another guffaw from Troy. "I had an absolute romp."

She tore a bit from her dinner roll and pelted Michael with it. It bounced off his arm. Too late she realized how inappropriate it was to lob bread at the Lord Prince, but he didn't mind. Troy laughed even harder.

"You could have warned me, you know," she admonished the dark-haired man.

"Could have," Troy agreed. He drank to that.

She sent a glare around the table at both of them, though she couldn't pump any real anger into it. They met her look with wide grins. Though she'd been played, the prank wasn't mean-spirited. Just... juvenile.

"You two," she muttered. She grabbed her empty glass. "I'm going to get more juice."

She tossed her napkin to her chair and got to her feet. Troy looked at her, his brows arching in a hopeful way. She thought he might apologize, but what he said was:

"Could you bring me back some carrot cake?"

She sent him a sour look. "I should bring you back eyeball soup."

She breezed away from the table, smiling only when she was sure the men couldn't see. She wasn't going to give them the satisfaction. It would only encourage them.

"I'll take that as a yes," Troy called to her back.

CHAPTER 12

The next day blurred by for Raina. The laundry load was staggering as people dumped their clothes before the weekend. Occupied with work and her mind on the upcoming party, time flew by. She and Beth soldiered through the stacks, washing and folding a huge amount of dark clothing.

By the end of the day, Raina's hands were water-logged, and her back was stiff, but she was too excited to care. As soon as her shift ended, she hurried up to her room to get ready.

In a flurry of nervous anticipation, she flitted about putting on cosmetics and pieces of her outfit. It was the first time she used the makeup Desiree left behind. The colors were darker than she would pick herself though still pretty. Smoky black kohl eyeliner and burgundy lipstick evoked the cat goddess she was going for.

She tested her work in the mirror. She didn't look at all like herself, especially when the mask covered half her face. The dark eye makeup brought out her green eyes. Setting the mask aside, she touched her long hair. She didn't often style it. A ponytail sufficed for work. Tonight, though, something different was in order.

She recalled people in hieroglyphs often wore braids. She eyed her reflection and started separating locks of hair.

It took her most of her prep time to finish the hairstyle. After a couple of false starts, she went with a single braid coiled in a crown atop her head. The finished effect put her in mind of the headpieces many Egyptian goddesses in art wore.

Donning the rest of her outfit, she put her mask on and checked her reflection one last time. It was amazing how unlike herself she looked. Gone was Raina the laundry girl from outside the Walls. The woman reflected was bold, powerful, alluring. A dangerous and confident beauty.

She was everything Raina secretly desired to be. And for the night, she could pretend she was that woman.

—

The others were waiting in the lobby when she came down. Nerves got the better of her and she paused. Breathe in. Breathe out. If she fainted on the stairs, not only would she get hurt, but everyone would see. Not the entrance she wanted to make. When she was sure she wouldn't fall, she finished her downward trek.

Even from across the room the costumes the group wore cut an impressive image. Trixie was a perfect Aphrodite, close to nude in her curve-hugging wrap of white. Her long blonde hair curled down her back like a cape, topped with a gorgeous shell tiara. Gold serpentine bracelets wound from her wrists to her elbows, matching her sandals.

Troy, dressed as Dionysus, was wearing even less than she was. A scrap of crimson cloth hung scandalously low on his hips. The only other thing he wore was a grapevine laurel on his head. His dark hair was free of its usual ponytail and fell loose about his broad shoulders. A metal amphora hung from a strap across his well-toned chest. He was barefoot.

Michael was stunning as Ra in a knee-length gold and white loincloth. A wide indigo belt held the Egyptian kilt in place. His muscular torso was bare save for a fancy gold collar and runes painted on his pale skin. Most impressive was his headpiece: A gold crown in the shape of a falcon's head. Striped, blue fabric flowed from the crown, becoming a navy cloak. An authentic lapis ankh pinned the cape around his shoulders. Black eyeliner intensified his dark eyes.

Seeing Raina, he stared for a moment, captivated. Then he smiled and put out a hand, inviting her to join him. As she teetered over on her platform sandals, Troy and Trixie also looked at her.

No, not her. Bastet.

She remembered the confident, bold cat woman in the mirror. Her walk shifted to a saunter.

"Now that's what I'm talking about," Troy said when she reached them. "Two goddesses of love, Greek and Egyptian. Jackpot!"

"Hello," Michael greeted, taking in the whole of her appreciatively. "You look exquisite."

Flattered, Raina would have ducked her head modestly, but the neck corset refused. She settled for lowering her eyes. Found herself looking at Michael's hips and immediately looked up again.

"Thank you," she said. "Trixie's help. You look... great."

The word was hardly adequate, but everything else that sprang to mind felt too crude: Sexy. Hot. Luscious. Not classy, but true.

Compared to the others she was overdressed. She recalled what Trixie said about wearing nothing but chains and wondered what sort of event she was getting herself into.

"The driver is waiting outside," Michael said. "Are we ready?"

"Just a mo'," Troy said and uncorked the amphora.

He lifted it to his lips. Tipped his head back for a deep drink that ended with a happy sigh. Wiping his mouth with the back of his arm, he stuffed the cork back into the jug. He beamed a rosy-cheeked smile around at the group.

"All right. Ready."

Michael offered his elbow to Raina. She took it but she was staring at Troy.

"You have alcohol in that?" she said.

He grinned bigger and patted the amphora. "You bet. Would you expect anything less of the god of partying?"

Trixie rolled her eyes. "You don't have to get *that* into character," she said as they headed for the door.

"But it's much more fun that way," he said as he trailed after her.

—

Raina expected a car or a limo, but the vehicle waiting for them was a bona fide coach. Hitched to the front were two glossy black horses with ostrich plumes decorating their heads. Red velvet curtains hung at the side window, pulled back to allow a peek at the interior.

The coach had two padded benches facing each other upholstered in quilted red velvet. Red carpet covered the floor. The driver opened the door for the group.

"Well, this is fancy," Raina said as she settled into a seat.

Michael sat beside her. Troy settled on the bench across from her and Trixie took a seat across from Michael.

"I like to ride in style," he said. "Some situations require a little extra."

Troy made a face. "I prefer a car with armrests."

He waved his elbow at the door to show there was nowhere to lean.

"Form over function," said Michael loftily.

He reached into his pocket and pulled out a handful of gold claw-tipped rings. Raina watched as he put them on. They fit snugly over his fingertips. They looked wickedly sharp.

Raina regretted not taking the time to paint her fingernails. Then she put thoughts of her costume out of her mind. If she were overdressed or under-accessorized, no one complained.

"So, what are these Society parties like?" she asked, to further distance herself from stage fright. Bastet wouldn't be nervous or care what others thought of her wardrobe.

Trixie looked to the men too, as she didn't know either. The coach lurched forward and with a clip-clop of horse hooves, they were on their way. The road rumbled beneath them, providing background percussion to the journey.

"Crowded," Troy supplied. "Loud. Lots of people dancing and trying to outdo each other."

Michael tipped his head, considering. Troy's description was accurate. "Just about any vice you wish to indulge in can be found there. And it's wise to keep an eye on any drink you have."

Troy patted his amphora. "Part of why I bring my own."

Michael smirked. "I doubt anyone would slip anything into your drink. It's common knowledge you'll do anything without the need for a Mickey Finn."

"Heeey," Troy objected over Trixie's giggle. "There are some things and people I wouldn't do."

"Name one."

Troy thought fast and blurted: "Abraham. From the Order."

Michael gave a derisive laugh. "Only because he despises you."

"Lenore," Troy tried again.

Michael wrinkled his nose in distaste. "Same situation as Abraham. She'd sooner kiss a carrion crow than you."

"Her sister isn't so judgy," Troy volleyed.

Michael rolled his eyes and put his last claw ring on. Flexed his fingers. Admired the way the claws glimmered in the light from the mounted lantern outside the window.

Trixie stared at him. "You slept with Ligeia?"

"Slept?" he grinned wolfishly. "There wasn't any sleeping."

Raina busied herself twisting her left wrist cuff into the right place. She was by no means a virgin, but it was strange hearing so much about Troy's sex life without warning. It was also weird to picture him having sex with Ligeia. The woman was in fine shape, but old enough to be his mother.

"Those are my relatives you're talking about," Michael reminded blandly.

"You're the one who brought it up," said Troy.

"I did not," Michael said. "I made a point that there's no one you'd say no to. And you just proved it."

———

The coach pulled into a long driveway where it joined a line of fancy cars and carriages depositing people dressed to impress. Some were virtually naked. One man wore a jewel-encrusted cock sock with a rainbow array of precious gems affixed to his body. Another guest was decorated with a spray of peacock and turkey feathers. Ornate makeup and high heels were her only other accessories.

Michael helped Raina down from the carriage. She would ordinarily find it excessive, but in those tall platform sandals she was grateful for a hand to hold onto.

The masquerade was held at the old Beverly Hills Hotel, a meandering estate of unique design. Its sunset pink paint had faded over the years, but the iconic entryway was still an eyeful. A long colonnade sheltered arriving guests under a ceiling striped green and white. The carpet to the glass doors was a brilliant red splash under amber gas lanterns.

The mood in the air was electric. Exotic scents, perfumes, and cigar smoke mingled. Michael escorted Raina, with Troy and Trixie coming up the red carpet behind them. People lingering near the entrance took notice of the Lord Prince and his entourage.

All eyes were on him and the woman on his arm. Raina felt like royalty by proxy. Giddy and overstimulated, she gaped at the people who were waving at them. Michael gave a few token waves. Raina didn't feel entitled to wave to his admirers, but she smiled at those who smiled at her.

A valet opened the lobby door for them without question. No need to prove who they were. Raina flashed him a smile as well. He touched the brim of his hat to her. Then she stepped into the darkness.

Inside the hotel, she was transported to some other reality in some other time. Live music played, thumping a sensual beat directly into her flesh and bones. Red and gold lights flashed in the dark lobby, bouncing off a large chandelier.

The furniture was cleared away for the occasion, turning the area into a social space. Double-wide doorways stood open to the Crystal Ballroom where the music came from. The dining room was open too. Several tables and chairs waited for guests to rest between dancing and merrymaking.

Raina's group entered the ballroom. Despite the thrill, the atmosphere was daunting. The lights disoriented her, strobing and swinging in random directions. It was impossible to see the far side of the room through the mass of moving bodies. Costumes changed the silhouettes of people from expected to fantastical. They were a singular dark creature writhing ecstatically to an industrial beat.

Michael led her on a wide circuit around the room, past the stage where the band played. The music was deafening up close. The vibrations in her lungs threatened to steal her breath away. They continued past. Soon she could feel her heartbeat again.

Raina could tell Michael was looking for someone. When they reached the far side of the dance floor, he abandoned the search and turned to her.

"Drinks? Or dancing?" he asked over the sound of the party.

"I'm fine with doing both at once," Troy said loudly, patting his amphora. He offered Trixie his hand.

She accepted it with a smile and the two of them disappeared into the gyrating crowd.

"Let's dance," Raina decided.

Michael took her hand and waded into the throng. The crowd parted around them, instinctively moving out of his way. When they reached a point near the center of the masked group of people he released her.

They began to dance, though not exactly together at first. She watched the way he moved, and he did the same with her. Finding the rhythm together. Silently deciding the terms of the dance with subtle body language and glances.

Raina liked to dance, but she generally did it by herself where no one else could see. She wasn't insecure about her skills. Her mother taught her how to move. That's what made her reserved. Self-conscious. Lyra's provocative steps were tailored to draw the eye to the female form.

Holding back the natural motion of her body was difficult. Especially when the music grew more spirited. The throbbing beat demanded certain moves Raina grew tired of fighting. As she let go of her inhibitions, Michael drew closer. He read her well. It was as though he knew what she was going to do even before she did. He matched her fluid motions with masculine prowess. Brought power to the dance that made her want more.

The longer the song went, the closer they got. His body brushed against hers. Her heart was pounding, her breath short. Exertion? Or the magnetic presence of the man who had been preying on her thoughts for days?

The song wound down and before another could start, she took the opportunity to call a break.

"Drink?" she said, motioning in the direction of the bar.

She needed to catch her breath, to calm her heart. To give herself time to sort out the emotions and impulses that threatened to carry her away.

Michael nodded and took the lead again, clearing a path for them off the dance floor. They joined the line at the bar, which was short since most folks were still dancing.

"You dance well," he said as they waited.

The compliment gave her a little thrill that made her smile. "So do you. I'm not used to dancing with someone else. I mostly do it at home. Alone."

"That's a shame," he said. "You should come to the Bunker sometime. Weekends they play all kinds of great music."

"I don't know..." she hedged.

She was saved from having to defend her reluctance because it was their turn to order.

"I'll have a Zombie," Michael told the guy who was working the bar. Then he looked at Raina expectantly.

She planned to have water, but the mood in the room made it feel like a waste. What the hell. It was a party, after all. The only problem was what to order. The blackboard behind the bar was no help. It just listed names like Ocean Breeze and Sex on the Beach.

"I'll have a zombie, too," she told the bartender.

Michael's brows went up at her choice. Had she made a mistake?

"I've never had one." She felt the need to explain. "I figure I may as well try it."

He smiled. "It's a potent cocktail, but it goes down like Kool-Aid."

"I haven't had Kool-Aid in years," she said nostalgically.

The bartender sluiced several things into two glasses. His movements were smooth and deft from lots of practice. It was a performance art worth watching.

"You can also get Kool-Aid at the Bunker," Michael advised. "With or without vodka."

She lit up, impressed. "Do they have the blue kind?"

"They do."

"Oh, now you've sold me on it."

The bartender handed them their drinks. Each glass was full of liquid that started green at the bottom and faded to orange at the top. Art indeed. Michael dropped a couple of coins on the bar, more than the cocktails were worth, and led her away.

"Do you want to sit?" he offered, motioning to the dining area with his colorful glass.

Raina looked at the dancers and then over to the doorway. "Yeah," she decided. "Let's get out of the noise for a bit."

CHAPTER 13

Michael and Raina retired to the other room where there were less people. Though the lighting was dim, it was brighter than the ballroom. The music was less intense there, too. Normal conversation was possible. The couple made their way over to an open table. He set his drink down and pulled a chair out for her before seating himself.

Raina sat down, moving her skirt so that it kept her lower half covered. Then she had her first sip of the mixed drink. It was sweet, citrusy, and delivered a hefty alcohol kick when she swallowed. She blinked and cleared her throat. Alcohol fumes burned their way down to her belly, lighting a fire there.

Michael grinned at her reaction. "I told you it was strong." He had a long pull from his glass, only wincing a little.

"That was like ice down the back of your shirt. Or lava. More like lava." She suspected she could light her breath on fire if she had a match to breathe on. "Oh, hey! There's a chunk of pineapple in it."

"Let it soak. It'll absorb the alcohol, but it won't taste as strong as the drink."

"Sounds dangerous," she said. "How long do I let it sit?"

"As long as you want. The longer it does, the more potent it gets."

He had another long sip then used his straw to shove his fruit down to the bottom of his glass.

Raina eyed her pineapple wedge then did likewise. In for a penny, in for a pound. "You know, I'm starting to think you're a bad influence on me."

She had another drink. It went down with the same sweet bombastic burst as before. The heat spread outward to her limbs, relaxing them. A couple dressed as Eros and Psyche passed by their table carrying their own colorful drinks. A cloud of expensive-smelling perfume followed the woman.

"Me?" he said. A little too innocent. "Whatever would make you say that?"

"I don't drink. And I never dance in public."

Michael drank more of his zombie and set his glass down. Shifted his position so there was less room between them. "You should do at least one of those more often."

"See?" she said. An impish smile played on her lips. "That's what I'm talking about. Bad influence."

In the other room, the song ended, and another started. Heavy bass and a raucous industrial squeal paid homage to Nine Inch Nails. The crowd bounced and bobbed in time to the music, strobed by the flashing lights.

"Heeeey!" Troy's voice cut through the music.

Raina looked over her shoulder and saw him and Trixie heading toward their table. He had a neon blue drink in his hand. She had something pale and bubbly in a wine glass.

"I just had the best Blow Job," he announced proudly. Trixie laughed at Raina's shocked look. Troy clarified: "It's a shot. Of alcohol."

Recovering, Raina sent him a crooked smile. "And what's that you're holding? A Sixty-Nine?"

It was Troy's turn to look surprised. Michael's eyes were on her too. Her cheeks warmed but her smile didn't waver. If Troy could be obnoxious, she could too. She didn't set the ground rules. She played by them. The costuming and the alcohol empowered her. Made her feel more at ease with being herself than she had in days.

Which was good because she liked herself. She didn't like the Raina that second-guessed herself and felt out of place. Michael and his social circle were just people in the end. Powerful people, but people. And they were becoming her friends.

"This is an AMF." Troy raised his glass. Held it out to her. "It's like... the heavyweight of cocktails. Want some?"

"She doesn't want to suck on your straw, Troy," Trixie said, rolling her eyes.

"How do you know?" he fired back full of mischief.

Raina lifted her own glass. "I'm fine with what I have, thanks. Zombie."

"Oo," Troy said. "Good choice."

"I've never had one before. It's... different."

"I can't stand mixed drinks," said Trixie loftily. "They make my stomach hurt. I prefer champagne or wine." The music shifted and she perked up. She set her glass down. "I love this song! It's my jam! Michael? Come dance with me?"

"Would you mind?" he asked Raina.

He could dance with whomever he wanted to. He was the prince. But she appreciated his manners. Very considerate of him. "No, I don't mind. I'd like to sit a bit longer and try to catch up to you with this."

She lifted her glass. It was still more than half full whereas Michael had finished over half of his already. As potent as the cocktail was, her stomach wouldn't tolerate a faster pace. The heat was fine in moderate amounts, though. She wasn't going to risk making herself sick at the first and only Society party she'd been invited to.

"I'll keep 'er company," Troy offered. He kicked out a chair and straddled it like he was mounting a horse.

Michael rose and joined Trixie who beamed with pleasure as she latched onto his arm.

"We'll be back in a bit," he told Raina and Troy. Then the pair disappeared into the ballroom.

—

Troy sucked down some of his bright blue cocktail through the paper straw. "So. Having fun yet?"

Raina had another sip of her drink and winced at the bite of the rum. Hopefully she would get used to it if she drank more. If nothing else, it might numb her tongue, as strong as it was. "I am. This is pretty amazing. It's very loud though."

"What?" he said, acting like he hadn't heard her. Then he grinned. "Yeah. I think most of these people don't have a lot to say. So, it lets 'em pretend like they're being social without actually having to talk."

"There are a lot of people here," she said. "More than I expected. I guess I thought it'd be a smaller party."

"I like small. Smaller gatherings are more intimate." Troy tipped his glass toward her to punctuate his point. "The Society does have 'em, but they're more exclusive. Scenes like this are for the masses."

His drink slopped over and dribbled on his exposed thigh. The unexpected splash of icy wetness made him yelp and wiggle. Grabbing the edge of his toga, he blotted it up starting with the area between his legs.

"Are you all right?" Raina couldn't help giggling at his spread despite her sympathy. If he spread his legs any wider, she would know whether he was wearing underwear or not.

"Yeah. It's just cold." He patted his leg a few more times, then grinned big. "That's one way to cool down after dancing."

"I think I'll keep mine in the cup."

She had another sip then looked in her glass. "Michael said I should let the pineapple soak up the alcohol. But I don't think I'm going to get it back unless I drink this whole thing. And if I do that, it'll be the end of me. I'm already feeling it."

"Zombies are no joke," Troy agreed. "You want me to get it out for you? The pineapple?"

"How?"

"With this." He plucked the straw from his own drink. "Wanna see?"

Curious, she nudged her glass toward him. He took it. Eyeballed the sunken bit of fruit. Then he sank the straw into the zombie and skewered the pineapple. He lifted it, moving with slow precision so as not to lose it. Once it was clear of the glass, he flipped the straw over and offered it to her. It dripped on his hand.

"Nicely done," she said.

She leaned forward and took the pineapple with her teeth. Troy watched fascinated as she tugged it off the straw. Acutely aware of his attention, she smiled and tipped her head back to catch the fruit in her mouth. It went in neatly, without making a mess or her dropping it.

"Whew," said Troy appreciatively. Then he licked the drips of alcohol off his hand. "You have some hidden talents there, Raina."

She started to laugh and almost inhaled the pineapple. Chewing it up, she swallowed, hardly noticing the spicy rum flavor as it went down.

"You nearly made me choke." Her tone was too playful to be truly accusing.

"Have another drink," he plied, dropping the straw into his drink again. "It'll make you feel better."

"Sure, it will," she said sarcastically. She had another sip anyway.

As she lowered the glass, she noticed a woman approaching Troy from behind. She wore a magnificent pair of silvery feathered wings on her back. Her toga was a gray shimmering waterfall over her lean form. Her face was angelic by nature and she had long black curly hair pinned with a pair of silver combs. She was the prettiest woman Raina had seen outside of a painting.

Putting on a comical air of sneaking, the woman held a finger to her ruby lips to include Raina in the act of stealth. Then she slipped her hands over Troy's eyes and mouthed to Raina:

"Tell him to guess who I am."

Troy startled and reached up to touch the hands that blinded him.

"I'm supposed to tell you to guess who it is," Raina said, playing along.

Everything was funnier at the moment. She felt an instant camaraderie with the mischievous angel behind Troy. The woman gave her a warm smile in thanks for the assist.

"Umm..." Troy said. He petted the hands. "Ahh. I'd know those fingers anywhere."

He grabbed one the hands and used it to tug the woman down into his lap. She squeaked in mock protest. One of her wings buffeted his face. Troy didn't care.

"Hello, Holly," he grinned. He gave her tiny waist a friendly squeeze.

"Spoilsport," she chided, smacking him playfully on one of his broad, bare shoulders. Her voice was a husky Southern drawl. "You're supposed to guess."

"But I didn't need to guess. You think I'd pull just anybody into my lap?"

She pouted a little longer, then decided she was over it. She pecked his cheek. Looked over at Raina. "This one knows how to play," she praised. "What's your name, sug?"

"Raina. Nice to meet you."

"Raina!" Holly chirped. She squirmed out of Troy's lap. He was reluctant to let her go. "Oh, my gosh. Michael told me about you. I'm so glad you could come!"

She thrust a hand out to Raina, palm down. Her nails were the same red as her lips, tapered and long. Raina wasn't sure how to receive the hand. It didn't seem like a handshake move. She grasped Holly's fingers in a gentle squeeze. That seemed to appease the hostess.

"Someone broke into my house and stole my mother's necklace," Raina explained.

"That's what Michael said. I know everybody who deals in jewelry," Holly boasted. "Including the pilfered kind. Got me a boy here who's workin' on tracking it down... He's over there in fact."

She wiggled her fingers at a good-looking young man with messy hair who loitered in the doorway nearby, a cigarette between his lips. He had on an outfit that went with Holly's, though his wings were smaller, and his toga covered more. He lifted a hand in acknowledgment but stayed where he was.

"He's goin' by 'Evan' these days," Holly went on. "I swear he changes names more often than some people change their underwear."

She reached over and grabbed Troy's drink. Had a sip and gagged. "Good God!" She set the glass down and fanned herself frantically. "There's tequila in there! You should've warned me!"

Troy held up his hands in defense. "You didn't give me time."

Holly turned to Raina in desperation. The very picture of a damsel in distress. "Can I have a swig of your thing, sug? I'm dyin' here."

The woman's drama was amusing in the cutest way. Raina was starting to see how Holly got her status as the most social socialite. "Sure. I don't think it has tequila in it. It's a Zombie."

She handed the glass over. Holly took a long gulping drink, sighed in relief and passed it back.

"Only thing a Zombie's got is rum and more rum," Holly said. She smacked her lips, enjoying the aftertaste. "Much better. Thank you. Y'know, they don't call it 'ta-kill-ya' for nothing."

"It's not that bad," Troy said. He had a deep drink from his own glass to prove his point, almost draining it. He finished with a satisfied burp.

"He's gonna be pukin' tonight," Holly warned Raina. "I hope you weren't planning to go home with him."

She liked Holly and regretted not going with Michael to meet her before. Another opportunity missed. In a fit of alcohol-fueled resolve she decided she was going to seize more moments when they came by. Life was for living and first times weren't always necessarily a bad thing.

"I'm staying at the hotel," she said. "But we don't share a room."

"Good. You don't need this cretin keepin' you up with his suffering," said Holly. Despite the criticism, she ruffled Troy's hair. The affectionate gesture came close to dislodging his grapevine laurel. "Michael told me what your necklace looks like, but why don't you tell me. Just so Evan knows exactly what he should be scouting for."

Raina described the necklace and locket to her. She also added the description of the people who broke into her house in case that helped. When she finished, Holly looked impressed and scandalized on her behalf.

"Bless your heart," she said with utmost sympathy. "Well, don't you worry, sug. We'll get your mama's necklace back one way or the other. I promise."

She swooped in and before Raina knew what was happening, Holly glomped her in a big hug. She smelled of musky spice and honey. Black curls tickled Raina's cheek and then Holly retreated in a swing of feathered wings.

"It was nice to meetcha, Raina," she said. Then, to Troy: "Stay outta trouble, sug."

She kissed her fingertips and pressed them to his mouth, receiving a kiss from him in return. Then she ambled over to where Evan was waiting. Together, they disappeared through a side door across the room marked 'Employees Only'. Raina watched them go.

"Wow," she said. "She's... something."

Troy grinned. "Isn't she just, though?"

He drained his cup and Raina drank with him. There wasn't much left of her drink, but she credited that to Holly.

Troy set his empty glass down. "I'll grab us another round," he volunteered.

Before she could tell him no, he was up and gone. Loud music crowded in as the zombie warmed her. Holly's liberal affections played in her buzzing mind. The woman was a hurricane of good feelings. The most social Society member, Michael called her. Raina couldn't imagine herself being so free, but it wouldn't hurt to touch others more. Touching was nice.

She watched the dancers while she waited for Troy to return. The action was heating up on the floor. Dancers were at that peak where many were drunk enough to forget to be shy, but not so drunk that they were falling over. Good times all around. Eventually Raina spotted Troy. She waved happily, realizing just then how much she had missed him.

He had a whole tray of drinks with him that he carried over to the table. There were four glasses on the tray, two tall and two short. He set the tray down and dropped into his chair with a broad grin.

"What did you get?" Raina eyed the drinks. "They're very... brown."

"Fun stuff." Troy grabbed the short glasses and set one in front of her. "That's a Gold Digger shot. You down it in one go."

She looked closer at it. The drink had three layers. The top was golden brown. The next layer was a milky tan. The bottom was clear with gold flecks floating in it.

"Is that real gold?"

His grin got bigger. "Yep. Don't worry. It's safe to drink."

She lifted the glass and swirled it. The flecks danced and glimmered. Pretty! "I've never drank gold before."

"Here's to first times," Troy saluted. He clinked his shot glass against hers and tipped it into his mouth, straight down his throat.

She raised her glass. "To first times," she agreed and then did the same.

It took her two swallows to get the full shot down. A wave of flavors seared their way from her mouth to her stomach: Cinnamon, Irish cream, and coffee liquor. Sweet and creamy. Like a dessert soaked in alcohol.

"Nice job," Troy said despite her struggle. He passed one of the tall glasses over to her next.

"What's this?" She wiped her mouth with the back of her hand. She tried to rub her hand on her dress but missed and smudged it on her thigh instead.

"Long Island iced tea."

"I've heard of those." She took her glass then slid a suspicious look his way, exaggerating it. "You're trying to get me drunk."

He took the other glass. Mischief flavored his smile. "Maaaaybe. Hey. It's a party. If you're not going to get drunk now, then when?"

"I don't like getting drunk," she said. She sipped the Long Island. It was a nice refresher after the burn of the shot. Sweet, but not too. Easy to drink. Too easy.

"Why not?"

She had another swallow and shrugged. "I make bad decisions when I'm drunk."

The heat in her belly spread outward, numbing her shoulders and thighs, and warming her crotch along with rest. She felt better than she had in days, no—weeks. Relaxed and at ease. Happier. Stress was a hundred miles away. The thumping music caressed her, making her sway to the beat.

"I won't let you make any bad decisions tonight," Troy vowed and drank to that.

She snorted. "You already have." She lifted her glass to show how.

"I won't let you make any *more* bad decisions."

"I'm holding you to that." Turning suddenly sincere, she patted him on the knee. Making good on that resolve to touch more. "I like you, Troy. You're awesome."

"You're pretty awesome yourself," he toasted.

They both drank to that. Mutual admiration society. Out in the ballroom, the music shifted to something slower. The song was full of bass but had a sultry waltz beat to sex it up.

"I feel like dancing some more," he said. "Want to?"

Raina looked over at the ballroom. A thin haze hung in the air, catching the bouncing lights. Ethereal beauty. She couldn't make out Michael or Trixie in the silhouetted throng of moving bodies.

"Okay," she said. "Sure."

CHAPTER 14

They both had a few more gulps from their glasses in case someone cleared them away while they were gone. When Raina got to her feet she wobbled a little. Gravity was her enemy when she was tipsy, and the platform sandals she wore conspired with it. Troy took her hand.

"Careful," he said.

He was her life preserver. She clung to his arm as he escorted her to the dark dance floor. Unlike when she was with Michael, the crowd didn't budge for them. So, they kept to the outer fringe. Troy pulled her close in a languid sway to the rhythm. His arms were strong around her, his hands prone to wandering up and down her back.

Raina's blood was alight with the alcohol she'd consumed. She melted into the moment, hooking her arms around his neck as they moved to the beat. The dance grew more intimate. His hips rubbed suggestively against hers. Desire was plain in his brown eyes—an unspoken offer to take things further if she were willing.

———

Not far from them, Michael was still partnered with Trixie. The girl was doing her best to lure him in with her moves, throwing him longing looks and sultry pouts. Pushing her breasts and hips out as she gyrated in a 'come hither' way. While her flirtatious display entertained him, he didn't encourage it. Dancing with her was strictly diplomacy tonight.

The song was almost over when he caught sight of Raina and Troy. The way they moved together cooled his good humor. He wasn't prone to jealousy. He and Troy shared women before without issue, sometimes at the same time. But seeing the two of them grinding on each other bothered him.

Noticing his distraction, Trixie moved closer. She wriggled up against him in a bid to regain his attention. He tried to focus on her, but his eyes kept straying to the other couple. As the song came to an end, he stepped away from his dance partner.

"Excuse me," he said to her. Then he moved through the crowd toward the other couple.

Trixie saw where he was going, and her dismay shifted to anger. She was too proud to follow him. However, she didn't want to stick around and watch Raina get all the attention either. So instead, she picked her way off the dance floor. She paused to take one last disgruntled look back and then headed for the exit.

Michael didn't notice. He only had eyes for his destination. When he got to them, he tapped Troy's shoulder. The other guy looked at him, first surprised, then all smiles.

"Heeey," he greeted as the next song started.

"May I cut in?" Michael said.

Even though he was well on his way to a good drunk, Troy could read between the lines. His enthusiasm dwindled.

"Yeah, okay."

He stepped back and the prince took his place. Troy, not one to waste time on a lost cause, went to look for Trixie. Michael offered his hand to Raina. She took it and he pulled her close.

"Hi," she smiled up at him.

The innocence in the greeting made him smile.

"Hello."

His arms settled low on her waist while hers draped over his shoulders. She relaxed against him, conforming nicely to his bare chest. He felt the press of her leather corset against his skin and the softness of her breasts above it.

"Oh! I met Holly," she said over the slinky music. Even through the loud tune he could hear the slight slur of her words.

"Did you?"

He nuzzled her hair, inhaling the smell of her. Alcohol and arousal. The erotic scent made him want to take her someplace private and do something about it. The hotel wasn't completely out of service. It just didn't rent rooms out to the public since the Society took it over. He could get into one quite easily...

"I did!" said Raina, unaware. "She's a real peach. She said she'd help me find the necklace."

Michael turned with her, rocked her back then brought her up and close again. Closer than before. He pressed his body against hers and felt her press back. One of his hands found the loose end of her braid. He had to resist the urge to wrap it around his hand and use it as a lead to kiss her. He made himself release it and stroked her back instead.

"Wonderful." He wasn't thinking about the conversation.

She put her cheek against his shoulder. Skin on warm skin only charged him up more. She said something then, but her words got lost in his cloak and the music.

"What?"

"Nothing," she said louder, the word bounced on a giggle.

She lifted her head to speak again but nothing came out when their eyes met. He wanted her. More than a means to restore his lost abilities, he wanted all of her. Every inch, every ounce. He could see in her deep green eyes she sensed his desire. Welcomed it. Her lips parted, an invitation to a kiss. He bent to accept and...

A loud burst of static crackled from the speakers, disrupting the song and raking the ears of those listening. The music died. People stopped dancing. Their attention flew to the stage. Raina and Michael looked over as well, their intimate moment dispelled.

A woman dressed as Athena was atop one of the large speakers. She stared wild-eyed out into the crowd. Two of the band members tried to get her down. She paid no attention to them.

Her crazed eyes found Michael. She jabbed a finger in his direction. "Prince of Darkness!" she bellowed. Her voice was unnaturally distorted, a throaty and powerful intonation. "Your reckoning is upon you!"

Scowling at the intrusion, Michael took a step toward the stage. The woman raised her arms. Acted like she was pulling something heavy from the air above as she shouted arcane words. There was a deep crack overhead.

Michael looked up and flew into action. He grabbed Raina. Dove to the side. They both went down in a heap. He flattened himself on top of her.

A thunderous crack sounded overhead, and the huge chandelier came crashing down. A deadly spray of jagged crystal pieces shot out in all directions.

People screamed.

—

Pinned and covered by Michael, Raina couldn't see what was happening. All she could see was his face close to hers. He grimaced. There was a flare up of bright, hot light behind him from the direction of the stage. More screaming.

Michael held his position until the light died down. He glanced over his shoulder then looked down at Raina.

"Are you all right?"

"I... think so," she said. "What—"

Before she could finish the question, he was on his feet. He grabbed her hand and pulled her up. She stumbled, propelled too fast by his strength. He caught her so she wouldn't fall. She clung to his side to steady herself. Once she was sure she had her footing, she looked around.

Troy stood near the door to the lobby, both hands on fire. His eyes were wide, his expression uncharacteristically serious.

There were people crushed under the fallen chandelier, moaning and crying in pain, skewered with pieces of broken crystal. Many fled the room while others tried to move the heavy light fixture. On stage several fires were burning, including one atop the melted speaker.

Michael saw the blaze and his face darkened. "Dammit, Troy! You incinerated her!"

The flames on Troy's hands went out as he approached the prince. "She was going to pull the ceiling down!" he defended. "I had to!"

"I can't find out who sent her if she's DEAD," Michael stormed, unmoved by logic.

The men squared off. Raina hugged herself as she looked on in concern. It was scary to see them both so angry and to see Troy butt heads with the Lord Prince. Could he do that? Apparently so.

"Oh, my God!" Holly cried from the dining room.

She and her winged companion heard the crash and came to see what was going on. The horror of the sight was plain on her cherubic face.

"What the hell happened?" she lamented, looking around in dismay at the tragic mess the ballroom had become.

Michael turned to her. "Someone has been playing with powers they shouldn't."

"A party crasher," Troy added. "We took care of her."

Michael gave him a nasty look.

"Oh! Michael!" Raina gasped. "Your back!"

Several glittering shards of crystal had lanced through his cloak, pinning it to him. Blood seeped through and soaked the blue material a deep purple. He glanced back but couldn't see what she saw. He could feel it, though, now that his attention was called to it.

"Dammit!" he swore again. "Troy, put out those fucking fires! Holly, bring medical supplies. Gauze or whatever you can find for these people. Raina—" He looked at her. "I need you to pull this shit out of my back."

"What? Me?" she blinked. "I—"

"I can't function like this," he said with forced patience.

The others were already on the move.

"I don't want to hurt you more," she objected. "Shouldn't we get a doctor or—"

"I don't need a doctor!" he flared. He pulled a quick breath. Exhaled. "Just. Help me. You won't hurt me. I'll be fine as soon as this glass is out of my back. Trust me."

She didn't. But she followed him to the dining area anyway. He went to the table they had been sitting at earlier and put his hands down on the surface. Holly returned and dumped rolls of gauze in front of him.

"I brought some peroxide too," she said. "Evan, darlin', get on the radio and call the medics. We're gonna need all the help we can get."

The young man had shed his wings while they were off getting medical supplies. He hustled two first aid boxes out to the ballroom and gave them to a couple of people who were helping others. Then he darted out to the lobby.

"I'm gonna go see who I can help," Holly said. "Holler if you need anything else."

She made good on her statement, leaving Raina and Michael alone with the pile of medical supplies.

"Grab one of those cloth napkins," Michael instructed. "You don't want to cut your hands."

Raina looked around and, finding a linen napkin, shook it out. She approached him, her confidence fading as she eyed his bloody back.

"I'm sorry," she said as she reached for the biggest shard.

She grabbed hold and tugged. He tensed up and she lost her nerve, releasing it.

"Don't stop," he snapped. "Just yank it out!"

"I'm trying!" she snapped back, too rattled to think about propriety.

She seized the shard again and pulled it. It slid out, tinted with his blood. She dropped the two-inch chunk onto the table and reached for another. His nails scratched audibly on the wood surface, and he grunted in pain, but he held still.

One by one Raina plucked the chunks from his back. There were seven big pieces and several smaller bits she had to remove before the bloody cloak hung free. As soon as the last piece was out, he shed the ruined accessory and let it drop to the floor. Blood streaked his back.

It was an unpleasant sight, but Raina wasn't the squeamish sort. She grabbed the peroxide and wetted a large gauze pad with it. Troy came into the room, his toga smudged with ash. His amphora was gone.

"Fires are out," he reported. "They're so much easier to start than to stop."

"Scoop up the remains," ordered Michael.

Raina gently blotted his injuries. Despite the size of the shards she removed, the wounds didn't look as bad as she feared. Had the cloak reduced the penetration?

"There's nothing left to scoop," said Troy.

"Great." Sarcasm dripped from the word. Michael huffed an agitated breath.

Raina swabbed away more blood and squinted. What she thought was a cut was only a smear of blood. In fact, the more she wiped, the less injuries she saw.

"Are... Your wounds..." she faltered.

Michael's ire eased as he noticed her confusion. A hint of a perverse little smile tugged one corner of his mouth. "I'll be fine in a few. I just can't heal while there's something in the injury."

"Oh." Stunned beyond words, Raina didn't know what else to say. "Wow."

Troy gave her shoulder a squeeze. "Welcome to our world."

CHAPTER 15

Michael's wounds closed rapidly. He had Raina gather the blood-stained crystal shards and put them in a napkin. He wrapped the bundle in his ruined cloak and tied it to his belt for safekeeping. Once his injuries healed, he, Troy, and Raina went to help Holly.

Michael and Troy helped to move the fallen chandelier, freeing the people who were under it when it came down. Raina provided basic first aid to those that needed it. She didn't have any medical training, but she could bandage simple wounds.

At one point she saw Michael tending to a badly injured man. The prince had his hand on the man's bloody chest, his brow furrowed in concentration. Someone in need of bandages approached her for help then, so she didn't see what he was trying to do.

Soon the medics arrived and took over. She, Michael, and Troy retired to their coach. Trixie was nowhere to be found. Troy had searched for her earlier, before the light fixture was destroyed, and had heard from the doorman that she'd left. He didn't have a chance to check on the matter, but she wasn't among the injured.

No one said much as the coach trotted them back to the Bradford. They were all tired. Troy sagged into the corner of his bench, almost asleep. Michael was awake, staring out the window at the darkness. Despite her fatigue, Raina's curiosity got the better of her as she sat there watching him.

"There was a man you were with," she said. "You had your hand on his chest. What were you doing?"

He stirred on the padded seat beside her and gave a soft sigh that was almost a growl. "I was trying to heal him."

"You can do that?"

A sour frown crossed his face, quickly replaced by a neutral mask. "Apparently not. I could, before."

She took a breath to ask more, but he cut her off.

"You should speak to Ligeia about her helping you learn some protective measures," he said. "You need to be able to defend yourself if something else happens."

Raina laced her fingers over her knees. Though her feet were aching, she resisted the urge to remove her shoes. The Bradford was close. She could take her shoes off once she was inside the hotel.

"I'll do that tomorrow," she said. "I'm willing to learn whatever she wants to teach me."

"Good," Michael said. He looked back out the window again and resumed brooding.

—

Troy rousted when the coach came to a stop outside the hotel entrance. He mumbled a good night through a huge yawn then he wandered up to the front doors and let himself inside. Michael stayed behind to help Raina down out of the carriage.

When she made it to the sidewalk, she expected him to let go, but he kept hold of her hand. His gaze was intense when her eyes met his.

"Thank you for your help tonight," he said in a low voice.

Not entirely sober, she wasn't sure if he was thanking her for helping with the injured people or for helping him specifically. It didn't really matter. What mattered was the way he looked at her. An echo of the way he looked at her on the dance floor before the chandelier fell.

"Oh. It was no trouble," she dismissed awkwardly.

He was so close, for a wild moment it seemed as though he might make good on the interrupted kiss from earlier. But then he released her hand and turned to start up the front steps. He held the door for her when he got to it.

She went inside, trying without success to sort out how to feel. His angry outburst at the party and moodiness afterward confused her. Almost as much as his blatant desire for her had made her yearn for him. It was a mixed bag to sort through and she was too tired to do it.

"I should, um, go up," she said in the lobby. "Get clean before bed."

"You do that. Good night, Raina."

He headed toward the bar while she angled for the stairs. She paused at the base to watch him go. Without the cloak there was nothing to interrupt her view of his well-built upper body. There was no sign of the injuries he'd suffered earlier. Just smooth, toned muscle. Muscle that she longed to run her hands over. She turned and started the long trip up the stairs, silently scolding herself for staring. For wanting him. Her life was already messy enough without the distraction of infatuation.

To take her mind off things she focused on the pain in her feet. Soon she would be in her room and able to shed the clunky sandals that hated her toes. Afterward she could soak in the tub and just not think for a while.

———

Michael needed a shower too, but he wanted a drink even more. There was no one tending the bar this late, but he considered the hotel his personal property and wasn't shy about fixing himself a glass of bourbon. He didn't even bother with the "right" glass. He dumped the liquor into a tumbler and sank down onto a barstool to brood some more.

The evening had started off well enough, though it certainly didn't go the way he would've liked. Not that anything ever did. As far back as he could remember, people told him he would be in control when he was grown. Yet he was even further from that goal than ever.

At least when he was younger, he had the false comfort of believing he was invincible. He could do things no one else could. For a brief time, he truly believed himself to be a demi-god. And then everything changed. The power he'd taken for granted before was no longer his to command. Forget about controlling the world. He couldn't even make it through a simple social gathering without disruption he couldn't stop.

Halfway through his second round, he sensed Pietre coming up behind him. He hunched his shoulders and hunkered over his glass. The warlock ignored the antisocial signals and took a seat beside him.

"Troy told me about your little... adventure."

"Really?" Michael's tone scraped between casual and irritable. "I thought he would have gone and face-planted somewhere, as burnt out as he was."

"Oh, he tried," said Pietre. A smile laced his words. Then, more seriously: "Your enemy grows bolder."

"Tell me something I don't know," Michael grumped.

He had another gulp from his glass. The liquor warmed his throat, but it didn't make him feel better. He wished Pietre would take the cue to leave him alone. The warlock could read his mood. He was just choosing to ignore it.

"Tomorrow, I'm going to conduct a ritual on the remains of the landlord. We should be able to find out who killed him."

Michael looked at him, his interest baited. "Yeah? Well. That's something, anyway."

"Hopefully."

"What're the chances that's related to what happened tonight?"

Pietre shrugged and slid off his barstool. He went around the bar. Looked at a couple of bottles before selecting a chartreuse.

"It's been fairly quiet since your return," Pietre remarked as he poured a glass for himself. "Up till now. I wouldn't bet on it, but it seems likely the two events may have some common backbone to them."

"Yeah. Sort of what I was thinking."

Pietre swirled the bright yellow-green wine to de-gas it. "Whoever they are, they're sloppy. I'm sure we'll find something of interest in the dead man's corpse. A shame you couldn't take the would-be assassin alive."

Michael's irritation heated up again. "Fucking Troy. It's all or nothing with him. Either he stands there like a stump or he goes all scorched earth. He has absolutely no common sense. Can you teach him that?"

Pietre chuckled. "If only I could. But his impetuousness isn't without some merit. Every now and then."

He lifted his glass to his lips.

Michael snorted. He didn't argue, though. As annoying as Troy's inconsistency was, it had been useful in taking an enemy off guard more than once. "When you're done with the dead guy, I want to start Raina's training."

Pietre's brows arched. "Yes?"

"Yeah. After tonight..." Michael huffed a sigh, annoyed. "I tried to heal a man there and I couldn't. I know—I know it's still there. Somewhere inside me. I can feel it! I just... can't... reach it."

"The girl doesn't have to be trained in witchcraft for you to do the ritual," the warlock reminded.

That was the last thing Michael wanted to hear now. His temper, held in check all evening, erupted. "I know that, but I want her to survive it! You know the ritual could kill her. *I* could kill her." He set his glass down before he broke it by accident. He glared at the other man. "I'm not going to just use her up like a rag and toss her aside."

Pietre's knowing smile crept back. "You've never had a problem with it before. Do you have... feelings for her?"

"No." The word was flat. It was also a lie, but Michael wasn't about to give Pietre the satisfaction of an honest response. "She's useful for more than a single pass. I'm sure you've sensed her potential."

"I have," said Pietre with more than a hint of hunger. "But I would have started teaching her the first night she arrived if it were up to me."

"Yeah, well," Michael said, ignoring the dig. "Start tomorrow, after you get done with the corpse. I'll be joining you when you do. Once she has some of the basics down, Ligeia can help strengthen her."

"You're ready to continue your lessons as well?"

Michael reached for his glass again. "Yes. But don't make me look bad."

Pietre spread his hands. "Why would I do that?"

"Because," grunted Michael. "You're a fucking sadist."

He drained his glass. Set it down with an audible thunk.

Pietre laughed. "Guilty as charged. But I won't try to make you look foolish," he said graciously. "It's on you whether you do or not."

—

On his way up to his room, Michael encountered Trixie on the landing. She had changed out of her costume into a more mundane set of satin pajamas. She was having a cigarette on the small bench against the wall.

He nodded to her. She sucked on her cigarette and got to her feet when he reached her.

"Are you all right?" she asked. "I heard about what happened at the party after I left."

He paused and looked down at her. "It was nothing that couldn't be handled. Some people were injured. I don't believe anyone died, apart from the person responsible."

"Well. That's good."

"I suppose," he allowed. "Except the person who did it was... I think she was under someone else's influence."

"Possessed?"

"Possibly. Hard to know for sure since Troy destroyed the remains."

Trixie put her cigarette out. Stepped closer to him. "You know ever since that new girl showed up things have been weird."

He cocked his head. "Indeed."

"Are you sure it's safe to keep her around?"

Her concern was curious to him. He sifted through her mood without prying directly into her mind. Just took in the surface flavor of her emotions. She was always a variegated tapestry of feelings, tonight even more so. Concern, bitterness, and paranoia were the top notes.

"Are you worried?" he asked.

Trixie gave a tight shrug. "I'm just wondering if having her here is a good idea. She seems to attract trouble and we don't really know anything about her."

"Are you concerned for my sake? Or your own?"

She frowned and folded her arms. Looked away. She didn't like him calling her out, even in a subtle way. "Yours. She's no threat to me."

"No. She isn't," he agreed. "Nor to me."

He reached over and brushed two fingers down her jaw. Her eyes met his again. Her lashes fluttered. She leaned into his touch, but he let his hand fall away.

"I don't trust her," she said, cutting to the chase. "I don't think you should, either."

"I appreciate your concern. It is duly noted, if misplaced."

Although she wasn't satisfied with the response, she let it go. She'd said what she needed to. "Care for a nightcap?"

"Already had one," he demurred. "I'm going to shower and sleep. Tomorrow comes too soon."

She didn't try to hide her disappointment. "Okay. Rest well."

"And you." He flashed her a smile and continued upstairs.

CHAPTER 16

The next morning, one of the triplets intercepted Raina on her way out of her room. The pale woman had her hair in braids when they first met. Now her straw-colored locks hung in loose waves down the back of her shapeless white dress.

"Pietre is ready for you," she said without preamble. "Come with me."

She turned and walked away. Raina glanced down at herself. She followed after the other woman, hoping her clothing was adequate. She dressed in the expectation of doing laundry.

"What's your name again?"

"Tisi."

"Tisi," repeated Raina. She made it a point to remember it this time. "Do you know what he'll be teaching me?"

Tisi's lips thinned but she didn't slow her step even when they reached the stairs. She took them with the sure-footedness of a mountain goat. "How to survive."

Raina followed, one hand sliding down the polished wood banister. Gravity was never her friend, and it had been especially unkind to her of late. After last night, she wasn't her most stable. A little extra caution never hurt.

"Yes, but... I mean. Will he be teaching me spells? Or..?"

"He'll teach you what he thinks you need to know."

The blunt answer was hardly helpful. Raina tried again. "Am I going to have to memorize incantations?"

Tisi stopped and turned on her so fast Raina almost ran into her. The woman didn't react to the near collision.

"It will be easier for you to wait and see than for me to guess," Tisi said. Her words were stripped of emotion, her face a perfect blank. "If you have questions, you should save them for Pietre. Only he knows what he is going to do."

She turned and resumed her quick trot down the stairs. Raina watched her for a moment, then hurried to catch up. She couldn't decide how to react to the woman's deadpan behavior, so she let it slide though it was peculiar.

Tisi took them to the far side of the hotel on the ground floor, down the hall from the dining area. At the end of the corridor a frosted glass door led into the pool room. Tisi opened the door for her then left without another word.

"Thank you," Raina called after her, to be polite.

The other woman didn't turn or acknowledge her at all. Rude.

The pool room was a wide and echoing space. Long windows took up one of the walls, though tall bushes outside blocked the sunlight. Their jagged tops allowed only a glimpse of blue sky. Instead of natural lighting the room was lit by overhead halogens. Raina's neighborhood was sparing with electricity due to the cost. Candles and lanterns were the norm. At the Bradford Hotel, hot water and indoor lighting were a given. Incidental luxury of the elite.

The tiled room had a damp, musty smell though the salted water was clean. Three steps led into the shallow end. A pipe ladder poked out of the deep end where a diving board extended over the blue pool.

Michael and Pietre sat at one of the deck tables. Pietre wore his standard black pants and shirt and was barefoot as always. Michael had relaxed his style and had on a loose-fitting pair of burgundy pants and a white linen shirt buttoned only halfway up. Raina ran her hand over the skirt she'd borrowed from Desiree's closet. Not exactly poolside attire.

Several jars on the table held a variety of substances. Other items cluttered the surface too: Bowls. Candles. A bell. A long, unsheathed knife. When she headed over to them, Michael put out his cigarette in a crystal ashtray among the clutter.

"Good morning," he said.

"Ah, Raina," said Pietre. "So glad you could join us. Michael informed Beth you won't be helping today. I'm sorry to say you'll be skipping breakfast. I hope that isn't a problem."

The drinking she'd done last night tempered her appetite. "Thanks. I'll be fine."

"Excellent." Pietre smiled. "Shall we get started?"

"The sooner the better," said Michael.

Raina was unable to contain her curiosity any longer. "What is it we're doing?"

"Basic protection," Pietre answered. "First, you're going to learn how to make a circle of protection with salt. Michael? Would you care to show her?"

The young man rose and took a large jar of salt from the table. "Anyplace particular?"

"Over there near the ladder."

Michael went over to the indicated spot.

"A Circle of Protection is generally five feet in circumference," instructed Pietre from his seat. "But it can flex as big or as small as needed. You can make it just large enough to stand in. It can surround a house. Size only matters when you are trying to hold a specific entity. Then it is critical."

He gathered four candles and a long box of matches from the table.

"Outdoors, a sword is used to draw the Circle in the ground. In a pinch your knife—we call it an athame—can be used... once you have one, that is. Indoors, ritual circles are painted or drawn in chalk. White. A temporary circle like ours can be made with salt or a white cord."

Having no instruction on size, Michael made the circle five feet. Large enough so both he and Raina could feasibly stand inside it, if necessary. It put the southern edge of the circle only a couple of feet from the edge of the pool.

"The Circle is always started from the east and drawn clockwise," continued Pietre. "Notice how he walks backward. It is easier to control the line that way. Less risk of scuffing it by accident. Never break the circle."

Michael finished the circle and brought the salt container back to the table. "Candles?"

Pietre handed the candles to Raina but kept the matches. He took the knife from the table. "Come," he said to her.

He went to the easternmost edge of the circle, where Michael had started the line. "Indoors, you must consecrate the Circle with the sword or athame. The tip of the blade is pointed at the Circle. You start and end at the east."

So saying, he walked completely around the circle with the point of the long knife angled toward the salt line. Once he rejoined Raina, he waved her toward the Circle.

"Place a candle at each cardinal point. East, north, west, south."

"On the line?" She wanted to be sure she did it right. She hated messing up while learning something new. Though it was unrealistic, she liked to do things perfectly the first time. Especially when others were watching.

"Yes. On the line."

She set a fat, stubby candle down at each point, as centered on the line as she could get without breaking it.

"The incantation?" Michael said, showing off his expertise for Raina.

Pietre waved a hand. "For this exercise we are forgoing the standard dedication." Then, to Raina: "In a Circle designed to protect you from a true enemy, you infuse each cardinal point with energy. White is often used for smaller rituals. Our Coven uses red for... bigger things. Angels are often invoked during the incantation said as you dedicate the Circle."

Fascinating. Raina had studied angels in her mother's art books and in some reference books on their shelves. It was a subject Lyra had many resources about. The *Dictionary of Angels* was one of the books Raina saved from the trashed house. Books in general were a weakness of hers. Every book was a potential friend.

"Does it matter which angels?" she asked.

Her question pleased the warlock. "It does matter. It would do you no good to call on the Fallen if you serve the Higher Power, and vice versa. Likewise, a Vodoun would do best calling to the lwa rather than relying on Judeo-Christian saints and angels."

"Why aren't we doing an incantation now?"

"Because you are only protecting yourselves from each other."

Michael shot him a peculiar look. He opened his mouth to ask, but Raina beat him to it.

"How do you mean?"

The warlock handed Michael the box of matches and a fifth candle.

"Go and stand in the Circle. Light the candles."

Michael gave the warlock another dubious look. Then he took up a position in the center of the salt ring.

"See how he enters the Circle from the east?" Pietre moved to stand behind Raina. "North of the eastern candle. That is how we always enter and leave the Circle."

Michael lit the candle he held and set the matchbox on the pool deck. He systematically lit each candle with the one he held, again starting at the east. As he turned from one candle to the next, he kept his over the line. Once finished, he set his candle down where he'd left the matches.

Pietre leaned in close to Raina, speaking just to her. "Now. Focus your energy. Imagine it as a cord. A thick, strong cord of power. Loop it around Michael. Imagine yourself using it to pull him out of the Circle. Toward you or away from you, the direction does not matter. Focus."

She looked sidelong at him. He was close enough for her to smell the peppermint on his breath. "And then what?"

"Then do it."

"You want me to push him?" Surely she misunderstood. Push the prince?

"Not with your body. With your spirit. Use your energy."

"How?"

"You can sense others, yes? For example, though we are not touching, you can sense where I am right now even if you are not looking at me. Yes?"

He passed a hand near her shoulder. Followed the curve down her arm without actually touching her. She most certainly could sense where his hand passed. It was almost electric. It was energy connecting with energy.

"Yes..."

"Sense Michael."

Raina focused on where he stood inside the salt ring. When she was close to him on the dance floor she had sensed him even when they weren't touching. There was a lot she'd sensed then. And she discovered she *could* sense him now that she tried. Not only could she feel his presence, but she sensed his attention on her. When she made eye contact, she could tell he sensed her as well. It was an awareness that went beyond sight. Closer to communication than seeing.

It wasn't the first time she had noticed his awareness of her either. She was just fully conscious of the press of his attention now, knowing what she was sensing with nothing to distract her.

It occurred to her she had also sensed Troy at the party. And Tisi a bit ago in the hall. The sensation she'd gotten from the woman was far less welcoming than Michael's attention was now. It occurred to Raina why the woman's blankness had thrown her so: Tisi was deliberately closed off. Nothing there to sense. She had intentionally shut Raina out of her psychic space.

"I can feel him," she said, warming to the exercise now that she understood it. "I can feel him!"

Michael smirked at her choice of wording. Then he stretched, showing off his physique.

"Good," Pietre purred. He paid no mind to Michael's peacocking. "Good. Now. Push him. Use your hands to direct the energy, but do not cross the Circle with your body."

Raina hesitated. She didn't particularly want to push him. Physically or mentally. "But he's the prince."

Pietre gave another soft laugh. His peppermint breath tickled her neck. "This is just an exercise. He understands. Don't you, Michael?"

"Of course, I do," he said. His smirk grew bigger and more self-assured. "But I don't think she can do it."

The smug comment caught her off guard. His blatant lack of confidence stung her pride. Shoving thoughts of rank aside, she focused on the sense of him—the energy that was him. Visualized shoving that energy out of the ring and into the pool. With that image in mind, she thrust her hands forward.

Though Michael didn't move, Raina met instant resistance. It was as though an invisible wall sprang up between them. A magnetic sort of energy, except it repelled her rather than drew her. A flicker of surprise crossed Michael's chiseled features.

"Try again," Pietre encouraged her. He swept his foot forward, using his big toe to break the line of salt.

"Hey!" Michael objected. "That's not—"

He didn't get to complete the sentence. Raina's psychic shove pushed him clear out of the Circle. He flipped sideways into the pool, landing with a splash. He surfaced, sputtering.

Raina laughed. Regretting the involuntary reaction, she clapped a hand over her mouth. Pietre grinned wolfishly.

"Not fair!" Michael exclaimed. His hair was plastered to his face and his shirt clung to him as he swam to where he could reach the bottom.

Raina tried to look remorseful but had to keep her hand over her mouth to hide her smile. Still, it leaked into her eyes.

"Oh, you think that's funny?" Michael accused.

He brought his right hand up and tightened it into a fist. With a swift motion he brought his arm back, his bicep rippling with the force he applied.

"No, I—" Raina broke off in a squeal when she sailed into the pool.

Cold water shocked her senses. She rocketed to the surface, sputtering as Michael had. When she flipped her wet hair back, she saw him grinning at her. Full of himself.

"You..!" she said, too indignant to finish the thought.

He laughed at her outrage, which prompted her to splash him in retaliation.

"Now," Pietre interceded. "Let's not start that. Come out of the water."

Michael resisted the urge to splash her back, though his eyes followed her as she swam to the pool's edge. Her skirt floated about underwater offering distracting glimpses of her legs and panties. Once she was out, he joined her. Together they stood dripping on the concrete deck. Pietre clucked his tongue.

"Michael. You let your guard down."

"I didn't expect you to break the Circle," the prince grouched, his amusement evaporating.

Pietre picked up the salt container. "You should always be alert, especially when you know someone is about test your defenses."

Michael made a face. He couldn't really argue that logic, so he picked another point to nitpick instead. "This is supposed to be Raina's lesson."

The warlock repaired the Circle, going completely around it with the salt. "It *is* her lesson. If you happen to learn something along the way, all the better. Now, Raina. When I've finished consecrating it with the blade, you step into the Circle. Enter from the east."

She wrung out her skirt while Pietre reset the Circle. Once he finished, she entered north of the eastern candle, careful not to drip on the salt line.

"Michael," said Pietre. "Try to break the Circle. Raina? Don't let him."

Raina widened her stance and braced herself.

CHAPTER 17

"As you've seen, you can strengthen your energy when you use your gestures." Pietre lifted his hands for show. "Hands, arms, even something as small as a motion of the fingers can be impactful. That applies to defense as well as offense."

Michael moved toward the Circle. Remembering the woman who crashed the masquerade Raina put her hands up, palms out. She pictured the ring filling with her energy, expanding to push him back.

She soon felt resistance. As he leaned into the pressure, his body tensed under his clingy wet clothes. He was captivating when damp. She could see the outline of his muscles easily.

Michael took advantage of her distraction. The instant he felt the pressure ease, he asserted his own and lunged forward.

Swiped a foot through the line of salt, scattering it. Too late she tried to push him back. Rather than meet her in a psychic struggle, he grabbed her around the waist and hauled her up off her feet in a bear hug.

"I win," he said.

She wriggled in his grasp, infuriated with herself and him. "Put me down!"

"You lost your focus," chided Pietre. "If you do that in a real fight, it could be deadly."

"Lucky for you this isn't real," Michael said next to her ear.

His arms tightened around her for an instant, then he tossed her into the pool again. She landed in the water butt-first, sending up a big splash. Her legs tangled in her skirt as she kicked to the surface. She came up, sputtering indignantly.

"If I knew we were going to get wet, I would have worn something else," she complained. Water ran down her face. She swam to the side of the pool and pulled herself out.

As she got to her feet, Michael grinned at her. Gloating.

"You're a real piece of work," she said.

That's all the warning she gave before she shoved him. Hard. While she used her hands she also added a hefty psychic boost to the contact. His smug smile shifted to surprise. He wasn't expecting an immediate counterattack. He teetered on the edge for an instant then fell back into the pool.

Pietre sighed and shook his head. "Children," he said to the ceiling. There was a hint of amusement in the exasperated statement.

Michael surfaced next to the pool's edge. He grabbed Raina's ankle. She yelped and tried to snatch her leg back. Too late. Off balance, she had to let him pull her into the water or else she'd go down on the deck.

When she went under this time she caught hold of his shirt and used it to haul herself back up. She surfaced right in front of him, indignant. She tried to duck him by shoving his shoulders down, but he didn't let her, instead catching her around her waist again. He pitched her backward into the pool.

She came back up with an incoherent cry of frustration. Launched herself at him again, but he was ready for her. He caught her and spun around. The drag of the water almost pulled her skirt off. She had to scramble to not lose it. Michael laughed and let her go.

"You're bad at this," he commented.

She wrestled the skirt back up and fixed him with a baleful glare. "You don't fight fair."

His brows went up. "This hasn't been a fair match from the start."

"I think the lesson is over for the day," Pietre decided. "If you wish to keep playing in the pool, you might want to remove some of those clothes before you drown."

Embarrassed, Raina swam to the edge. "I'm sorry, Pietre." She pulled herself up to the deck, water raining from her clothing.

"No need for apologies," he dismissed, not at all bothered. "Though next time I may have you train next to the cactus planter."

Michael got out of the pool and flipped his wet hair out of his face. "You wouldn't."

Pietre turned his smile on the prince, showing lots of teeth. "Wouldn't I?"

He gathered some of the items from the table, including the knife, then took his leave. Michael went over to a dark wicker cabinet near the windows, and he dug up a couple of large hotel towels. He brought one to Raina and tossed his onto a chair.

"After we dry off, do you want to grab something to eat?" He stripped off his shirt. "I'm starving."

Unprepared for a show, Raina found herself staring at his athletic frame and the way the water trickled over his bare torso. The way his pants clung to his pelvis and thighs. Forcing herself to look away, she draped her towel over her shoulders and wrung out her skirt again. Wrung it till her fingers cramped.

"I suppose," she said, preoccupied with the effort of not looking at him.

He watched her without reservation, openly admiring her wet form. Being attuned to his attention now, she found it impossible not to feel it when he looked at her that way.

"You could wrap the towel around your waist and lose the skirt," he suggested.

It was decent advice, but she hesitated. She didn't want to disrobe right in front of him even under the cover of a towel. She'd already been virtually naked in front of him before and didn't want to make a habit of it. But she also didn't want to track water all over the hotel.

She chose the lesser of two evils. After swaddling her hips in the towel, she wiggled out of the sopping wet skirt. Scooped it up from the deck. When she straightened, he was still watching her.

"If you give me your, uh, your clothes, I can take them all to the laundry," she offered, avoiding eye contact.

His smile dimpled one of his cheeks. "Thank you. I'd appreciate that."

Fixing his towel about his waist, he shimmied out of his wet pants and handed them to her along with his shirt. She took the pile of dripping clothes. Noticed his underwear tangled up in the pants.

He was naked under the towel.

Raina's cheeks heated up again. She pretended not to notice and buried his clothes under her wet skirt.

"I'll take these to the laundry," she said unnecessarily. Her mind was on his towel, not what she was saying. "And meet you in the dining room after I've changed. All right?"

"They don't serve lunch. Meet me in the lobby," he said. "We'll go out."

———

They left the hotel in Michael's Bugatti. He drove fast, though not at the speed he had when Raina first rode with him. The Atlanta Rhythm Section played on the car stereo as they cruised. The local broadcast was exceptionally clear that sunny afternoon.

"Where are we going?" she asked.

"It's a surprise. I radioed an order ahead while you were changing."

Mystery food. A real lunchtime adventure. "I'm not a picky eater. I'm sure whatever you ordered will be fine."

They pulled into the parking lot of a long brick building with blacked-out windows. A large sign proclaimed it the TNT Grill. It only took a couple of minutes for Michael to dash inside and grab the bag before they were on the road again.

Minutes later they arrived at Elysian Park. Positioned behind the abandoned Dodger Stadium, the hilly preserve overlooked the river that cut through the outskirts of the walled section of town. Fall brought a touch of red, yellow, and brown to the arboretum, though most of the plants were persistently green.

They drove up the tallest hill and parked at a spot where the land had once been curated. It was overgrown now. Shifted in odd ways thanks to years of earthquakes. Despite the upheaval there was a flat grassy area at the end of a short trail with a good view of the river. A towering evergreen stood near the edge of the hill. Old graffiti coated its trunk, faded with time.

Michael carried the food. Raina brought a blanket he pulled from the trunk of the car. It was old and coarse but would serve to keep them off the ground.

She spread the blanket in the shade of the large, leaning evergreen tree. The thick, crooked branches made a nice canopy to keep the direct sun off them. The only sounds came from songbirds, the cool breeze, and the rustle of blackbirds that flew up to settle in the tree above them.

"It's so quiet out here," Raina observed.

"Not a soul for miles," agreed Michael.

He set the bag down once she got the black-and-white blanket positioned. She took a seat and smoothed her hand over the rumples in the blanket.

"I remember going to the park when I was little," she said. "It was nothing like this, though. The one I went to had playground equipment. You know? This place looks like it's always been wild."

"There's a playground." Michael sat beside her. "It's down the hill. This spot's better for eating at. More room to sit. Less prowling scavengers."

He took a couple of wrapped paper plates from the bag. Handed her one along with a thin wooden spork. He didn't open his immediately, instead looking out over the river and cityscape. The valley was visible all the way to the mountains. From their vantage it was quite peaceful. Innocent at a distance.

"I forgot how nice this place is," he said. "I haven't been here in years."

"Really?" Raina didn't open her meal yet either. Waiting for him. "How come?"

He looked at her and tipped his head. "I don't have a lot of leisure time. When I do go out someplace like this, it's usually to meditate. Not for fun."

A casual statement, but it gave Raina a thrill anyway. "Are you having fun?"

"I am. Shall we?"

He tugged the waxed paper off his dish, uncovering a steak so rare it was bleeding. It was nestled in another layer of waxed paper so it wouldn't soak through the plate. The grilled meat was precut into bite-sized strips, which forgave the absence of a knife.

Raina removed the wrapper her plate. Her meal was pasta with shrimp coated in garlic cheese sauce. It smelled delicious.

"I wasn't sure what you might like," Michael said. "Father Jeremiah enjoys that dish, so I thought you might too."

She resisted the urge to do a taste-test with her finger. She'd already done enough to convince him she was a hot mess. Instead, she poked the pasta with the spork. It wasn't easy to load noodles onto the flatware, but she made it work.

"It's very good," she said after a sample.

They stopped talking for a bit while they ate. Occasionally they made eye contact. It was a comfortable silence, unpressured. The sounds of nature filled the conversational gap—bird chatter and the whisper of wind through the trees. Glancing up, Raina noticed the blackbirds again.

"What are those?" When he looked at her quizzically, she motioned upward with her spork. "Ravens? Crows?"

He looked up. "Ravens. Crows are smaller. Some people mistake them for the carrion crows that were common here a few years back, but they're not the same."

"Did you train them?"

He smiled. "No. They're not pets. They're... companions. They follow me by choice."

He took a strip of raw meat from his plate and threw it skyward. Three large ravens leapt into the air. Two caught it and pulled in different directions. The meat tore, leaving them each with a chunk. They gulped down their prizes, circled a few times in hope of more, then settled again in the tree.

"I only ever see you eat meat," Raina said. "Why is that?"

"Because it's the only thing I've eaten in front of you."

An artful dodge. She tilted her head and studied him. His expression was inscrutable, though she sensed playful amusement.

"Do you eat other things?"

He smiled at her tenaciousness. "I do."

"Isn't it bad to eat so much meat without vegetables or anything?"

He finished his meal and tossed the plate to the side with the spork in it. "Not for me."

"Why? Does that have to do with the way you heal yourself?"

"Something like that."

He moved closer to her and took her plate. Set it aside. She had a follow-up question, but she forgot what it was when he brushed his knuckles along her jaw. His hands found hers and he rose, tugging her to her feet along with him.

"What are we doing?" she asked as she got up.

His answer was another enigmatic smile.

He led her around the tree where a rope swing hung from a thick branch. He helped her on. She took hold of the thick old ropes. The seat was sturdy considering it looked like something salvaged from a construction site.

Moving behind her, he took hold of the ropes above her hands. "This is the secret swing. No better view in New Salem."

He drew the swing back and released it. Gave her a gentle push. The arc took her out past the edge of the hill. The ground fell away and for a few seconds she was flying high above the city. Unprepared for the sight of the whole valley beneath her, she gripped the ropes tight. If she fell, she would die. But what a death it would be, freefalling long enough to know it was coming. Powerless to stop it.

"Oh!" she exclaimed. "It's so high!"

The ground came back into view beneath her feet as the swing sailed back. With it came a rush of relief mingled with adrenaline. Her relief was quickly overcome by a strong urge to fly again. The earth held her down. The air was freedom.

He gave her another push and the ground dropped away again. She could almost touch the sky. A real bird's eye view. She let go of fear and the wonder of the experience filled her. It was exhilarating. The wind tugged her hair and clothes, begging her to play with it. When she shut her eyes, she lost all sense of her position. The only thing that existed was motion and fresh air.

After a couple more swings, Michael grabbed the ropes and reeled her in. Coming around in front of her, he slipped his arms around her waist to help her down. He kept his arms about her even after her feet were on the ground. Her heart pounded in her ears. Meeting his eyes, she felt that thunderbolt of attraction again.

"What are you?" she asked, her voice soft with awe.

His eyes met hers and she felt like she was flying again. Desperately in danger of falling.

"I'm a man," he said, leaning in closer. Their lips were inches apart. "One who finds you very... captivating."

Her cheeks grew hot. She turned her head, afraid he might try to kiss her. She didn't want him to taste garlic on her breath.

"I'm just me," she floundered.

"I want to make love to you."

Stunned by his straightforwardness, she looked up at him with rounded eyes. "I... Don't know what to say."

All playfulness was gone from his demeanor. His body telegraphed his desire, and his strong arms tightened around her. "Say you'll come to my room tonight."

She had to look away or she would be lost in those penetrating dark eyes. His words whipped her emotions into a storm of uncertainty and longing. His intensity was exciting, but it also scared her. If she said yes, what then? She hardly knew where she stood with him as it was. Sex would only complicate things.

"Come to my room tonight at ten." He hooked her chin with a finger, encouraging her to look at him. "We'll have drinks. Talk about your training. We won't do anything you don't want to."

She teetered on the edge of the unknown for a heart-stopping moment. Then she let go. There was no room for fear. Or words. She made do with a simple nod.

He rewarded her with the warmest, sweetest smile. Then he pressed his lips to hers in a chaste kiss. No tongues. Just a brief, electrifying seal to their plans. It was over so fast, she barely had time to kiss him back.

But she did.

CHAPTER 18

When they returned to the hotel, they parted ways with another light kiss. He went to tend to his duties. She was scheduled to meet Ligeia after lunch. The lunch hour was almost over, so Raina sat down by the firepit in the lobby to wait. Her mind was still reeling. Lost in a fog of new horizons.

Ligeia wasn't long in coming. Dressed casually for her, she wore a black bodycon dress, velvet stilettos, and a wide-brimmed hat. She had a lit cigarette in a long, tapered filter. Her fine brows arched when she saw Raina in one of the white wingback chairs.

"You're early," she said. She swept the younger woman with a critical eye and sucked on her cigarette filter. She exhaled smoke toward the ceiling. "I like that."

Could she sense Raina's giddy preoccupation? Or was Ligeia playing straight? For the sake of her nerves, she decided the older woman was being earnest. "I prefer early. I can always wait. I can't gain more time if I'm late."

"Well. That puts you a step ahead of half of my past apprentices. Shall we get started?"

"I'm ready when you are."

"Let's go." Ligeia crushed her cigarette in an ashtray on a side table and left the empty filter there.

"Where are we going?" Raina asked, rising.

"The cemetery."

———

Ligeia had her driver take them to a graveyard near the Bradford. An elegant rectangle sign out front read:

Hollywood Forever: Funeral Home, Cemetery, Cremation

One of the two broad iron gates was open. It allowed access to a strip of pavement that resembled a street from the Hills more than it did a cemetery lane. They cruised past an old three-story chapel overgrown with generations of ivy that choked the weathered bell tower. Thorny pink roses grew wild in brick planter in front of it.

The driver parked the Rolls Royce Phantom in a roundabout that was surrounded by tall palm trees and the ladies stepped out into the mild afternoon sunshine. There were in-ground graves to the right, row upon row. Hundreds of markers dotted the patchy field. Massive oaks and sycamores cast perpetual shade on portions of the burial lawn, killing off more of the ill-tended grass.

Ligeia led the way to the left-hand side of the graveyard where above-ground monuments and sarcophagi stood. They passed many ornate headstones, including a towering obelisk made of white marble and a crypt that looked like a cottage, complete with a mailbox. A black cat watched them from atop a tombstone shaped like a bench. Its yellow eyes were alert, unafraid. This was his territory.

"This is beautiful!" Raina exclaimed.

Not just the statuary. The whole place was artful despite the neglected state of the landscaping. The warm climate and lack of employees to care for the place was understandable. All of New Salem had that problem, even the most active areas.

"It's one of the city's oldest cemeteries," said Ligeia. "This way."

They angled toward a small lake in a portion of the cemetery designated as the Garden of Legends by brass signposts they passed. At the center was a crypt in the shape of a scaled-down mansion. It was a two-story white brick building with ionic columns on all sides. The crypt even had its own yard.

"I can't believe people used to get buried like this." Raina was star-struck. As much as she admired the pyramids in Egypt and the necropolises of Greece, this was a wonder she could touch and sense.

"Only the filthy rich, my dear."

Ligeia paused to look out over the placid gray water through dark glasses with large oval lenses. The autumn breeze teased the blunt ends of her blonde hair.

"They're expecting me to teach you some basic cantrips." She glanced at the younger woman and huffed a short, fussy breath. "Before I do, you need to understand a few things."

Her serious attitude drew Raina's full attention. The cemetery was beautiful, but she was there to learn.

"First: Even though a man is technically in charge of our Coven," Ligeia sneered the word 'man'. "Our true power lies within us: The fairer sex. Pietre is powerful, but nothing you can't handle if you know how. Don't confuse his casual attitude with weakness. If he were a snake, he'd be a black mamba. You should never let your guard down around him. He will take full advantage."

Raina fidgeted. Pietre had said something similar about staying on guard. "He seems so... nice."

Ligeia barked a bitter laugh. "Of course, he does. You haven't challenged his authority. If you do, you'll see his true nature. He's a beast. You can't trust him or those apprentices of his. The triplets are his eyes and ears."

She lit a cigarette and strolled along the walk that skirted the pond. Raina kept pace with her, wrapping her arms around her middle.

"I'm supposed to learn from him."

"And you should," the older woman said. "Just don't make the mistake of thinking he's your friend."

"What about Michael?"

Ligeia arched a fine brow above her dark glasses. "What about him?"

"Can I trust him?"

Ligeia laughed. Though light and amused, there was a sharp edge to her laughter.

"You can't trust any man. There are some you can rely on more than others, but they are always on the prowl. Always out to prove themselves. They're a territorial, domineering species by nature. They're best managed by a strong hand in a velvet glove." She pulled a slow drag from her cigarette. "Michael can be a treasure. He can also be a terrible brat if he's thwarted. He has his Father's temperament."

Raina chewed on that bit of information. She'd seen his temper at the masquerade. "I think... he likes me."

She knew he did, yet she felt the inexplicable need to downplay the knowledge. The whole conversation had her doubting herself.

Her confession prompted another laugh from Ligeia. "I'm sure he does. You're young. Sweet and pretty. Unsullied. A rare commodity. He probably has a standing bet with the others as to who'll bed you first."

Stung, Raina paused. The older woman strolled on. Even though she wore high heels, they didn't slow the witch.

"I'm not a virgin," Raina said, needing to defend herself. She hurried to close the distance between them.

"Good," said Ligeia and she meant it. "Less for them to take from you."

"Why do you hate men so much?"

Ligeia glanced sidelong at her. "I have many reasons for not trusting men. But I don't hate them. They can be useful for many things, not the least of which is pleasure. What I'm telling you I say for your own damned protection. You're too easy to hurt. Too naïve. Soft. You need to get your defenses up before you find yourself in a situation you can't handle."

There was that word again: Useful. A twist of worry knotted Raina's stomach. What sort of group was she getting involved with?

"Okay. So. Don't trust the men," she said, trying to sound less anxious than she was. "Is… is that why Desiree left? Because of them?"

Ligeia stopped and turned on her, a sneer curving her red lips.

"Desiree." The word was a curse on her tongue. "Was a traitor to us all. She was a disobedient bitch who dabbled in trade with some of the darkest spirits out there. Had a weak spot for the undead. She abandoned the Coven because she didn't want to play by our rules. Ran off and got herself killed or worse."

"Or worse?"

Ligeia peered at her over the sunglasses, her dark eyes cold. "There are worse things than death."

She started walking again, crossing a short bridge to the small island in the center of the pond. Raina followed. The peace she'd enjoyed when they entered the cemetery was gone despite the lovely view.

"This will do," Ligeia decided.

"For what?"

"I'm going to teach you how to lynchpin a cantrip." The witch took off her sunglasses and hooked them on the low collar of her dress. "Then you're going learn how to defend yourself."

———

Though nerve-wracking, studying under Ligeia was also quite educational. Lynchpins involved pre-casting an entire spell and leaving out essential words or gestures. Sometimes both. By saying the key words or making the correct gestures, a more complicated incantation could be evoked in less time.

It was tiresome work. Especially when it came time to put the stowed magic to use in what Ligeia called "practical field training". By the time they finished Raina needed a shower. It took a while to scrub all the graveyard off her. It was well into dinner time when she finished. She hurried to dress, dabbed on some jasmine scented oil, and went downstairs with her hair still damp.

Michael and Troy were the only two at the table when she got to the dining room. Used plates at other places suggested they'd had company earlier. Both men had eaten. Troy was on his second plate of dessert.

Raina grabbed some food from the buffet, not minding what she piled on. There wasn't much to choose from this late. Once she had a full plate, she carried it over to their table.

"Hi," she said as she sat down.

Troy smiled a welcome at her.

Michael eyed her hair. "Did Ligeia take you to the pool?"

Raina patted her damp curls. "No. I just had a shower. I needed it. We went to the Hollywood, um. The cemetery south of here."

"Hollywood Forever?" said Michael. "Interesting."

"Mm-hmm." Raina smeared butter on a roll. "She taught me how to use lynchpins. Had me use them on some dead guys she brought out of the crypts. I think they were famous when they were alive."

Troy laughed behind a fist to keep from sharing his brookie with the table. "Sounds like something she would do."

"Animated corpses are excellent practice dummies," said Michael. "She's thrown a couple at me, too. Though no one famous that I know of."

"I wonder what it'd be like to fight Bruce Lee's corpse," mused Troy. "Think he'd still use martial arts?"

Michael swirled his wine as he considered. "I don't think animated dead are that coordinated. Besides. Isn't he buried in Em City?"

"Huh. I don't know. Maybe."

"I think he and his son both are," Raina put in after she swallowed the food in her mouth. "My mother had a thing for Brandon Lee. I'm pretty sure they're both buried up there somewhere."

"Huh," Troy said around a bite of cake. He had no qualms about talking with his mouth full. "Weird place for a couple of movie stars to be buried."

"I wouldn't mind it," said Raina. "The weather's nicer up there."

"If you like cold rain."

"Do you even have to worry about the cold?" she asked. With his firepower, it didn't seem like something he should be concerned about.

He pushed his empty plate away and gave a satisfied belch. "I can make fire, but I still feel the cold. Michael's the living heater. Not me."

She looked over at the prince, curious. He sat back in his chair with a confident smile. The expression dimpled his cheeks, and he arched a brow at her.

"Cold doesn't bother me," he said proudly. "No temperatures do. I could run around buck naked in the dead of winter, and it wouldn't matter."

That made for an interesting mental picture. Raina coughed. Tried to refocus her thoughts on the original topic. It was difficult with that visual hanging around in the back of her thoughts. She cut into her grilled chicken breast to help distract herself. The meat was a bit dry but tasted fine.

"Does it bother you to get wet?" she asked Troy.

"Nah. I'm not made of fire."

"I'm sorry if I'm asking a lot of questions," she said, remembering her manners. "I haven't heard much about what you guys can do. Just that you have 'mysterious abilities'."

Troy grinned at Michael. "Hear that? We're mysterious."

Michael gave a short laugh. "Not how I would describe you."

"I don't want to hear how you would," Troy said. He didn't sound offended.

Michael had a sip of wine then he reached for the half-eaten roll on Raina's plate. "May I?"

She blinked at him, puzzled. "Uh. Sure? Um. They still have some up at the buffet if you want one."

"No need."

He took the bread and pulled it apart. Then he did it again. And once more.

"Oh!" Raina exclaimed.

Each of the four roll halves were the same size. He gave her back the original one, the corner of his mouth quirking. She took them and gave them an experimental squeeze. They all felt the same. Amazing.

"That trick came in handy during the Flood," he said. "It's not easy to keep a whole town fed in an emergency."

"I bet," marveled Raina. She looked at the roll half. It looked no different than when he'd taken it.

Not one to be outdone, Troy plucked up one of the roll halves. "But can you toast it?"

He concentrated and soon the bread was steaming. Then it burst into flame, surprising even him.

"Crap!"

Without thinking it through, he dropped the flaming roll into Michael's wine glass. It hissed, put off a puff of smoke, then went out. The blackened bread disintegrated into unappetizing chunks in the red alcohol.

Michael looked at his glass then favored Troy a dour look. "Nice. Real nice."

Raina giggled. It wasn't diplomatic, but she couldn't help it.

"So, I haven't perfected toasting," said Troy. "It's the thought that counts."

Michael looked pained. Shook the wine glass to see the bread bits swirl then set it aside in disgust. "Here's a thought: Don't set your dial to 'charcoal'."

Troy tucked his hands behind his head and smiled, unfazed. "Would you tell the sun to shine less? Or a volcano to chill out?"

"Yes. I would."

"Well, that's because you're a spoilsport," said Troy. "Don't you agree, Raina?"

Her eyes rounded and she held up a hand. "I'm not taking sides. I'm eating."

She proved it by doing just that.

———

After dinner Michael had business that he needed to tend to. Troy went to trivia night down at the bar. He invited Raina to come, but she declined on the excuse that she was too tired to go out. It was partly true. Though mostly it was because of her plans to meet Michael later. She didn't tell Troy, to spare his feelings and avoid an awkward conversation she wasn't ready to have.

In her room she stewed over what to wear. It was a difficult decision complicated by the fact that she was having second thoughts about going. She didn't want to stand Michael up, but Ligeia's words haunted her. The things the witch said echoed her own doubts. What would she be getting into if she went to his room? Nothing would change if she didn't go. If she went, she would be heading down a foreign path that led to the unknown. One that she might not be able to backtrack from.

He'd said they wouldn't do anything she was uncomfortable with, but her main concern was she would get too comfortable and make a fool of herself. If she did go, she decided she would abstain from alcohol. Drinking relaxed her too much. Sober, she would be in better control of herself and the situation.

She finally picked an outfit to wear: A modest button-down blouse in her favorite shade of peacock blue and a pair of comfortable black lounge pants. Nothing risky. She pulled her hair back in a ponytail and checked her reflection in the full-length mirror. She was channeling some serious librarian vibes. To casual it up, she put on her slip-on sandals.

That did the trick. She looked nice, but not too nice. She just wished she had her mother's necklace.

CHAPTER 19

When the bell struck ten Raina left the shelter of her room. Her heart was racing. Her emotions were all tangled up. She was excited, scared, thrilled, and uncertain all at once. It was exhilarating, but it was also nerve-wracking. A heady cocktail—one she really shouldn't be indulging in. The past two years she'd done fine without another person in her life. But she also hadn't met anyone like Michael in that time.

She went upstairs to the third floor, the old carpet muffling her steps. She could see the door to the prince's suite down the hall as she got to the landing. She paused there and looked at it for a moment. Room number three. Just another door in a hall full of them and yet it was special because it was his.

Why the third suite, though? Why not the first or second? Was there something special about the third one? Perhaps he liked the number. It was probably nothing meaningful, but wondering about it kept her mind off her nerves. Mostly. The only true cure was in crossing the threshold of that door.

After a few steps, she paused again. Glanced back to the stairway. Her heart was in overdrive, and not just because of the effort it had taken to climb the stairs. Every last nerve was on edge with doubt and fear of another big change.

She could still go back to her room. In the morning, she could claim she'd fallen asleep by accident. But she was already on the third floor. His room was only a few feet away. It would be silly, cowardly even, to back out now. She wasn't even sure why she was so nervous. What harm could there be in spending time with a man she was attracted to? True, he was the Lord Prince. But underneath the station and fancy clothes, he was a person.

Michael was the first man in a long time who had occupied Raina's imagination so much. The things he said, the way he looked at her, made her want to get closer to him. To know him better. And she couldn't deny her raw physical attraction to him. Ligeia warned her to keep vigilant. She could do that while she explored where this intoxicating path led.

She took a steadying breath. Exhaled slowly. Then she approached his door. Beneath the jangle of nerves, she was looking forward to this. Thrilled about it, even. She was finally getting to spend time with Michael when they weren't busy with other concerns. Without anyone else around or waiting for them. Just him and her together. Alone.

After another deep, bracing breath, she knocked on the door. Seconds later, it opened. Amber light spilled out into the hall.

"Hello," Michael said. "Come in."

He stood back to allow her entry. To her surprise, his clothes were casual: An untucked dark red poet's shirt and a pair of loose-fitting black velvet pants. His hair was unbound, falling in untamed waves down his back. He was barefoot. Comfortable and at his ease, he was even more beautiful.

"This is the first time I've seen you without shoes... outside of the pool," she said as she entered his suite. She was trying to play it cool though she was anything but.

He smiled and pushed the door shut, locking it behind her. Her heart skipped a beat when she heard the bolt slide into place. Privacy guaranteed.

"No reason to wear them if we're not going anywhere."

"Good point." She kicked off her sandals in the entry hall. She lost a couple of inches, but her feet were happier. "Now we're on equal footing. More or less."

"Indeed," he said, his smile turning enigmatic.

He led her to the sitting room. There was a small kitchen on one side of the room. An island with barstools separated the sitting area from the kitchenette. Three closed doors hid other areas. A couch and a loveseat faced a console where several lit candles flickered. Incense burned there too, earthy and woodsy. A scent becoming of a man.

"Wow," Raina said, admiring the layout. "This place is huge!"

"Ambassador suite." He went into the kitchen. "Would you like a drink?"

"Just water, please."

He paused at the counter where he had a bottle of D'usse XO cognac on ice. "Water?"

"I'm not up for alcohol tonight." She offered him an apologetic smile, rubbing her middle to show her reason. Her stomach was fine, but it made a good dodge.

He shrugged and reached for the liquor. "You won't mind if I drink straight from the bottle then?"

"Have at."

He pulled out the stopper and set the bottle down on the counter. Made of bell-shaped black glass, there was a silver double cross etched on it, the end of which resembled a sword point. He poured a glass of water for her.

"I'm afraid it'll have to be tap water," he said. "I don't keep bottled."

"Not a problem," she dismissed. "I'm used to New Salem's local flavor. Ocean-fresh."

He chuckled and set the glass of water down on the island where she could reach it. Then he grabbed the cognac bottle. Coming around the island, he led the way to the couch where he settled on one side. She had a sip from her glass and set it down on the coffee table before joining him. The cushions were plush, soft and comfortable. She made sure to keep a polite distance between them.

"So, I have to ask," she said. "Why room number three? Why not the first suite?"

He had a belt from the bottle and looked at her. Tipped his head slightly. "The first two are smaller. Honeymoon suites. I guess the people who remodeled the place didn't expect newlyweds to do much other than sleep together."

Walked into that one. "Oh. Well. That makes sense."

"Eventually I'm going to move into the third-floor area of the building next door," he said, distracting her from the subject of honeymoon sex. "The hotel courtyard shares its back wall with an old theater. The bottom of the building was a shop, the second floor was the theater, and the third was a residential space. I'm having it restored, but it's taking forever."

"I bet. Restoration was difficult in the best of times. I can only imagine how tricky it is now, with supplies and good help hard to find."

"Indeed." He had another swig from the ornate bottle. "You've been doing well with your training."

She ducked her head, flattered. Though he had mentioned talking about her training when they arranged to meet, she wasn't prepared for him to lead with praise.

"Oh. Thanks." She gave him a quick smile. One compliment from him and she was off in awkward land again. "It's... not something I ever pictured myself doing. I mean... Since I was a kid, I knew there were... Well. I wasn't like other people. Except my mother. She taught me things like palmistry. But she was always so superstitious about it, I never tried to get into it. You know?"

Though her nerves had her prattling, Michael was genuinely interested. As she talked, she relaxed. This really was going to be a friendly chat.

"Was your mother a soothsayer?" he prompted.

"Not really. She studied a lot of things. She loved art and the obscure. The occult was sort of a fixation for her. She said we came from a line of fortunetellers. She predicted a wreck that totaled her boyfriend's cart."

"Really? Impressive." Michael had another deep drink from the bottle.

"Scared the pants off him," she said. "Mom read his fortune on Tarot cards for fun. He didn't believe in them. The cards turned up a nasty spread. That same weekend, he was almost killed. He came by the house to tell us about it. Broke up with her the following week. It was the last time she did anything with the cards."

Michael shook his head. "That's too bad. It sounds like she had the Gift."

"She did. I guess I always knew I did too. I just never knew how to focus it. Like... I've always been good at knowing things before they happen. Knowing what people are thinking..."

"What am I thinking?" he challenged, his enigmatic smile returning.

In the past, the ability surfaced at random. Impressions would come to her, and she would just know what was on another person's mind. What motivated them. What their most likely course of action would be. Could it work on command now that she understood better how to open her senses? Only one way to know.

She studied his body language and expression. Deliberately opened her mind to the feel of him. That's when things got strange. As with their exercise at the pool, when she focused on his energy, she found she could sense it. She could sense him. The nuances of his emotions were like paints on a palette, blending into each other in a wash of dominant and recessive impressions. An artful vibration of energy.

That vibration was palpable and warm—hot, even. Dormant but powerful. An active volcano at rest. When his lava glass eyes locked with hers, she saw nuances there as sure as if he were speaking to her. He was amused, but he was also intent on her presence. And he wanted something from her.

"You're thinking... I'm sitting too far from you."

She looked away, embarrassed. She should have said that some other way. Or not at all. Her eyes found the random collection of bottles and vials on the coffee table she plucked one up to study. If she busied her hands, she couldn't fidget.

"True. Well, I was actually thinking you should be closer to me. Same difference." He took another swig of cognac and set the bottle down on the coffee table. Then he scooted over. Right next to her. He tapped the bottle she held. "That's Helga's Magik."

She glanced up, intrigued by the name. His face was less than a handspan from hers. Intimately close. "What is it?"

"Cinnamon, cardamom, ginger, clove, and cayenne in a peach oil suspension. Here." He gave the glass stopper a twist and pulled a thin glass rod out of it. "May I have your hand?"

She put out her free hand. Catching it, he turned her arm so he could access her wrist. He rubbed the blunt tip of the glass wand in a circle against her skin, spreading the oil around. Then he lifted her wrist so she could take in the scent. It was spicy and sweet. Far stronger than the oils in Desiree's bottles.

He stroked the area with his thumb, gazing at her steadily. The oil warmed and tingled on her skin. His undivided attention warmed her in other ways.

"It's heating up," she said.

"Do you like it?" He gave her a crooked little smile. "It's perfect for massaging tired muscles with."

His thigh pressed against hers and the slow way he caressed her wrist whispered promises of sensual fulfillment. Everything about him was drawing her in despite her resolve to keep things polite. She wanted to feel that touch all over. Craved it.

"I'm sure it is." She met his eyes again and was awash in a tide of desire when she saw the way he was looking at her.

"Would you like to try it?"

She blinked a few times. Her gut impulse was to say yes, but she checked the urge. Michael was a well of mystery she hadn't yet begun to fathom. It wasn't her way to jump into unexplored territory feet-first. She should probably call it a night, in fact.

"I..."

She was going to say as much but her words failed her when he drew his fingers up her arm. It was the lightest caress, but it was steeped in sexuality.

"There's nothing to fear," he murmured. "No commitment. No strings."

The last of her resolve crumbled. Trying to resist him was like trying to resist the vortex of a tornado. "I... guess. All right. Sure."

His hand moved up to her shoulder and over to the front of her blouse. He caught the collar and tugged, freeing the top two buttons. When she didn't stop him, he tugged harder. The next button slipped free. The one after popped off completely.

"Oops," he said without an ounce of regret.

He eased the blouse off her shoulders, leaving her upper half bare save for the hand-made bra she wore. His strong hands slid over her exposed shoulders, caressing her in a way that went straight to her crotch. How could a single touch be so enticing?

He urged her with gentle pressure to lie belly-down on the sofa. She stretched out on the velvety cushion. Crossed her arms under her cheek to support her head. She was vulnerable, but she wasn't nervous anymore. She was in too far for that.

Shutting her eyes, she tried to relax. A futile attempt: His fingers found her bra clasp and unhooked it, exposing her back and freeing her breasts. The simmering heat within her became a full-blown fire, burning away uncertainty and leaving only desire. The sexual energy he gave off was impossible to deny.

She tried to pull out of the tailspin she was in. It was just a backrub. Just a backrub. That's where it would end. That's where she would put an end to it. And after it was over, she would say goodnight and go back to her room. Masturbate to relieve the mountain of sexual tension she'd built up. That's what she would do.

He poured some of the oil into his palm and set the bottle aside. Rubbed his hands to stimulate the slickery substance. His palms settled against her upper back, deliciously warm. Smoothing the oil over her skin, his hands glided in a slow, suggestive sweep that covered every inch of her back. Despite his earlier promises, his intentions were clear in that sensual move. This wasn't a massage. It was foreplay.

And still she stayed.

His hands moved in broad strokes down her back to the waistband of her pants, caressing the oil into her skin before moving back up again. He covered her whole back in Helga's Magik. Then he started to massage in earnest.

With skilled fingers he coaxed her body to unwind, his touch gentle but firm. He found trigger points and stiff kinks in her muscles she hadn't been aware of until that moment. Even without the oil the massage would have been heavenly, but the warming ointment made it so much better. She sighed and the stress of past days melted away.

As she surrendered to the moment, the massage evolved, shifted from therapeutic to intimate again. His hands explored, his fingers grazing the curves of her breasts and teasing the waistline of her pants again. Her breath quickened with her pulse, wanting more of those stimulating touches.

After several delicious minutes of the slow, hot tease, he leaned in close. The heat of his body added to that of the oil. A stray lock of his long hair tickled her cheek.

"It can get warmer," he murmured in her ear.

His suggestive words spurred in her a hot rush of need. She should get up. Leave, before she lost herself completely to the yearning desire that was consuming her. It wasn't too late.

She turned her head to say something to defuse the situation. Anything. He was so close she could kiss him without trying. It was an invitation she was helpless to resist. Her lips brushed his. Far from sating her need, it only heightened it.

He helped her turn over and pulled her closer, deepening the kiss. His mouth tasted of berries and chocolate with an alcohol kick. Made her wish she'd tried the cognac. Her arms settled around his shoulders, the kiss stoking her inner fire into a wild blaze. She was burning up in lust, and she no longer cared. Consequences be damned.

The rest of their clothes soon joined her blouse on the floor. Hands and mouths explored, eagerly touching and tasting. As they kissed his strong body pressed against hers in a slow, grinding simulation of sex, fanning their erotic flames until he finally penetrated her.

For two hours they made love. Moving together in a sexual symphony that brought them both to a sweaty, gasping, and deeply satisfying climax. Raina tingled all over afterward. Not just where the oil had soaked into her skin but clear down to the tips of her fingers and toes. Overdosed on pleasure until she was numb.

She drank most of her water in a single go, parched from exertion. He had some more of the cognac and when he offered her a sip from the bottle, she accepted. The sweet, smoky alcohol burned its way to her middle as she settled in his arms. His body fit perfectly against hers.

They stayed on the couch for a time after their passion cooled, simply enjoying the closeness. No words. None were needed. And when the hour grew late and sleep threatened, he gathered her up in his arms and carried her to his bed.

They fell asleep holding one another.

CHAPTER 20

In the morning, Raina woke to the unfamiliar sensation of someone beside her. The scent of the bedclothes reached her next. The smell of clean linen and of Michael. She'd slept with Michael.

Rolling from her side to her back, the soft sheets slithered against her bare skin. She never slept nude. Last night was a rare exception. Last night was full of all sorts of exceptions. She sighed and opened her eyes. Michael was already awake, propped on his side. Watching her. She smiled, self-conscious.

"Hi."

He favored her a gentle smile in return. "Hi."

He leaned in and kissed her. It was meant to be a 'good morning' kiss, but it kept going. His hand found her side and stroked down over her hip, warm on her skin. He moved in closer, deepening the kiss.

Her heart beat faster. She should pull away. Put a stop to this before things went further than they already had. She needed time to think. To figure out what she was doing. But his hand was between her thighs, fingers exploring.

He teased her to a back-arching climax without letting her escape the kiss. It was only when he pulled her toward him that he broke from it. Positioned her thigh on his hip and entered her. Her arm went over him, clinging to him as he rocked her with languid strokes. Sex was unhurried, sensual, and deeply satisfying for both of them.

A good morning indeed.

They kissed again before he slipped out of bed to go start the shower. She stayed twined in the sheets; her thoughts finally free to wander. The conflict she'd felt on waking was a distant shadow on the horizon now. Whatever was happening was too good to deny.

And really nothing had changed. There were no claims staked simply because they'd shared a passionate night and morning. Sex was a pleasant sideline to what they were already doing. No strings, he had said. No commitment. Friends with benefits. Nothing to slow her down or curtail her freedom. Just a good time between two adults.

"Water's ready," he called from the bathroom.

He was inviting her to shower with him. She'd never bathed with another person before. She smiled and stretched. Her limbs were stiff thanks to all the intimate exercise. A hot shower would be nice.

"Coming," she called back.

She slid out of bed and padded nude over to the bathroom. Gone was the vulnerability from earlier. There was liberation in moving naked through his private space.

He was already in the water when she came in. She pushed the door shut and joined him in the hot spray. He welcomed her with a hug and a kiss.

Showering with another person wasn't as efficient, but it was more enjoyable than doing it alone. They took their time washing one another, becoming ever more familiar with each other. Hands explored muscular angles and gentle curves, petting as much as cleaning. It was a long time before they finally emerged into the steam-filled room. Tooth-brushing and grooming took more time as well, distracted as they were with one another.

They were late for breakfast.

...

"What about the laundry?" Raina asked as they finished their tardy morning meal. They were two of the last people in the dining room apart from the staff who were clearing the buffet.

"That can wait," Michael said. "There will always be more laundry to do. Today, we need to speak with Father Jeremiah."

"I feel bad for not doing my part," she protested. "Beth needs the help."

Michael tipped his head. "You'll be doing your share. This is more important. We'll leave as soon as you're ready. We can stop on the way out and tell her you won't be there today. She'll understand."

—

The Remington mansion stood proud against the gray sky. Michael and Raina followed the leaf-strewn walk to the porch. The front door swung open for them. More attuned to such things now, Raina could tell it was the house's doing, not Michael's. A building that could move on its own should be unnerving, but more than anything she found it intriguing. Made her want to learn more about it.

Michael entered first. As Raina crossed the threshold, she opened herself to the place. Tried to sense it as she had sensed Michael's energy.

She wasn't prepared for the major psychic surge that slammed into her. It swept over her, robbing her of air. She staggered and clutched at her chest. A flood of images crashed over her. Tidal waves of feelings, sounds, and sights. Violence. Sorrow. Fear. Anger. Joy. Love. Death. So many faces. So many voices. Generations of memories unlocked to her all at once.

Michael touched her arm, concerned.

"Raina?"

The surge subsided. She drew a shaky breath. There was no malice in the ebbing wave. It was raw, potent energy and emotion. She could still feel it all around her, but at a distance now.

"I... I was sensing the vibe of this place," she said with a quaver to her voice. "I'm fine. It was just... a lot."

He put an arm around her shoulders and gave her a supportive squeeze. "If a house were a battery, this one would be nuclear-powered. It has a long, long history. Many spirits call this place home."

"Michael," a woman's voice greeted from the stairs. Her tone was an odd blend of delight and reproach. "I didn't know you were coming by."

A woman who looked a lot like Ligeia breezed down the boxy steps. She wore a loose floral print summer dress made of a material that flowed behind her as she moved. Her platinum blonde hair was swept up, held in place with a blue and green kerchief.

"Ligeia's twin," Michael advised Raina in an undertone. Then, to the woman as she came off the stairs: "Mother Lenore, this is Raina. We're here to see Father Jeremiah."

Lenore turned a stony gaze on Raina. There was more than a passing resemblance between Lenore and her sister. They both could freeze water with a frosty glance like that.

"Charmed," Lenore said, insincere. She forced a smile as an afterthought then looked at Michael. "Jeremiah's in the nursery with the boys, sweetheart. Why don't you run on up while Raina and I fetch some drinks for everybody?"

"Thank you, Mother Lenore." Michael eased his arm off Raina's shoulders and brushed a light kiss on her cheek. Then he headed up the stairs, taking them two at a time.

Lenore watched him go then she turned her attention back to Raina. Her expression cooled and hardened. Molten lava on ice.

"I don't know what you and Michael have going on," she lied. "But I wouldn't take it too serious if I were you."

Raina wrapped her arms around her middle, an instinctive defense against the unwarranted if subtle animosity. "We're just friends."

"Uh-huh." Lenore was unimpressed. She swept through the dining room without a glance back. "Michael's an impetuous boy. Lets his feelings carry him away without thinking of the consequences. Be careful you don't get carried away too."

Raina frowned and followed her into a large kitchen. The dark wood cabinets had beveled glass panes that stared at her. Watching what she would do.

"I'm not a threat," she said to Lenore—and to the house.

Lenore laughed, sharp and derisive. At the central island she turned and fixed a strange look on Raina. A superior gaze, for sure, but there was something else in her dark eyes. Pity? "Don't be stupid. If you were a threat, you wouldn't have made it through the front door."

Raina hugged herself tighter. She wanted to be polite, but Lenore was straining her good graces. "I like Michael. A lot. I would never hurt him."

Lenore rolled her eyes and turned to the double-door refrigerator. Yanking it open, she rooted around inside. Pulled out unlabeled liquor bottles and a jar of olives. She set them down on the counter with restrained force. Then she took a crystal pitcher out of a bottom cabinet.

"Open those," she said with a brisk wave at the olive jar.

Raina took the jar and tried to open it. The lid was on tight. She wrestled with it. It popped open quite suddenly, splashing her and the floor with brine.

"Oh, for the love of—" Lenore snapped. She whipped out a dish towel and thrust it at Raina. "Clean up and go sit down. I'll take care of the drinks myself."

Raina's ears burned with embarrassment. She swabbed the floor then flipped the towel over to pat herself dry. After hanging the towel up, she moved to the far side of the island, out of the way.

Lenore mixed up a batch of martinis in the pitcher, working brisk and silent for a few minutes. It wasn't until she pulled cocktail glasses out of the cabinet that she finally spoke again.

"Do yourself a favor. Don't get too attached." She set the glasses and pitcher on a tray and finally made eye contact with Raina again. Turned on a hostess smile like she'd flipped a switch. Her next words were sickly sweet. "Now be a dear and take these upstairs. Do you think you can do that without spilling?"

———

Raina carried the drink tray down the second floor hall toward the sound of voices. Lenore's condescending words rankled her, but also made her wary of tipping the tray. The pitcher weighed down one side of the platter, forcing her to concentrate.

She was halfway down the hall when the sound of whispering reached her. Someone was behind her. She paused to look back. The whispering stopped. There was no one in the hall.

Senses keened, she waited. Listened. The hall was deathly still. Maybe it was the echo of the voices up ahead. That must be it.

She continued toward the sound of Michael's voice and found him and Jeremiah in a pastel nursery. Two toddler beds sat alongside each other near the window. An antique toybox spilled a variety of playthings on a thick rug where the twins played. They were stacking blocks, making towers while the men chatted.

"Raina. Hello," Jeremiah greeted.

She didn't want to appear rattled by the conversation with Lenore, so she put on a smile she didn't feel. "Hello, Jeremiah."

"Here. Let me help you." He took the tray from her and set it atop the bureau, high enough that the boys couldn't reach it.

"Ah, martinis," said Michael. "One of Mother Lenore's finest recipes."

Jeremiah filled the glasses on the tray. "Michael was telling me you've been training with Ligeia and Pietre."

Spying an old rocking chair with a crocheted blanket over it, Raina went and had a seat. "I have. It's been quite an experience. I've learned a lot in a short time."

"That's good." He brought a martini glass to her.

She hadn't planned to drink. It would be rude to refuse, though, so she took the glass and held it.

Michael shoved his thumbs in the pockets of his slacks. "She's been learning defense. I thought you could teach her some other things."

Jeremiah offered another glass to Michael, who freed a hand from his pocket to accept it.

"Other things," the older man said carefully. "History? Or..?"

On the rug, Gabriel knocked over the tower. The wooden blocks clattered as they tumbled to the hardwood floor where the rug ended. Zachariel squealed in surprise and then raked the scattered blocks into a pile.

"Can you teach her endurance?" asked Michael. "Defense is all well and good, but she needs to be prepared for things she can't defend against."

Father Jeremiah helped himself to the last martini. Sipping it, he considered what to say to that request.

"What kinds of things?" Raina asked.

Michael shrugged and had a gulp of his drink before answering. "Psychic attacks. I mean, just opening yourself to this place stunned you."

"Anyone would be," put in Jeremiah.

A flicker of annoyance crossed Michael's face. "Can you teach her?"

"What you're asking is... not a tangible thing that can be taught," said Jeremiah carefully. "Only experience can do that."

Across the room, Zach tried to stack the blocks again, but they fell over in another noisy clatter. His brother wasn't helping. He kept throwing blocks at him. Raina set her glass down on the table next to the rocking chair and joined the boys on the floor.

"Can I try?" she asked Zach.

The little boy eyed her for a moment, then he held a block out to her. She took it. Gathered a few others and arranged them in a single layer on the rug. Gabe, intrigued, stopped throwing blocks to watch. Soon, she had a sturdy base constructed. Behind her, the men continued to talk. She tuned them out. Focused on what she was doing. The boys were fascinated by her arrangement. They handed her more blocks.

"Put this one on next," Gabe demanded, shoving a blue one at her.

Zach pushed an orange one into her hand. "Now this one."

As she added blocks the twins fell into a natural rhythm, taking turns in an instinctive way. The three of them made a great team, with the boys supplying blocks and Raina doing the stacking. The whole set went into the pyramid they made.

"A triangle is the strongest shape," Jeremiah said, taking note of the design.

She glanced back and saw he and Michael were watching her. The attention made her sheepish. She'd meant to help, not take over. Not that the boys minded. They were quite happy with what they had made together.

"It's less likely to fall." She looked at the pyramid. "Look," she said to the boys. "See what happens when I do this?"

She nudged one of the bottom corner blocks out. Gabe sucked a deep breath certain the whole thing would fall. The pyramid wobbled, but it held its shape. The twins gazed at it in awe. Thoroughly impressed.

"Oooo!" chirped Zach. "It's magic!"

Raina laughed. His enthusiasm was contagious. "It's not magic. It's just..."

"Natural strength," finished Jeremiah.

She pushed the block back under the pyramid, making it whole again. Gabriel stared at the stacked blocks longingly. It wasn't hard to guess what he wanted, even without reading his vibe.

"You want to smash it, don't you?"

He grinned big at her. Nod-nod-nodded.

She turned to Zach. "Is it okay if he smashes it?"

Zachariel gave it serious thought. "Okay."

With a happy whoop, Gabe scrambled to his feet and kicked the pyramid. Blocks flew in all directions. Raina shielded herself with an arm and put up an energy bubble to keep the flying missiles away from herself and Zach. The blocks were toys, but they had sharp corners that could hurt.

"Careful, Gabe," Jeremiah said belatedly.

"Make it again!" the little boy demanded of Raina.

She smiled and started gathering blocks.

"Make it again, please," corrected Jeremiah.

"Make it again, please," Gabe repeated dutifully. He and his brother hurried to collect blocks for Raina, each trying to get the most.

"I'll see what I can do," Father Jeremiah said to Michael. "But I have a feeling Raina can manage on her own."

CHAPTER 21

Lenore stayed inside to serve the boys a snack while the other adults retired for tea in the garden gazebo. The trellised shade occupied one side of the yard and offered a view of neatly tended plants that were kissed with autumn hues. Many refused to bow to the cooler temperatures, stubbornly clinging to their summer greens.

An antique teapot nestled beneath a knit cozy on a table in the center of the gazebo. Shelley porcelain cups stood ready for the tea, a vintage line from the 1940's embellished with gold detailing. A jar of honey and a fifth of brandy completed the spread.

"Psychic resistance is a matter of willpower," Father Jeremiah explained as he stirred his cup. "Not all that different from what you've been doing with Michael and with the animated corpses Ligeia threw at you. Just more... internal, I suppose?"

Raina sipped her tea. It was a delicious rosehip and lemon. She went heavy on the honey. The wooden dipper was fun to use. "How can you defend against something you can't see coming?"

"There's the rub," said Jeremiah. "You can't live in a state of constant readiness. You'd wear yourself out. But you can keep alert to your environment without being paranoid about it."

"You just have to recognize a threat when you feel one," Michael added. He splashed a little more brandy into his drink.

"When Michael was little, he was constantly testing me." Jeremiah smiled at the dour look the younger man gave him. "It wasn't until I started pushing back that he decided it wasn't fun anymore."

"You never played nice," Michael muttered into his teacup, only half serious.

"Is that how you learned to defend yourself?" Raina asked Jeremiah.

He shook his head. "No. No, I was trained before I met him. The Order made sure of it. I was born into the mission. But that's a long story I'd rather not bore you with."

Raina suspected she would find his tale anything but boring. He didn't wish to share, though, so she didn't press. For now.

"Perhaps Michael could test you," Jeremiah went on. "Nothing is a better teacher than experience."

He finished his tea and set his cup down while the two younger people exchanged a glance.

"I'm going to head in and see if Lenore needs help. Raina, it was a pleasure to see you again."

"Likewise, Jeremiah." She smiled at him. His genial demeanor was refreshing. Comforting. It was rare to meet someone she felt so at ease with. Especially these days.

Michael set his teacup down and studied her intently. She found the attention curious given the situation but then she felt him pressing her with his presence. As Jeremiah said, it wasn't that different from the exercise at the pool. Only this time Michael wasn't trying to move her physical body. He was digging into her mind.

She set her cup down. If there were to be a contest of wills, she wanted her hands free. He invaded her thoughts, pressing harder until memories rose to her mind unbidden. One came to the forefront, of her dancing in secret the way her mother used to dance for men. Touching herself afterward.

Horrified, Raina shoved his presence back. He slithered past her defenses. She tried to block him by thinking of a catchy song. It was dispelled by a memory of her making a fool of herself as a teen over an uninterested boy. Then came the memory of dinner with Michael's inner circle, and her without underpants.

Raina couldn't shut him out. He was too quick and knew this game too well. So, she did the next best thing: She dove into his mind. It wasn't difficult. He was distracted by trying to ferret out her secrets and provided an open channel to her. It allowed her access to his innermost memories.

She orientated herself on something that pulse in her mind's eye. Tapping into it, she was rewarded with a memory not her own. It was an intimate way to experience his past firsthand.

Michael was with a woman he adored. He held her in his arms and Raina felt his heart breaking as if it were her own. The woman, his woman, was dead. He held her shade, a tangible ghost. He kissed her tenderly then she swirled into vapor and disappeared into the ring he wore. The one with the milky opal.

The memory came to an abrupt end. Michael had closed his mind to her. He fell back in his chair, eyes wide. Raina slumped, physically drained. Like she'd run around the block a few times. They sat in mortified silence, too overwhelmed to speak.

It was Michael who broke the silence.

"You... learn fast."

Raina gave him a tired, sardonic smile. "Pressure does that to me." She hesitated, then added: "Was that... The boys' mother?"

He reached for the brandy. After a gulp straight from the bottle, he winced and nodded. He didn't look at her. "Evangelina. She's the first woman I truly loved."

"And... she's in your ring?"

He fidgeted with the jewel on his finger, turning the ring around and around. "She is."

Raina eyed the ring. Could Evangelina hear them? "Is she all right with that?"

Michael bowed his head. Took a breath and released it in a heavy sigh. "She doesn't know. For her, it's a dream. A never-ending fantasy of the life we should've had."

Stunned by the confession, Raina blinked a few times. Though it didn't surface on his face she could sense his heart-wrenching pain. She wanted to reach for him but held herself back. This was delicate territory she was treading on.

"You said she died in childbirth."

He nodded. Still not looking at her. "When she came to me as a phantom, she was already losing herself. Ghosts... often do that. Reduce to their most basic personality traits. Especially if they don't understand they're dead. I couldn't lose her to a never-ending nightmare, so... I put her in a perpetual dream."

He had another swig from the bottle. When he lowered it, she took it from him. He looked at her, the agony of that unhealed wound in his troubled eyes. Setting the bottle on the table, she got up and moved to his side. Wrapped her arms around his shoulders.

"I can only imagine how difficult it was," she said with heartfelt sympathy.

That must be why Michael was so dedicated to helping her find her mother's locket. He understood how much a simple piece of jewelry could mean when someone was grieving.

He put his arms around her and pulled her down into his lap where he could press his face against her shoulder. They sat that way for a while, just holding each other. Time seemed to stand still for them. Not even a breeze stirred.

"I never shared that with anyone," he said at last. His voice was tight.

He lifted his head to look at her. There was raw vulnerability there she never expected to see from him. Still waters ran deep. It made sense, in reflection. Everything else about him was intense. A loss like that would cut to the core. And he was too proud to wear it on his sleeve. Vulnerability was not an asset to the Lord Prince.

"I'm sorry." She petted his forelocks back from his brow. "I didn't mean to hurt you."

He caught her hand and caressed his cheek with it. "Don't be sorry. I'm glad you know."

"I wish I could say the same about what you saw in my thoughts."

A smile tickled the corners of his lips and a hint of a sly glimmer returned to his dark eyes. "I'm glad of those things, too."

She sighed, but it was mostly for show. It was a relief to see his sense of humor rebound so readily. "You would be."

"Will you dance like that for me sometime?"

Raina's throat and cheeks grew warm. "Maybe. I don't like dancing like that."

"That's not what your memory said," Michael pointed out. "You liked it enough to—"

"One thing we need to agree on," she interrupted, pressing her hand over his mouth. "Is to not hold our memories against each other."

He plucked her hand away. She didn't resist. He gave her a rakish smile. His humor was back to full strength, as was his mischief.

"I would never," he said.

Then he kissed her. It was a gentle kiss but heated. She tasted his desire. His arms tightened around her.

When the kiss broke, he said in a low voice: "Come to my room again tonight. Please."

She wanted to say no, if for no other reason than to exert some amount of control over the situation and her own feelings. But when he looked at her like that, she couldn't resist. She didn't want to resist.

"I will."

—

As soon as she entered his suite that night Michael swept her into his arms. Eager kisses and heated caresses became needy, hungry ones. His fervor drove her own desire to a frenzy. A wildfire which consumed them both.

They pawed at each other. Shedding clothes, they stumbled to his bed where they fell in a passionate tangle. The bedframe creaked with the intensity of their lovemaking—a counterpoint to their ardent moans. There was no grace to the rough joining. Just deep satisfaction for both of them.

Afterward Raina lay exhausted, her head on his bare chest. Listening to the strong, steady rhythm of his heart. He stroked her hair, gentle and lazy.

"I never want to hurt you," he said softly.

She stirred, finding his words dissonant with the blissful moment. "Then don't." She pressed a kiss to his chest, right over his heart. "I trust you."

His hand stilled on her hair, then drifted down to settle between her shoulder blades. "Should you?"

She lifted her head to peer at his face. What she found surprised her. Instead of relaxing, he was troubled. Brooding. "Why wouldn't I?"

His lips pressed together briefly, and he gave her a sulky glance. "I used to be able to take a single step and move clear across the world. I could bring a man back from the dead. I could fight a demon—and win. There was little I couldn't do."

She pushed herself up to sit beside him. While his claims were weighty, possibly exaggerated, she had seen him do amazing things. So, she accepted what he said without reservation.

"Can't you do those things now?"

He shook his head and rolled away to take a cigarette case from the bedside drawer. He offered one to her. When she shook her head, he lit his. Dropped the case and lighter in the drawer.

"I lost most of my powers two years ago."

Another stunning disclosure. "How?"

Not subtle, but Michael didn't mind.

"My Father took them from me." He exhaled spicy smoke. "He wanted me to do something I didn't want to do, so He crippled me. I've regained a lot thanks to the Coven but... it's nothing like it used to be."

She reached for his free hand and laced fingers with him. The gesture did nothing to soothe the crease between his brows.

"Jeremiah did that?" It was difficult to imagine him taking the prince's powers from him as a punishment. The older man seemed too kind.

Michael huffed an amused breath that wasn't quite a laugh. "Jeremiah isn't my Father. He's a priest of the Order. My Father..." He sucked on his cigarette again. "Is far more powerful than anyone you know."

Raina gave his hand a comforting squeeze. "He must be, if he's able to take away your abilities."

Michael's mouth twitched. "His power is infernal."

"Infernal?"

He hesitated before saying: "Diabolic. So was mine, until I defied Him."

Diabolic. Infernal. Quite a bombshell.

Raina's response was crucial. How she reacted would decide where their relationship went. He was braced for the negative. His body tensed. His jaw set. As much as she wanted to reassure him, she didn't rush sifting through her feelings. It was important to understand her position before she could make it clear to him.

Though she was raised to accept there were powers beyond her understanding, she had no religious leanings. Her mother was an occultist. Church wasn't a place where they spent much time. But learning her lover was the son of someone connected to the underworld was big. Bigger than big.

"Then what you have now is completely of you," she said at last. "Whatever comes next is all you. You're a great man. You don't need infernal power to be who you are."

He regarded her with open interest. He had no trouble with self-esteem, but her opinion mattered to him. "I've been trying to regain what I lost without Him."

"That's wise," she said. She lifted his hand and brushed his knuckles over her lips in a light kiss. "That sort of dependence is a prison, regardless of its source."

He had a last drag from his cigarette and crushed it out in the small ashtray on the bedside table. He'd only smoked half of it. He pulled her into his arms.

"It felt like freedom," he admitted, wistful.

"You'll be free again," she said, though she had nothing to base that on except how fast she was picking things up. If she could bend energy to her will, he could do much better. "I'm sure of it."

"We'll see."

They lay together for a few moments before another point of curiosity stirred Raina to speak.

"So... Mother Lenore is your grandmother."

"Yes."

"And Father Jeremiah isn't any blood relation to you."

"Correct."

She pushed herself up so she could see his face again. "You told me about your Father. But... what about your mother?"

Michael did a little shrug that became a full-body stretch. "Just a woman. An artist. She died when I was born."

"Really?" An artist. Raina liked her already.

"Mm-hm. My twin died with her."

She sat all the way up. She needed to be upright to take that in. "Well. That's... wow. You had a twin?"

He nodded and sank back into the pillow pile. "The cord got wrapped around his neck. They were able to save me with an emergency surgery, but my brother and mother both died."

"I'm sorry," Raina said. Not only for his loss, but for adding more gravity to the moment.

"I never knew them. I don't mind talking about them. Mother Lenore and Father Jeremiah gave me more than enough attention growing up. Being an only child was often inconvenient."

That she could relate to. "No one to blame when you break something."

He chuckled and reached for her again. She relaxed into his arms, but in a way that allowed her to see his face. To study his features and the nuances in his eyes. They were darkest chocolate, not black as she had first thought.

"What about you?" Michael said. "You told me about your mother. What about the rest of your family?"

"She's it. I never knew my father. His name was Stefan. Mom didn't like to talk about him. He got her pregnant then left when he found out. I guess he wasn't ready to be a dad."

"He missed out on knowing you." Michael didn't dwell on the subject, asking instead: "You said you had no siblings, right?"

"Yeah. Mom stopped with me. Said I was all she needed. I wanted a little brother or sister." She nuzzled his shoulder. "I used to think it was so I could have a live-in playmate. But I think I also wanted someone to boss around."

"I suppose I was lucky in that regard," he said. He stroked her back with one hand, starting at the nape of her neck and petting down to her waist where the blankets covered her. "I had an agemate to play with next door. Not the same as a sibling, but close. He was always getting me in trouble."

"One of those friends," she sympathized.

He gave a short laugh. "He broke my arm once. It was an accident, but Mother Lenore was furious. She wouldn't let us play together for a long time."

Raina nuzzled his neck. "Couldn't you just heal it?"

"I couldn't do that back then."

"Oh. No?" She was curious again. "How does that work?"

"It just does."

He pulled her close and kissed her on the lips, effectively stopping further questions. He wasn't interested in conversation any longer. His hands roamed her body. As one slipped between her thighs, she lost interest in talking too.

CHAPTER 22

Waking next to someone was an experience Michael was starting to like. Raina was a soft, sweetly scented addition to his bed. When she was asleep, he could stare at her as long as he wanted without her becoming self-conscious.

And though she was attractive, it wasn't her beauty he was studying. He was sorting out his growing attachment to her.

He had been with many women. His status and popularity ensured he never wanted for companionship, sexual or otherwise. There were precious few who'd given him more than physical pleasure. The intangible connection he had with Raina fascinated and bothered him.

It was peculiar how much stronger he was when she was near. It had nothing to do with metaphysical power. She grounded him—in a good way. Before her, his entire being was devoted to the prophecy of who he was meant to be. Even when he defied his Father, he was still thinking of what was best for the people of New Salem and the world.

She made him want to steal time from the pursuit of the future to dally with her. Like now.

———

He was still watching her when she woke. She smiled sleepily up at him, and her natural beauty stirred him. He kissed her, slow and deep. Last night's kisses were hungry and fervent. This was tender. Loving.

When it ended, she snuggled into his arms. They lay together for a long time. He liked the feel of her. She was warm and curvy in all the right places.

"We're going to be late for breakfast again if we don't get moving soon," she said at last.

He stroked his palm down her bare back. The silken feel of her smooth skin went straight to his groin.

"We can be late," he said.

She giggled softly and, seeing his arousal tent the sheet, she eased herself on top of him. A short fumble later she was guiding him inside her. A soft groan escaped him at the hot hug of her around his stiff cock. She rode him slowly at first, rocking her pelvis at a measured pace. Need soon overcame him. He took her hips in his hands, thrusting faster and faster until they were both moaning in ecstasy.

Afterward, they shared another shower. It wasn't quite as time-consuming as the last one, but they didn't exactly hurry either.

"I'm going down to help with the laundry today," she said as they toweled off. "After breakfast."

"Be done by three bells." He stole another quick kiss. "We're supposed to meet with Pietre."

...

That afternoon they spent three hours in an abandoned mall parking lot with Pietre and Troy, playing with fire. Raina was intimidated at first when Pietre had her draw a Circle of protection around herself with sulfur and Troy set it ablaze. Being at the center of a ring of fire flew in the face of all her self-preservation instincts.

"Harness it," Pietre told her. "Lock onto its energy and steer it away from you."

The flames were too close for comfort. Raina focused on the energy of the heat and tried to lasso it, but fire wasn't solid. Trying to latch onto it was like trying to hold water in her hands.

"Capture the fire, Raina," the warlock urged.

His prodding only frustrated her. "I can't! It's too slippery."

"You will," Pietre asserted. "Troy? Bring the heat up."

Troy flicked an uncertain look at him. Pietre met the glance with an expectant expression. Troy refocused and did as he said. The flames intensified as he concentrated on them, growing taller and hotter. Michael folded his arms. There was nothing either of them could do to help in the lesson.

 Sweat formed on Raina's upper lip and dampened her blouse. Between the heat and her own fear, her system was in overdrive. She tried again to wrap her will around the flames. Using her hands as a focus, she grabbed at the air and pictured herself harnessing the fire.

She could sense the energy, but grabbing it simply wasn't working. So, she tried a new approach. Instead of trying to take hold of it, she tried buffeting it with a wall of force. That worked—a little too well. The flames whooshed and licked forward, right at her, singing her hair.

Hastily she reversed the push, sending the flames outward in all directions. The fire went out as it left the sulfur ring.

"Good," said Pietre, satisfied. "Not exactly tidy, but good enough."

"You okay?" Troy asked.

She touched her hair and nodded. "Yeah. Just lost a little fringe."

"It's always best to move the fire *away* from things you don't want to burn," said Michael. Since she was okay, he was entitled to poke fun.

"I figured that out, thanks," she said, sarcasm coloring her words.

As they continued the lesson, Raina got more adept at controlling the way the fire moved. Experimentation taught her how to fine-tune that control to smaller motions. And with practice she gradually lost her fear of being burned.

That's when things got interesting.

Troy shot a jet of fire at the parking lot pavement and Raina spun it into a whirling column. She made it skip and dance across the stretch of flat ground while Troy kept the blaze going. It left a winding black trail of melted asphalt where it went.

Michael tried his hand at controlling the fire spout next. It surprised no one when he was able to whip it into a frenzy. It quickly became a fire tornado of biblical proportion. Raina helped him steer the spectacle, keeping it well away from them. Even at a distance the heat was impressive.

They kept it up until Troy exhausted his firepower.

On the way back to the hotel they discussed the history of witchcraft, paganism, and other occult practices. There were so many different faiths and offshoots, Raina found it difficult to keep up with the conversation.

"I used to think all witchcraft was the same," Raina admitted.

Her confession brought a halt to the conversation and Pietre punished her lack of education by assigning her several books to read. Michael told her she could borrow them from Father Jeremiah the next time she was at the mansion.

They had supper when they got back to the hotel. Raina planned to relax afterward, but as they discussed her training over the meal, the subject of the pool session came up.

"Sounds like a blast," Troy said after hearing about the fiasco the exercise devolved into. "Now I want to go swimming."

"I'd be up for a night dip," Michael said.

Troy looked at Raina. "How 'bout you?"

The fire exercise was a workout both physically and mentally. She was stiff all over, even in places where she was pretty sure had no muscles. The idea of swimming sounded more like exercise than fun to her at the moment.

"I don't know," she hedged. "I'm kind of tired..."

"Aw, come on," he cajoled.

"It's a great way to relax." Michael turned on his most winning smile.

Double-teamed, Raina sighed with dramatized resignation. "I don't have a swimsuit..." She was fighting a losing battle, but she was going to put up a token struggle.

Michael had a quick solution for that. "Just wear some shorts and a shirt. Nobody will care. I promise."

She looked from one man to the next. There was that look again. The one she couldn't resist. Doubled. She didn't stand a chance.

"All right." She was such a push-over. "Fine."

———

After dinner was over, they parted ways to go change clothes. Raina dug up an old pair of shorts and a tank top that she knotted around her waist. It wasn't a stylish look, but it would keep her covered. That was all that mattered.

When she got to the indoor pool Troy and Michael were already there. Troy was in the water. Michael sat at a table near the deep end having a cigarette. He was in a pair of black knee-length shorts.

"I have to admit I'm surprised you enjoy swimming," she said to Troy as she approached Michael's table.

Troy swam from the shallow end up along the side near them. His wet hair was slicked back against his head. "Why's that?"

"Fire and water don't normally go together."

He hoisted himself up out of the pool to sit on the edge. He wore form-fitting striped bottoms that left the majority of his muscular body bare and very little to the imagination. The wet bottoms looked suspiciously like briefs rather than swimwear.

"I told you," he said. "I don't mind being wet. I throw fire, but I'm not made of it. I love the water. And I love having access to an indoor pool in fall. Better than freezing your balls off outside."

"Fortunately, I'm not at risk of that," Raina laughed.

Michael put his cigarette out and rose from his seat. "Ready to swim?"

Raina shifted her smile to him. "That's what I'm here for."

"Good."

He grinned and opened his arms to her. She stepped into his embrace, expecting a kiss. Too late she saw his smile turn wicked.

"Michael—!"

That's all she got out before he jumped into the pool with her. The huge wave hit Troy, who tried to duck. He got splashed anyway.

They spent the next hour splashing and dunking each other like kids, until they exhausted themselves. It was fun to be silly. Raina was able to put aside the seriousness she'd been facing of late and enjoy the moment. In the rollercoaster her life had become, she was learning to take pleasure in the highs before the next lows came along. Balance was a necessity.

...

"She's almost ready to be initiated," Pietre said the next morning.

Court was over. It was just Michael, with Pietre and Ligeia left in the chapel of the First Church. They sat to either side of the prince. Pietre was barefoot as always. Ligeia was decked out to her typical fashionable standards.

"Do you agree, Auntie?"

Ligeia nodded, though she was far from enthusiastic. "In another week or so, she'll be ready. Have you told her why she's been training to be a witch?"

Michael propped his elbows on the arms of his chair and laced his fingers together. "If you're talking about the ritual..."

"Of course I'm talking about the ritual," she snarked.

He fixed his gaze on her. Lesser individuals would squirm. She didn't even flinch.

"No."

Ligeia exhaled sharply. Her expression soured. "She should know."

"She will," Michael said. "There's no point in bringing it up yet."

His response irritated the witch all the more. "You don't think it would help her prepare if she knew what you were planning?"

"It might scare her," said Pietre.

"She should be scared!" Ligeia glared at him. "That archaic piece of predatory sorcery is dangerous and disgusting, invented by a—"

She stopped herself saying "man" but had no ready follow up. Michael and Pietre both looked at her, expecting her to finish her thought. She brushed imaginary lint from her sleeve.

"—person who cared nothing about the consequences of their actions," she finished somewhat lamely. "I understand you want your powers back, Michael, but Raina deserves to know."

"What she doesn't know can't hurt her." Pietre's smile was smug with superiority.

Irked with herself for backing down, Ligeia got to her feet. She would only get angrier if she stayed. "I'll tell her about initiation." Her words were curt. "She'll need a sponsor."

"I'll be her sponsor," Michael said as though it were obvious. "The triplets can assist with the ritual."

"All the more reason for you to tell her what's really going on," Ligeia said. "If you sit on this, she's going to feel betrayed when she finally finds out."

Michael's expression darkened. "I know what I'm doing, Ligeia. Your opinion has been noted. If that's all, you're free to go."

She bristled at the dismissal but managed to keep her temper in check. "Thank you," she said with the delivery of a curse.

She marched out of the chapel. The bright autumn sun turned her into a black silhouette as she pushed through the door. Then she was gone.

Pietre looked from the door to Michael, his smile spreading. "You do know how to push her buttons."

"I'm not trying to push her buttons," Michael said, insulted by the insinuation. He sank deeper into his chair, scowling. "She's just wrong."

Deep down he knew she made a valid point. However, he wanted to present the idea to Raina in his own time and way. He was sure if he put it to her the right way she would understand. What he was still unsure of was why it mattered so much to him.

Pietre gave a nonchalant shrug. "Whatever feelings Raina may have about the ritual are easily cured. One way or the other."

CHAPTER 23

Over the next week Raina's days were split between learning from Ligeia, Pietre, and Father Jeremiah. When not at lessons she helped Beth in the laundry room. Her evenings were consumed by navigating the social whirlpool that revolved around the prince. Her nights belonged to Michael.

She got to know his children as she spent more time at the mansion. The boys decided she came by just to entertain them. Fortunately, her time with Jeremiah was mostly lecture. She could divide her attention, listening to him and keeping the twins happy with block towers and fingerpainting.

Though her life was packed, she still cradled the hope Evan would bring news of her missing necklace. In the meantime, she kept at her lessons, which included memorizing lines for her upcoming initiation into the Coven.

Initiation was a huge and scary step for her. It made sense that the Coven didn't want to train someone who was not part of their Family. Raina understood that. It was the process itself that rattled her. It was designed to separate a person from their old life so they could embrace the new one without inhibition. It was a drastic and deliberate acknowledgment of change for someone who was generally set against change.

The evening of her initiation crept up on her, arriving all too fast. People filled the hotel, abuzz with muted excitement. Though most were not privy to the ritual ceremony, they would attend the party afterward. A small mercy. Some Covens had every member present for the full ritual.

She dressed as Ligeia instructed clad only the white robe she had sewed for herself. She was bare beneath it. She wore no makeup, no jewelry, not even the scented oils she'd gotten in the habit of using. She was clean. Pure.

As she waited for the hour of the event to roll around, Raina went over her lines. Though she'd practiced them for days now the repetition soothed her. Staved off her stage fright. Kept her from thinking about all the people who would be there. They would be there to support her. Being the center of all that attention was an exciting idea but also intimidating. She sequestered in her room through dinner, too anxious to eat. No one disturbed her until the ninth bell rang.

As the last bell sounded a knock came from the hall.

She opened her door to Alec and Meg. Both wore ash gray robes. Meg gave her a bolstering smile then she and her brother escorted Raina to the stairs. They descended in silence, Raina first, followed by the pale siblings. Once they made it downstairs, they flanked her.

Several of the Coven members gathered in the lobby to watch the procession. A large fire flickered in the central pit, casting long shadows that danced on the walls. Raina kept her gaze forward, not meeting anyone's eyes. Focus kept her anxiety at bay. Beneath her robes, her knees were weak. Despite being sober, she had a sense of detachment. Like she was somewhere slightly off to the side of herself.

The three proceeded down the hall to the double doors that connected the hotel to the old theater. Troy waited at the end and held one of the doors open for them. He smiled encouragingly at Raina. She gave him a frail smile in return, glad to see him. Then she was through the door. It shut behind her and the siblings.

The small anteroom had two sets of double doors on the far wall. Two copper braziers stood on either side of one set, marking the entrance to the Temple. Fire in the braziers burned bright gold, illuminating the small space. Meg and Alec passed through one of the marked doors into the room beyond. The door closed silently.

Raina was alone.

Her heart raced, making her dizzy. To steady herself she took in the ambience of the anteroom. Homed in on the smell of age the old building put off. Dust and ancient wood and history. The theater was close to 200 years old. Even in the sliver of space she stood in, she could sense its venerable personality.

The energy it held was mysterious, dark, and beautiful. The peace it gave off filtered into her. She put a hand on the wall and sensed that it appreciated her touch. She might only be telling herself that, but it helped settle her nerves.

Voices from the Temple room reached her, muffled by the wall. She couldn't make out what they were saying. She didn't need to. She knew from practice. She was being formally introduced to the leaders of the Coven. She tried to meditate but found it difficult to tune out her surroundings now that she'd opened herself to them. She was rooted in the now.

There was a palpable vibe around her, an ambient sense that both warmed and dwarfed her. It was like the impression she'd experienced when she met Michael, that of standing over a yawning chasm. Only now she was about to jump in.

She heard a bell ring three times. Not the clock bell outside but a hand bell rung within the Temple. Her heart fluttered. That was the signal. The introduction was complete.

The door opened and Meg returned, this time accompanied by Michael. He wore a floor-length robe of black velvet and carried a coil of red braided cord. A long knife hung in a sheath from his belt. Meg had a blindfold in her hands.

Excitement and fear gripped Raina. She was dizzy again. The world swam. It was the closest she'd ever come to passing out. Fainting at her own initiation would be embarrassing. She couldn't let that happen. As a last, desperate resort she said a silent prayer to the Powers.

Her nerves calmed instantly. She could breathe again.

The immediate response fascinated her, but she had no time to analyze it. Meg stepped behind her and tied the blindfold over her eyes. Raina kept breathing deep and even. Meg's gentle hands went to her shoulders. Removed her robe. Chilly air rushed over her bare skin. She trembled with the chill and her own excitement.

In the darkness she sensed Michael take Meg's place behind her. At his touch she lifted her left arm, as they had practiced. He tied the cord he carried around her wrist. Then he repeated the motion with her right arm, binding her hands at the small of her back.

The bonds were secure though not tight. Still, it was humbling to be naked and bound, blind to the process. Anticipation, intimidation, and wonder warred within her. Everything was so ethereal. Unreal, yet very real.

He drew the silken cord up around her throat where he tied it. Again, the bonds were not uncomfortable, but she was as vulnerable as it got. Her heart pounded in her ears. For better or for worse, her life was about to change.

Though she knew what was coming next, Raina was startled when Michael banged on the door with the pommel of his knife.

"Who knocks?" Pietre's voice was as clear as if he were in the room with them.

"We come with one who would join our number," Michael responded. He spoke in a normal tone of voice, yet they heard him perfectly fine on the other side.

"What is her name?" Ligeia's voice was in the room now.

Raina pulled a quick breath. Focused her energy around projecting her voice, as she was taught. "My name is Raina. I beg entry."

"Enter this our Temple," answered Ligeia.

The door opened and hands were on Raina's elbows, guiding her forward. She had to trust them to steer her. The room beyond was warmer than the anteroom. She heard fire crackling.

"Raina," Ligeia said from somewhere in front of her. "Why do you come here?"

Her tongue darted out to wet her suddenly dry lips. This was it. "To worship the Powers in which I believe and to become one with my Brothers and Sisters of the Craft."

"Enter the Circle," came Ligeia's response.

Michael's hands steered Raina into the Circle. She felt dizzy again, though this time it was a natural—or supernatural—high. A response to the archaic energy filling the Temple room. When they stopped at the far side of the Circle, Michael remained beside her. Cool water sprinkled her front. Salt water from the censer Ligeia shook over her. The bell rang again, a clear note that resonated.

"Do you wish to end the life you have known so far?" Pietre said somewhere off to her left.

She expected he would ask something to that effect, but his wording was grim. More than final. Spiritual death.

"Yes," she said. "I do."

"So be it."

She could hear the smile in the warlock's words.

Michael touched her head. There was a soft scrape of metal near her ear as he cut off a lock of her hair. He moved away and the smell of burning hair reached her. Then he was guiding her again, steering her to the east. He took her to each cardinal point, introducing her to each of the Elements. Then he brought her to the center of the Circle.

"And now," Michael said. He stood close to her. "Face those whom you seek."

He removed the blindfold.

The cavernous room was lit with braziers of flame positioned around the painted white Circle on the floor. Nearby was a cloth-covered table—an altar cloaked in dark red velvet. Pietre stood on one side of the Circle, in a long black robe like Michael's. He had his hair slicked back in a severe ponytail. Ligeia, to his left, was also in a black velvet robe. She had her hair pulled back, pinned with a silver comb.

A silver circlet with a crescent moon emblem sat on the side of the altar closest to her. A golden, horned helmet was on Pietre's side. Behind them a black tapestry emblazoned with a white pentagram hung on the wall. They both held a knife. Each blade was personal to the one who had it.

"As we need the Powers, so too do they need us," Michael said to Raina.

"I speak for the Lord and welcome you," Pietre said to her next.

"I speak for the Lady," said Ligeia. "And welcome you."

"I honor the Lord and Lady," recited Raina. Her heart was still racing. It might never slow again. "I pledge my love and support to my Brothers and Sisters of the Craft."

The High Priest and Priestess held out their knives and Raina bent to kiss the blade of each. The black iron of Pietre's knife was ice cold. Ligeia's, silvery steel, was warm by comparison.

"And do you abide by the Rules set out by the Coven?" prompted Ligeia as Raina straightened.

"I do."

"Then let your bonds be loosed and be reborn," Pietre said.

Michael tugged the red cord around her neck, untying it. It slipped away and he untied her hands, stroking each of her wrists affectionately. He draped the cord over his shoulder and accepted a bowl of olive oil Ligeia passed him. He dipped his forefinger into the oil and his eyes met hers. She saw love reflected there. Her spirit soared.

"With this sacred oil I anoint and cleanse you," he said.

He drew a cross on her forehead, between her brows. Then he drew a pentagram over her heart, moving with slow intimacy, replenishing the oil on his fingers as needed. He touched her crotch next, then brought his finger to her right breast, then the left, and back down to her womanhood once more.

"You are now one of us," Ligeia said. "And will share in our mystic arts and learn as you progress."

"Ever remember your oaths to the Coven," added Pietre. "And to your Brothers and Sisters of the Craft."

They both hugged her and kissed her, Pietre on her left cheek and Ligeia on her right. Michael embraced her next and kissed both of her cheeks. Then he took her robe from Meg, who stood nearby with it. He slipped it over Raina's shoulders. Meg and then Alec hugged and kissed her as Ligeia rang the bell three times.

"Now is a time for celebration," Pietre said, full of pride.

———

The group escorted Raina from the Temple room to the courtyard in the center of the hotel. The outdoor area was decorated with autumnal flare: Black and dusty purple swags hung over the doors and windows. Garlands of grass and late-blooming flowers crisscrossed the space between balconies. There were cinnamon brooms and candles everywhere.

Tisi met her at the door with a laurel woven from sage flowers, eucalyptus, and baby's breath. After placing it on Raina's head she kissed and hugged her. The typically stoic woman even smiled. Then the rest of the Coven descended on Raina. It was customary to greet a new initiate with a hug and a kiss. There were over thirty individuals at the Bradford Hotel. Raina had never been kissed by so many people.

There was food, drink, and music. Many Coven members surprised her with gifts. And while she had been avoiding alcohol, she broke the self-imposed ban to share hand-crafted honey mead which Brother Darien brought in her honor.

His soft-spoken, unassuming presentation of the liquor endeared him to her. The paper labels on the bottles featured images of wolves he'd drawn. Each bottle had a different label. There were no ingredients listed. The drink was sweet with a hint of citrus, fizzy and strong.

Meeting everyone at the party was a blur of faces and rapid conversation. She wouldn't recall later exactly what was said but she was left with the impression of a good time. A few interactions would stick with her. An older woman with a genial smile and the demeanor of a fairytale grandmother. A large man with tattoos who laughed deep and merry.

There was an impromptu bout of swordplay between Pietre and two other Coven members, a stout woman with frizzy red hair and a tall, lean man with a long beard. The bearded man dueled them both at once while balancing a tankard of mead in his other hand.

They laughed and had fun smacking each other with the flats of their steel sword blades. Thighs and calves were favorite targets. Though they were careful not to strike with the sharp edge, it was still a painful game. Inevitably the man with the tankard spilled on himself, putting an end to the mock fight.

At two bells past midnight the festivities finally died down. Overstimulated and exhausted, Raina said goodnight to those who still remained. When she went inside, Michael went with her. She was about to head up the grand staircase when he caught her hand and reeled her in. His strong arms circled her, enveloping her in the warm familiar scent of him.

"It's been a big day for you." He gazed at her with unmasked desire. "It's late, but I'd be lying if I said I want to let you sleep."

She smiled up at him and slipped her arms around his waist. "I'm not so tired that I can't stay up a bit longer."

He pulled a breath like he was going to say something but kissed her instead.

They went upstairs to his suite. In his bedroom he pushed her white robe from her shoulders, letting it drop in a heap on the floor. Removing his robe was trickier for her as he was already kissing her neck. It was a delightful surprise to find he was also naked beneath his robe.

His kisses traveled from her neck to shoulders, then to her breasts. Easing her onto the bed he gave her nipples attention with his tongue before kissing a trail to her nethers. He took his time pleasuring her, bringing her to trembling orgasm. When her delightful spasms subsided, he joined her on the bed. He left her no time to catch her breath before he penetrated her.

The pace was slow and sensual at first. Then faster. Faster. He kissed her, lunging harder as his tongue explored. She moaned into the kiss, drunk on pleasure. His arms slid under her. Gathered her hips so he could deepen his thrusts.

Untamed ecstasy stole her breath. She had to pull away from the kiss to breathe. She clung to him, lost on stormy waves of intense pleasure. When she came her whole world went dark for a few seconds. She was still fighting for breath when he climaxed with a strangled groan. Spent, he sank down atop her. She could feel his heart pounding, strong and fast. His body was coated with sweat, and she realized hers was too.

It took them several long moments to recover. When he pulled out he kissed her gently. Then he climbed up the mattress to flop on his belly, his face buried in the pillows. Raina crawled after him and dropped beside him. Her whole body thrummed with afterglow. She lay there for a bit, then reached over to pet his back. His skin was almost dry already, back to its normal heat. She pressed against him to steal some of that heat for herself.

"We should start using protection," she mused. "If we're going to keep having this much sex."

He stirred and turned his head so he could see her. His long hair caged his face.

"You don't have to worry about that. After the boys, I learned a neat little trick that neutralizes the chance of my accidentally impregnating someone."

"Let me guess. Pietre taught you?"

Michael grinned. "Who else?"

She smiled and petted him some more. Brushed the hair back from his eyes. "Well, that's good. I'm not ready to be a mother."

He draped an arm over her waist. "With my luck, it'd be twins again."

"Definitely not ready for that." Her eyes rounded.

He chuckled and pulled her close. They kissed again. A stillness crept over them as they lay there enjoying the closeness of the moment. Gradually the stillness faded into sleep.

CHAPTER 24

The morning after her initiation, Raina was working in the laundry room when she received a note from Trixie. The woman said Evan delivered it. The message was that "D" wanted to meet her at the Bunker that afternoon about her necklace. Raina was thrilled but checked her reaction. It might be bad news.

Michael was occupied with his princely duties. Troy was off on some errand for him. Raina wasn't due to meet with anyone for lessons, so she took a pedicab alone up to the Bunker.

She didn't know where the place was, but the driver did. On the way she tried to enjoy herself, however the weather was misty and chilly. Her coat wasn't waterproof. Damp, she huddled in the open-air cab and waited for the clammy ride to end.

When they reached the Hills, the driver stood up on his pedals to use his full strength to get them up the sloping road. The way grew darker as overgrown trees and shrubs crowded in.

Arriving at the club was a disappointment. Raina had pictured a nightclub from films with velvet ropes and neon lights. This place was unadorned cinder block. It looked like the military installation it had been converted from.

Set into the side of the hill, the club entrance was a pair of solid steel doors, drab gray. Above the doors hung an old theater marquee. Black blocky letters proclaimed it the Bunker. A smaller hand-painted sign screwed to the bottom read: "Leave your inhibitions at the door."

Raina paid the driver with one of the coins Michael had gifted her at the party. She waved off the change, not wanting to dicker.

"Will you need a ride back?" the driver asked.

Raina tore her eyes off the bleak structure. "Oh. Um. Yes. But I wouldn't want to keep you here and cost you fares."

"Nobody'll be wanting rides in this weather. People in New Salem think they're made of sugar."

She chuckled. He was right. Even a light sprinkle sent shoppers running home from the market. Weather like today ensured most were tucked away and would stay that way until the threat of rain was gone.

"Well, if you don't mind waiting, that would be great. But I'm not sure how long I'll be."

"No worries," the man said. "I keep a book in my cab for wait times. *The Count of Monte Cristo*. I'm about halfway through it."

"All right then," said Raina. "Stay warm."

The driver smiled and tipped his cap. "Will do."

She approached the imposing doors. She expected them to be heavy, perhaps locked. When she tried one it swung open easily on well-oiled hinges. She took a last glance back at the pedicab then went inside.

The door swung shut behind her. She was in a small foyer. The floor was polished concrete, scuffed in the center by foot traffic. The walls wore a skin of flyers, posters, post cards, stickers, and other advertising. A bare bulb overhead lit the cramped space. Ahead, the paper-plastered wall boasted a small window and a dark brown metal door. A steady beat thumped behind the door.

A young black woman with navy blue hair sat behind the window. She had on a black and white striped turtleneck sweater and was looking down at something. Her eyebrows were pierced, as were her nose and lips. She looked up when Raina came to the window. Got up just enough to push it open a few inches. The bass thump got louder.

"Hi," Raina said. "I'm, uh. I'm supposed to meet someone here. D?"

The attendant swept her with a scrutinizing look. "Who's asking?"

"Raina."

The woman slid all the way out of her seat. "One sec."

She shut the window and left her post, disappearing from Raina's line of sight. With nothing else to do, she idly tried to see what the woman had been looking at. It was hard to tell from that angle, but it looked like a black and white comic. Some kind of illustrated magazine.

Unable to see more, Raina turned her attention to the media on the walls. Weird art overlapped photos of Bunker patrons. There were ads for local establishments. Others promoted bands and live performers. Several were for personal services: Masseuses, pet-sitting, house cleaning, delivery, psychics, and instructors. There was even a flyer for the First Church. Someone had drawn a cartoon penis on it. Juvenile vandalism, but it made Raina smile.

The brown door opened. The heavy bass beat escaped again and the woman from the window poked her head out.

"Your party's waiting for you in Suite D."

She stood back to let Raina pass. The hallway on the other side was a dark mirror of the foyer with lots of ads covering the concrete walls. The lighting was wan, a flickering blue-green fluorescent fixture. As the brown door shut, the attendant ducked back into her windowed booth, trusting Raina to know where to go.

She could only go forward or back, so she forged into the darkness ahead. A curtain of shiny black beads separated her from the source of the pulsing beat. There were more layers of instruments now, higher notes and voices. Classical music with an EDM makeover. Flickers of light blinked through the curtain, making the beads glitter with intermittent rainbows.

She pushed through the rattling strands of beads. A wide, dark room stretched before her. It was lit by strobing, swinging laser lights which sliced through a swirling layer of smoke. The place had a scent all its own, tobacco and incense and something sweet she had never smelled before.

Fat dark-upholstered couches hugged the walls. There were a few armchairs and tables scattered randomly around the perimeter. The center of the cavernous room was empty, the floor barely visible through the smoke. The lights came from a DJ booth at the far end, the source of the deafening music.

This was the club Raina had expected—mostly. Except it was empty. No one manned the DJ booth. No one was on the dance floor.

The absence of people gave the room an uncanny quality. The flash of lights and rambunctious music should be paired with a packed crowd. The empty room clashed with the vibe. Closer inspection proved it wasn't entirely deserted, though. Bodies sprawled on the couches. Some were slumped in cuddled-up pairs. One couch had four people heaped together. Occasionally a body would stir to tap an ash from a cigarette or to lift a glass. Most of them didn't move.

The mood in the room felt plain wrong. The place was too loud, too big for so few people. People who were living shadows. The music infested her thoughts, making it difficult to think. Dizzy and disoriented, Raina looked around.

She spotted a hallway near the restrooms that looked promising. A sign above it in neon paint glowed under a purple spotlight: The Rabbit Hole. She decided to try it. At worst she would have to backtrack. Anything would be better than being the only person standing on the dark dance floor.

Down the long hallway the music was less intense though the musky-sweet smoke still fogged the air. The walls to either side were dark gray concrete set with narrow black doors made of sturdy industrial metal. Each had a sloppily painted letter on it in white. Some had other drippy symbols as well, none of them familiar to Raina.

She found her way to the door marked with a runny D. She paused outside. Should she walk in? Or knock? Her thoughts were cottony. The floor felt like it was swaying beneath her.

A knock on the thick door probably wouldn't be heard, so she decided to let herself in. The door wasn't locked. It opened into a small sitting room. Black loveseats and chairs crowded a central circular table. Several candles burned on the stone surface.

A woman sat in one of the chairs, exotic and beautiful. She had braided burgundy hair down to her waist. The strappy white dress she wore made her honey-colored skin glow in the candlelight. A white leather collar hugged her throat. Necklaces spilled down to nestle in the ample cleavage exposed by her v-neck.

There was an older man with her, standing to her right. His outfit was a creamier shade than the snow-white she wore. His salt-and-pepper hair was trimmed short under his off-white Panama hat. Even his wingtip shoes were ivory. He had a thin cigar in his mouth.

"Hi," she said. "I'm Raina. Am... I in the right place?"

"Raina." The woman gave her a smile that showed straight, pearly teeth. "Hello." She glanced up at the man beside her. "Please excuse us, Henri."

The man touched the tip of his hat and moved toward the door. He repeated the gesture as he passed Raina, offering her a smile around his cigar. He pulled the door closed behind him when he left.

"Please. Have a seat," the woman invited. She made a fluid gesture to the chair beside her.

"I'm sorry," Raina said. She approached the chair, her step slow to combat the swaying floor. "Are you D?"

"Depends on who you ask. The Coven knows me as Desiree."

Raina's eyes widened as she sank into the seat. "Ohh. Wow." She shook her head and blinked hard, trying to clear her head. It didn't work.

Desiree lifted her chin, proud. "You've heard of me."

"Yes. A little." Raina had heard a lot about her, yet not enough to draw any conclusions. "I heard you ran off."

"Is that what they told you?" Desiree laughed, sharp and indignant. She flipped her braids over her shoulder. Propped her elbow on the arm of her chair and leaned closer to Raina. There were old scars on her forearm crossing over one another. "Did they tell you *why* I left?"

Raina pressed her teeth to her lower lip. Thinking took effort. "Just that you got into some sort of dark, uh, magic."

"Cowards." Desiree was visibly disgusted. "Who told you that? Never mind. It doesn't matter." She leveled a stony look at Raina. "The Coven is vile. Corrupted. You shouldn't trust anything they tell you. They turned away from their purpose and listen only to Michael and Pietre now. Evil incarnate."

"Michael isn't evil," Raina objected. Remembering what he said about the source of his abilities, she amended: "He doesn't use infernal powers anymore."

"Really, now." The other woman was unconvinced. "Even if that were true, Michael remains the son of Satan. He's killed dozens of people. He allowed that bastard Pietre to take my baby from me. You have no idea what I went through to get her back."

Raina rubbed her forehead, pressing her thumb between her brows. Why were her thoughts moving like cold molasses? Desiree's accusations were too heavy to fully take in. "I'm sure there's been some mistake..."

"There is no mistake!" Desiree slapped the armrest of her chair. She caught herself when she spoke next, her words were steady again. "Michael allows horrible things to happen under his watch. He commands others to commit atrocities on his behalf. He beguiles and violates and destroys. He will destroy you, Raina, if you continue to serve his interests. Mark my words. If you let him, he will be the end of you."

Raina shook her head slowly, not wanting to hear such awful things. A cold lump settled in the pit of her stomach. "No. You're wrong. He wouldn't hurt me."

"I'm right," challenged Desiree. "You doubt me? Ask around. Every woman he has been close to has either died or was a demon. Are you a demon?" Her sculpted features took on a sympathetic cast. "I was infatuated with him too, once. He is sinfully easy to fall for, isn't he? But there is no love in him. He doesn't feel. Not like you or me. He is an alien to this world. A monster."

Raina kept her hands still, fighting the urge to fidget or hug herself. She didn't want Desiree to see the effect her words were having. Michael had been nothing but kind to her. She had seen how loving he could be as recently as last night.

The outcast witch leaned closer. Her almond-shaped eyes reflected the gleam of the candles. "Leave the Coven. Join me and I will show you what true witchcraft is supposed to be—without the influence of the Devil."

"What influences you?" Raina challenged. "Is it true you made deals with dark spirits?"

Desiree's answer was slow in coming. "I made a single contract with a Petro lwa years ago. I did it for the sake of saving two people the Coven locked in the basement. I paid my debt."

The woman's logic was confusing. "You say Michael is evil, but you use evil spirits when it suits you?"

"Petro spirits are not evil," Desiree disputed. "They represent the negative balance of the universe. That is not the same as wantonly following the son of the first Fallen, the enemy of the Righteous. He who leads the whole world astray."

Raina was done listening. "Do you have my mother's necklace or not?" She wished her voice didn't tremble.

Desiree's lips pressed into a fine line. "Your necklace is safe, but it's not with me now. If you want it, I will give it to you."

"You will?"

"The Society is holding a costume ball Halloween night at the old Wattles Mansion. Bring Michael. Prove to me he isn't the vile man I think he is, and I will give you the necklace."

That seemed more than a little suspicious. "How can I prove that? You've already made up your mind."

"I'll know," Desiree assured her. "If you can get him to come, I'll know."

CHAPTER 25

The smoke in the hall blurred Raina's senses. She wandered through a hazy, shadowed dream. The music had shifted from heavy bass EDM to retro Goth, dark and slinky. There were more people in the cavernous main room now. Several were on the dance floor, moving in fluid undulations that stirred the fog. Green and blue lights skimmed the haze, lending the place an eerie, watery quality.

Wandering out onto the dance floor, she was entranced by the motion of the dancers. Everything slowed down. Even blinking took forever. Drowsy euphoria settled over her, putting billowy distance between her and the upsetting conversation with Desiree. Even the cabbie who waited for her vanished from her mind in the waking dream.

Sucked in by the music and the moment, she was sleepwalking through a beautiful vision. A languid whirlpool of darkness and light. Flitting shadows. Hypnotic drums. It was an exotic, hazy dream. No fears could reach her, no stress or sorrow. It was pure bliss.

Sweet-scented mist swirled around her. She was in the center of the dance floor now, bathed by the cool, swiveling lights. Bodies drifted past her in the fog. Brushed up against her. She was one with them.

It felt so right.

She shut her eyes and let the music move her. Gave in to lure of the dream. It was like shedding a skin. Liberating.

After a while she became aware of someone behind her, moving with her. Their energy was familiar. Dark and alluring. Michael. She was dancing with Michael. Their bodies connected and she realized it wasn't Michael after all, but Pietre who shadowed her.

Raina tried to turn. The action made her dizzy, unstable. She was walking on water. Pietre caught her before she could fall. Pulled her into his arms. He swayed with her, his front to her back.

"I didn't expect to see you here," he said close to her ear.

He didn't have to raise his voice for her to hear him over the music. The intimacy of his tone gave her goosebumps.

"Hi," she said and giggled because it wasn't exactly a response to the unspoken question.

"Are you having fun, my dear?"

"Am I?"

She leaned against him because it was easier than standing on her own. The watery floor couldn't claim her as long as she had him to prop her up. They moved together in time to the music, his arms wrapped securely about her waist.

"Perhaps too much." His smile laced the words.

"Never."

—

Time slipped by in a liquid blur. The dance floor dissolved. They were in the Rabbit Hole, doors floating by in the fog. Pietre's arm was around her shoulders and hers were around his waist. She was warm and secure. It was nice to have someone like him in her life, mature and strong. Someone who taught her powerful secrets.

The world blurred again. She was in a room lit by dozens of candles. All sizes and colors, they covered the sideboard and end tables. Melting wax spilled down their sides in glistening rivulets. Flickering light played on the dark walls and ceiling. She was sprawled on a bed, a plush blanket beneath her bare body. She couldn't stop petting it. It felt so nice under her hands. Against her skin.

Perfect. Everything was perfect.

Weight settled next to her then Pietre's lips were on hers. His tongue slid into her mouth. Her surprise melted straight into pleasure. Her hands found his hair and it was soft, too. He tasted of peppermint and lust. She devoured the kiss, instantly alight with desire.

He moved on top of her. His body was bare, too. Where had their clothes gone?

Then he was between her legs, entering her. He knew what he was doing, how to deliver pleasure and how to make her body respond. Soon she was clinging to him, gasping and moaning. Tumbling into an intense climax that made her thighs shake.

He kept going. Deeper. Harder. It seemed like he would never stop. She was delirious with passion. Her thighs were wet. She clawed his back as she came again, drawing a sensual moan from him.

Everything blurred again and she was in his car. There was a strong smell of peppermint in the warm air. Her clothes had found their way back to her. She was a blissful sort of numb. Worn out. The view outside the window was rosy with the sunset. The city sped by as they headed back to the Bradford Hotel.

She nodded off before they got there.

...

Michael was getting impatient. Troy, Ligeia, and Trixie were at the table with him but there was no sign of Raina. He'd gotten into the habit of waiting for her before he ate, and he was hungry. It was well past sunset. Almost eight bells.

"I wonder where Raina is," he grumped to relieve tension.

"I don't know if she's coming," Trixie volunteered.

"What? Why?"

The black-haired woman set her fork down. "She went to the Bunker earlier today. I understand she had a meeting with Desiree, then she and Pietre... Well. I don't like to gossip. But I heard she was pretty wiped out when he brought her back."

Michael sat back in his chair. He needed a moment to process the verbal slap.

Troy was quicker to recover from the surprise. "You're not trying to say she and Pietre—"

"Desiree?" Ligeia said at the same time. Her dark eyes were alight with malicious affront. "At the Bunker?"

Trixie looked around the table, suddenly less sure of herself. When she intercepted Evan's message warning Raina the note warned against trusting Desiree. Trixie wanted to get the initiate into trouble. She'd swapped the note for one of her own encouraging Raina to go. She hadn't considered exactly how her gossip might be received.

Michael's hand came up in a sharp move, motioning his companions to silence. Ligeia lit a cigarette and puffed it angrily.

"Tell me what you know," he commanded Trixie. His words were deceptively soft.

—

Raina stirred. She was drained. Sluggish. Her head felt pressurized. It took her a moment to realize she was in her bed at the Bradford. Atop it, actually. Still dressed as she had been when she left earlier that day. For a moment she just lay there, taking in where she was and in what condition. Her body was stiff and her mouth sticky-dry.

After a few seconds she brushed her hair back from her eyes and squinted at the window. There was no light behind the heavy curtains. Night had fallen. Her brain was foggy. What happened? She'd gone to the Bunker. She spoke with Desiree. Things got fuzzy around that point.

She didn't remember leaving Desiree's room, though she did have a vague recollection of being in the main room of the club. And dancing. Dancing with Pietre. Pietre was there.

Flashes of memory followed, like shaky photographs viewed in a strobe light. They'd had sex but she couldn't remember what led to it. Her impression of the joining was fragmented. Passionate moments and intense pleasure. Then... nothing. She had no idea how she got back to the hotel.

She rolled to her side as a sick feeling grew in her stomach. Had Desiree done something to her? That didn't seem likely. Raina hadn't eaten or drank anything her room. That she could recall. Caught between wanting to remember and wanting to forget it all, she groaned. Pushed herself up and swung her legs off the bed to sit on the edge. That's where she froze.

Michael was sitting in a chair near the bed, staring at her. His expression was perfectly neutral.

"Michael!" Guilt quickly overcame her surprise. "How long have you been there?"

"You weren't at dinner," he said, ignoring her question. "Are you well?"

The vibe he gave off unsettled her. It was blank, just like his expression. "I... think so. I went to the Bunker earlier. I think there was something in the air... Made me, um. Tired."

He took a black cigarette from a silver case on the table and struck a match to light it. Then he resumed staring at her. "They often smoke opium at the Bunker during the day. I didn't expect you to go there alone or I would have warned you."

Opium. Raina read about the stuff in the old manuscripts her mother had. A section in one told of wooden and ceramic head pillows from China that patrons of opium dens favored. The idea of resting one's head on a hard block snared her attention because of how uncomfortable it sounded.

"Ugh," she said and hugged her middle. She wasn't sure if she was hungry or close to vomiting. "I won't make that mistake again."

"Why were you there?" He tapped his ash in a glass of water he had on the table for that purpose. "If you don't mind my asking."

She tucked a leg up under her other knee. Despite how casual his tone was, the whole conversation had her on edge. "I went to talk to someone. About my necklace."

Cautiously she probed his aura, trying to define his mood. He frowned and pushed her thoughts back.

"Don't." The word was sharp. Forceful though he didn't raise his voice.

She shrank into herself. "I'm sorry. I just... you're acting... strange."

His mask of calm was fractured. He sucked on the cigarette hard, hotboxing it. "You're hiding things from me. I don't like that."

She pulled a deep breath and let it out slowly. She got the distinct impression she was on trial. Not at all what she needed. She was still wrestling with her own feelings about what happened at the Bunker.

"I'm not hiding anything."

"Then tell me who you went to see."

She hugged herself, then made herself relax. She didn't want to look defensive. "I saw Desiree. She has my necklace. She said she would give it back to me."

"If?"

"She wants me to come to some Halloween party at the, um. Some old mansion outside the Walls. I think."

The details eluded her, but that didn't seem to matter to Michael. His posture relaxed, if only a little. She could only see that as an improvement.

"Interesting," he said. "Why didn't she give you the necklace while you were at the Bunker?"

Why indeed? Raina struggled to recall.

"She didn't have it with her."

"Hm." Michael hit his cigarette again and tapped his ash into the glass.

Raina remembered something else. "She wanted you to come, too. To the party."

She still had no idea what had happened to cause a rift between the Coven and Desiree, or how it affected Michael. Ignorance, in this case, was not bliss.

"Did she." It should have been a question, but Michael's tone flattened it into a statement. "What do you know about her?"

"Just what Troy and Ligeia told me." What she wouldn't give to be back in yesterday instead of tonight. "That she got into some dark magic and ran off."

A thin smile tugged Michael's lips. It vanished quickly. "I suppose that's an accurate, if abbreviated, account."

"Look, if my talking to her is a problem, I'm sure there's another way to get the necklace back."

A bleary memory stirred of Desiree telling her Pietre and Michael were evil. She shoved it away.

The prince puffed on his cigarette one last time and dropped it into the glass. The ember hissed when it hit the water. His moves were short. Staccato. His expression was still a perfect picture of neutrality.

"I'll go to the party with you."

"You will?" Raina's heart leaped. She hastily bridled it. His statement wasn't exactly a proposal for a date.

"I'm curious to know why she wants me there," he said. "It's been years without so much as a peep from her. Now she surfaces right when things get strange."

"Do you think she had anything to do with my landlord's murder?"

Michael shrugged. "Perhaps. She's not the type to kill, but it's possible someone or something she's working with is."

"Dark magics mean dark spirits," Raina murmured.

"Generally, yes."

He was staring at her again. She felt him probe her mind. She resisted the urge to shut him out in the same manner he had when she'd tested his energy.

"If there's anything you want to know, you just have to ask," she said quietly.

The psychic pressure eased. Michael's brow dipped, a faint line appearing between his brows. "I would rather not have to ask."

She could guess what he was fishing for. Which meant he already knew or at least suspected. Why, then, was it so difficult for her to tell him? She laced her hands over one knee to keep from fidgeting.

"I slept with Pietre." Better to get it out there. Like ripping off a bandage. "I didn't... mean to. Exactly. It just sort of happened."

Michael's neutral expression didn't waver. "I see."

"I think it was the opium," she went on. His continued blankness was disconcerting. Any reaction would be better than nothing. "I really don't have an excuse. We were dancing and..." She stopped herself. "I'm sorry if I hurt you."

"You haven't hurt me." He looked up at the ceiling. Searching for words. "If anything, I'm... disappointed." He focused on her again. The blank mask was ever present. "You've been training to stay on your guard. It would be one thing if you chose that path. But to let yourself blindly go? I thought you were stronger than that."

His statement was a direct hit on her biggest source of insecurity. Tears stung her eyes. She blinked them back. "Well. Apparently, I'm not."

Michael tipped his head, studying her. "We're not married. It's up to you who you share your body with. But you should be certain about what you want when you do."

She squinted at him, totally lost. Lost and hurt. She hated that his words hurt her. "Then why are you— Are you upset with me?"

He pursed his lips and considered the question. "No."

She sagged as confusion overtook her. "Then why does it feel like you are?"

"Perhaps I should go."

She sagged more. They weren't fighting and yet she was miserable. Worse, she didn't know how to fix things. "I don't want you to go. I just want—"

He did that head-tip again, like a dog listening to a peculiar sound. It was impossible to read him. Or guess what he was thinking.

"Do you forgive me?" she asked. "I mean. Are we... okay?"

He sat back in his chair and thought some more. "I don't intend to hold today against you, if that's what you mean. But I think it would be best if we didn't share a room tonight."

She wrapped her arms around her middle, hurt spreading from her heart to her stomach. She didn't trust her voice, so she nodded instead.

He sat there a moment longer, then rose. She stayed seated as he let himself out. When the door closed, she collapsed. Buried her face in the pillow so she could cry without being heard.

CHAPTER 26

Hours later, Michael let himself into the mansion he called home. The Remington was his retreat when life was pressing too hard. His sanctum sanctorum when he needed something. At the moment, he needed a shower.

He still hadn't eaten when he left the Bradford Hotel and was ravenous by the time he hit the streets. He needed sustenance, but more than that he wanted to stalk something. So, he drove to Elysian Park hoping to find one of the monsters that still prowled there. Anything with sharp teeth.

It wasn't difficult to find a worthy opponent. He found the creature skulking around the weathered playground. It was as big as a lion, with the stocky body of a dog. No hair. Huge fangs and claws. An infernal predator from the fog that covered the city for years. Most of the fog was gone now, but many of the beasts remained.

Michael brought no weapons with him. He fought the thing bare-handed. It was a vicious battle. The monster refused to surrender to its fate. It gave him the challenge and distraction he needed.

The massive beast bit his arm. The pain motivated him to fight harder. They were well-matched but Michael was a more formidable hunter. Hunger fueled him as well as the emotional fallout he refused to share with Raina. The fight ended when he broke the monster's thick neck. He'd gorged himself on its hot, bloody remains.

Covered in blood and coming down from an adrenaline high, he trudged up the boxy central stairs of the old house. No one bothered him on his way to the second-floor guest bathroom.

He ran the water in the shower so hot it fogged the walls as well as the mirror. Shadowy, indistinct shapes darted over the misty glass as he scrubbed the gore from his body. Blood swirled in the tub drain, circling away until the water finally ran clear.

Once he was clean, he shut off the shower. His wound was healed by the time he stepped out onto the bathmat. Despite the humidity, the air was cold on his skin. Supernaturally so.

"Whoever's there," he addressed the room as he toweled off. "Go away and leave me alone."

The temperature eased up to normal. Satisfied, he slung the towel over the shower curtain rod. Part of living in a haunted house hinged on knowing how to manage it.

He was getting dressed in his room when someone knocked on the door.

"What?" He shrugged on a plain black T-shirt. It matched his boxers.

The door creaked open. Father Jeremiah stuck his head in. "I thought I heard you come in."

Michael pulled his long, damp hair free from his shirt collar. He raked the uncombed mess back into a loose ponytail and secured it with a band he took from the top of the dresser.

When he didn't say anything, the older man stepped all the way in. "Everything all right?"

"I'm still figuring that out."

"That doesn't sound good." Jeremiah crossed the room to the bed and sat on the edge. "What's going on?"

Michael sighed and leaned back against the dresser. "When did you know you loved Mother Lenore?"

Jeremiah blinked in surprise. "I don't know. It just... sort of snuck up on me, I suppose. Over the years." He gave the matter more thought. "The first time I told her I loved her was in the middle of a fight. Do you remember when you wanted to be a veterinarian?"

Michael rolled his eyes. He didn't like to be reminded of the stupidity of his youth. "Yes."

"The first time I said I loved her was that night, after the blow-up. After she canceled your birthday party. She was drunk and raving about those things you put in the freezer. You were already in bed. I had to hold her to stop her doing something she'd regret. She said something to the effect of 'why are you doing this?' and that's when it came out."

"That's not love."

Jeremiah chuckled. "Oh, but it is. Love is the reason I put up with her when she's like that. That and my love for you."

Michael turned back to the dresser and dug around in the drawers. He wasn't looking for anything specific. He didn't even see the clothes he pushed around. "Why does love come with so much unpleasantness?"

Jeremiah clasped his hands between his knees, steepling his fingers downward. "I think there's more pleasant about love than unpleasant. But everyone has problems in a relationship. Any relationship. Just look at the rest of your family."

"Again, I'm hesitant to call that love," muttered the prince.

"It is what it is."

"What if you love someone and you don't want to?"

Jeremiah's brows arched up. Interesting line of questions. "We don't often have a choice in who we love. We care for whom we care for." He paused. "Are you having issues in that department?"

The response chafed. Michael pushed the drawer shut without taking anything from it. "I don't know. Maybe. Maybe not." He ran a hand over his loosely bound hair, suddenly antsy. "I don't want to— I don't want what happened to Evangelina... I don't want that to happen again. Ever."

Jeremiah regarded his grown ward with gentle concern. "Should be easy enough to avoid."

"I don't know." Michael started to pace. Moving soothed him. "I don't like feeling this way. I don't like the thought of it."

"What is it you're worried about?"

Michael paced as he tried to pinpoint the answer. When he found it he stopped in his tracks. "Raina. If I care for her, *He'll* take her. My Father always wants what's mine. I'm not strong enough to protect her. Already Pietre has—"

He stopped as frustration knotted his insides. He wasn't angry at Raina. He wasn't even angry at Pietre. Though it disgusted him that the warlock took advantage of her, it didn't come as a surprise. No, Michael was angry at himself for feeling anything about her in the first place.

Jeremiah's hand on his shoulder startled him out of his brooding. He turned to see the older man wearing that stoic face he always got when things needed doing.

"You've stood up to Him before," he reminded.

"And look where it got me!" Michael shrugged off the hand and paced to the other side of the room. "I hate love."

With effort Jeremiah kept himself from smiling. "It is the worst of tyrants."

"I'm tired," Michael grumped.

Jeremiah took the hint. "I'll let you sleep," he said solicitously. "If you need me, you know where to find me."

He let himself out. Michael went over to the bed and flopped face down. He expected to crash immediately, as tired as he was. However, sleep proved evasive. It was near dawn when he finally stopped tossing and turning.

...

Raina had a restless night as well. She woke at six bells, stiff and run down. She was hungry, but she didn't want to go to the dining room. She wasn't ready to face Pietre or Michael yet. Especially not Michael. Not after last night.

Thinking about the conversation upset her all over again. She should get up and start the day. She had a lesson with Father Jeremiah later that morning. But getting out of bed was a tremendous chore. She dawdled, drifting in and out of sleep for the next three bells.

Sometime after the tower struck nine, there was a light knock at her door. Her heart leapt. Was it Michael?

"Just a minute," she called.

She scrambled out of bed and threw a robe over her nightshirt. Then she hurried to the door and pulled it open without checking the peephole.

Troy stood on the other side with a large breakfast plate in his hands.

"Hey." He smiled, a friendly gesture that almost masked his concern. "Didn't see you last night or this morning. I thought you might be hungry."

She considered turning him away but seeing the food sparked her appetite. Though she didn't want company, taking the meal and turning him away would be rude.

"Thanks," she said. "Um. Come on in."

She accepted the plate and carried it over to the table. He pushed the door shut and followed her, taking the chair across from her. He fished a fork and knife from his back pocket. Wiped them on a napkin before offering them to her.

"I would've brought you some juice, but I was kind of short on hands."

She flashed a smile she didn't feel. "Thanks," she said again as she took the flatware.

He watched her eat in silence for a bit, then ventured: "You okay?"

"Yeah," she said around a bite of ham. He had done well with his breakfast selections. It was obvious he'd noticed what she liked from the buffet.

Troy shifted in his chair, settling into a casual slump. "Well. If you wanna talk or whatever... I'm here." He hesitated, then added: "Nobody thinks less of you over what happened with Pietre. Hell, half the people here have been his plaything at one time or another."

She froze, a chunk of syrup-soaked waffle poised midair on her fork. She stared at him. Word traveled fast in the Family. How many of them knew about her night with the warlock?

Realizing from the look on her face he'd said the wrong thing, Troy tried to smooth things over.

"Sorry. Too personal?" He lowered his chin, contrite. "If it helps, he jumped me, too."

Her first instinct was to get irritated, but his confession tempered her reaction. "He did?"

Troy nodded, sincere. "First time I met him. I'd never even been with a guy before. Or a girl, for that matter."

Raina couldn't help her stare, amazed by his candor. "How did you... I mean. Afterward."

Though her words were a tangle, Troy got the gist of what she was trying to say. "I figured it this way: Either I could make a big deal about it, or I could roll with it. I decided to roll." He sat forward and gave her a poignant look. "If you don't want him touching you, tell him. If he doesn't listen, tell Michael. He'll make sure it doesn't happen again."

Raina set her fork down as fresh misery swept in. "I don't think Michael wants to talk to me, much less speak for me."

Troy reached out and took her hand. Gave it a squeeze. With the contact came an electric tingle she'd experienced the first time he touched her. It didn't startle her this time.

"Michael's feathers might be fluffed right now," he told her. "But give him a day or two and he'll get over it. He knows Pietre too well."

"I just don't want him upset with me," she said. "We're not... I mean. Michael and I aren't a couple. He has a problem with the fact that I let my guard down. And... he's right. I did. I guess I was high, and I wasn't thinking..."

The truth of that bothered her all the more. Jeremiah, Ligeia, even Pietre himself had cautioned her time and again to stay alert. She'd gone with the easy flow of what was happening, not thinking about the consequences.

"We all make mistakes," Troy consoled. "Even Michael. I could tell you a half dozen dumb things he's done, right off the top of my head."

She was sure he was only trying to make her feel better. It was working.

"You're sweet."

He grinned crookedly and ducked his head. He let go of her hand. "Nah. I'm not. I just don't want you in here moping. The world's a little less sunny when you're not around to brighten it up."

"Charmer," she accused, her tone bordering playful.

"What can I say? I like the sun. Comes with being a walking fireball."

He snapped his fingers, and a puff of orange flame sparked up. He caught it and it disappeared.

His antics made her smile for real. She tucked into her breakfast with renewed vigor.

CHAPTER 27

Later that morning, Raina went to the Remington mansion to meet with Father Jeremiah for her lesson. He let her in and took her to the formal front sitting room which she'd learned the residents referred to as the Great Room. In her old home, there was only one living space, the family room. She had seen the family room at the mansion and preferred its casual furnishings to the hard, fancy furniture in the Great Room. But as a guest, she kept her opinion to herself.

Tea spread was on the glass table: The pot under its quilted cozy; Shelley teacups and saucers gilded with lines of gold; lemon wedges, sugar cubes, and cream in matching bowls. Silver spoons with handles in the shape of rosebuds. There was even a plate of petit fours, sweet little teacakes with fancy colorful icing. It was all quite posh.

"I think it's just me today," she said as she sat down. "I haven't seen Michael today."

Jeremiah took the cozy off the teapot and began to pour out caramel vanilla tea. It had a lovely aroma that sweetened the cool air.

"I heard from him," he understated. "He had matters to tend to. Just as well. We're covering history on a subject he grew bored with years ago. Nothing he'll miss."

He filled a cup and was starting the next when there came the sound of small running feet from the hall. Headed toward them at great speed.

"Raina!" Gabriel cried as he dashed into the room. His brother followed close behind him.

The boy in the lead launched himself at her. She opened her arms both to catch him and to defend herself from the impact of his tackle-hug. The five-year-old squirmed and latched onto her neck in a fierce embrace.

"Ack." She tugged one of his arms to loosen his grip. "Hi, Gabe. Hi, Zach."

Zachariel reached the sofa. He was trying to keep a polite distance, but when he saw Raina hug his brother, jealousy reared its head. He climbed up next to her and hugged her waist. It wasn't easy with Gabe in the way. She gave him a one-armed squeeze.

"I missed you," Gabe told her. Then he saw the tea. "Cakes! I want one!"

Jeremiah eyed the treats. "I suppose. You can have one each. But don't tell Mother Lenore I let you have sugar right before naptime."

Both boys clambered down and crowded the plate of teacakes to debate which was the best. Raina watched them, amused. Their warm reception restored her faith in her place in the universe. It was comforting to have such a ready source of voluntary affection.

Motion at the doorway caught her attention. There was another boy peeking around the corner. When he saw her looking at him, his eyes widened. He took a step backward, then changed his mind and came fully into the room. He was around eight years old and looked so much like the twins he could be their older brother. He had the same sandy blond hair and slim build. The dark eyes were definitely a match.

"Hi," she greeted. "I'm Raina."

Father Jeremiah looked over. "Hello, Ethan."

The boy shoved his fingers into the pockets of his jeans. There was a frayed hole in the right knee of the faded denim. The twins always wore expensive clothes. Ethan's t-shirt and jeans were more in line with what Raina was used to seeing kids wear.

"Hi." He stared at her with open curiosity.

"Raina, this is Ethan," Jeremiah introduced since the boy didn't seem inclined to. "He's a cousin to the twins."

"Wow," Raina said to the boy. "You sure do look it."

Ethan's mouth quirked up on one side and a dimple appeared in his cheek. "Strong recessive genes. I saw you last week, but you didn't see me."

Raina was taken aback by the boy's vocabulary. He looked too young to know what recessive genes were.

"Did you?"

He smiled bigger, enjoying the attention. "Yeah. I'm pretty good at hiding."

"Would you like a cake?" Jeremiah asked him.

The twins finally made their choice. They both plopped down on the hardwood floor to eat just shy of the Persian rug that was under the furniture.

Ethan considered the tray of treats. "Nah," he decided. "I don't like frosting. Well, that's a lie. I like chocolate frosting. But not that white glaze stuff. Or buttercream. Buttercream's gross."

Jeremiah finished pouring the tea and offered a cup to Raina. She took it and scooped sugar cubes into it. Ethan continued to watch her.

"How old are you, Ethan?" she asked. She had a sip of tea. It was good but needed a dose of cream.

Ethan rocked on his heels, his well-worn sneakers squeaking on the wooden floorboards. "Age is a state of mind. Not a state of being."

She glanced up from doctoring her tea. "That's an interesting philosophy. I may have to steal it, if you don't mind."

He grinned, pleased. "Sure. I'll let you."

She found herself liking him. His mannerisms were peculiar, but in a good way. He was smarter than most boys his age she had met. Intelligence and eccentricity seemed to run in the family.

Ethan went over to where the twins were finishing up their cakes. He nudged Zach's bottom with the toe of his grubby shoe. "Hey. Dork. We were going to play hide and seek."

Zach frowned at him. "I want to stay with Raina. You cheat."

The older boy turned on a false look of shock, his eyes widening. "I do not. Hey!" That last was aimed at Gabe. "Don't eat crumbs off the floor, doofus. That's where people walk. God. You're so gross."

Jeremiah cleared his throat. "Why don't you boys go play?"

Zach turned the glower on his guardian. "I want to stay with Raina," he repeated in a firm tone.

"Come on." Ethan grabbed his arm. "The grownups don't want us here."

"No!" Zach pulled away from him.

Gabe, who had been eating as many crumbs as he could, looked over at the other boys. Then he looked at the cakes still on the table. Calculating.

"Zachariel," Jeremiah warned.

"NO!"

Zach burst into tears. He jumped to his feet and ran over to Raina. Flopped his upper half into her lap where he wailed. She hastily set her teacup down before it spilled on them both. Hands freed, she patted his back. Awkward.

"I think it's nap time," Jeremiah said sternly.

Zach cried harder and grabbed two fistfuls of Raina's shirt. He wasn't going without a fight. "I want Raina!"

"You're gonna get it now," observed Ethan, amazed and gleeful.

"Hey," Raina said to the drama in her lap. She rubbed his back to get his attention. "Maybe I could read you a bedtime story. How about that?"

She was asking Father Jeremiah as much as she was Zach. The little boy's sobs dwindled. He lifted his head and looked up at her with red-rimmed eyes.

"Okay," he said, his voice thick with tears. He sniffled. Dramatic to the last.

Jeremiah looked less than pleased, but he said: "All right. One story then you're to stay in bed until I tell you nap is over." His tone brooked no further argument. "You too, Gabe. Gabriel!"

The other boy had seized his opportunity to nab another cake while everyone was distracted. He'd eaten half of it already. When Jeremiah came for him, he gobbled down the rest.

Ethan covered his mouth with his hands but that didn't stop his mischievous laugh. Father Jeremiah shot him a black look.

"You are not helping."

Ethan had the decency to look contrite. "Sorry."

Jeremiah picked up Gabe. Crumbs fell from the boy's clothes and hands. "Just... clean that up while we're putting them to bed. Please."

Raina lifted Zach, who rested his cheek on her shoulder. She suspected he was using her as a shield. He didn't even look at Jeremiah.

They carried the boys upstairs to the nursery and cleaned them up before putting them into their low-to-the-floor beds. Jeremiah wasn't happy, but he was a quiet presence in the rocking chair while Raina read a Beatrix Potter storybook. It worked to calm the twins. Neither said anything when she finished the book and put it away.

Soon she and Jeremiah were back downstairs in the Great Room. Ethan had cleaned up the mess on the floor and was nowhere to be seen. The house was quiet once more. Raina hoped they would get on with the lesson, but Jeremiah wasn't about to let the situation slide.

"You shouldn't let them tantrum you into doing what they want," he said once they were seated.

It was the first time she'd heard him use a stern tone with her. And while his words were still well within the realm of gentle, his displeasure was clear. Fatherly disapproval was new to her.

"I'm sorry. It seemed the easiest way to handle things. It was... getting pretty crazy."

Jeremiah made a small frown. "The easiest way is rarely the best way. That goes double when you're dealing with Michael's sons."

Raina took up her teacup. Fiddled with it without drinking from it. The easiest way wasn't the best way. She knew that all too well from her recent experience with Pietre.

"I'm sure you're right," she said. "But how should I have handled it? He was crying on me."

"And he'll do it again now that he knows he can manipulate you. The best way to manage that sort of behavior is to be firm with him. Tell him it isn't the way to get what he wants."

The man made a lot of sense. "I'm not used to dealing with kids," she admitted. "Was Michael like them when he was little?"

Jeremiah's expression relaxed and he gave a short laugh. "He was worse. But there are twice as many of them, so I suppose it all evens out."

Just like that, the tense moment was over. Raina appreciated the fact that he didn't feel the need to belabor his point. Still, she suspected he could be quite intimidating if he had a real mad on.

"How long have you been... with him?" she ventured.

She followed the question with a sip of her tea. It had cooled. Still tasted good, though. She'd yet to have tea at the mansion that failed to please. The stuff at the Bradford was plain breakfast tea. Drab by comparison. Maybe she could get some of the good stuff sent to the hotel if she found out where it came from.

It occurred to her she might be getting spoiled on tea.

"Michael was close to their age when my Order sent me to mentor him." Father Jeremiah drew a breath and released it in a soft sigh. "It seems like only yesterday, and also a lifetime ago. So much has happened over the years. Things have changed a lot. It's a new world now."

"That's the truth. I think back to when I was a kid and it's like... the whole planet went into nightmare mode. And when the nightmare stopped, the world we knew was... Just. Gone. You know? Sometimes it feels like the before-part was all some happy fantasy. And this—what we have now? Is what life always was."

Her words had a profound effect on Father Jeremiah. He seemed to power down. "Sometimes it feels as though the nightmare isn't over. As if it's just... on hold for a while. Like being in the eye of a tornado."

Realizing how dreary he sounded, he cleared his throat. "But enough melancholy. If we're going to talk history, we should make it something useful to you. How much do you know about the fallen angels?"

...

Outside of paintings, Raina didn't know much about the legacy of the Fallen. Just that they used to be angels and were cast out by the Supreme Being. So, they started with the basics. They discussed John Milton's works and the apocryphal religious text, the Book of Enoch. Jeremiah told her about angelic theory and how other religions viewed angelic entities.

The subject was fascinating. Time flew by.

When they finished for the day, Raina returned to the hotel. She spent the afternoon with Beth in the laundry room, losing herself in the monotony of washing and folding, her mind full of fantastic images of the Fall from Grace.

The way Jeremiah described things made the biblical characters more real to her. Sparked in her an interest to learn more about religions and history in general. Linking the religious tales with historical dates and happenings was a fun way to put them into context. They weren't just myths and names any longer. They were stories about actual people, individuals who walked the earth and ruled the heavens—and hell.

And while it was a fictional tale inspired by a whimsical muse, Raina found Milton's works, both *Paradise Lost* and *Paradise Regained*, to be strangely truthful. Like the poet had truly been inspired by a Muse to write them. And who was to say he hadn't been?

At four bells, Beth shut things down. Raina dried her hands and went up to her room. She intended to go outside and practice the cantrips Ligeia taught her. Instead, she wound up thumbing through Desiree's sketchbook.

She flipped to the back and found the picture of Michael sleeping. Her heart cramped. She missed waking next to him that morning. In such a short time she'd gotten used to him being there.

She was being foolish. More than foolish. People kept telling her to steer clear of him. This mess was a big part of why she'd shied away from relationships. When she got comfortable with a person, she relied on them. With reliance came the painful risk they would leave her.

She never knew her father but had suffered from his absence. The club fire that killed her mother wasn't Lyra's doing, still her loss was devastating. Not to mention Raina had a track record of poor decisions where it came to men. She gravitated to people who were no good for her. All signs pointed to Michael being another dubious choice.

She ran her finger lightly over the drawing, tracing his cheek. Despite the delicate touch the pencil line smudged. She snatched her finger back in dismay. It didn't help. The damage was done.

She flipped back a few pages, not wanting to see her mistake yet unwilling to put the book down. There were more pictures of people, mostly women. A drawing of Ligeia was all sketchy, hard lines. One image showed a funeral. Michael was there. His expression was masterfully captured: Determined, stoic. There was sorrow in his eyes. Was it Evangelina's funeral?

After a few more pages she closed the book and put it back in the drawer. What was she going to do about Michael? She couldn't avoid him forever. Nor did she want to.

And then there was Pietre. She couldn't avoid him, either. She was due to meet with him the next day. She needed to find a way to move forward.

Troy's solution was to "roll with it". She could follow his example or make it an issue. Which she didn't want to do. She'd taken part in the tryst willingly. Enjoyed it even. While she regretted her actions, she couldn't deny the wicked pleasure in her fractured memories.

She hoped he would just let it go. Then she could pretend nothing happened. If he tried to make another move on her again... well. She would deal with that if it happened.

Needing to get away from her circular thoughts, she grabbed her coat from the closet. A brisk walk in the crisp evening air would help clear her thoughts. Help her figure out what she was going to do in the morning.

CHAPTER 28

Michael woke that afternoon to a quiet house. Throwing on some pants, he went out to the hall. Passed by the nursery. He could hear Zach and Gabe chattering to one another behind the closed door. He opened it and stuck his head in. Both boys were in their respective beds.

"Daddy!" Gabriel cheered.

Zach pushed himself up to a sitting position. "Can we come out now?"

That was a strange question. They never asked for permission to leave their room except...

"Are you being punished?"

The boys looked at each other with wide eyes.

That was answer enough. "Before you say anything," cautioned Michael. "Remember what I told you about lying."

The twins looked at him again. "You can lie to anybody except family," they said in unison.

"So. What did you do?"

There was another beat of silence. Then Zach said: "Gabe ate an extra cake when Father Jeremiah said we could only have one."

Offended by the betrayal, Gabriel sat up. "Zach didn't do what Father Jeremiah said either! He threw a big fit!"

Michael looked from one boy to the next. Zach was angry. Gabe was clouding up, ready to cry.

"Sounds like you both were bad."

Both boys fidgeted.

"Is Raina family?" Gabe deflected.

Though unprepared for the question, Michael fielded it without missing a beat. "No. But I don't want you lying to her. You respect her like you would family. Understand?"

Both blond heads bobbed in synchronized nods.

"Can we get up?" pressed Zach.

Michael made a show of consideration. "I think you should stay here until I speak to Father Jeremiah. We'll see what he says."

The twins had enough experience with their father to know better than to argue. He wasn't around all the time, but he had disciplined both of them in the past. They knew not to push him.

"Can I have a hug?" Gabe wiggled his fingers.

A reasonable request. Michael went to the boy's bed and stooped to give him a quick hug.

"Me too!" Zach threw in.

Of course. What one had, the other wanted. Michael went to him next and gave him a squeeze.

"Be good," he told them as he headed for the door. "Father Jeremiah will tell you when you can come out."

———

Downstairs, Jeremiah filled Michael in on what happened that morning. When the priest went upstairs to deal with the twins, Michael spent time with Lenore who insisted on feeding him. She kept raw meat in the fridge she seasoned herself. He preferred it fresh and unseasoned, but he never told her. It made her feel useful.

After he ate, he went to his room to change. He liked to dress well in public. No one would criticize him, but clothes made the man. Once presentable he said his goodbyes and hit the road.

After a few necessary stops he went back to the Bradford and parked out front. Not ready to jump back into the social pool, the prince got out of the car. The evening air was brisk, scented with distant smoke from a fire. Dry leaves skittered across the cobblestones. The sunset stained the sky purple and pink. Michael loved this time of year. The span between summer's oppressive heat and the damp cold of winter never lasted long enough.

He crossed over to the garden, a circular park in the middle of the old plaza. A giant tree grew from its center. Concrete paths intersected within the maze of plants, many in autumn colors that brought the fall he longed for. He came to a dead end where a stone bench marked the end of the path. He sat and lit a cigarette. The spicy smoke and crisp air cooled his lungs.

Keen to his surroundings, he detected a person approaching before he saw them. Raina came into sight, rounding a rosebush. She stopped when she saw him. He gave her quiet regard. Her wide eyes and skittish stance put him in mind of a young deer. They stared at each other for a silent moment. He sucked on his cigarette and exhaled a thick plume of smoke. Dropped the butt to the stone walk. Pressed it out with the heel of his boot.

"Nice evening." His words were soft.

Her skittishness eased. "It's starting to get cold."

"October's always like that. Warm, warm, then suddenly: Cold."

She took a couple of steps closer. "I was just... walking. Thinking of what to wear to the, um. The party. On Halloween."

Her approach was cautious. Michael sat still, letting her come to him. A cool breeze rustled the leaves and tousled her long curls.

"Are you familiar with Carnivale?" he asked.

"I am." She was only a couple of feet away now. "I don't know where I'd get a costume that would fit the theme, though."

"Couldn't you sew one? You said you sew."

Raina ducked her head. "I do. But there's not enough time to make a whole dress." She looked over at him again. "Are... you still planning to... to go with me?"

He sensed her energy, exploring her mood. She didn't try to block him. He tasted uncertainty and longing. Longing for him.

"Why wouldn't I?" he said.

He rose and with a supernaturally quick motion he was right in front of her. Near enough to smell the jasmine oil on her skin.

"I don't know," she said absently. Captivated by his gaze.

His hands settled on her shoulders. Pulled her close. She pressed against him, her lips parting. He seized the invitation and kissed her deeply. Her arms went around his waist. The world disappeared, scaled down to that connection between them.

He broke the kiss, one hand cupping her cheek. There was so much he wanted to say but the words tangled up in a rush of heated emotion. More than anything he needed her to understand he wanted her, too. Past, present, future.

They kissed again. Intense and driven. Needful. Then he lifted her, cradling her close to his chest, and carried her to the bench where he sat with her on his lap to resume the kiss. His hand went up under her peasant blouse. Plucked at her bra clasp. The undergarment surrendered. His hand found her breast, skin to skin. Her breath quickened. He nipped at her lower lip, and she responded by deepening the kiss. His other hand found hers, guided it to his crotch to show her the desire he couldn't pin words on. He reached for the top button of her pants.

"Not here," she whispered. "Someone will see."

"Let them."

Her cheeks pinked. "Michael..."

His lips crushed against hers, urgent. He needed her. Now. She softened and when he tugged at her pants this time, she helped.

No one disturbed them. Only the ravens witnessed their frenzied joining in the fading sunlight.

...

They returned to the hotel together and were having dinner when Ligeia and Troy joined them. Troy set his wine glass down and went to grab food. Ligeia settled across from Raina. She lit a cigarette, ignoring the fact the other two were eating.

"I've been wanting to talk to you," she said, jabbing her cigarette at the younger woman.

Her tone was stiff, the way Lyra used to sound when Raina had done something wrong. Even though Ligeia wasn't her mother, the tone had a similar jarring effect on her.

"What about?"

"Please," Ligeia snarked. "You know what. You were out socializing with that bitch."

Raina's heart sank. It took her appetite with it. "I did see Desiree."

Ligeia made a soft sound that might have been a superior laugh or a derisive snort. It was too short to tell for sure. "Why?"

Raina poked at her food. "She has my necklace. I went to get it back."

"And you didn't think to tell anyone before you waltzed off into an unknown situation?"

Though she struggled to keep her expression neutral, Raina's brows pinched. She was a grown woman. Not some teenager in need of scolding. In front of the prince, no less.

"I didn't know who I was meeting," she said. "I got a message that the person who had it wanted to meet at the Bunker."

The guttural sound Ligeia made was one of outraged distaste. She looked away, as though it angered her just to look at Raina. "And you just went. No questions asked." She shifted her attention to Michael. "Real smart one you have there."

The prince refused to be drawn into the fray by taking a deep drink of wine.

Flustered by the criticism, Raina reddened. "She didn't do anything. We just talked."

Ligeia's obsidian eyes were on her again, sharp as daggers. "Oh, she didn't? Is that why Pietre had to carry you in?"

Raina set her fork down and looked at her lap. Everything she said dug the hole deeper.

Knowing she'd taken that round, Ligeia sucked a long pull from her cigarette and blew smoke at the younger woman. "In the future if some unknown person asks you to meet them, you will tell me. You're lucky you got out of there alive."

Raina's temper got the better of her. "I'm not a child."

Ligeia gave a sharp laugh. "Yes, you are. You're a fledgling witch. An apprentice with no understanding of the dangers in this world. Until you *grow up*, you're not going anywhere alone."

Troy arrived bearing two heaping plates of food. He looked around, reading the table. He'd overheard the last of what Ligeia said. "I'm happy to go with you wherever."

"Now you have no excuse," said Ligeia. "Is the rule clear enough for you?"

Raina gave a short nod. "Crystal."

———

After dinner she and Michael left the dining room together.

"Don't let her get to you," he said. "Being a bitch is her way of showing she cares."

Raina gave him a half-smile. "I could stand a little less care."

He took her nearest hand and squeezed. "She just wants you to be careful. We all do."

Raina's shoulders sagged. "I know. I will. I feel stupid about everything that happened."

"You're not stupid. Experience is a merciless teacher."

"What happened to Ligeia to make her so full of hate?" Raina asked as they reached the foyer.

"She's been through a lot." His expression grew more serious. "When she and Mother Lenore were born, there were prophecies about them. Ligeia embraced hers while Mother Lenore ran from hers."

That drew Raina's interest. "What prophecies?"

They reached the stairs. Michael paused. "Ligeia would be the leader of women. Lenore would be the mother of men."

"What's that mean? The leader of women I can guess. She's meant to run the Coven. But what about mother of men?"

"It has to do with me. Possibly my sons, too."

The subject made him uncomfortable. As curious as she was, she didn't want to pry into things he didn't wish to share.

"We don't have to talk about this."

Their eyes met. His were shadowed with deep inner turmoil. Impulsively she leaned forward, tilted her head and kissed him. Desiree accused him of not having feelings, but Raine knew if anything, his ran stronger than anyone's she'd sensed.

When the kiss broke, he said: "Want to go somewhere?"

———

Somewhere was a parking lot in an abandoned strip mall. A traveling circus took advantage of the space to set up their sideshow. It had an enchanting vintage flair to it. After paying the entry fee and buying tickets hand-printed on recycled paper, they wandered the row of booths and wagons. The only ride was an old Ferris wheel. The rest of the sideshow was made up of individual acts and games of chance.

They paused to watch a scantily clad tattooed woman swallow fire and spit it out in a burst. Raina would have found it more impressive a few months ago.

"It surprises me you don't have a partner," Michael said.

She chuckled. "I've had plenty of wanna-be suitors. Several were nice, but..."

"But?"

"I guess I wasn't interested. I had... a long relationship with someone who was bad for me. When it went south, it was uhh-gly."

They angled toward a booth where a thin man painted a caricature of a customer with his feet. His hands were withered and useless, but he made up for them with the dexterity of his long toes.

"What about you?" she asked. "How are you still single?"

They watched the man paint, then they wandered on. The crowd was getting thicker. Lanterns with colored panes lit the midway, adding festivity. The scent of popcorn and distant barrel organ music carried on the breeze.

"I've had a few lovers. Mostly one-night stands."

"Really?"

"Some were two nights."

He'd spent more than two nights with her. That padded her ego but also made her nervous. She decided to change the subject.

"When you were little, did you know you were going to be... well. This?"

"This?" He paused to watch a contortionist who was bending over backward. "You mean Lord Prince of New Salem?"

"Yes."

"Sort of. There were prophecies Father Jeremiah reminded of me constantly when I was younger. I came into my powers early. By the time I was a teen I'd already performed minor 'miracles'."

"I remember hearing about you on the news. Something about a marketplace healing..."

He made a face. "Word got out I was helping a sick boy. Next thing I know, I'm laying hands on three hundred people."

The woman on stage passed herself through the space between her legs, putting her head beneath her own pelvis. Smiling broadly, she did a little jig to further showcase how limber she was. A couple of people dropped coins in her locked donation box.

"You... lost that ability, though." Raina said. "Right?"

He frowned. "I did."

She didn't mean to make him brood. She kissed his jaw. Felt the scratch of his blond stubble. "You'll work back up to it."

"Mm. I don't plan to do three-hundred person sessions again, regardless. That fiasco was the reason the Church got started. Gives me a place to see people without being mobbed."

He fished a coin from his pocket and dropped it in the woman's moneybox. Then they moved on. The next booth they stopped at was a game run by an elderly man in a purple top hat.

"Step right up," he invited, waving his cane. A small carved head topped the cane. The head wore a miniature hat just like the one on his head. "Win the lady a prize!"

Michael looked at the stuffed toys on display. The booth had some of the biggest at the sideshow. Mass manufacturing was no longer a thing, so the toys were unique to the booth.

"I'll give it a try," Michael said. "What do I have to do?"

The old man grinned. Waved his cane at three wicker baskets. "Get a ball in the basket. One ticket for three balls. One in, you get a small prize. Two gets a medium. Three gets ya one of the big fellas."

Michael fished in his pocket for a ticket. The man snatched it up and set three grubby whiffle balls down. Michael gathered them before they could roll away.

"You know these things are rigged," Raina mentioned.

Michael didn't respond. He eyed the basket in the middle then pitched a ball. It went in and bounced right back out.

"Ohhh, so sorry!" the old man said. "Try again."

Michael tossed another ball in with the same result.

"One more try," said the carny happily.

Another ball sailed into the basket and bounced out again.

"Ohhh, so sorry!" the man exclaimed, not sounding sorry at all. "Them's the strokes."

Michael dug another ticket from his pocket. Raina favored him an incredulous look.

"You're not seriously going to try again, are you?"

He glanced at her, winked, then put a serious face back on. Put his ticket down and the carny gave him three more balls. Michael picked them up. Fidgeted with one as he eyed the basket. Then he tossed the ball underhand. It struck the bottom of the basket and rolled in, settling in the back.

"Ohh!" the carny barked, surprised. "Winner-winner chicken dinner!"

Michael kept his focus on the basket and took another ball in hand. Shifted his stance and tossed it underhand with a slight twist. It smacked the side of the basket. Dropped in beside the first.

"Well!" the old man said. "I'll be jiggered. Betcha can't do that again."

Michael tossed the last ball. It hit and went in. Raina clapped enthusiastically, bouncing on her toes. She didn't care about prizes. She liked seeing Michael beat the shyster at his game.

"You see that, Stan?" the old man asked his cane's head. No sore loser, he. He actually seemed impressed. "We got a real sure-shot here. Name your prize, young man."

"Let's have the dinosaur. The two-legged one."

The old man used his cane to knock the bipedal dino from its spot. A couple of blackbirds perched above startled into flight.

Michael smiled and accepted the stiff plush toy. "Thanks."

"I can't believe you did that," Raina marveled as they walked away.

He laughed. "After everything, this impresses you? It's just physics. I threw the first round to make the old guy happy."

She grinned. "Well, it was nice of you to win a toy for me."

"For you?" Michael said. "This guy's for me."

For a moment she thought he was serious, then she caught the mischief in his smile. "I wouldn't want to come between a man and his dinosaur," she said, playing along.

They strolled on for a bit, taking in the sights.

"I might give him to you as a trade," he said as they drew near the end of the carnival.

She looked at him with dramatic interest. "For what?"

He eyed the oversized stuffed animal as though weighing its value. "I'd settle for... a kiss."

She pretended to give his offer the same consideration. "I suppose that's fair."

They stopped then and, smiling, sealed the deal. After the kiss, she tried to claim the toy. He didn't let go.

"I don't know..." he hedged. "Two kisses is more fair."

"A deal's a deal." She gave him another kiss anyway.

They explored the full length of the show and started back the way they'd come. He stopped to buy some popcorn to share. They munched as they went.

"So, I have an idea for our costumes," he said. "But we'll need your skills as a seamstress."

"There's not enough time to—" she started.

"Trust me," he said.

CHAPTER 29

The next morning Michael and Raina drove to a place near the Walls that sheltered New Salem from the rest of the world. The junk barrier threw a long shadow over the imposing structure they parked next to. A huge marquee on its left side proclaimed it the Hollywood Museum. The name was repeated in red block letters above the front double doors.

It was unlike any museum Raina knew. Built in the late 1920s, it had four columns on its façade and three stories of barred, concave windows. Detailed pediments framed the topmost windows. Large spotlights were grouped along the edge of the flat-roofed structure.

It looked like an ornate prison.

"A museum?" She loved the idea of spending time with Michael around a collection of art, though she didn't see how it connected with the upcoming party.

He slid out of the car. "This place was closed forever after the Time of Troubles," he said as she joined him on the sidewalk. He linked his arm with hers and ushered her in through one of the windowed doors. "A local group runs it now. It has so much history. For instance, the lower level used to be a speakeasy."

"Wow. What a neat place!"

The entryway was dark and had golden wooden floors. A black unfinished ceiling gave the illusion of infinite space. It was colder inside the building than outside. Fortunately, Raina had her long coat on.

"They have a bunch of creepy displays from horror movies and whatnot in the basement." Michael was obviously a fan of the place. "The upper floors are where they keep all kinds of old Hollywood memorabilia."

They moved down the corridor to a reception desk. The first floor was visible from there. It featured red walls, pinpoint spotlighting, and lots of glass cases framed in black. The mood of the place was elegant and austere. A busy eyeful due to what all was on display. And for Raina, who was used to tightly budgeted electricity, the amount of power that was being used to light the place made it all the more decadent.

An older woman behind the ticket counter got to her feet. "My Lord. It's a pleasure to see you again." Then, to Raina: "Miss."

Raina smiled at her. The docent smiled back then focused on Michael again. "Are you here for a tour?"

"In a round-about way, Francine. I need to borrow something. There's a formal masquerade at the Bunker on Halloween. Raina and I need something traditional to wear."

The woman grabbed a massive ring of keys from a drawer and came out from behind the counter. "Of course, my Lord. Let me just lock up."

She scurried to the door and flipped a "Closed" sign in the window to face the street. After she locked the doors she rejoined them. Raina was impressed with how swiftly the woman complied with Michael's wishes. Had he borrowed from the place before?

"We have several masquerade costumes." Francine led them deeper into the museum. "Let's see... there's *Labyrinth*. Or *Marie Antoinette*. *Fifty Shades of Gray*. Oh! What about the *Man in the Iron Mask*?"

"Not familiar with that one," Michael admitted.

The docent glanced back at him. "The film was all right. Leonardo DiCaprio as King Louis XIV. So-so script, but the costuming was to die for."

She led the way upstairs, through valleys of cases and podiums. They passed more wax statues and cardboard standees than Raina had ever laid eyes on. It would be fun to tour the place and forget about costume 'shopping'.

"Could we come back sometime?" she asked Michael, squeezing his arm. "And see everything? There's just so much!"

"Decades and decades," agreed Francine proudly as she led them to a locked glass case.

Michael kissed Raina's hair. "We can. We'll make a day of it."

"Maybe we could bring the boys."

He looked surprised. Then he smiled. "I suppose. Though that would change the experience."

"We could bring Father Jeremiah, too," she amended.

His smile grew. "That might be best."

"Here we are." Francine unlocked the display.

Inside the case a pair of dress dummies supported two breathtaking outfits. The king's garb featured a gold brocade overcoat and knickers, with a cravat so thick and fluffy it hid the linen shirt beneath. The lady's dress was a similar shade of gold, with a bell-shaped skirt and puffy sleeves. Large pearls adorned the neckline which was cut low to frame the cleavage area. Hundreds of seed pearls nestled in the lace trim.

"We'll need to alter them, I'm sure." Michael stepped up to finger the fabric of the coat. Seeing Francine's look, he added: "Nothing permanent. We won't cut anything. I promise."

The matron wasn't placated. "The fabric is old. Whoever alters them should know that."

"I'm doing the work." Raina suffered a stab of conscience. The docent's treasures were being threatened so they could have something to wear to a party. "I'm an expert seamstress. I won't do anything to damage them."

Her reassurances were met with the slightest bit of relief from the curator. "If you're that good, maybe you could do some restoration work for us sometime."

"Really? I would love that!" Raina meant it, too.

"Let's see how you do with these." With utmost care Francine lifted the heavy dress off the mannequin. "I'll get a garment bag."

...

Michael had work to do so he couldn't be with Raina the next day when she was to meet with Pietre, so Troy went with her. They rode out to the beach on his motorcycle, with Raina on the back. A thin fog haunted the streets, billowing out of the way as they cut through it. The ride out to the beach reminded her again that she still had Troy's jacket in her room. She just never thought about it unless she was actively on his motorcycle.

A wide, empty parking lot overlooked the sand where Pietre waited. Apart from the warlock, only animals were on the beach. Ground squirrels and wharf rats scurried about searching for food.

Shorebirds hovered above the white-capped waves. The heartbeat of the ocean surf was the only sound for miles.

"I would've thought there'd be people here," Raina said as she climbed down off the bike.

Troy dismounted. "The public beach is further south. The Coven and Michael claimed this section. I think it used to be a park or something."

They headed down the wind-sloped dunes to where Pietre stood on the pale sand, a stark pillar of black against a blue ocean and cloudy gray sky. He was facing the water, positioned near the rolling surf. The foamy waves threatened his bare feet. He had his hands together before him, fingers pointed down.

"I see you made it here without trouble," he said. He looked back over his shoulder then and gave them a crooked smile. "Since you're here, Troy, you can assist."

He held up his hands defensively. "I'm just transportation."

Pietre turned toward them. Raina stopped a few feet away. Despite her resolve to "roll" like Troy, she wasn't comfortable with getting too close to the warlock yet.

"Nonsense, my boy." Pietre fixed the younger man with that quirky smile. His eyes were steel. "You'll help."

Troy shifted his weight and hooked his thumbs in the belt loops of his jeans. Looked down at his motorcycle boots. "These aren't exactly beach shoes..."

"Take them off if they're a burden." Pietre turned his attention to Raina. "What about you, my dear? Do you need to strip your footwear as well?"

"I'm fine."

Aware of their destination, she had chosen to wear sandals. Her toes were cold, but not as cold as they would be if she were barefoot. Socks would have been prudent but as bad as her sense of fashion could be, she couldn't bring herself to wear socks with sandals. Socks would only catch sand anyway.

Troy plunked himself down and pulled off his boots. He dumped the sand out of them before setting them aside. He was wearing socks, which he left on.

"All right," he said. "What do I do?"

"You'll pass your energy through her to me," the warlock instructed. "As Michael did with you at the mansion a few years back."

"That energy didn't go into you." Troy got to his feet and dusted off his butt.

"It doesn't matter. You're not aiming to kill. Simply to transfer power."

"Whoa." Raina held up a hand. "Wait. What are we doing?"

Pietre turned his odd smile on her. "You are going to be a conduit. Like... a string of lights. Troy is going to send psychic energy into you, and you will pass it to me. Think of it as an advanced game of 'hot potato'. Troy? Stand behind her and take her hands. It will be easier that way."

Raina didn't like the sound of this 'game' or the uncertain look on Troy's face as he moved to stand behind her. She needed more information but wasn't sure what questions to ask.

"This won't hurt, will it?" That was important to know.

Pietre moved closer to her, within arm's reach. "Not at all."

She glanced back over her shoulder when Troy's hands took hers. He gave her a quick, apologetic smile. Then Pietre closed his hands over both of theirs, bringing her attention back to him. Scant inches separated them now. Her pulse quickened and she fought back anxiety and an odd rush of desire, reaching for anything else to take her mind off her tangle of feelings.

"Nervous, my dear?" the warlock asked. Amusement sparkled in his blue eyes. He was enjoying her discomfort.

Raina shored up her resolve and lifted her chin. "I'm fine. Ready whenever you are."

His quirky smile spread. "Now, Troy."

Troy's grip tightened and a feeling of warmth flowed into her. Not just through her hands but through her whole back like she was standing with the sun directly on her. The energy saturated her. Soon her whole system jittered. She was wired up as though she'd drank eight pots of coffee.

"Oh!" she gasped. "Oh, my God."

"Hardly." Pietre chuckled. "Release it into me now. Quickly. Holding onto it could be... detrimental."

The intensity of the sensation increased. An elevator ride up with no ceiling. She needed to release the energy... but how? Her thoughts were a hyperactive blur. Recalling her time at the pool, she shut her eyes. Visualized the energy as a swirling, fast-moving mass she could push out of her body and into the warlock. Instantly she felt the psychic pressure ease. The flow was unblocked. Energy moved through her rather than into her. It was exhilarating.

"Good," Pietre purred. "Good girl."

The effect was a lot like being drunk. She was giddy. Swept up in the sensation. The press of the men's bodies warmed her. Distantly knew she should be uncomfortable, but she wasn't. The moment was too sensual, too wonderful to be unpleasant.

Pietre began to pull then, actively siphoning the energy from Troy through her. The rush of energized pleasure increased. She heard Troy's breath catch. He was feeling it, too. Without warning, Pietre reversed the flow. Not expecting the shift, she resisted briefly then released the energy back into Troy. Again, his breath hitched.

The flood of back-and-forth sensation continued for several seconds and then tapered off. It left Raina's heart pounding.

"That's enough," the warlock murmured.

His face was just inches from hers when she opened her eyes. He released her hands. The drunk feeling subsided. Acutely aware of how close they all were, she tugged her hands from Troy's and slipped out from between the men.

The world wobbled a little and she stumbled into the water. She had to pause to catch her balance. An incoming wave lapped over her ankles, ice cold.

"Wow." She pressed a hand to her forehead. There was still pressure in the center, slowly diminishing. Not painful, but impossible to ignore. "That was... Weird."

Troy untucked his shirt to hide the effect the exchange had on him. "You've never done that before," he said to Pietre.

The man gave him a smug smile, eyes hooded. "Not to you. Did you like it?"

Troy looked away. "I think you know the answer to that."

Pietre laughed.

As Raina's equilibrium returned, she stepped out of the frigid surf. "I'm wet."

"I imagine you are," the warlock said, making her blush hard. "I believe the lesson has been learned. Shall we return to the hotel?"

Raina suspected if she said yes without qualifying it, she might find herself in a situation she didn't want to be in. "I'm ready to go back. Get cleaned up. Maybe have a nap. I'm... pretty tired."

She could tell from his self-satisfied smile that Pietre wasn't fooled. But he said: "Let's head back then."

The return ride seemed to take less time than the trip out. Soon they were pulling up to the Bradford. She slid off the motorcycle, forcing herself not to bolt as soon as her feet hit the ground. Pietre arrived right after she and Troy did. Inside the hotel, she beelined for the stairs. The men followed at a slower pace.

At the top of the stairwell, she paused to send them a quick smile. "I'll, uh, see you guys later."

She headed for her room then, trying to appear casual as they bid her goodbye. She didn't look back.

CHAPTER 30

The next morning Raina went to meet the High Priestess in her suite. Like Michael, Ligeia had a room up on the third floor. It was down the opposite end of the hall, room number six. Raina lifted her hand to knock but the door swung open before she could even touch it.

"Enter," the older woman's voice reached her.

Raina stepped across the threshold. A variety of scents greeted her: Cigarette smoke, vanilla, rich perfume, and something musky she couldn't put a finger on. The door slammed closed behind her with a startling bang.

Heart racing, she entered the sitting area of the suite. White and gray featured, from the drapes and paneled walls to the fur rug on the floor. There was a wood-burning stove in the corner, an old-fashioned black potbelly retrofitted into the wall to let the smoke out.

"Sit."

The word was a command, not an invitation. At a gesture from Ligeia, a chair slid from its place near the wall and struck the backs of Raina's knees. She dropped into the seat. The chair skidded over to where Ligeia sat, regal in a white wingback chair. Nearby a coffee table held her ashtray and glass of red wine.

Despite being in the comfort of her room, Ligeia was impeccably dressed, her black wardrobe a sharp contrast to her surroundings. Her long legs were crossed, tapered to wicked points by patent leather stilettos.

The witch sat forward to grind her cigarette out. "We need to talk."

Nothing good ever followed those words. Especially when they came after a greeting like Raina received.

"All right." No need to panic. This was just a talk.

Ligeia's dark eyes pinned her. "First: Pietre. When we were at the graveyard, what did I tell you about him?"

So much for casual conversation. Had she heard about the beach session? Raina shifted uncomfortably under the older woman's dagger-like gaze. "Not to trust him."

"I told you to never let your guard down around him. What happened at the Bunker?"

"I..." Raina faltered. What indeed? "I wasn't myself. There was opium—"

"No excuse!" Ligeia snapped. "That man can get into your head even when you're stone-cold sober. It's your job to protect yourself against him and anyone else who tries to manipulate you. It doesn't matter if they're using sorcery or substances."

Ligeia had a sip of wine to let her message sink in. Then: "Never let your guard down."

Raina gave a mute nod. Tried not to think about yesterday at the beach. She didn't even have the opium excuse for that.

"Now. The second matter." Ligeia stared hard at her.

"Yes?" She was fidgeting again.

"I heard you're going to that bitch's party."

Raina crossed her ankles and smoothed a hand over her skirt needlessly. Anything to avoid meeting the tension in the room head-on. "Michael and I are going. Together."

Ligeia's expression pinched. "Tell me. Are you a complete moron? Am I wasting my time on you?"

"I don't understand why you're so upset." Despite her attempt to keep her emotions in check, Raina's words came out tight. Petulant, even to her own ears. Not the way she wanted to come across.

And it was the wrong answer. Ligeia's dark eyes hardened. "Since this is so difficult for you to grasp, I'll educate you." She rose from her seat and circled Raina's chair with slow, measured steps. Predatory. "Once upon a time there was an untrained young witch who attached herself to a prestigious Coven."

She prowled around Raina's right side, forcing her to turn her head to keep Ligeia in sight. The hostile energy the witch put off was even more intimidating up close.

"The Coven took her in." Ligeia continued. "Taught her virtually everything she knew. Then the end of the world came. She and the Coven moved to New Salem to be near a warlock prophesied to bring about the New Age. She was trusted with certain duties. Such as caring for a pair of troublesome undead creatures the High Priestess kept in the basement."

Ligeia was behind her now. It was nerve-wracking to have that barely restrained anger behind her. But her only other choice would be to twist awkwardly in her chair. So, she kept facing forward, her hands locked onto the edges of her seat. Maybe that would keep them still.

"The young witch decided freeing those creatures was more important than anything," said Ligeia. "More important than the Coven, more important than her vows and her own future. She made dark deals with terrible spirits to break the wards that bound the undead, ensuring their escape."

Her hands came down heavy on Raina's shoulders, who tensed up instinctively.

"The idiot girl ran with them. A Wild Hunt was called. Chased them to the edge of the sea where the undead were destroyed. But their destruction didn't end the bargain the young witch made with those vile spirits. Exiled from the Coven, she fell deeper under their spell. She lives to serve darkness now."

Ligeia's grip tightened on her shoulders. Long red nails dug into her skin through her shirt.

"Now. What do you suppose she might want with someone like you?"

Raina squirmed. "Ow."

Ligeia squeezed even tighter. "You have a purpose to serve, Raina, and it is with the Coven. Troy didn't stumble on you out of blind luck. You were meant to be here."

Michael had said something to that effect as well. Raina turned her head, wanting to see the woman's face. Ligeia obliged her, releasing her death grip to come around to her side.

"What is my purpose, then?" Raina flexed her aching shoulders.

She wasn't being impertinent. She genuinely wanted to understand why the Coven all thought she was there for a reason. What reason could there be?

"You are her replacement."

"What do you mean?"

Ligeia's expression hardened again. "What I mean is you need to be vigilant if you're going to that party. There's only so much Michael can do to protect you in his weakened state."

"You aren't going to tell me not to go?"

"And have you defy me?" Ligeia gave a sharp laugh. "No. I'm not going down that road with another of my initiates. Go. Do what you have to, since that necklace means so damned much to you. But don't make the mistake of believing you're safe."

Ligeia went back to her chair and settled herself in it. She crossed her legs primly.

Raina knew she should leave it at that, but something was eating at her. "Desiree said Pietre took her baby. Is... that true?"

The witch cocked a thin brow. "The baby she birthed on the kitchen floor? She left the infant here when she ran off with the creatures she freed. Pietre's apprentices cleaned it up and sent it to the mansion. It was cared for alongside Michael's own children."

Raina didn't know what to believe, but she could sense truth in the woman's words. "What happened to the baby? She's not there now."

"Hell if I know." Ligeia lit another cigarette. "The bitch showed up at the house and as far as I'm aware, they let her take it. I haven't heard anything about it since."

As cold as her words were, again Raina could feel the truth underpinning them. She wished she could remember what else was said during her meeting with Desiree, but the only other clear thing she recalled was a warning: Women close to Michael tended to end up dead.

"I'll be careful," she said to Ligeia and to herself.

"You do that. And if you get the chance, nab a lock of her hair for me. Now go on. That's your lesson for today. Learn it."

...

Despite everything, Raina finished the alterations to the costumes by the time the day of the party rolled around. She basted the borrowed garments using long stitches to do as little damage to the old fabric as possible and was rather proud of the results. The gown was fit for nobility, exquisite in its construction. It would be fun to wear the gold taffeta gown in public.

She got ready in her own room, and Michael in his. Over the busy days, the reason behind their going to the masquerade had faded in the shadows of all that needed doing. As she took the dress from the closet that night she couldn't stop thinking about the reason.

Desiree had her necklace. She said she would return it. Raina would finally have her mother's pendant back. And she was certain once Desiree met with Michael, she would see what Raina herself saw. Michael might be mischievous at times, but he wasn't evil.

What was evil, anyway? Actions were evil. If other people did things in his name without him asking them to, that was on them. Not Michael. And if the rumors about Desiree were true, the outcast was hardly pure herself. What dark spirits had she appealed to that would help loose undead creatures on the world?

Raina wormed her way into the golden gown, moving carefully so as not to strain the old fabric. Being engulfed by the layers of skirts was akin to being under a collapsing circus tent. There seemed to be no end to the fabric. After some searching her head finally found the boxy neck hole.

As she adjusted the hang of the voluminous skirts, her thoughts skimmed back to that horrible experience at the altars. Michael wasn't responsible for that. However, he did allow sacrifices to take place there. At first, she believed him responsible or at the very least negligent for allowing such a thing. After spending a few weeks in his world, though, she understood how easy it was to get swept up in other concerns. To forget things that weren't right in front of her.

She was also guilty of letting the matter of the ritual killings slide now. She hadn't meant to forget. Other people had met their end on the bloody trio of stone and if it weren't for Troy, she would have too. But the days had been so full, it had been sinfully easy to just flow with them as those days turned into weeks.

"I really need to do something about those altars," she muttered to herself. The promise felt hollow given that she knew she wouldn't be mentioning them to the prince tonight.

With some contortion she got her zipper up. Then she retouched her hair. She'd styled it and applied her makeup before dressing so she wouldn't have to do it while wearing the borrowed gown. She looked at her reflection in the full-length mirror by the door. A baroque fairytale looked back at her.

She lifted the fancy golden mask. The illusion was complete. "I'll talk to Michael about getting rid of them," she said to her mirror self. "Right after the party."

———

Mask in hand, Raina left her room. With each step her bell-like skirts swished around her legs over the wispy crinoline that gave it form. Made her feel like she was floating instead of walking. Turning toward the stairs, she saw Michael waiting for her.

A fantasy in regal gold, the borrowed outfit looked so right on him it could have been made for him. He wore his long hair in a low ponytail secured with a gold satin ribbon matched to the brocade of his jacket. His golden mask dangled from his hand as he chatted with Troy.

Both men fell silent at her approach, drinking in her presence. Their enchantment was plain on their faces. The attention filled her stomach with butterflies even as her confidence soared. There was heady power in a dress that could stop conversation. She gave them a demure smile.

"Man, I'm starting to wish I was going to that party," Troy said, half-joking. "The two of you... whew. You look great. Gonna knock people's eyes out."

"Why aren't you going?" Raina asked.

Michael offered her his arm. She took it and he reeled her into an embrace. Her skirts swallowed his legs.

"Ahh. Trixie's going to be there," Troy said. "After the last party... Well. I thought it'd be better if I went down to Love's Pub instead. They're doing some karaoke and a costume contest thing. Laid back. Nothing fancy."

"Are you dressing up?" prompted Michael, eyeing the other man's clothing. Troy was still in his normal clothing.

"I have a T-shirt I wrote 'Designated Drinker' on. I figure that'll get me by."

"Master of 'low effort'," Michael scoffed. He looked at Raina then. "Are we ready?"

"Yes," she said. "You look great, by the way."

"And you are radiant. Gold looks quite nice on you."

He led her to the stairs without releasing her arm. They started down the stairs. Raina glanced back. Troy was watching them from where he was leaning against the banister.

"Bye, Troy. Happy Halloween."

He lifted a hand. "Happy Halloween. Don't do anything I would."

CHAPTER 31

The masquerade was located across the freeway from the Bunker.
Nestled at the base of the mountains, the lavish Wattles estate took
up four city blocks. Michael drove, which meant finding a place to
park when they got there. Several vehicles already lined the
surrounding streets. They had to walk a block to get back to the
mansion grounds. That suited them both fine as it gave them a few
moments alone.

The winding road led them through scenery that was pretty
yet eerie. Deserted luxury mansions surrounded them, many
damaged and falling in on themselves. Overgrown properties
crowded with a riot of bushes, evergreens, and untrimmed palm
trees. Suburbs gone wild. Behind the screens of foliage, the hills
rose up to blend with the mountain where more dilapidated
mansions lurked in the shadows.

"During the Angel War, people abandoned this area," Michael noted as they strolled down the old sidewalk. "So much affluence gone to waste. A lot of these houses had swimming pools that went sour. We had clouds of mosquitos in the valley for years when they festered."

"I remember that. My mother and I moved here about four years before the War," said Raina. "Just in time for the mosquito clouds. We had nets over the windows and the beds."

Michael plucked a late-blooming moonflower from a nearby vine and tucked it into her hair. "Where were you before you came here?"

"Nevada. Our town was destroyed by a huge sand tornado. Flattened everything. We got through it hiding in an old bomb shelter. There was nothing left to rebuild afterward. Nobody even wanted to. We were looking at moving to Sin City or here. Mom thought it would be better here. That it would be safer... closer to you."

That sounded weird. Raina bit her lip and wished she could take it back. Or at least phrase it in a way that didn't come across like she was some sort of groupie or fanatic. She'd thought she was past such awkwardness with him. Apparently not.

Down the block music echoed from the grounds of the mansion they headed toward. It was one of the only sources of light in the dusky evening. In the cool shadows of the overgrowth night insects began their nocturnal songs.

"All things considered Sin City didn't fare so badly during the War." Michael hooked her arm with his elbow and took her hand in his. "At least they didn't have to deal with being flooded."

"True," she agreed, glad to move past her awkward statement. "But I heard the giant dust storms that hit were awful."

"Mm. Is it better to drown in water or dirt?" Michael wondered. Then he quoted: "Some say the world will end in fire. Some say in ice. From what I've tasted of desire, I hold with those who favor fire. But if it had to perish twice, I think I know enough

288

of hate to say that for destruction ice is also great and would suffice."

He noticed her stare and smiled. "*Fire and Ice*, by Robert Frost. He's one of my favorite poets. He was born in California."

"I don't know much about poets," she said. "I'm mostly familiar with Edgar Allen Poe and Lord Byron. Dante."

"You have a taste for the grim."

He wasn't wrong. "I suppose," she said. A smile tickled the corners of her mouth.

They reached the entrance to the boxy mansion. The walled garden behind it was aglow with flickering firelight. The windows of the old manor house were lit warm yellow. They followed the sidewalk through a covered driveway and around to the terracotta front porch. The doors of the estate were wide open.

In front of the building a long yard sprawled, dead from lack of watering. That area was dark; the masquerade was being held in the back gardens. The dichotomy reflected the neighborhood: Luxury underpinned with decay.

Lilting strains of classical music poured through the building, inviting them in. They went up the stairs together. Raina had to hold up the hem of her skirts to avoid stepping on them. Moving in the gown took more effort than regular clothing, but it was worth it. She felt like a noble lady.

"I wonder if there are more stairs or doors in the world," she said as she climbed. Then, on reaching the landing: "Oh. Wow."

The entry vestibule was posh. White decor with dark wood accents. Greek statuary haunted the corners. Old paintings hung from the ceiling, supported by thick black chains. The sparse furnishing had a severe design. It was there to be seen, not used. The whole place bled artistic showmanship.

"It is nice, isn't it?" said the prince.

A few people milled around the entry, dressed in masquerade finery. A sign to the right pointed the way to the Ladies Lounge. One to the left pointed out the Gentlemen's Lounge. A hand rendered sign above the northern glass doors showed the party was ahead.

As Michael escorted her through those doors, Raina noticed they had the same rounded-top shape as the Bradford's. Opening herself to the feel of the place, she took in a similar sensation of mellow age and experience. The Wattles mansion felt sadder, though. Empty in a way the Bradford didn't.

"When do you think this place was built? It reminds me of the hotel."

Michael glanced around as they passed through the doorway to the formal gardens. "I don't know. Probably around the late 1800's or early 1900's. Father Jeremiah's history lessons didn't include much about Hollywood architecture."

"We should pester him about that," Raina joked. Then she saw the area they were walking into, and her words failed her completely.

The gardens were a beautiful, living dream. Breathtaking at night. Unlike the front grounds, the back held well-tended planter boxes full of lush greenery. Wide steps from the porch led down to the first third of a wide brick terrace where more guests mingled, decked out in costumes ranging from simple to exquisite.

Beyond the recessed area two flights of steps led up to the second level where the firelight came from. Raina and Michael headed that way, taking the steps slow so she could manage her voluminous skirts without tripping.

"This is amazing," she breathed. "Like a fairytale."

"I'm sure the Society would appreciate your glowing praise," said Michael, amused by her awe. "They've spent most of their time and money fixing this place up. It was in sad shape even before the Time of Troubles."

They reached the landing. More steps led further up, a flight on each side, screened with box hedges. Planters gave way to single bushes and neat rows of flowers. A deep concrete pit in the center of the landing took up most of the floor. Raina peered down into it. The bottom was filled with hundreds of candles, the source of the flickering light.

"Old fountain?" she guessed.

Michael looked down into the pit as well. "Looks like it."

"A shame it doesn't have water."

"Probably too hard to care for. They already suck up too much water just keeping the garden alive as it is."

"I suppose that's true," she sighed.

Despite the practicalities, it still made Raina sad to see it dry. The candles were a nice touch, but it would have been so much prettier with water there, spouting up to the night sky. It would have provided a nice splashing sound as well that would further the tranquility of the garden.

"The water plant is well maintained." Michael took her hand again and they continued up the next flight of steps. It was longer and steeper than the last. "But clean water doesn't happen overnight. There's a reason it's rationed."

His statement brought her back from the fantasy of the garden to grounded reality. "You really do have a lot to manage, don't you?"

The statement triggered a shift in Michael's expression, bringing a serious, rueful edge to his features Raina regretted inspiring.

"More than I want," he said. "You're probably right: I should delegate more. There's so much going on that should have my attention. Things beyond New Salem or even this side of the continent. It's just... difficult to let go. I don't want to lose touch with what I have here just to—"

He shook his head, cutting himself off. "Never mind that. It's a party. We should be enjoying it."

She regarded him with open concern. She wanted to press him to continue, but he flashed her a winning smile. He was determined to leave the somber subject matter behind. She made a mental note to revisit the subject later. Perhaps when she talked to him about the issue of the altars.

Instead, she said: "This is the longest I've seen you in a public place where people weren't flocking around you."

"Maybe I should wear a mask more often."

She laughed, struck by the mental image of him running around town in disguise. "I think people would notice if you were the only person wearing one. You'd make quite an impression."

"We could make it a law that everyone has to," he suggested, not at all serious.

"But that would ruin the fun of dressing up," she bantered playfully.

He gave a dramatic sigh. "I suppose you're right. We'll have to leave the mystique of masks to the theatre."

They reached the top of the stairs. The brick path made a perimeter around tall, boxy hedgerows in the center of the terrace. An arch cut into the bushes opened onto a large plot of dark earth where the main festivities were taking place.

A small ensemble of musicians sat in one corner of the party space on a temporary stage, playing dark waltzes on stringed instruments. To the left of the stage was a long table laden with treats and drinks. An ornate silver beverage fountain tumbled with a cocktail made to resemble blood. Red, orange, and black were the theme colors, seen in swags adorning the stage and bows tied to the guest tables and chairs. Halloween colors. A temporary floor of wooden planks filled the center area where a few couples danced. Tall candelabra provided the area with light.

Michael and Raina took in the party, then he turned to her.

"Shall we?" He took her by the hand and pulled her toward the dance floor.

She hesitated, frozen by the idea of dancing where everyone could see. It was different at the last party. It was dark and crowded. No one could see her. This dance floor was well lit with a few people on it.

"I don't know how to ballroom dance," she excused.

"It's easy. Just follow my lead."

He led her to one side of the dance floor where they wouldn't collide with anyone. Her skirts swept the boards. He took her right hand in his left and positioned her left on his shoulder. Then his right hand found her shoulder blade, his right arm supporting her left arm.

"When I step forward with my right foot, you step back with your left." He slowly walked her through the steps as he spoke. "Then bring your right foot back and to the side when I bring my right foot forward and to the side. Right. Just like that. Now slide your left foot over to meet your right foot. Then we reverse it. Step forward. Right, left, slide. And back again: Left, right, slide."

She followed along, steps unsure, feeling out the cadence of the music as she moved. She didn't slide her feet with the grace he did, but she found she was able to keep up. She relaxed as she got into the rhythm of the steps.

"And that's a box step." He smiled. "See how easy it is?"

He turned her, not missing a beat. She fumbled and found the beat again. The longer she danced with him, the surer her steps became until their dance grew smooth. Her eyes met his and there was that connection that transcended the need for words. His psyche mingled with hers and they began to move together in a natural rhythm. Elegant and easy.

She was swept away. A faint smile teased his lips. Her heart raced, whether because of the dance or the way he looked at her, she wasn't sure. Everything was magical. For an ethereal moment she lost touch with the world.

A few months ago, she was entrenched in the dull rigor of daily life, unsure if she would have enough money to make ends meet. Now she wore gown of gold and was dancing in the arms of the prince.

Everything had changed so drastically, it hardly felt like her life anymore. But if it wasn't hers, whose was it?

The music reached a pitched peak, swirling upward toward its finale. He released her shoulder and twirled her in a motion so sure and quick she was spun around and in his arms again before she knew what was happening. She laughed and fell against him as the song ended. He hugged her and gave her a quick kiss.

"Drinks?" he offered.

"Please."

He took her arm, and they left the dance floor. Headed over to the table of treats beside which the red fountain flowed. In addition to that fountain, two bowls of colored punches were arranged on the table. One was creamy with slices of orange floating in it. The other punch was a vibrant green.

After a moment of sizing up the fare, Michael took a cup and dunked it under the stream of the red fountain. Raina did likewise. She tended to dislike green things, and the orange stuff reminded her of a drink she sampled at a wedding once. It had too much grapefruit in it. She never wanted to risk the bitter flavor again. Red was safe.

They were looking for a vacant table when a woman in a black and teal gown approached them. A man dressed from head to toe in red velvet accompanied her. Peacock feathers covered her half-mask, and she had a pair of long peacock tailfeathers poking out of her updo. The man had a full devil's mask on a stick he held in front of his face.

"Lord Michael?" she inquired. Her excitement said she already knew it was him.

"Wilhemina," he greeted. "A pleasure."

They shared a cordial embrace. She had to bend forward to reach him over her wide skirt.

"Raina," Michael said. "This is Wilhemina. She's the Society's head of events. Mina, this is Raina, my—" He glanced at her, then looked back at Mina. "Date."

"Pleased to meet you," Mina cooed, extending a hand.

Raina took her hand and gave it a light squeeze. Date. He had paused before calling her that. Had he wanted to call her something else? Their hostess didn't notice. She was already gushing at Michael about the event.

"And you are?" Raina asked the man in red. If she occupied herself she wouldn't think about what was unsaid.

"Henri," he said. He had a faint French accent. "I do believe we have met before."

He lowered the mask. Raina recognized him.

"Oh! You were at the Bunker."

Henri extended his free hand. When Raina took it, he turned hers so he could brush a kiss across her knuckles.

"Classy." She reclaimed her hand.

"Do you have a moment? Madam Desiree would like a word with you."

He motioned across the clearing to a woman standing near the tall hedgerow. She wore a beautiful white dress and mask reminiscent of a swan. A splash of glittering red covered her front from throat to waist. She lifted a hand when she saw Raina looking her way.

Raina looked at Michael. He was listening to Mina go on about the décor.

"I'm going speak with Desiree," she told him when there was a break in Mina's chatter. She pointed out the woman in white. "I'll be back soon."

A faint wrinkle appeared between his brows, but Wilhemina was already yammering about the logistics of hosting such a gathering on Halloween.

Raina turned to the man in red who smiled and raised his mask again. He led her around the dance floor, to the far side of the terrace where Desiree waited.

CHAPTER 32

Across town, Father Jeremiah followed the twins down the dark street with an oil lantern to light the way. Their own neighborhood was largely uninhabited and not trick-or-treat friendly. So, he had driven them to an area near town center where plenty of homes gave out candy to youngsters on Halloween.

Lenore chose the boys' costumes. They were dressed as sheep, with Zach in white and Gabe in black. Jeremiah humored her by dressing the part of the shepherd.

Ethan came with them as well, but he refused to be a sheep or a shepherd. Instead, he wore an old scarecrow costume, which she grudgingly allowed. She rejected his first choice: A wolf. The scarecrow was a compromise. She didn't know about the papier-mâché mask he made. Once they were out of the house, he donned it. It covered his whole face and had a hideous, sharp-toothed smile painted on it. He'd outlined the eyeholes in runny black paint.

Gabe and Zach didn't mind the mask, so Jeremiah didn't object to it. Growing up around Ethan, they were immune to his attempts to scare them. The mask was tame compared to some pranks he'd pulled. They knew it was him under the toothsome face.

Their treat sacks were already half full. The family festival at the square would bring them even more goodies. Preoccupied with conversation about what they would do, they didn't notice the people following them.

—

When Raina reached Desiree, the man in red faded back, leaving the ladies room to talk.

"You look lovely," Desiree greeted Raina.

"You do, too." Raina admired the woman's outfit.

Desiree's gown was made of white feathers. The only part without plumes was her corset. Red crystals encrusted the sweetheart bodice, splashing down her front like blood. A red crystal choker emphasized the slashed throat look. Her costume was ghastly and gorgeous at once.

"A friend made it." Desiree fluffed the feathers that padded her hips then her expression turned serious. "Have you given thought to what we talked about? Will you join me?"

"I can't," Raina said. No sense in beating about the bush. "I know there's bad blood between you and the Coven, but they've done so much for me... I can't just leave. Things are different than you think. Really."

Desiree looked away, disappointed. "I wish I could believe you. But as long as they listen to Pietre and Michael, it will never be the way it was." She looked at Raina again, her eyes intense. "You don't know what it was like before. If you did, you would understand how far down the left-hand path they have gone."

"Maybe." Raina didn't understand what she meant about the left-hand path. It didn't matter at the moment. "But I think if you just gave them a chance—"

"No." Desiree's tone was firm. "I would never return to them unless I was the High Priestess. I will not follow evil men. I wish you would join me. I hate to see another innocent fall prey to their wicked ways."

"Michael came like you asked," Raina pointed out. "You said if he came, you would know—"

"Yes. I see him. He's heading this way."

Raina turned and saw him cutting through the milling partygoers. The Society woman was no longer with him. Instead, Trixie was tailing him. She wore a black and white dress, and a matching mask painted with black and white diamonds. Her black hair was teased up high.

"I don't wish to speak to him," Desiree said. She fished in her bodice and drew out a folded piece of paper. "But would you give this note to him for me? Then I will return your necklace."

Raina accepted the paper. "Thank you. I would appreciate that."

She went to meet Michael, who was a few steps away.

"Desiree said she'd prefer not to talk," she interpreted. "But she wanted you to have this."

He looked down at the paper she offered him. Puzzled, he took it. Unfolded it. Suspicious confusion clouded his features as he read it.

The writing was bold enough that Raina could see it:

"GOT YOU."

Michael looked at Raina for clarification, but she was just as lost. That's when she spotted Henri again. He melted out of the crowd behind Michael and leaped at him. Slapped a band of metal around his neck and clamped it place.

Trixie backpedaled from the sudden assault. Michael whirled on his attacker. Hit him with a hard uppercut to the jaw. The man in red fell back. Michael grabbed the metal collar and tugged. It didn't budge. Locked.

"Shit!" he swore. He fumbled with the back but couldn't find a way to release it.

Raina turned to demand an explanation from Desiree and saw her motioning with her hands. A cantrip. Raina had to do something. Fast.

The only thing close was a candelabrum. She envisioned an energy cord looped around it and pulled. Hard. The standing candlestick flew at Desiree.

Flames jumped eagerly from the falling candles to the feathered skirt. In an instant, the outcast witch was ablaze. She screamed. Her spell fizzled at the interruption. Raina grabbed Michael's hand and tugged. Time to run. He resisted only briefly then outpaced her, practically carrying her. Trixie followed them.

Desiree tried to shed her flaming dress. Henri scrambled to his feet and grabbed a punchbowl. He doused her in green liquid. By the time the flames were out, Michael and Raina were on the porch.

"I will have the Coven!" Desiree cried. Her voice amplified, carrying her anger clear across the gardens. "It's ten o'clock, Michael! Do you know where your children are?"

He hesitated at the exit to shoot her a mistrustful glance. Then he and Raina hurried through the old mansion. They didn't stop running until they were to his car.

Once there he tried again to pull the collar off. It held firm.

"Dammit!" he swore with more vehemence. "That bitch!"

"Let me—"

Raina started to reach for the collar, but he pulled away.

"Did you know?" He advanced on her then, towering over her in his rage. "Did you?!"

She shrank back from his anger. "No! I don't know what's going on! She just told me to give you that note. I had no idea—"

He turned away. Balled his right hand in a fist. Looked like he was about to punch the car, but after a tense moment he uncurled his fingers. Ran both hands over his hair. "Dammit!"

"Michael, what is it?" Raina tried again. She kept her distance this time. He was scaring her.

He grabbed at the collar, tugging hard on it in frustration. "This thing! It's a warding collar. It strips the wearer of their power. Pietre perfected the damned thing. He had one on Desiree for a while. That's probably where she got the fucking idea!"

Trixie caught up with them, winded and limping in her high heels. Raina became aware of her own pinched toes and the punishment they'd taken during the mad flight from the estate.

"We should go," Trixie said with a glance back over her shoulder.

No one was following them. Yet.

Michael growled angrily and went around the car. He yanked the driver's side door open. Raina got in on her side. Trixie squished in beside her. Their wide skirts filled up that side of the car. Trixie barely got the door shut before Michael started the car. The engine roared and he peeled away from the curb with a screech of rubber on asphalt.

———

They stripped their masks and drove in unhappy silence. Michael brooded at the wheel. He took them to the mansion at top speed. Pulled up to the curb fast and slowed at the last moment to slam on the brakes. Once he had the car parked he jumped out and rushed to the front door.

The women turned wide eyes on each other. A look of fear was plain on Trixie's face. Raina didn't know what to feel apart from miserable.

"Let's get out," she said. The other woman was blocking her way.

Trixie opened the door and clambered out. She lingered beside the car, hugging herself. Raina hesitated then went through the iron gates up to the sheltered porch. The front door was still open, so she went inside.

She could hear Michael's angry voice coming from the upstairs hall. She didn't want to see him so upset, but she couldn't stand staying downstairs either. She climbed up the boxy staircase, skirts in hand so she wouldn't trip.

Michael and Lenore were together in the second-floor hall. Ethan was in a nearby doorway, his expression dark. It was obvious from his red-rimmed eyes and tear-streaked face that he'd been crying. Seeing Raina, he ducked out of sight.

"We need a plan," insisted Lenore. "You don't even know where they are!"

"He should have stayed with them!" Michael stabbed an accusing finger at the doorway where Ethan had been.

"He came back here to warn us."

"Some warning! He can't even tell us where they were taken!"

"He was scared."

"He's a ghost!" Michael stormed. "They couldn't hurt him!"

"It's Halloween," Lenore snapped back. "You know that means he—"

She saw Raina then and her lips thinned to a grim line. She tipped her head that way and caught Michael's eye. He turned as well. He was furious. Livid with anger. His expression tamed some when he saw Raina. Coming down out of reaction mode, he drew a deep breath. Then he turned back to Lenore.

"I'm going to get Pietre to take this damned thing off," he said to her, yanking on the metal collar. "Then I'm going to talk to my Father. I need my powers back. All of them. Now."

Raina took a few steps toward him, not liking the sound of that. "You don't need infernal powers. You have the Coven. You have me."

He turned on her again. There was a vicious look in his dark eyes. It was scary to see.

"Do I?" He looked her up and down. Took a broad step in her direction. "You wanted me at that party. How do I know you didn't set me up?"

The accusation struck deep. Her insides curdled. "I wouldn't do that," she said stiffly. "When the collar's off, you can search my mind if you don't believe me."

"I will."

———

The ride from the mansion to the hotel was smothered in pensive silence. When they arrived, they bypassed the main front entrance and went around back.

In the plaza behind the hotel the Coven was celebrating Samhain Eve. A huge bonfire burned. Many people, not just witches, danced and socialized. Near the back entrance of the hotel a long table held the remnants of the Silent Feast. Flowers and gifts for the departed covered a chair at the head of the table.

The group encountered Ligeia first. A black sheath dress hugged her shapely body, paired with black stilettos. A pointy netted hat obscured her face, but her outrage was plain when Michael showed her the collar.

"How?" the witch wanted to know.

Michael's jaw set. "I don't want to get into that now. I just want it off. Where's Pietre?"

Ligeia eyed him. "He's around. We'll find him. But I want to know what happened."

"Desiree tricked us." Michael's temper flared again. "She used Raina to distract me while her henchman snuck up on me. She has my boys, Ligeia, we don't have time for this!"

She slid a hard look at Raina. "Fine." Her tone implied the conversation wasn't over.

In no time she tracked down Pietre. He was with the triplets on the far side of the fire, chatting with other partygoers. His relaxed smile faded when he saw the group heading his way.

"Excuse me," he said to the people he was with and moved to intercept the new arrivals. "Trouble?"

Ligeia looked at Michael, who motioned to the collar at his throat.

"Oh, my." Pietre leaned in for a better look. Then he gave Michael a perverse little smile. "Never thought I'd see one of those on you."

Michael was not amused. "Can you get it off or not?"

"I'm sure I can," said Pietre. "But not here. Let's go to the Temple room."

CHAPTER 33

A few minutes later they were in the cool darkness of the Temple. Ligeia stayed behind to maintain an official presence at the bonfire. She would rather be in the sanctum with them, but priorities took precedence. Pietre lit the braziers then turned his attention to Michael. Raina and Trixie stood by, ready to help.

The warlock examined the collar, circling Michael as he did. "Hmm. Who put this on you?"

"Desiree," the prince grumbled. "Her lackey did, anyway. I'm pretty sure it's her enchantment, though."

"You don't seem drunk," observed Pietre. "How did they manage to get it on you?"

Michael glanced at Raina, who looked down at the floor. It didn't stop her feeling the weight of his feelings though.

"They distracted me."

Pietre examined the back closure, which had no visible lock or trigger mechanism. He gave it the lightest of tugs. It didn't budge.

"I keep telling you: Never let your guard down."

"I don't need lectures right now." Michael's frustration boiled over, heating his words. "I need you to get this thing off me. Her people took my boys. I have to find them!"

"I can do it," Pietre decided. "But it will take time." He looked over at the women. "We won't be needing your assistance."

"Are you sure?" Raina didn't want to go.

Not wanting to be left out, Trixie added: "There's nothing else I'd rather do than help."

Pietre waved them away without looking at them. He was focused on the collar. "There's nothing either of you can do, unless you have a way to track the children."

Raina had no way of doing that. Still, she wasn't going to admit defeat. If there was anything she could do to help fix things, she was going to try.

"I'll see what I can do."

She retreated. Trixie hesitated, then she left too. Out in the hall, she caught up with Raina.

"Where are you going?"

Raina sighed, suddenly weary. "I'm going to go change. This is a borrowed dress. It's already taken enough abuse."

Trixie glanced down at her own gown and ran a hand over her wrinkled skirt. "Not a bad idea. My feet are killing me. Are you going to go back out to the bonfire after you change?"

"I doubt it. I don't want to run into Ligeia."

"I'll manage Ligeia," Trixie offered.

Raina was unconvinced Ligeia could be managed, but she was too worn out and dejected to argue. They trudged upstairs, each stewing in her own troubled thoughts. At the landing they went their separate ways. Raina went to her room. Changed into more comfortable clothing. She wore only her clothes—nothing from Desiree's closet. She hung up the gown and tried to smooth it out. It needed cleaning, but that would have to wait.

As she brushed her hair, she replayed the events of the evening in her head. Picking apart each moment and questioning what she should have done differently. She'd been so easily played, letting Desiree use her. Why had she been so trusting?

The moment at the car was the worst. Seeing Michael's barely restrained rage was scary, but more awful than that was knowing she had been the cause for it. His heated words came back to her: Desiree had been collared before by Pietre.

Setting the hairbrush down, Raina went to the sideboard and pulled out the sketchbook. Flipped to the page with the drawing of people in cages. They were both wearing collars. The one in back, the person facing away from the camera. Could that be Desiree?

It was possible. More likely, though, it was the other "undead creature" the outcast witch freed.

When had Pietre collared Desiree? And why?

Raina shut the book and sighed. Massaged her forehead in a futile attempt to soothe away the headache she was getting. She wasn't sure why she even cared. Desiree claimed Pietre had taken her baby, which was horrible. But then the woman had kidnapped Michael's children. Two wrongs didn't make things right.

The boys. Were they scared? Hurt? What was happening to them? Where were they? Were they wondering why no one was coming to save them? Were they caged? Collared? Dead?

Her stomach cramping from anxiety, Raina smudged tears from her eyes. Desiree not only used her as a distraction to get a collar on Michael, but the party itself was a ruse to occupy him while someone stole the twins. Raina blamed herself. She couldn't have predicted things would turn out the way they did yet she still felt responsible. Ligeia had tried to warn her, and she hadn't taken the advice to heart.

She slipped her sandals on and left her room. She needed to do something. She didn't know what, but anything was preferable to sitting in her room alone with her thoughts.

—

As she came down off the steps in the foyer, Troy entered through the front doors. He was wearing his "Halloween costume" T-shirt and his cheeks were flushed—with cold or from drinking at Love's. He greeted her with a smile.

"Troy!" Raina hurried over to him.

His smile faded as he took in her worry. "What's wrong?"

She grabbed him in a fierce hug. Surprised, he hugged her back. The embrace brought a familiar electrical jolt with it which she ignored. She was too upset to care about such things.

"The party," she said. "It was a setup. Desiree put this collar thing on Michael that stops him using his powers. And she had someone take his kids. We don't know where the boys are."

Troy's expression darkened. "Holy shit. I never thought she'd sink so low." Then he realized Raina was crying. He gave her a squeeze. "Hey. It'll be okay. We'll figure this out."

"It's all my fault," Raina lamented. She couldn't stop the tears now. "I never should have asked Michael to that stupid party. I never should have trusted her."

"Hey," Troy repeated. He released her and made eye contact with her. "Desiree's no slacker. She's a witch who's dealt with Michael before. None of this is your fault."

Raina appreciated the support even though she didn't believe him. She pulled a shaky breath and released it. Mopped her face with her shirt tail to dry her tears. Crying wouldn't fix things. It didn't even provide relief or release. It just made her feel worse, physically and emotionally.

"Pietre's working on getting the collar off." She paused. "What happened with her and Pietre anyway? I heard he put a collar like it on her. Why did Pietre collar her?"

Troy held his hands up to fend off the questioning. "I don't... I don't really know. I mean."

"What?"

"I don't know. She bolted with Ligeia's prisoners. When they brought her back, Pietre wanted to make sure she couldn't run again until the baby was born. Something about... I guess there was some question of paternity?"

Paternity. "Was the baby his?"

"I honestly couldn't tell you. I'm just telling you what I picked up on the side."

There was too much Raina didn't know about the situation. She couldn't hope to outthink an adversary she didn't even understand. Overwhelmed with the possibilities and unable to string anything together, Raina shifted gears.

"Can you help me find the boys?" she asked. "You said you find things for people."

Troy's shoulders drooped. "Not without Michael's help. He gives me these marker things." He flexed his left hand. "Sort of like a map. Or homing device. It's hard to explain. Easier to show. But he hasn't been able to do it since his powers were taken away."

"Dammit!" Raina swore, at her wit's end. "They're out there somewhere and they need us!"

Troy took her by the shoulders and said quite sincerely: "We'll find them. Just as soon as Pietre gets the collar off."

He gave her another hug. She put her arms around him, and they stood like that for a while, supporting each other. Then he pulled back so he could look her in the eye again.

"Do you want a drink to take your mind off things?" His words were gentle. "Or we could go chill in my room."

"I don't think that would help." She wasn't certain, though, and it surfaced in her vulnerable tone.

"Can't hurt."

They looked at each other for a moment, then he leaned in and kissed her. His tongue pushed into her mouth, and she felt a strong zing, like licking a battery. It was electric and sensual, and she was tempted to let herself fall into the moment. If for no other reason than it was a pleasant distraction from her emotional train wreck. But she pulled away and stepped back.

"I'm sorry," he said. "I thought—"

She wrapped her arms around her middle. She didn't want to hurt him with her rejection. "No. It's okay. I just—"

He shoved his hands in his back pockets. Looked sheepish. "I've had a few drinks." He hesitated, then added: "I really do like you, though. Always have."

His honesty was both sweet and painful. "I... I know. I like you, too," she admitted. She liked him more than she wanted to say. There was such a thing as too much honesty. "But... I love Michael."

Troy's brows went up. Then a crooked smile took over. "Not surprised."

"I'm sorry."

"No worries. I understand. Really."

She looked down as unhappiness spread inside her. Being truthful certainly didn't make her feel better. "I probably ruined any hope I have with him tonight."

His smile grew. "I doubt it. But if things don't work out..."

"Troy." She was in no mood for jokes.

He lifted his hands again. "Just saying." Then: "Let's go out to the bonfire. Maybe roast some marshmallows."

"I don't think that's possible," she said. "The fire's too big."

She was still leery of running afoul of Ligeia but felt braver with Troy beside her. She couldn't stay inside. Sitting around idle would only lead to more stewing and unresolved worry.

"Never know till we try. All else fails, I can roast them for us." He made a grand motion toward the door.

She thought about it. "All right. But if Ligeia comes around, I'm hiding behind you. She was pretty pissed when she found out about the collar."

"I'm not afraid of her," Troy said boldly. "I've had far too many rum shooters."

———

"Raina!"

Though the hour was close to midnight, the party outside the Bradford was still going strong. Raina turned at the sound of a familiar voice in the crowd, astonished to hear it at the bonfire.

"Maurice?"

Sure enough, her former neighbor was ambling out of the crowd of revelers toward her, a yard glass in his hand. He wore a black outfit covered in patchy black feathers. A raven or a crow. A crow, she decided, because he was shorter than Troy. Crows were the small ones.

"Hi!" Maurice greeted.

He pushed his glass into Troy's hands and grabbed Raina in a tight hug. She hugged back, but as the embrace lengthened, she patted his shoulder to signal the end. He was drunk and didn't get the message. He just kept hugging her.

"I missed you so much!" he said.

"It's been a while." It was the best she could come up with.

"It's so good to see you again!"

She patted his back again. Awkward. "I'm surprised to see you here."

He squeezed her uncomfortably tight. Almost lost his balance. She had to bear his weight to stay on her feet. For an instant she genuinely feared he would knock them both over.

When he finally got his balance back, he let go. She took a step away from him, closer to Troy.

"How've you been?" Maurice asked, oblivious to her reaction or the fact that he was the cause.

She glanced at Troy. He'd ditched the yard glass during the extended hug. There was no sign of it. And though he smiled, Raina knew him well enough to notice it didn't reach his eyes. Despite being well into his cups, Troy's steady gaze was fixed on the shorter man. He had a similar look in his eyes at the masquerade after the chandelier came down.

"Oh. Well," she said to Mitchell. "I've been busy. I've been working a lot since I, uh, lost my house."

The conversation was devolving into the same old pattern. Meet, greet, small talk, then he would ask her out. After so much upheaval, it was strange to see that some things remained unchanged.

"I wondered what happened to you," Maurice said. He didn't pause to give her time to tell him. "Hey, if you're still looking for a place, I got into the old Cecil building. There's a flat next to mine available. I could help you move in."

Yep. Same old Maurice. Before, she found him tedious. Now, after so much stress, she found him unbearable.

"I've got a place." She didn't even try to sound friendly. "I'm living here. With Troy."

She sensed Troy's eyes on her now, and his surprise. Unfazed, she kept her attention on Maurice whose expression crumbled. She didn't take pleasure in crushing his hopes, but she did take hope in it.

"You are?"

He looked at Troy, who donned a more sincere smile and draped a casual arm around Raina's shoulders. Gave her a light squeeze.

"Yep," he agreed proudly. "Might be tying the knot soon. We'll send an invite to you at the Cecil."

"Er. Congratulations," Maurice said, deflating. "I'm, uh, glad you, um. You got things sorted out."

He pretended to see someone he knew across the plaza. Lifted a hand, nodded and smiled a fake smile. Then he turned that same thin smile on Raina.

"I should get going," he said. "It was nice seeing you again. Don't be a stranger."

He started to come at her for another hug, but Troy kept his arm around her shoulders. Passively thwarted, Maurice settled for shaking each of their hands then he wandered away. Soon he was lost to the party.

Raina waited until he was gone then she smiled at Troy. "Tying the knot?"

He grinned back and let go of her. "Got rid of him, didn't it?"

"Thanks for covering for me."

Dealing with Maurice's clinginess was something she'd made herself tolerate for the sake of getting along in her old neighborhood. It was a cycle that never should have gone on so long. She was glad it was finally over.

Troy gave an amiable shrug. "Anytime you need me to get rid of someone for you..."

His tone was flippant, but she suspected the offer was sincere. She studied him. Firelight danced on his face and in his eyes. She sensed his conviction beneath his glib demeanor.

"You mean that, don't you?"

He lifted his chin and shifted his weight. "Yeah. I do. Don't get me wrong. I don't like making people disappear. Or roasting them alive. But I protect what I care about."

His words brought back the night at Holly's party. He showed no hesitation burning the woman who attacked Michael. No remorse, either.

"I'm glad you're my friend," she said. "And not my foe."

He smiled. "You'd have to try hard to be my foe."

"I think I won't."

"There are people who think I'm a monster," he said more seriously. "And Michael, too."

Desiree among them. She'd made that plain to Raina.

"You're not monsters," Raina said, believing it now more than ever. "You do what you have to do. Just like anyone else does."

He got a funny look then, sort of wistful. "That's how I try to live in these weird times."

The wind picked up, carrying smoke from the bonfire their way. She reached for his hand and squeezed it. She didn't mind the zing of static electricity when she touched him.

"Me too."

CHAPTER 34

It took Pietre a little over half an hour to remove the cursed collar. Far too long for Michael's limited patience. By the time it came off he had a plan and was more than ready to act on it.

"You might want to rest," the warlock suggested. "Before you attempt to communicate with your Father."

"There's no time. It has to be now."

Michael only took time to change into his ceremonial robes and to grab some candles, his knife, and the Coven's sword before he left. The weapon was a longsword with a two-handed grip and double-sided blade. Etched into the cross guard was the phrase "*Non ducor — duco.*" I am not led — I lead.

He took off from the hotel in his Bugatti and sped to the nearby Elysian Park. Mount Baldy would have been a better choice, but it was too far away. He pounded his fist on the steering wheel, frustrated by his limitations. This wasn't the way things were supposed to be!

Tires squealed as he whipped across the broad plain of neglected pavement surrounding the old Dodger stadium. A few lonely tents dotted the otherwise empty parking lot, small homeless camps. His car sailed up onto the wide sidewalk outside the main gates and screeched to a halt. He hopped out, slamming the door behind him.

His anger fueled him. Made him potent. He was never more empowered than when he was angry. When he got to the rusted gates of the stadium entrance, he tore through them with a more violent version of the lock-breaking cantrip. A section of the barricade buckled and tore free. It flew inward and landed with a loud clatter. Sparks lit up the darkness where metal struck concrete.

He stalked out onto the untended dry land that was once a baseball field. A few feet from the center he sank the point of the sword deep into the earth and dragged it in a wide circle, tearing up dirt and dead grass as he went. Clouds gathered in the night sky, drawn to energy that was already taking shape.

Once the Circle was complete, Michael etched the sigil of Lucifer in the middle. It was crude but it was true to form. Stepping outside the Circle, he plunged the sword into the ground beside him. Taking the candles from the deep pocket of his robe, he set four of them at the cardinal points and lit them with a fifth one. When finished he set the fifth candle next to the sword. Pulled his athame from his belt and aimed the sharp point at his palm.

"Father!" he called. His voice echoed in the empty stands. "*Rachem alai Adonai. Betzel k'napheka an ir motsem machceh.* Hear my call!"

He speared the meat of his thumb with the knife. Blood welled up. He held it over the eastern candle where it dripped crimson drops that glistened in the candlelight. Focusing his thoughts and energy, he lifted his head.

"The blood is life. *Sanguis vita est.* Hear my call, Father, and come to me."

His words resonated though he didn't raise his voice. The wind stirred, whispering through the empty stadium seats.

He moved to the other candles, stopping at each to drip blood on the ground around them. He had to reopen the wound once as his body automatically tried to heal itself.

As he completed the circuit the wind grew stronger. The candles flickered and the atmosphere grew dense. Heavy, as it did before a storm. Above, the stars were blotted out by dark clouds. Ravens perched on the broken stadium floodlights ruffled their feathers and cawed, perturbed.

Within the Circle, the air coalesced and thickened. Energy swirled, darker than dark, and took on form.

Lucifer had arrived.

He was stunningly radiant. Pure dark beauty. A collapsed star gone supernova, he pulled at the senses even as he spread fear. Despite his urgency Michael was awestruck. He never got used to the presence of his Unholy Father. Lucifer was so dominating and otherworldly, it was impossible to not be fascinated by the fallen angel.

"Father." Michael forced himself out of his stupor. He wanted to dive right into his purpose for the summoning, but he remembered protocol. "Greetings."

"*Child,*" the celestial being returned.

He spoke not with his mouth but through word-feelings pressed directly into Michael's mind. It was like rolling thunder inside his skull. The first time they communicated that way his nose bled. The next few times Michael was left with a migraine. It was still uncomfortable, but experience taught him to control the flow.

"I need my powers back." There was no time for subtlety. "The rogue witch Desiree has my sons. Our sons. I need to get them back and I need my full strength to do it. Will you restore what you took from me?"

Lucifer gave him cool regard. Unmoved. "*So quickly you change your mind.*"

Michael's temper rose but he tamped it down with effort. "I haven't changed my mind about anything. I don't want to step down from this place or my role in it. I just want to rescue the twins. For that, I need the power I had. Will you *please* grant me what you took?"

"*I will give you what you desire,*" Lucifer agreed. "*As an exchange.*"

Michael's heart sank. Of course. It wasn't a deal with the devil unless both sides got something out of it.

"What do you want?"

Lucifer moved closer to the edge of the Circle. The candle nearest him dimmed, its light sucked into his presence. The physics of the material plane were meaningless in the company of infernal divinity.

"*I want your bride.*"

The demand confused Michael. "I have no bride."

"*Your companion,*" the fallen angel clarified.

A vision of Raina appeared in Michael's thoughts. He recoiled, mentally and physically. Of course she was his target. The prince knew she would be, yet the move still struck him like a physical blow.

"Why?" he demanded, outraged. "Why not anything else?"

"*She is most important to you.*" The flavor of the thought implied that much was obvious. "*I will take her for a night and a day.*"

"No! You killed Evangelina when you took her!"

"*The act of giving birth in your dwelling killed her.*"

"Because of what You did!" Michael was infuriated they were even discussing the matter. "She would have been fine if You hadn't planted Your seed in her alongside my baby!"

"*Do you accept the terms?*" the entity pressed.

Michael shut his eyes to rein in his emotions. He knew the diabolical angel could sense his struggle. He needed to react precisely. Not hysterically.

"There has to be another way. Something else You want."

"*There is nothing else of yours I desire.*" Lucifer was inflexible.

Michael's hands balled into fists. Desperate frustration rolled over him like a tidal wave. His head dropped in defeat. This whole meeting was pointless. Doomed from the start.

"I can't accept Your terms."

"*Then there is no bargain.*"

There was no venom in the statement. No judgment or pleasure. Just cold fact. There was to be no compromise or clemency. It was all or nothing.

"Depart then," Michael said. His disappointment and anger seeped into his words despite his attempt to restrain himself. "I will find my way without You."

"*Peace be with you, child.*"

Michael sensed the sardonicism. "Peace? I hate the word."

The Shakespearean dig wasn't lost on the angel. He smiled, amused at last. "*So you say.*"

Michael made a sweeping motion with one arm, extinguishing the candles. Lucifer disappeared, gone with the light.

...

Fatigue got the better of Raina and she retired to her room. She wanted to wait for Michael, but it was already past one bell. Losing sleep without having anything productive to do was literally a waste of time. Some rest, however minimal, was better than none at all. So, she tried to sleep.

Though bone-weary, she discovered she was still too worked up to relax. Too worried. After a few minutes fretting in the dark, she turned on the lamp and rose from bed. Reading would take her mind off of things. She started toward her collection of books but paused at the sideboard. Her fingers traced the handle of the drawer that held Desiree's sketchbook.

An uncanny warm breeze tickled her skin. The sultry smell of smoke and musky incense rode the eddy. Glancing at the sideboard mirror, she saw someone standing right behind her.

"Don't be afraid." His honeyed voice was as warm and smoky as the scent that preceded him.

She whirled around and her fear melted to wonder. The man she faced was nothing short of beautiful. Masculine perfection that could spark instant longing in the stoniest of souls. No artist could do justice to his allure. He was divine perfection.

He resembled Michael—rather, Michael resembled him. Tall and lean. Obsidian eyes. His hair was a similar shade of golden blond, tumbling loose to mid-torso. The white floor-length tunic he wore shifted around him as if made of fog, allowing enticing glimpses of his athletic form. A silvery-white cloak of feathers spilled down his back. No, not a cloak. Wings.

His strong aura was as easy to sense as it was to see him. Intense. Vast. Stunning. An intimidating wellspring of power a black hole would envy. Raina found herself mesmerized by him in spite of the awesome fear he inspired in her.

"Are you— You're..." she stammered.

"Light-bringer. The Daystar, Son of the Morning. I am Michael's sire." His smile pierced Raina's heart. "He came to me tonight."

He moved closer to her, putting off an unnatural amount of body heat. The exotic scent in the room came from him. He was the incense. He reached out and stroked her hair. It was a tender touch, imparting intimacy. Her own temperature crept up.

How did one address the infernal? In a scramble she recalled her lessons with Jeremiah.

"What do I owe the honor of Your presence?"

His satisfied expression assured her that was proper.

"Michael refused My assistance, but he will not succeed without help. He hopes to rely on your strength. It will not be enough. You... will not be enough, alone."

She wasn't quite following, but the gist of his words was cause for concern. "Michael asked for Your help?"

"I offered to restore him in exchange for a night and day in your company." He lifted a lock of her hair and touched it to his flawless lips. "He refused."

He was too close, muddling Raina's thoughts with his arousing scent and alluring presence. Even as she resisted the impulse to touch him, fleeting fantasies darted through her imagination. Visions of carnal pleasure with him. Fiery kisses and mind-blowing ecstasy. She craved him so strongly it frightened her.

He was messing with her mind, incidentally or deliberately. The temptation was real and oh so terribly inviting. This was danger on a level that surpassed anything she'd experienced. Her very existence as she knew it was on the line with no warning. A part of her was already in his arms, in her mind and heart.

"You don't need his permission." She instantly regretted the phrasing. She hadn't meant to give him the notion that she was approachable or willing.

The fallen angel chuckled. It was a rich, melodic sound. "We all have codes of conduct. I will not take what he wants without consent. Nor will I give without compensation. But without My help... he will fail."

He was so close, if she shifted her weight her hip would touch his. She yearned to do just that. To feel his arms around her, his firm body against hers. She hungered for the connection. For that one-way tumble into the unknown.

Was he bare beneath that misty robe? He looked to be. What would it be like to kiss him? To feel him inside her?

Mustering her will, she tried to drive back the persistent, impure thoughts. Focus. She needed to focus. She had to keep her guard up. Shore up her resolve. She was never one to jump headfirst into the unknown. He was messing with her on the most basic level. Yet it was almost impossible to clear her thoughts when she yearned for his touch as much as a starving person desired food. There was a fire that burned in her only he could quench.

"The Coven and I... we can help him," she said, sounding feeble even to her own ears.

He laughed. Not mocking, simply amused by her resistance. "By the time you rally, your enemies will have made their next move. Time is short."

She looked away. Staring at him wasn't helping. "We don't have a choice."

"But you do."

His fingers brushed her chin, lifting it to get her to look at him again. His touch was glorious. Melted her will. She gave only token resistance then she was falling into the fathomless darkness of his ancient eyes.

She needed him.

"I... don't..." She couldn't think beyond her need.

"You can consent," he said. "If you agree, I will restore him *pro tempore*. He will be able to do what he needs to reclaim his children and mentor."

He leaned in closer, his lips bare inches from hers. She could feel his warm breath on her skin. Her heart thundered with wild desire. Her lips parted, breath coming quick and shallow.

The door to the hall swung open and banged against the wall. Michael had bypassed the lock. He wasted no time taking in the scene. He'd sensed his Father's presence the moment he got to the hotel. The sight was enough to send him into an intense rage that defied logical thought.

"Get away from her." Not a threat, but certainly a command.

The fallen angel didn't budge, though his gaze slid over to Michael. He sensed the challenge implicit in those words. "Raina and I are talking, child. If she wishes Me to depart, she only needs say so."

It was the first time in years Michael heard Lucifer use a spoken voice. The infernal entity could be easy on the senses when he chose to be.

Raina looked at Michael then at the fallen angel. She didn't want to tell him to leave, but the presence of the Lord Prince helped clear her head. Some. His being there reminded her of her priorities—and concerns.

"I need some time. Please."

The Morning Star appraised her anew, intrigued. He smiled a perfect smile. "Very well. But remember: Time is short. I will listen for you only until evening comes again."

The vapors of his robes swirled thicker and thicker, swallowing him up. When the mist cleared he was gone.

Michael rushed to her, dispelling the last of the fog. He took her by the upper arms and studied her face with open concern.

"Are you all right? He didn't do anything to you, did He?"

She expected him to be angry. Far from angry, he was worried about her. She had come so close to caving to temptation.

The effects of overpowering lust still lingered, though it was subsiding. Her eyes stung with tears of guilt and regret she quickly blinked away.

"I—no. I'm fine. He wanted to make a deal with me."

Michael's head dropped. "Son of..." He looked at her again. "Did you agree to anything?"

She shook her head. He pulled her into a fierce hug.

"Whatever he says, don't listen to him." Michael pushed her back again to see her face. His was grim. "He destroys the things I love."

The confession pierced her heart. She put a hand over his. "I love you too, Michael."

He froze. Stared at her. A flurry of emotions crossed his features, too quick for her to define. Pain surfaced last.

"I don't know what to do." His voice cracked. He released her and ran his hands over his hair. "I don't want to hurt you."

She took one of his arms with both of hers, hugging it close as she guided him over to the bed to sit.

"We'll figure this out. Together."

CHAPTER 35

"Our options are limited," Michael said. He looked at Raina, troubled. "We can conduct a Wild Hunt. Or there's... a ritual. One that would allow me to absorb your personal power for my own. The ritual... reopens doors that He closed to me."

The way he put it set off warning bells for Raina. "Your Father was of the opinion my 'strength' alone wouldn't be enough. That it would take too long. I should have asked Him why. I didn't even think to."

Michael sighed. "I hate to agree with Him, but He's probably right. The energy transfer would be immediate, but..." He faltered. "The effects aren't. And it would likely keep you bedridden for at least a day afterward. It isn't easy."

"But I've learned how to transfer my energy to others," she pointed out. "It didn't bother me at all. It was... fun."

Fun. That was one way to put it. But clarification at this point would do no good.

"There's a big difference between passing energy to another person and what happens in the ritual. It... drains the subject. Completely. In ways you can't imagine. It's great for the recipient, but hard on the donor."

She could tell there was something he wasn't saying. And what he did say was troubling. She drew a knee up and hugged it to her chest. "Well. I can't be much help afterward if I'm bed ridden."

"The Wild Hunt will take time," he said. "But is marginally safer."

"Are you sure we shouldn't talk to your Father again?" she proposed. "I mean. Didn't you say you'd be able to find Jeremiah and the twins if you had your powers back?"

"Yes. But I'm not willing to have you pay the price."

"That should be my choice to make."

He took her hand then and looked at her. Concern darkened his features. "The reason Evangelina is in my ring now is because He took her from me. I will not let that happen to you, Raina."

She squeezed his hand. "I understand. And I appreciate your position. But what if we made it part of the deal? That He couldn't do anything that might hurt me?"

Michael's frown deepened. He didn't like what he was hearing. "He would find a way to get around any promise He made. He's the Father of Lies. Don't you understand? He *is* Original Sin. He shows you what you want to see, tells you what you want to hear. He ensnares and then takes what He wants. Has He clouded your mind so much?"

"No," she insisted. Though he wasn't entirely wrong. Some wicked part of her still yearned for the fallen angel. "But the people who have your family aren't going to wait. We need to do something now. Not in five hours or however long it will take to get the Wild Hunt under way."

"No." Michael released her hand and got to his feet. Irritated. "I'm going to ready the Wild Hunt."

"Michael, I want to help you," she said as he started for the door. "I really think we should ask your Father—"

"No!" He stopped and turned on her but didn't come back. "Do NOT talk to Him. That isn't an option."

"It's my choice," she reasserted.

Michael's lips pressed together in a firm line. His jaw set. "Don't, Raina. I mean it."

He turned and left then, shutting the door hard enough to rattle the floor-length mirror.

She sat there on the edge of the bed, gripping the blanket tight with both hands. "Way to work this out together," she muttered.

For a fleeting moment she considered praying for guidance. But she didn't know who to pray to. The Coven revered the God and Goddess, but who they were was a matter of opinion.

Some of the Family believed the Powers to be Pan and Diana. Some thought of them as Samael and Lilith. Others believed them to be the masculine and feminine aspects of a single nameless deity. At least one person she knew believed the Powers were within—the source of the essence they used to manipulate energy.

Whatever or whoever might answer any prayer she had right now would likely only stir up more trouble.

Raina sighed. It was close to two bells in the earliest part of the morning. She had until the evening to decide what to do. She should be tired, but she was more alert than ever. She couldn't sleep if she wanted to.

She decided to go with Michael. Perhaps his way would work. And if they got close to evening without results, she could intervene. It seemed the best plan of action.

———

The hotel was alive with activity when Raina went downstairs. In the lobby several people milled about. Michael was at their center with Pietre and Trixie. They faced away from the foyer and as Raina approached, she was privy to their conversation.

"I'll start the ritual to summon the Hounds," said Pietre. "Will you be bringing Troy and Raina as well?"

"You shouldn't bring her," Trixie said. "You still don't know if she set you up."

She stood close to him, her hand on his shoulder. Practically pressed to his side. Her body language spoke volumes. It dawned on Raina then that Trixie was not her friend. She'd been blind to the rival right beside her.

"Possibly," Michael said. "But—"

"I didn't," Raina interrupted. The three turned toward her. "I told you to search my mind if you don't trust me. Do it now."

Trixie's reaction was priceless, a blend of anger and alarm. Though Raina picked up on it she kept her eyes on Michael. He glanced at Trixie then he looked at Raina again. He stepped closer to her, intense with emotion.

"Open your mind to me." It was a simple command. Not hostile but quietly dominating.

She spread her hands. She was as open as she could be. He stared at her, and she felt the familiar press of his thoughts. Unlike before he wasn't gentle. He invaded her mind completely, flooding her with his presence. Rapidly sifted through her memories, contacting everything she experienced in the past weeks.

The process was so fast and thorough, it overwhelmed her. A blur of impressions rushed by as Raina's memories played in super fast-forward. She wobbled in his grasp, woozy. Several times Trixie sprang to the forefront of the flood of recollections.

Abruptly he pulled back and her mind was her own again. He held onto her, steadying her while she regained her sight and balance. He wasn't looking at her, though. He was staring at Trixie.

"Now you."

The black-haired woman blinked, surprised. "Me?"

"You." Michael stepped into her personal space. "Don't make me repeat myself."

Pietre looked on, visibly engaged by the unfolding drama. He enjoyed watching people squirm.

Trixie flicked a look Raina's way. Was that fear in her eyes? Then the other woman shut her eyes and shut out the room.

"I'm ready," she said.

Michael put his hands on her shoulders and focused on her. Intent. Seconds passed and his expression tightened. His jaw set with the strength of his determination. Trixie tensed up. Went pale.

Without warning one of his hands flew to her throat and squeezed. Her eyes snapped open. There was no mistaking the fear there now.

"It was you!" he snarled.

"No, Michael! Please!" she squealed. She flailed an arm in Raina's direction. "It was her! I was trying to get rid of *her*! I never meant for anything to happen to you!"

Michael kept his eyes on Trixie and his hand around her throat. She put her hand over his, but she didn't dare pry at his fingers.

"I'm sorry, my Lord!" she said, words strained due to his grip. "Forgive me! I didn't know Desiree planned to collar you. I swear!"

"You did nothing to stop it." His bicep twitched with the restrained urge to squeeze tighter. "I should kill you now."

"Do you know where Desiree is?" Pietre's placid calm was a direct contrast to Michael's barely contained rage.

Raina rubbed the spot between her brows. Though Trixie had never been a welcome wagon, she had no idea the woman disliked her so much. Enough to risk everything just to be rid of her. It was a shock, but it also hurt to be so despised for little reason.

"No," Trixie said. "I don't. But I can find them. I'm sure of it. Please! Give me a chance!"

Michael's grip tightened. Her face reddened as he cut off her airflow and circulation.

"If she can locate them," Pietre said with the same mellow lack of concern. "Perhaps we should let her. We can summon the Hell Hounds in the meantime."

Raina stared at Trixie's purpling face, too stunned to effectively hate her yet.

Michael held on a bit longer then released Trixie with a rough shove. "Go. Find them. Tell me where they are."

The woman staggered. She gulped air and massaged her bruised neck. She didn't answer but nodded vigorously. Then she stumbled toward the front entrance.

"Trixie," Michael said. When she paused his next words were ice. "Don't do anything you'll regret."

She looked at him wide-eyed then she hurried out.

"You're just going to let her go?" Raina looked from the door at Michael.

"I'm sending Troy after her. If she tries to run or do anything other than find Desiree, she will suffer." He gave her a long look then, a peculiar expression crossing his features. Then he turned to Pietre. "Start the summons for the Hounds. Bring the triplets. We'll need them."

"And me?" Raina asked.

When he looked at her, Michael got that funny look again. Like there was something he wanted to say but was holding back. "Do as you wish."

The answer stung but it also irritated her. "I want to come on the Hunt."

"I don't think that would be wise." He started across the room to speak with Troy.

Refusing to be brushed off, Raina followed him. People gave him space, but she had to elbow a few to keep up with him.

"You said I could do as I wish," she reminded him. "I wish to go with you."

"I don't have time to argue with you," he said, not slowing.

"Then don't argue! I'm coming."

He flicked an agitated glance her way. She was angering him, but she didn't back down. It was too important.

"Fine," he said. "Be ready when we're set to go, or we'll leave without you."

She stopped. Watched as he talked to Troy. His shift in attitude toward her baffled her. Hurt all over again, her irritation turned inward. Why did she always fall for men who hurt her? It was an inconvenient habit. One she seriously ought to break.

All around the room people were gearing up and heading for the back exit. Many were armed. Most were wearing clothing that could take a beating: Leather coats and pants. Boots.

She looked down at her nightshirt and pajama bottoms. She needed something fit for a fight. Even if she didn't engage directly, it would be better to wear something she could move in. Clothes that couldn't get snagged or trip her up. As she hurried toward the stairs, she ran a hand over her hair. She needed to do something about it, too.

—

Raina threw on jeans and an old T-shirt tucked into her waistband. Grabbed the leather jacket she'd borrowed from Troy but didn't put it on yet. She left it near the door so she wouldn't forget it then went into the bathroom. Grabbing a couple of hair bands, she braided her hair and bobby-pinned it around her head like a headband. It was sloppy but it did the job. Nothing to grab.

As she worked on her hair, she tried to figure out her plan. While she'd had some training, she wasn't cut out to battle an experienced witch and whatever Desiree had waiting for them. Michael knew it, too. But she couldn't stay behind. She would go nuts waiting and wondering.

She would have to wing it and hope she didn't have to resort to calling on infernal help. Grabbing Troy's jacket, she hurried downstairs to join the others.

CHAPTER 36

Before Michael lost his powers, tracking people was a piece of cake. He would place a sigil in the palm of Troy's hand that acted as a radar or beacon. The closer to the center of his palm the red dot got, the closer he was to his quarry.

Troy had to rely on stealth. Trixie was a few blocks ahead of him in her little corn-powered coup. He rode his motorcycle with the lights off, trying to stay back far enough to keep out of her rearview mirror. It was hard to tell how far that was, so he played it safe.

They passed town square, which was dead at this late hour. Even Love's Pub was dark. The streets were empty except for the clammy fog. It reminded him of the time following the disasters.

Creeped him out. The town was safer now and the fog thinner, but the urge to avoid the night streets still lingered.

The first stop Trixie made was at an old Presbyterian church minutes away from the First Church. Troy used his tank-mounted CB to radio their location back to the Bradford. He'd just finished the transmission when she came out of the cathedral. She took the steps two at a time and got back into her car.

Soon they were on the move again.

"We're on the road," Troy radioed Alec, who manned the receiver at the hotel. "I think she's got a bead on their location now. She's driving pretty fast. I'll stay on her unless Michael wants me to double back to the Church."

"Copy that," Alec replied. "I'll update him. If he wants you to change course I'll let you know. Otherwise, I'll keep radio silence until I hear from you."

"Roger," said Troy. "Over and out for now."

He dropped the receiver into the magnetic holster behind him and leaned into the ride to catch up.

———

Fifteen minutes later, Michael paced near the bar. It would take time to find Desiree, but it had been forever since Alec updated him last.

"This is taking too long," he grumbled. "I should have gone with Troy."

"Do you want me to check on Pietre's progress?" Raina offered. She sat on a barstool at the midway point of his restless track.

"No. He'll let me know when he's finished, though you'll hear the hounds before then, I'm sure."

He walked the length of the bar and started back again, his hands jammed in his pockets. He wanted a drink but needed his wits sharp. He hadn't slept. He wasn't confident he'd remain alert if he drank.

"What are you going to do when you find Desiree?"

"Kill her."

His bluntness gave Raina pause. She tried again. "I mean... She has the boys and Jeremiah. She's not going to just let you kill her."

Michael didn't want to think about the details. He wanted to be mobilized already. "I'll figure it out when I get there."

"Isn't that dangerous? We should have some sort of—"

"I'll figure it out when I get there." He repeated with emphasis. His warding look warned her to back off. The last thing he needed was a lecture.

She frowned and hugged her middle. "I can't help you if I don't know what to do. No one can."

"I don't know what we're facing yet, Raina," he snapped. "Until I do, I can't plan. Sorry if that inconveniences you."

"It's not..." She huffed a short breath. "I'm just trying to help."

"I didn't ask for your help."

Raina wavered. Torn between backing off and digging in, she chose to dig in. She hopped down from the barstool and put herself right in his pacing path. He stopped. Glowered at her.

"We'll get through this," she said. "Together. If you want to leave now, then let's leave. Pietre can lead the rest to where we are once he's finished his ritual."

Michael wasn't happy, but her words cooled his temper somewhat. He thought about it then nodded. She made sense.

"You want to go get the car while I tell Alec?" she said.

He gave her another nod. She started to turn away, but he grabbed her wrist. Pulled her in close for a short, fierce kiss. Then he headed for the door. Each step brought him closer to saving his boys.

—

Troy marveled at the impressive monster that was the I-10. When the world ended, it took most of the population with it. He'd never seen the city in its before-time when it needed such a wide river of pavement. Eight lanes divided in the center by a concrete barricade. Seemed excessive in the absence of traffic, especially in the dead of night.

The radio crackled to life.

"Hey, Fireball." Raina's voice came over the speaker on the private channel. "North Star here with Prince Charming. What's your twenty?"

Troy grinned and grabbed the receiver. "North Star, huh?"

"Better than the handle I had as a kid. My mom's boyfriends called me Short Stack."

"I like North Star. Definitely an improvement over pancakes," he agreed. "I'm up on the Santa Monica. Just crossed the San Diego. Looks like our little bird's flying to the beach, but that's a guess. I'm hanging back so she doesn't get nervous."

"We've cleared the Walls," Raina said. "We're coming to join you. The rest will meet us when the dogs are ready."

"Ten-four. Should I back it down?"

There was a pause, then Raina came back. "Prince Charming says negatory. We'll catch up to you. Keep on doing what you're doing."

"Roger," said Troy. He sped up. "Watch out for the hole at the Overland exchange. Don't know what happened there, but it's a big 'un."

"Copy. Thanks for the heads-up."

—

"She's exited at 14th, south bound," Troy's staticky voice came over the CB in Michael's car minutes later. "Heading into Woodlawn Cemetery. Should I keep on her?"

Michael shook his head. His eyes were locked on the dark, foggy road ahead. "I know the place. It's in a residential area. Tell him to park someplace nearby. Tell him... tell him to meet us at the southeast corner of the cemetery. And tell him to relay the location back to Pietre."

Raina squeezed the button on the CB receiver. "Prince Charming says negatory. Find a place to park and meet us outside the southeast corner of the boneyard. Pass the word on to Home Base."

Moments later Troy responded. "If I do that, I'll lose visual. You sure you want me to?"

"Yes, I'm sure," Michael said peevishly, as though Troy were in the car with him. "There are only two exits from the place, both of them on the south side. If we lose her, we can send Pietre and the dogs to find her. I have a plan."

"That's an affirmative, Fireball," Raina paraphrased into the receiver. "Prince Charming has a plan."

"Ten-four, North Star. See you guys soon."

It wouldn't have surprised her if Michael complained about her adapting his responses, but he didn't. He didn't even seem to notice. The car sped up, flying down the expressway toward their destination.

—

The sprawling L-shaped cemetery beside the freeway ate up eight blocks. One of the oldest graveyards in the abandoned part of the city, ivy choked its fences. Thin fog swirled over the ground, turning trees and gravestones into indistinct silhouettes. The night sky was black with clouds. The moon and stars wanted nothing to do with what was happening down below.

Michael parked between the two southern entrances. A clattering of pinfeathers sounded overhead when he and Raina got out of the car. A large flock of ravens circled down, winging around them in a fast-moving swarm. Raina pressed closer to Michael. She'd gotten used to the birds following them, but they'd never done that before. To the eye, Michael just stood there, yet Raina sensed his energy moving with the spiraling flock. Communing with them. The tornado of birds angled up and flew out over the graveyard. Apart from the rattle of their wings, they were silent.

"Wow," Raina murmured. Now that they were gone, she found their coordination impressive. "Are they going to look for Trixie?"

"They're going to look at everything. There's Troy."

Though Michael said to meet them on the corner, the dark-haired man was jogging their way. Rather than intercept him, Michael remained where he was. So, Raina stayed with him.

"I saw a car leave," Troy said when he got to them. "I was already away from my bike so I couldn't radio you. There was a guy behind the wheel. Didn't see anybody else in the car."

"Shit." Michael thought for a moment, then: "Shit. Okay."

A lone raven winged back over the fence. It gave a couple of raspy caws before flying back to the cemetery. Relief flashed across the prince's face, then he turned resolute.

"Desiree's at the central mausoleum. We need to move in now before anything else goes down."

"We're not going to wait for the others?" asked Raina.

"No time." Michael was already making long strides toward the nearest entrance. "We need to engage before she decides to run. Be ready for anything."

"No sweat." Troy was being cheeky, but there was an authentic air of 'been there, done that' to his attitude.

"Don't roast her. I want her taken alive."

"Got it. Bend but don't break her."

"Raina," Michael said to her. "I need you to do whatever I say. I may not have time to explain myself. Can you do that?"

She blinked fast. Working on the fly was not her strong suit. But what choice did she have? "I... can. Yes. Okay." Though she didn't like agreeing to such a broad scope, there was no time for strategy.

He gave a short nod and trotted up the long paved lane into the foggy cemetery.

—

Darkness shrouded the vast graveyard. Towering maple, ash, and hemlock trees were shadows in the misty night, their presence made known as the wind hissed through their branches. Shorter trees, Devil's walking stick, lined the driveway. Their dagger-like spines tore at the group when they passed too close.

The only light came from the mortuary at the center of the cemetery. Flame-filled industrial barrels flanked the entrance. The lower windows of the blocky building were lit as well. Along the edge of the roof dozens of ravens marked the place with their presence. Michael's group moved fast over the dead grass alongside the main path to reduce the amount of noise they made. Despite having to avoid the thorny trees, it was a wise choice—until something hit Raina's legs from the front. Something heavy. She sat down hard in the ditch.

She found herself face to face with a dead body. Only this body was moving. Badly decayed, it rasped a snarl. Grabbed at her, dry lips curled back from its gnashing teeth in a permanent leer. She scrambled back from it in a crab-crawl. It grabbed her leg.

There was a sharp clang as Troy's machete came down on the corpse's arm, cleaving off its hand. Michael was right there too. He stomped the thing's head, caving it in. Raina scrabbled to her feet. The severed hand was still locked onto her ankle. She kicked it off and punted it into the fog.

"God! I hate zombies!" Now that the thing was gone, she could be properly disgusted. She shuddered. She could still feel its bony grip.

"You okay?" Troy asked.

Michael paused. "They're everywhere."

"I'm all right," Raina said, then she looked around too and saw the horrible truth.

There were corpses all around them, cloaked by the fog. White bones stood out where skin had peeled or been eaten away by scavengers. Several crawled their way, too far gone to rise or move fast. The one that hit Raina had used her forward momentum to its advantage. Clever for something with little brain left.

"They're probably from the mass uprising a few years ago," said Michael, moving to the paved path. "Stay alert."

"I hate zombies," muttered Raina. She shuddered again and joined him.

"Now that we know they're there, we can easily dodge 'em," Troy said, far too chipper.

His optimism wasn't reassuring. She didn't fear the shambling undead. Even before lessons with Ligeia at the cemetery she could handle them. She just hated them. The disconnect between the body and the person who had piloted it was unsettling. Dead flesh was gross, even if it wasn't moving.

"Let's go," Michael urged.

They stuck to the road after that.

CHAPTER 37

Though the group passed several writhing corpses on their way to the central building, none gave them trouble. Most were so far gone they'd lost the putrid scent of rot. Instead, a mustiness rose from the bones. Old death.

At the doors of the mortuary Michael paused. Listened. Tried without success to use senses out of his reach. There were no wards on the doors. Apart from that he couldn't tell what was ahead. Marching into an unknown situation wasn't ideal, but there was no help for it.

"Get ready," he told Raina and Troy.

He pulled the heavy oak door open.

Golden light flooded out of the hall, pushing back the night. Moving cautiously, first Michael entered, then Raina. Troy brought up the rear.

The columbarium within was a cold stone vault. Torches lined the walls, guttering and gleaming on a floor of dark, polished granite. White marble slabs covered hundreds of niches where urns of the dead rested. At the end of the hall a statue of the Blessed Mother stood. Beyond her an arched doorway yawned into darkness.

In the center of the vault was a large pile of wood. There was a pole erected in it where Zachariel and Gabriel were tied, gagged, and blindfolded. They still wore their Halloween costumes, grubby and ruined from their mistreatment.

Desiree stood beside them in a white sheath dress, a black satchel on her hip and a windproof lighter in her hand. A bandage around her left arm was evidence of injury from the Halloween party. A chalk Circle of Protection surrounded her.

"Stop right there." She stroked the flint of the lighter. It sprouted a bright flame. "Unless you want them extra crispy."

The group stopped.

"Let them go." Michael's words were steady and firm, masking his rage at seeing his sons treated in such a fashion. It would do them no good for him to lose control at this crucial moment.

"Come on, Desiree," Troy plied. "This isn't you. You wouldn't hurt kids."

The witch was unmoved. "They aren't children. They're the spawn of Satan. But their fate isn't mine to choose. It's yours, Michael."

She focused on him as she held the lighter over the pyre. Reaching into the bag at her hip, she pulled out a collar similar to the one Henri had put on him at the Halloween party. She bent and slid it across the floor in his direction. He stopped it with his foot.

"Put it on," Desiree said as she straightened. She lifted her chin, proud and haughty. "Surrender to me. Denounce your leadership of the Coven."

He picked up the metal band. It was cold. Heavy.

"You really do intend to take over," he said.

Suddenly her plan was clear to him. If he did as she said, she would use him as a pawn to make the High Priest and Priestess step down. Perhaps that would work on Ligeia, but he doubted it. Pietre was even less likely to care. Desiree's faith in their loyalty to him was grossly misguided.

"Yes. I do. Ligeia was an idiot to let you and Pietre in. We never should have come here."

"No," Michael said. "*You* shouldn't have."

He moved then, faster than the others could track. Diving into a slide that propelled him through the line of chalk, he broke through the Circle. His body smudged away a good quarter of the chalk markings and he slammed into Desiree, knocking her feet out from under her. The lighter flew from her hand.

Michael hoped it would tumble harmlessly to the floor, but it landed in the pile of wood. The pyre burst into flame. She must have put combustible fluid on it for it to catch so fast.

There was a wild scramble as he tried to get the collar on Desiree. Wriggling violently, she opened her mouth to say something. It could be a lynchpin. Michael slapped his free hand over her mouth. The move silenced her but made it even harder to wrestle the collar onto her neck.

"Ring of fire!" he hollered. He only hoped the others would understand.

———

At his call Raina shook off her shock and, realizing what he must mean, she made a grabbing motion at the fire. She seized the energy of the flames. She found she could pull a column of fire from the pyre, but the wood quickly reignited. All she was doing was spreading the fire more.

"Troy!"

He sprang into motion, extending both arms toward the bonfire. He tried to help her move it, but the wood was stubborn. The fire wasn't his and was harder to control. Though they could draw the flames away from the boys, the wood pile continued to burn.

"Fuck!" he swore.

What they were doing wasn't working. Raina had no time to think of a better plan. Zach and Gabe were in danger, crying out in fear as the fire crackled around them. She had to do something.

"Keep it away from them!" she said to Troy.

Meanwhile, Michael wrestled with Desiree. She was not about to give up. He got a knee on one of her arms, pinning it, but she lashed out with the other, her athame in hand. The short dagger struck his left eye, blinding it. He grunted in pain and flipped her over onto her belly to limit her range with the blade. Blood from his ruined eye dripped off his face.

Raina ran to the pyre, took a deep breath and flung herself through the wall of flames. Heat seared her exposed hands and face. She didn't feel it. Her focus was on the twins. She had to trust Troy would keep the fire a safe distance away from them.

Pulling out her athame, she hacked at the rope that held them to the post. It was taking too long. Troy was keeping the flames away from the boys, but the heat was uncontained. Turning, she concentrated on the wood and gave it a hard psychic shove, thrusting her left arm out to reinforce the move.

Flaming wood exploded outward in a spray of sparks, igniting her sleeve. She slapped the fire on her arm to smother it. Then she turned and shoved at the other side of the pyre. Charcoal and embers scattered.

One large fiery chunk of wood skidded near Troy. Grabbing it, he ran to where Michael struggled with Desiree. He gave her a hard whack to the head. The hit dazed her long enough for Michael to shut the collar around her throat. He punched her for good measure.

Raina cut through the rope that bound the kids. With a final slice, it fell free. The boys yanked off the blindfolds and tore off the gags.

"Raina!" Gabe screeched.

He burst into tears and grabbed her leg. She had to pick him up to stop him climbing her side. Zach clung to her other hip. He wasn't crying, but his eyes were wide. Full of anger.

Weighed down by the children, Raina shuffled away from what remained of the pyre. She was starting to hurt, but she didn't stop to assess her injuries. Though the scattered fires wouldn't burn the stone mortuary they were still dangerous to the living. The boys needed to be as far away from the fire as possible.

"Raina, bring me the rope," Michael ordered.

She went to set Gabe down in a safe spot. He wailed in protest and held fast to her neck.

"I have to put you down," she insisted. "Daddy needs help."

"I'll get it," said Zach.

Before she could stop him, he let go of her hip and dashed back to the pole, weaving around the smaller fires. He grabbed the rope and ran it over to his father, who was sitting on Desiree. Michael took it and quickly bound the woman's hands. He wasn't gentle.

A howl rose in the distance, a terrible sound that caused everyone to stop what they were doing and listen. It was an unearthly racket that sent a bolt of primal fear through all who heard it. Michael shook off the effect first.

"Pietre's coming."

He got up and tied Desiree's hands to her feet. The bonds were tight. She wouldn't be able to stand. Once he had her secured, he grabbed the cloth she gagged his children with. Shoved a wad of it into her mouth and fixed it in place with another strip. Beyond the doors, the frightful baying of the hell hounds got louder. Closer.

Michael looked at his sons with his good eye. Gabe was still in Raina's arms. Zach had returned to her side, though he was no longer clinging. The boy watched the door, leery of the approaching hellhounds.

"Your eye!" Raina said, horrified.

"It's already healing," Michael dismissed. "Are you all right?"

Zach nodded stoically. His father wasn't afraid, so he wasn't going to be either.

Gabe looked at his brother and then at Michael.

"I'm hungry."

If Gabe could think about food, he was all right. "We'll eat soon," Michael promised. "We need to find Father Jeremiah first."

As the adrenaline rush subsided, Raina was beginning to feel her burns. She refused to stop and assess the damage, though. Focusing on that would only make it hurt more, and she had no time for that. The immediate danger was over, but they weren't safe yet. Troy kicked out the small fires, quashing them under his sturdy leather boots.

The oak door swung open and Pietre came in, Tisi by his side. Beyond him in the darkness of the graveyard were disturbing sounds, growls and snarls. The crunch of old bones.

Tisi shut the door on the grotesque noises.

"Pietre," Michael greeted, genuinely glad to see the barefoot warlock.

"Looks like you've had quite an adventure," Pietre observed on seeing the state of things. "Are you...?" He motioned to the prince's injured face.

Michael rubbed at the blood on his chin. "I'll be fine. Bitch stabbed me in the eye."

"Ouch."

"Find out what Desiree knows. We still need to find Jeremiah... and Raina's necklace."

"It would be my pleasure." The older man smiled. As much as he loved a good hunt, it was even more fun to play with prey that couldn't get away. He closed in on the trussed witch.

"We should get these guys home," Troy suggested, hooking his thumb at the twins. They didn't need to see the witch tortured. "Want me to take them?"

Michael threw him a look. "On your motorcycle? I don't think so."

"Aww," said Gabe. He liked Troy's motorcycle.

"Take the Bugatti," Michael said. He fished the keys out of his pocket and gave them to Troy who traded him the motorcycle keys. "Head for the mansion. And drive *safe*. Anything happens to it or my kids..."

"No worries," Troy grinned. He tossed the keys and caught them, then looked at the boys. "How fast do you want to go?"

Gabe wiggled until Raina put him down. He ran to Troy, excited by the idea of a car ride with someone who . "Can I shift the gears?"

"No," Michael said. He was already regretting the decision to let Troy take his car. "Drive safe," he repeated as Troy left with the boys.

The three paused outside the door when the hell hounds snarled at them. The infernal dogs looked even worse than they sounded. Huge, hairless beasts with fiery eyes, slavering mouths, and huge fangs. Alec and Meg held them back with thick black chains. Skirting the hideous pack, Troy hurried the twins to the street and Michael's car.

CHAPTER 38

Pietre crouched down in front of Desiree. His smile took on a cruel edge, his eyes alight.

"Sweet little Desiree," he cooed, rolling her to her side. "Always such a thorn in everyone's side. Michael wants to know where the priest is and what you've done with Raina's bauble."

He reached around and untied her gag. She spat out the wad of cloth Michael had further stifled her with. She coughed involuntarily, almost retching. Then she glared at the warlock. For a moment she didn't say anything, warring with her own pride and fear.

"I do hope you make this difficult." Pietre stroked a finger down the side of her face, an intimate and strangely gentle touch. I've missed the sound of your screams."

When he reached her ear he hooked the tip of his finger in it, right above her earlobe. Then he pulled. Hard.

She squealed as sharp pain lanced through her ear canal. "The necklace is in the chapel with the priest!" she bleated. "Henri tied him up!"

Pietre clucked his tongue disapprovingly. Releasing her ear, his hand moved to her hair. He lifted one of her braids and stroked her cheek with it. "You disappoint me, my dear. I prefer it when you're stubborn."

She tried to pull away from him. It didn't work.

"Who is Henri?" he prompted.

"A traitor," she spat. That information she gave more than willingly. "He's a warlock from the Garden who promised to help me in exchange for the book. He ran like a coward when he found out Michael was coming. He and Trixie both."

Pietre tipped his head, interest sparking. "Book?"

Michael had tried without success to heal Raina's burned hand. Both looked over. Book?

A vague sense of satisfaction crossed Desiree's face. "I'll tell you about the book if you let me go."

That made Pietre laugh. "You're hardly in the position to make demands."

"I'm not demanding," she said, a touch of desperation bleeding into her tone. "I'm bargaining. I don't want to be caged again."

He released her braid and stroked her cheek with his knuckles. She didn't try to duck him this time. His hand travelled down to her collarbone where his thumb settled into the divot between her clavicles. He pressed just hard enough to make her squirm.

"Tell me about the book," he said. "And I promise you won't be put in a cage."

He threw a glance Michael's way. The prince gave a slight nod.

"Henri took a book from the house where the necklace was. A grimoire. The necklace holds the key to the book."

"Interesting," said Pietre. He eased off pressure on his thumb. "Good girl."

He rose and went over to Michael and Raina, his smile smug.

"Our prodigal has been quite forthcoming. I thought if you don't execute her, I could keep her in the Bunker with Taylor."

"You can have her," dismissed Michael. "Just make sure she can't go anywhere or do anything."

Pietre nodded. "The grimoire." He looked at Raina. "What do you know of it?"

She shook her head, at a loss. "My mother had a lot of books. They were all over the floor when we went to get my stuff. I only grabbed my favorites. I never knew about any grimoire."

"Hm," Pietre said. "Was your mother a witch?"

Raina shook her head again, hesitant this time. "I... don't think so? I guess it's possible. But she never—she wasn't a practicing one, if so. I never saw her doing anything other than fortune telling."

"Let's get Jeremiah and your necklace," Michael said to Raina. To Pietre: "Stay here with Desiree."

———

Raina and Michael found Jeremiah in the chapel beyond the statue. He was tied to the decorative cross on the back wall, hooded and unresponsive. Michael tugged off the hood and gag, then lifted the man's head, massaging his cheeks with open concern.

"Wake up," he coaxed. "Father Jeremiah. Wake up."

The older man blinked awake and squinted at him.

"Sweet Lilith," he exclaimed when he realized where he was. "That bitch!"

"Help me," Michael said to Raina as he pulled out his knife. He set to work on the ropes that secured the man's left arm to the cross.

Raina moved to help with his right arm, ignoring the throbbing pain in her singed hand. It was going to blister no matter what she did.

"Can you stand? Are you injured?" Michael asked.

He positioned himself to take on Jeremiah's weight as Raina cut through the last of his bonds.

Jeremiah flexed his fingers to bring blood back to them. "They didn't hurt me. Not after they tased me. They kept me gagged and chained or I would've—" He paused. "The boys?"

"They're okay. Troy's taking them home."

The prince helped Jeremiah down off the dais that supported the cross and to one of the pews. Raina looked around. The chapel was small. Apart from the pews and the religious decorations, there wasn't much to it.

"I don't see my mother's necklace," she said.

Michael helped her look. They turned the room inside out, looking everywhere, even under the seats. It was nowhere to be found.

"Time to regroup," Michael decided.

Jeremiah waved off aid, feeling better after his brief rest. He limped but could walk on his own. The three of them returned to the columbarium.

Michael went to where Pietre was crouched beside Desiree. "The necklace isn't in there."

Desiree's eyes widened. "Henri. That son of a bitch."

"Where did he go?" Michael said. "Your man?"

"I don't—" Desiree started. Then: "Maybe back to the Garden. It's where I met him. East Texas. North of Bayou City."

"The runaway has her own runaway." Pietre was amused. "What a fitting end."

Michael didn't share his amusement. "Get her out of here. We need to find Trixie."

"I think she went with Henri," Desiree volunteered. The woman had betrayed her as well.

Michael's jaw set. "If she fled with him, she will pay."

"The hounds will be pleased to have twice the amount of game to pursue," said Pietre. He looked at Desiree then. "Time to lock you up, my dear."

The witch squirmed. "You said no cages."

Pietre smiled a lazy smile. "You won't be caged. What I have in mind for you is much better than a cage."

She looked worried but fell silent.

"We'll deal with this Henri guy in a couple of days," Michael decided. "And Trixie, too. Raina's hurt and I need sleep."

While his body could repair itself, it took a toll on his vital energy. It often left him quite hungry or, as in this case, extremely tired. It didn't help that he was running on no sleep.

"Of course," said Pietre. "If you wish me to come with you for the Hunt, I can leave Ligeia in charge of our captives."

Michael made a face. "Let me think about it. She hasn't been the best at keeping our prisoners contained."

Pietre shrugged. "Whatever you wish."

Michael turned his attention to the others. "Let's head to the mansion. Raina, you can sit in front of me. Father Jeremiah can take the back. Hold on tight."

It was a snug ride home.

———

It was close to dawn by the time they got to the mansion. They gathered in the dining room where Lenore doted on the twins and Jeremiah with food, drink, and attention. She even helped dress Raina's burned hand.

Though tired, Gabe wanted to tell them all about how brave he and Zach were after the 'mean men' kidnapped them during trick-or-treat. Zach wanted to know if they would get candy to replace what they lost when they were snatched.

Troy socialized briefly before excusing himself for some much-needed rest. He didn't bother leaving or even going upstairs. He went into the Great Room and collapsed on one of the hard couches fully dressed.

Lenore was able to get the twins to cooperate for bath and an extremely late bedtime by promising to replace their treats—and on the condition Michael and Raina tuck them in. Lenore was less than thrilled about including Raina, but she kept up appearances. She haunted the doorway, wearing a fake smile through the tuck-in process.

Once the boys were in bed, Lenore turned her attention to Jeremiah. Michael led Raina to the second-floor bedroom he considered his.

"I'm surprised you don't have the Master bedroom," Raina remarked as she looked around his room. It was nicely appointed but hardly a suite.

Michael gently shut the door. "Someone else uses it."

"Oh." Raina assumed it belonged to Jeremiah and Lenore. Would make sense, given they spent more time in the house than Michael did. "Well, this is still nice."

The bedroom was spacious enough. It had a queen-sized bed loaded with pillows and a thick comforter. A desk and chair cozied up to one wall and a dresser and an old-fashioned wardrobe hugged the far wall. The floor was antique oak, with area rugs to keep away the chill and echo.

Michael shed his shirt and headed for the wardrobe. "This has been my room since I was a child."

"Wow. I've never lived in one place for long. Hard to imagine having the same room for years."

She found herself staring at Michael as he stripped off his pants. She didn't mean to. After everything she'd been through and as tired as she was, she knew she should be thinking of sleep. But he was far more fascinating than the bed.

He opened the wardrobe. One side was dedicated to clothing on hangers, much of it black. The other side was a tower of short drawers. Longer drawers made up the lower half. He dug around in the short drawers.

"Do you want to borrow something for bed?" he asked, tugging out a white T-shirt. He looked at her then. Really looked at her. "Are you okay?"

"I'm fine," she said. "Just tired. Lenore gave me something for the pain."

"You sure?"

She rose and crossed the floor to take the T-shirt. "I'm positive."

He let her have the shirt. Then he took her in his arms. "I'm sorry. About... everything. I can be a real dick sometimes. It means a lot to me that you're still here. With me."

Raina hugged his waist but kept eye contact. "I won't lie. Your heritage... it scares me. But I love you. Maybe I'm crazy, but I do."

He gave a short, soft laugh. "You'd have to be crazy to choose this life. You'll fit right in with the family." He stole a light kiss. Then, more sincere: "I love you, Raina. More than I thought I could love someone. If there's anything you want from me, ever, you have but to ask."

"I want it all," she said, swept up in the moment. Then reality caught up with her. "But there is one thing you can do for me as soon as possible."

"Name it."

"Get rid of the altars downtown."

He regarded her for a silent moment. He nodded.

"Consider it done."

CHAPTER 39

The next afternoon Raina had a late lunch with Michael and the boys. Jeremiah and Lenore were there as well. Afterward they moved to the Great Room, waking Troy. He went to clean up and grab some food.

Zach and Gabe stayed close to their father and Raina, playing next to the sofas where the adults sat. As far as they were concerned, their daddy made the bad people go away. That was all they needed for now. Time would tell if their experience would leave lasting scars.

About an hour later, Ligeia arrived. She was overdressed as always, looking ready for a high fashion funeral. Lenore took it as her cue to usher the twins out to the back yard. More for her own sake than to spare the boys the adult meeting. Jeremiah went with her.

Ligeia settled in a chair across from Raina and Michael. She placed a black cigarette in her long filter stem and lit it. Crossed her legs imperiously.

"Quite a busy night last night," she remarked. "I'm surprised you're both up and active. Have you done the ritual yet?"

Michael and Raina exchanged a glance.

"No," he said. "Not yet."

Ligeia huffed. "You should do that sooner rather than later."

Michael and Raina exchanged another look. He sought an answer to a question asked without words. After a moment, she gave a short nod.

Michael shifted and looked at the High Priestess again. "We'll get to it," he said. "We can do it before we head out to find the grimoire that Desiree's man took when he ran off with Trixie."

Ligeia puffed on her cigarette filter. "Pietre told me about the book," she said. She wasn't even going to touch the topic of Trixie at the moment. "I'm most curious about it. I'm glad you're prioritizing it. However, there is one other thing that needs tending to before that."

He frowned, puzzled. "Pietre is taking care of Desiree."

"Not what I meant."

"Then what?"

Ligeia's dark eyes found Raina. Her gaze was ice. "There's the matter of your disobeying me."

Raina fidgeted and sat up straighter. She was getting that stomach-clenching feeling again. The one that came with matronly trouble. "What? I don't know what you mean."

"Don't you remember our conversation? How I told you that you weren't to go anywhere alone?"

"Yes..." Raina said cautiously. Though she was certain she'd followed the rule, her heart was still racing with anxiety. "I haven't."

"At Desiree's party, you went off to talk with that bitch alone," Ligeia's words were frosty.

Raina glanced at Michael. His lips pressed together in a brief grim line, but he said nothing. This matter was between the High Priestess and her apprentice. Raina looked at Ligeia. She raced to find an answer that wouldn't incriminate her.

"It was just across the, um, the courtyard."

"If you had followed the *one* rule I laid out," Ligeia said. She aggressively tapped the ash from her cigarette into the tray on the coffee table. "It's safe to say none of this would have happened."

"You can't be sure of that," Michael defended, unable to hold his tongue any longer. "Desiree—"

"Divide and conquer, Michael," Ligeia interrupted. She shot him a sharp look then her withering gaze swiveled back to Raina. "I warned you. You disregarded that warning. Consequently, you will be punished."

The fingers of Raina's good hand found her skirt and picked at the pilled fabric. "How?"

"That remains to be determined."

Michael frowned. "Raina helped take Desiree down. She saved my sons from being burnt alive, for fuck's sake!"

Ligeia pursed a tight little smile at him. She exhaled smoke in a narrow plume. "Correcting a mistake made after the fact isn't the same as following the rules. Don't let your emotions cloud your judgment."

"I want to be involved in the process," he asserted.

Ligeia arched a plucked brow at him. "Fine. When Pietre and I get together about it, you can sit in."

Her acceptance was a thin reassurance.

Raina made herself stop picking at her skirt. Folded her arms over her middle to keep her hands still. "Is there anything I can do to make this better?"

"If you mean to avoid punishment... no."

"Are you going to kick me out of the Coven?"

The witch gave a harsh laugh. "No. Don't be so melodramatic. Discipline is for correction. Learn from it."

She snubbed her cigarette out in the ashtray and rose. She paused to fix Michael with a serious look. "As soon as she's healed, you should do the ritual."

She left them then. They heard the front door shut behind her as she stepped out into the cold November afternoon. Raina relaxed her self-hug. Michael took her good hand and gave her a supportive squeeze.

"I'll speak for you," he said.

She nodded, but her stomach remained in knots. "Can we get rid of those altars before then? Like... tomorrow?"

He nodded and leaned in to kiss her. He put a hand on the back of her neck, staying intimately close after the kiss broke. His forehead touched hers.

"We'll get through this together. Right?"

She smiled on hearing him echo her own words back to her. "Right."

...

They didn't announce to the public what they were going to do. They only told the First Church. Still, word leaked out. There was already a small crowd waiting when the barricades went up around the altars.

A police cordon arrived to reinforce the barrier. The crowd grew as more people in the square noticed something interesting happening. A local vendor saw an opportunity and circulated the masses, hawking bottled drinks and snacks.

It was a full-blown event by the time Michael, Raina, and Troy arrived. The men were used to such spectacles and acknowledged their fans with smiles and nods. The noisy assemblage reminded Raina of the traumatic event that made her want the altars destroyed.

But that crowd was hateful. This group waved and cheered, excited to see the prince and his retinue. Excited to see her. Rumor had circulated in the past weeks that he was seeing a mystery woman. For some it was their first look at the newest celebrity in court.

She was surprised to see some wave at her specifically. Made her wish she'd put more thought into what she wore. A tie-dyed muslin poet's shirt, vest, and a circle skirt that clashed were comfortable but nothing she wanted to be remembered by.

She waved back at the people, earning smiles.

Michael touched her elbow to catch her attention. "Ready?"

Recovering from her stage-shock, she nodded. "More than ready."

"Let's do this, then."

He motioned to the head of the cordon, who signaled back. The captain cleared his officers to the other side of the barricades. It had the effect of pushing the crowd further back.

Michael took a position east of the three altars. Raina stood to the west. They raised their hands and focused on the bloodstained surfaces. Raina visualized the energy flowing from her to form a bubble over the altars. When she met Michael's bubble she connected to it.

"Troy," Michael cued.

The dark-haired man grinned and held out his hand. A ball of fire appeared, much to the delight of the onlookers. Ever the showman, he tossed it back and forth between his hands. Then he wound it up like a baseball pitcher. Lobbed the fireball at the end of a fuse that led to the explosives clustered at the base of each altar.

The fuse hissed and sparked. Seconds later the flame split down three separate fuses. The explosion that followed was tremendous. Debris shot out, held inside the energy dome Michael and Raina held over the area. She hadn't expected to feel the impact, but she did. Not as pain but as a bone-jarring rattle.

Bearing down, she held herself steady. Relied on Michael's strength to preserve the shield. The crowd cheered. Troy waved to them happily since his part was done.

When the rubble stopped flying Raina released her hold and staggered. She heard a few gasps behind her. Pride if nothing else kept her on her feet. She didn't want to topple in front of so many people. Talk about embarrassing.

Michael dropped his side of the bubble as well. Smoke and dust billowed out. Once she was steady, Raina moved to join Troy. Michael came over to them. The haze in the air slowly settled.

"There will be no more public sacrifices as of this day," Michael's voice traveled supernaturally so everyone could hear.

Another cheer went up. A reporter in the crowd snapped several photos with a vintage camera.

"Thank you," Michael said as the noise died down. "Spread the word."

He turned to Raina and offered his arm. "I don't know about you, but I'm starved."

"We could hit Love's," Troy suggested. "Fish fry."

"I was thinking of having something at the mansion."

"I like the sound of that," agreed Raina.

"Let's go home," Michael smiled.

The three of them left the square. Behind them, the cleanup crew moved in to shovel the wreckage away as bystanders snatched bits of rubble as souvenirs.

Soon Raina would have to face the combined heads of the Coven in a disciplinary meeting. For the time being she was content to enjoy the light mood that came with the destruction of the altars. Darkness could wait.

Reaching Michael's car, she glanced back over her shoulder at the area where the workers were cleaning. The sight filled her with joy. Smiling, she slid into the passenger's seat. Soon they were speeding away from the town square, Troy's motorcycle roaring along behind them.

About the Author

Leaf Graham is an award-winning screenwriter and author. The *Unhallowed* book series was inspired by a popular free web series he wrote that began in 2013 and ended in 2023.

When he's not writing, Leaf loves to create art, watch and make films, fabricate props for film, cosplay, and stage productions, play video games, and soak up horror in all forms of media. He also enjoys spending time with the two cats who have taken over his house.

If you enjoyed this book, please leave a review on Amazon. It helps me out and it makes the book easier for others to find.

https://amzn.to/42q8bwn

You find original artwork, short stories, and more at the *Unhallowed Garden*:

https://www.patreon.com/UnhallowedGarden